Colonel Fitzwilliam Takes Charge

The 8th Book in The Take Charge Series

A Pride & Prejudice Variation

By Shana Granderson, A Lady

CONTENTS

DEDICATION

This book, like all that I write, is dedicated to the love of my life, the holder of my heart. You are my one and only and you complete me. You make it all worthwhile and my world revolves around you. Until we reconnected, I had stopped believing in miracles, but now I most certainly do, you are my miracle.

Acknowledgement

First and foremost, thank you E.C.S. for standing by me while I dedicate many hours to my craft. You are my shining light and my one and only.

I want to thank my Alpha, Will Jamison and my Betas Caroline Piediscalzi Lippert and Kimbelle Pease. To both Gayle Surrette and Carol M. for taking on the roles of proof-readers and detailed editing, a huge thank you to both of you. All of you who have assisted me please know that your assistance is most appreciated.

My undying love and appreciation to Jane Austen for her incredible literary masterpieces is more than can be expressed adequately here. I also thank all of the JAFF readers who make writing these stories a pleasure.

Thank you to Rob Bockholdt: wyndagger@gmail.com, who was commissioned to create the artwork used for the cover.

INTRODUCTION

In this the 8th book in the Take Charge Series, it is the much loved character of Colonel Richard Fitzwilliam who takes charge. Along with the characters we love (some we love to hate) there are a few who I have introduced in previous books of mine.

We know Richard as a decisive military leader, but what style will he use when he points others in the direction he needs to?

Richard is severely injured in a battle during the Napoleonic Wars on the Peninsula which effectively ends his military career. Hence he is in London when Darcy is invited to join Bingley in Hertfordshire at his leased estate, Netherfield Park. He is familiar with several of the Bennets having met them 4 years previously in London.

How will he tolerate Miss Bingley? Will he be at the assembly when his cousin utters the infamous slight of our dear Lizzy? Will he be attracted to one of the Bennet sisters, and if so to which one?

How will, if they do at all, Lady Catherine, Wickham, and Collins play into the tale? Will Kitty and Lydia be their silly canon selves, and if so, how will the Colonel influence them?

I invite you to join me while Richard has his chance to take charge in his own distinctive way.

PROLOGUE

Second sons were required to choose a profession. It was no different for Richard Fitzwilliam, the second son of Lord Reginald and Lady Elaine Fitzwilliam, the Earl and Countess of Matlock. Lord Andrew Fitzwilliam, Viscount Hilldale, was three years older than Richard, who was born in 1782.

The Countess had wanted more children, but she was unable to bear additional offspring. Avoiding bitterness, Lady Matlock poured all her love and warmth into the two sons with whom she had been blessed.

Richard's family was not a large one. Thanks to an outbreak of smallpox, Lady Elaine was the only surviving member of her family. Lord Matlock was one of three siblings and the only male. The family's primary estate was Snowhaven in Derbyshire.

~~~~~~~/~~~~~~~

Lord Matlock's older sister, Lady Catherine de Bourgh, had married Sir Lewis de Bourgh in 1783; he was a wealthy knight who owned the estate of Rosings Park in Kent.

She had not wished to settle for a mere commoner, one such as the knight she married, but since her younger sister had married the wealthy but untitled owner of Pemberley in 1780, to avoid spinsterhood, Lady Catherine had accepted Sir Lewis, the only man who had offered for her.

When Catherine first noticed Robert Darcy's interest in her sister, she attempted to redirect the master of Pemberley to herself. He was a commoner, but his fortune was magnificent;

she would have been happy to marry a man with such wealth. Robert Darcy, however, never showed any interest in her; his affections remained fixed on Lady Anne.

It was mortifying to the eldest Fitzwilliam that her younger sister married three years before her. Not only that, Anne had already delivered a son and heir to Pemberley and the Darcy fortune in December of 1782. Catherine reasoned that at least her husband had a title and, although he was not nearly as wealthy as Robert Darcy, he had a reasonable fortune.

Lady Anne and Robert Darcy named their son Fitzwilliam, in keeping with the tradition that the firstborn Darcy sons are named with their mother's maiden name. They called him William. Thankfully, the current master's mother had been a Roberts.

A daughter, Anne, was born to the de Bourghs in October of 1784. As soon as she was churched, Lady Catherine attempted to browbeat her younger sister into agreeing to form an engagement between Fitzwilliam and Anne.

Both Lady Anne and Robert Darcy refused her entreaties roundly. They had made a love match, and they wanted nothing less for William, or for any of their children which they might be blessed with in the future.

~~~~~~~/~~~~~~~

Since the Darcy and Fitzwilliam estates were separated by barely ten miles, the residents of the two estates were much in each other's company. There was less than four years separating the three cousins. William was the youngest cousin, and Andrew the oldest. The three cousins were often together and became more like three brothers than two brothers and a cousin. Richard and William had been born a mere eight months apart and developed an especially strong bond. They often spent time at one estate or the other and took most of their lessons together.

The only times the Derbyshire families saw the de

Bourghs was during their annual pilgrimage to Kent for Easter. More often than not, that was when Lady Catherine harped on her favourite subject: the joining of Pemberley and Rosings Park via the marriage of her Anne and Fitzwilliam Darcy. As soon as she brought up the subject, the Darcys and the Fitzwilliams would cut their visit short.

In 1786, Pemberley's steward retired, and Robert Darcy employed a new man, Mr. Lucas Wickham. He came with a wife and a two-year-old son, George. Darcy had studied with Lucas Wickham at Cambridge, so when the position became vacant, the master of Pemberley was pleased to offer the post to his friend.

Lucas Wickham had read the law, but the amount Robert Darcy offered him made it well worth his while to leave his practice and move into the steward's house at Pemberley.

~~~~~~~/~~~~~~~

Starting at age ten, Richard told anyone who chose to listen that he would become a soldier one day. As he was so young, his parents, aunt, and uncle never took him seriously; after all, young boys who would eventually need one, changed their minds many times before settling on a profession.

Regardless of his parents and other family members calling it a boyhood fancy, Richard was sure he would become an officer at some point in the future. When it was his turn to choose a game, it was invariably one involving soldiers and officers.

Even at ten, Richard could see his mother was unhappy when he spoke of joining the Army. So as not to worry his mother, Richard no longer discussed his dream of becoming an officer when in her company.

Although still young, Richard understood the difference between his path as a second son and that of Andy and Wills. Andy would be the earl one day and would inherit Snowhaven; he already owned Hilldale, an estate in Staffordshire.

Wills would inherit Pemberley, other estates, a house in London, and a massive fortune. Neither his brother nor his cousin would ever have to seek a profession. Richard never begrudged them their futures and stoically accepted their paths would one day diverge.

Richard had a strong sense of independence and was not one to permit others to pay his way. Even at ten he was determined to make his way in the world and not live off the charity of others.

~~~~~~~/~~~~~~~

In September of 1792, the threesome was torn asunder when Andrew began his studies at Eton. Thereafter, George Wickham was included from time to time, but he did not make up for Andrew's absence. For a while, the two cousins were very close to young George.

Although George's and William's fathers were the best of friends, at a certain point, William began to feel uncomfortable around George Wickham. Richard also shared William's misgivings about the steward's son. When young Wickham was a little older, they caught him—more than once—making mischief and trying to fob the blame off on others, most often on William.

Due to the traits the two older boys saw in George, which he hid from his parents and theirs, they spent as little time with him as possible. Unfortunately, every now and again at Pemberley, Robert Darcy would command his son to spend time with young Wickham.

~~~~~~~/~~~~~~~

1793 was not a good year for the de Bourghs. Westerham in Kent, near Rosing Park, suffered an epidemic of Scarlet Fever. Both Sir Lewis and Anne became ill with the disease. They had serious cases. Anne survived, but her father did not.

By some miracle Lady Catherine did not contract the

disease. She claimed it was due to her rank, something everyone knew was stuff and nonsense. Rather than argue with her, family members merely shook their heads and did not respond.

One thing was certain, after she recovered, Anne was never the vibrant girl she had been before her illness. Although Lady Catherine did not want to acknowledge it, her daughter suffered lasting effects from the disease.

Lady Catherine was angry with her husband for daring to succumb to an illness, but it was nothing to the fury she unleashed after his will was read. All she received was an allowance, one—in her opinion—far too low for one of her exalted rank. Everything else had been bequeathed to Anne and the Earl and Darcy were named executors of the estate. The Earl was named Anne's guardian.

In the end, all her bluster about challenging the will aside, Lady Catherine could do nothing. When Anne turned three and twenty, the estate would become hers. Even more galling was a codicil which named Richard Fitzwilliam the heir if Anne passed away unmarried. If she married, then everything would belong to her husband.

At least Lady Catherine would remain mistress of the estate until Anne married or reached the age stipulated in her late husband's will.

~~~~~~~/~~~~~~~

Two years later, in September of 1795, the two younger cousins began their studies at Eton. Richard entered Eton when he was thirteen. William began early, at twelve. The two wanted to attend together, so they elected not to wait until the next term to begin their educations.

During their first term at school, Lucas Wickham saved Robert Darcy's life when his horse bolted for no apparent reason. It was discovered a thorn had worked its way under the saddle so when Darcy sat, it had driven the thorn into his horse's back.

When Richard and William heard about the incident, they both had a suspicion they knew how that thorn had found its way under the saddle. Not long before they were to leave for school, Richard had caught George Wickham trying to place a thorn between William's saddle and his cob's back.

The upshot was, in his gratitude, Robert Darcy became George's godfather and pledged to see he received a gentleman's education.

Richard and William wrote to Andrew about their suspicions. He replied that without proof positive, they could not accuse George Wickham of the deed. He recommended they all be vigilant when in his company.

~~~~~~~/~~~~~~~

Christmastide of the first year the two cousins were at Eton was celebrated at Snowhaven. They were happy to spend time with Andrew, who was home from Cambridge. There were a number of reasons the location pleased all three. Chief among them was they would not have to spend time in George Wickham's company. The cousins did feel badly for him because Mrs. Wickham had passed away from influenza in October, not long after the incident of the thorn under Robert Darcy's saddle.

Another advantage was their Aunt Catherine had refused to leave Rosings Park after her husband passed away, so none of the family members would be forced to listen to her inanities and nonsensical pronouncements.

Their aunt would never admit it, but one of the reasons she never left Kent any longer was that Anne's health was so poor it did not allow her to take long journeys, especially not into the frigid temperature prevalent in the north during the height of winter.

The day before Christmas, Lady Anne shared the news she was with child. She had felt the quickening almost two months ago but, given her two stillbirths and three miscarriages since William's birth, she had waited until her fifth month to tell anyone other than her beloved husband.

On the fourth day of March in 1796, Georgiana Bethany Darcy was born. Her birth underlined the fact God might give with one hand and take with the other. Lady Anne never recovered from the travails of childbirth and grew steadily weaker.

The seventh day after little Anna, as her mother had decided she would be called, was born, Lady Anne Darcy breathed her last. William, saddened at his mother's loss, was grateful his father had sent for him so he might arrive home before his mother passed away, allowing him to say his tearful goodbyes to his beloved mother.

At first, neither Darcy or his thirteen-year-old son wished to see little Anna; they associated her birth with the death of Lady Anne. It was Richard who pointed out the fallacy in their thinking. He simply asked them what Aunt Anne would have said to them about blaming her daughter for her death.

Richard's words snapped both Darcy males out of their haze. They realised that Lady Anne would have been the first to take them to task for their wrongheaded thinking. From that point on, father and son loved little Anna as she deserved to be loved.

The day before the two from Eton and one from Cambridge were to return to their schools, a de Bourgh carriage arrived at Pemberley. Lady Catherine came for two reasons: first, as she stated, she had come to manage Pemberley as it should be managed; second she had come to cement the agreement she had made with her late sister for Anne and William to marry.

Needless to say, she was sent away with a flea in her ear the very same day. She claimed to be seriously displeased.

~~~~~~~/~~~~~~~

When Richard and William began their final year at Eton, George Wickham, who was nearly thirteen, began his first year. The vicious propensities the cousins had oft observed over the years had become an integral part of young Wickham's character.

It was also plain he was envious of anyone who had more than him, which was almost everyone at Eton. The greater part of his jealousy was directed at William, hence the cousins avoided Wickham as much as they were able.

Christmastide was celebrated at Snowhaven again, as it had been every year since lady Anne Darcy's passing. Richard and William tried to inform Robert Darcy of his godson's behaviour at Eton, but Darcy dismissed their concerns, chalking up George's behaviour to youthful exuberance.

Thankfully, in May of 1798, after Andrew graduated from Cambridge and was planning a grand tour with friends, Richard and William completed their studies at Eton. This meant they would not be at the same school as George Wickham for at least two more years.

~~~~~~~/~~~~~~~

Richard and William rode up the bridle path at Pemberley to the lookout facing the distant peaks in the west. "Are you looking forward to Cambridge, Wills?" Richard asked as they dismounted from their new stallions.

Richard had been presented Invictus on his last birthday; William had been gifted Zeus as a reward for completing Eton.

"Yes, I am. What about you Rich? In all the years I've known you, your desire to choose the army as your profession has never wavered. I know Aunt Elaine and Uncle Reggie will not be happy if you go into the regulars, because you may end up on a battlefield one day," William stated.

"You know how you know your path is set as the heir to

all the Darcy holdings?"

"Yes, what of it?"

"Knowing it is your duty, would you change it if you could?"

"No, I suppose I would not. It is what my father taught me, and it will be my task to uphold the Darcy legacy—one day, many years in the future, I pray."

"Just as you know your path is the right one, so do I. Could you envision me making sermons or reading the law?" Richard challenged.

"I suppose not. I worry if you go into the army and something happens to you..." William stopped himself before he spoke the words.

"William, could you not have a riding accident as easily as I could be felled in battle?"

"It is always a possibility, but you must own the risks are much greater in the regulars. Why do you not go into the militia instead?"

"Because I want to be a *real* soldier, not a puffed-up peacock strutting to impress young ladies without knowing one end of a weapon from the other." Richard paused. "Just wait until you go into society. You will be hunted like a stag; just as poor Andy will be as soon as he returns from his grand tour. There is an advantage to being a poor second son, you know."

"Do not remind me. You know how much I detest interacting with people when I am not well acquainted with them."

"You can be a snob at times, William."

"Well, I am a Darcy of Pemberley, after all," William said with his nose in the air. It was a jest, but uncomfortably close to the truth.

The cousins sat in companionable silence while they

watched the sun begin to set over the peaks. The mountains took on a purple hue, save for their summits, which had reds, golds, and silvers from the setting sun shimmering behind them.

They remounted and rode down the bridle path to return to the manor house.

~~~~~~~/~~~~~~~

During their second year at Cambridge, Richard and William were walking to their shared apartments from Trinity College, when they heard the sound of fisticuffs. They discovered three young men beating on another.

Without thinking, the powerfully built Richard with William at his side, who was a rather well-built specimen himself, jumped in. Soon the three bullies found themselves on their backs holding bloodied noses.

"He is but the son of a tradesman; why do you care of we have some fun?" the leader of the three spat out.

"So, you think that gives you the right to act in such an ungentlemanlike fashion?" Richard demanded. "Should we have one of the masters adjudicate the rectitude of your actions here?"

"N-No, we will leave," one of the others stated nervously.

"If I hear of you or anyone else behaving in such a fashion again, you will answer to me," Richard threatened.

The three slunk away. William assisted the victim to his feet. He was a little shorter than Richard, was of medium build, and had strawberry blond hair.

"I am indebted to you," the young man said, extending his hand to Richard. "Charles Bingley of Scarborough, and as those *gentlemen* pointed out, my father is in trade."

"Richard Fitzwilliam of Snowhaven in Derbyshire. This tall one is my cousin Fitzwilliam Darcy of Pemberley, also in Derbyshire." Richard took the eager young man's hand and shook it.

William extended his hand, more tentatively than Richard, until his cousin gave him a pointed look. He shook hands normally after that. The cousins walked Charles Bingley back to his chambers. During their walk, they discovered he was a year behind them.

"You see, it is not so hard to meet new people," Richard stated as he and William made their way back to their apartments.

"I suppose," William allowed. "He seems an aimable sort, does he not?"

~~~~~~~/~~~~~~~

By their final year at Cambridge, which would end in May of 1802, a solid friendship had been formed between the cousins and Charles Bingley. The latter had not been shy about describing his sisters as fortune hunters and social climbers, most especially the younger of the two. It was Bingley's reason for not inviting either of his highborn friends to spend time with his family.

The only sour note was that George Wickham had arrived at the university. He spent most of his time running up debts, gambling, and wenching. Richard and William quietly bought up his debts and collected testimonials from young ladies he promised marriage to so that they would *anticipate* their vows with him. They told of how as soon as he bedded them, he was not seen again.

In May, the cousins returned home rather than plan a grand tour. Richard had already signed the papers to enlist in the Royal Dragoons as a Second Lieutenant; William decided to defer his tour until 1803, when Bingley would graduate.

Richard had saved his allowance over the years; with that—and a small loan from William—he had been able to purchase his commission. He was determined to earn any further promotions, not purchase them.

His parents were unhappy he was going into the regulars, but they vowed to support their second son in any way they could. The Earl had volunteered to purchase a higher rank, but Richard had respectfully declined.

One evening, with all four Fitzwilliams present, Richard and William presented the evidence they had collected regarding George Wickham's activities at Cambridge, including the fact one of the young girls he meddled with was with child and Wickham refused to take responsibility. Although Robert Darcy had not wanted to acknowledge his godson was so very bad, he was, finally, forced to accept the facts.

Darcy was sorry he had told young Wickham he would award him the Kympton living after graduation if George took orders. He summoned Lucas and George Wickham to meet with him. It was not a pleasant meeting.

At first George dissembled and claimed Richard and William were jealous of him, which led to their accusations. When he was confronted with the proof, he tried to claim his writing had been forged, which was easily disproved.

Robert Darcy, with Lucas Wickham's full agreement, withdrew as godfather and retracted his patronage from George. Although he said nothing, George Wickham was fuming silently, thinking of ways to revenge himself on those who had crossed him—including his traitorous father.

CHAPTER 1

By May of 1803, England and France were in a state of war. Richard Fitzwilliam had been promoted to lieutenant. His superiors had quickly identified his leadership skills and his ability for strategic thinking. It had become known he refused to allow his father, an earl, to purchase a higher rank for him. This marked Richard Fitzwilliam as a man worthy of being promoted on his merits.

When he had leave for Christmastide that year, Richard was happy to see all the family he cared about at Snowhaven. He commiserated with William who, having waited to take his grand tour after Bingley graduated, had been unable to travel to the continent, thanks to the Corsican tyrant's war of aggression.

William and Bingley planned a four-month-long tour of England, Scotland, Wales, and Ireland. Even that tour had been truncated when Bingley returned to Scarborough after his parents had been killed in a carriage accident.

It was during this visit Richard noticed that William had become haughtier and more taciturn. His cousin had always openly displayed his pride in the Darcy name and his position as the heir to Pemberley, but what Richard was seeing now went far beyond anything he had ever before noticed.

Before he confronted his cousin about his character change, Richard pulled his brother into a parlour. "What happened to William while I was away?" Richard enquired. "He seems to have developed the same attitudes as Aunt Catherine."

"You mean his arrogance?" Andrew responded. Richard nodded. "You must have noticed while you two were at Cambridge how uncomfortable William is in crowds, and his reaction to the huntresses of the *Ton*?"

"Yes, I saw that, but his attitude was nothing like it is now," Richard remembered.

"Since you went into the Dragoons our boy has been spending more time in London. He has already had one *lady* attempt to compromise him into marriage. He is hunted relentlessly."

"Andy, you have had to endure the same, if not worse. You do not behave as William now does."

"We are different people, Rich. You and I have always been far more sociable and easier in company than William. He has dealt with his discomfort by developing a forbidding mask; it scares away all but the most determined fortune hunters."

"When we were together, I was always able to deflect much of the attention from him. I understand it is hard for him, but he is a man full grown who has reached his majority. A man who should have learnt how to manage things without being rude and arrogant." Richard paused. "I assume with Bingley in mourning for his parents William has not been in company with him very much. Bingley always seemed to be able to cheer him."

"William did go to Scarborough to condole with Bingley. There he met the man's sisters. Miss Bingley was nineteen and Miss Caroline fifteen. William did not last a day in the Bingley house. He told me the sisters ignored the strictures of mourning and were falling over one another to fawn over and impress him with their *qualities*."

"Bingley was very forthright when he warned us about his sisters. However, William did the right thing by calling on his friend. I cannot blame him for escaping as soon as he did.

That being said, I wish I was able to spend more time with William. I am sure he would do better in society with me at his side."

"I have attempted to mitigate some of the societal pressure on him, but given the way I am hunted myself; I always have to be aware of my surroundings. I am unable to pay as much attention to William as I would like." Andrew paused. "The more time I spend in our so called *polite society*, the more I become convinced I will find my wife away from the *Ton*, just like Father did with Mother."

"Like you, I would hate being shackled to a lady without an original thought in her head, one uneducated other than in the so-called *accomplishments* society dictates. Come, let us return before Mother sends the servants to search the castle for us."

Before he could speak to William, Richard's attention was arrested by Anna, now six. Her golden ringlets bobbed up and down as she enthusiastically demanded her cousin come meet her new doll, Molly.

Richard did not miss Uncle Robert's indulgent smile as Anna pulled him to a little table in the corner of the drawing room where Molly was waiting to be served tea. As he looked at his uncle, it seemed to Richard that Uncle Robert's pallor was a little on the grey side.

With Anna demanding he join her and Molly for tea, Richard's attention was pulled from his musings about his uncle.

~~~~~~~/~~~~~~~

In early 1804, Richard was promoted to captain and assigned the duty of commanding a section of the Dragoon's training grounds, where he was to teach other officers and soldiers tactics and discipline.

He revelled in his new duties as much as he enjoyed earning his second promotion in the less than two years since he had been inducted into the regiment. His commanding officer was Colonel Grant Atherton, who Richard thought was just what an officer should be, so he studied the Colonel and adopted the laudable elements he observed in his commander's behaviour.

He was saddened when he learned that Lucas Wickham, Pemberley's steward, had been killed in June. He died after a riding accident. Since Richard knew the late steward was an excellent rider, he was rather surprised Mr. Wickham had met his end in such a fashion.

Although it had been some time since he had thought about George Wickham, he now wondered if that wastrel's father's support of Uncle Robert's decision to withdraw his patronage had something to do with the death. It would show a level of ingratitude Richard could not fathom.

The older Wickham had scrimped and saved so his son could complete his Cambridge education after Uncle Robert ceased paying for George. The ingrate had failed to graduate as he had been sent down for cheating on an exam in his final year at Cambridge.

Since then, anything Richard had heard of George Wickham described him as a dissolute, profligate, wastrel who thought the world owed him whatever he desired. As far as he knew, George wanted money without having to work for it.

Unlike the younger Wickham, Richard was not one to waste his resources. He was able to live on his wages, and saved some of what he earned. His father still insisted on giving him a generous allowance, so Richard sought out a place to save and invest his excess funds.

After a number of enquiries, he chose to invest with a man by the name of Edward Gardiner. The man's company, Gardiner and Associates, was primarily an import-export concern, but the man did business in other sectors as well.

He made his choice thanks to the reputation Gardiner

had of being scrupulously honest. His returns were more than double the banks' four percent. If that were not enough, his dividends were generally better than most other legitimate concerns that were accepting investments. After a few months' trial, during which his returns were ten percent or higher, Richard was so impressed he moved all of his savings into Mr. Gardiner's capable hands. He planned to recommend that his father, brother, and Uncle Robert consider investing with Gardiner and Associates as well.

Before he saw his family again, his memory of Uncle Robert's pallor—the one he noted at Christmastide but had not thought of since—came to his attention in the worst possible way. He received a black-edged missive in October; it announced the death of his uncle.

In September past, he had a sennight's leave and spent the time with William at Darcy House in London. Other than saying his father chose to remain at Pemberley with Anna, William did not so much as hint about his father's poor health.

Richard was granted emergency leave. He rode Invictus the more than hundred miles to the Darcy estate. He did not push his stallion beyond his capabilities, resting him every twenty miles. Richard arrived at Pemberly in the latter part of the afternoon on the second day.

Given the time since his uncle's passing, Richard expected the interment would have already occurred, given the time it took for the notice to reach him and for him to travel to Derbyshire. His supposition was correct. Uncle Robert had been buried the day before; his eternal resting place was next to his beloved Anne.

~~~~~~~/~~~~~~~

"Richard!" Anna, who had turned eight in March, exclaimed as she threw herself, crying bitterly, into her favourite cousin's arms. Richard used his handkerchief to dry her tears.

"I am so sorry I could not get here sooner, Sprite," Richard said soothingly.

"It is good you are here Richard," Lord Matlock stated as he sombrely shook his younger son's hand. "You are one of the executors of Robert's will so the solicitor would not allow it to be read until you arrived."

Richard hugged his little cousin again before her governess led her away. Anna did not seem happy to go, but was contented to leave after her aunt, Lady Matlock, agreed to accompany her to the nursery.

He approached William, who looked lost. "Wills, I was so sorry to receive the news of your father's death," he stated as he pulled his cousin to him for a hug. William was stiff to begin with, but Richard felt him relax a little before he released his cousin.

"It was his heart, Rich," William—now Darcy—stated. His voice was gruff with emotion and there was no hiding the fact he had been crying. "Father and his doctor tried their best to hide his illness from us, but in the last month or two, it became painfully evident that all was not well."

"Why did you not write to me about his health?" Richard asked. "You know I would have applied for emergency leave and been at your side."

"There was so much to do, so much to learn," Darcy averred. "I should have written to you even so, but I thought writing about Father's poor health would make it more real, so I concentrated on what I needed to learn and took lessons from Father—as much as he was able to teach me. Mr. Chalmers, the steward who replaced Mr. Wickham, has been a great help to me as I learn my duties."

"I had no warning Uncle Robert had made me an executor of his will," Richard related. "What could he mean by it? I am in the army and may be sent to the Peninsula at some point."

"Father valued your judgement, as I do. I have to believe that is why he wanted you to be one of the executors. Andrew is the other. He would have made Uncle Reggie another, but he already has his hands full administering Uncle Lewis's will, trying to rein in our aunt's excesses, and being Anne's guardian," Darcy explained.

Not long after the cousins spoke, the solicitor entered the room to read the will. As expected, his son was left Pemberley, four satellite estates, Darcy House, and the bulk of the Darcy fortune. There were small bequests to faithful retainers and to support some local charities, also not surprising.

"*To my nephew, Richard Fitzwilliam I bequeath ten thousand pounds*," the solicitor read. This surprised Richard; he had neither wanted nor expected any sort of bequest from his uncle. "*I appoint my son Fitzwilliam Alexander Darcy and my nephew Richard Fitzwilliam joint guardians of my daughter, Georgiana Bethany Darcy. As Richard is in the army, if he is lost before Anna's majority or she is married, I appoint Lord Andrew Fitzwilliam, Viscount Hilldale, co-guardian in Richard's stead. Under no circumstances is my daughter ever to be given over to the guardianship of Lady Catherine de Bourgh.*"

Again, Richard was knocked back. That William was to be one of Anna's guardians was expected, but he never thought his name would be read as one as well.

"*My daughter's dowry of thirty thousand pounds shall not be released if she is compromised, or both of her guardians' permission is not sought and granted before her wedding,*" the solicitor continued to read.

"*There is one last, not so pleasant, term of my will. I have no doubt my sister-in-law, Lady Catherine de Bourgh née Fitzwilliam, will arrive—if she is not already present—soon after my passing and claim an engagement between my son and heir Fitzwilliam and her daughter Anne.*

SHANA GRANDERSON A LADY

"No such agreement exists. Neither my dear wife, Lady Anne Darcy, nor I ever agreed to, or in my case signed, any marriage articles. As all of you listening to this reading know, Lady Catherine made up the supposed agreement from whole cloth. It exists nowhere but in her own mind. I hereby refute any claim she makes regarding such an agreement. Furthermore, should she, or any other woman, engineer a compromise of Fitzwilliam, I give him my permission to refuse to comply with such a travesty."

"That, my lords, Mr. Darcy, and Captain, is all of the late Mr. Darcy's will. I will leave an executed copy for each of the executors and for the current Mr. Darcy. I will retain a copy and will file one more with the probate court," The solicitor reported. He looked at the new master of the estate. "Your father wanted to ensure no one would be able to challenge the terms of his will, so he made sure he addressed everything. Are there any more questions for me?"

There were none, so the solicitor took his leave. Andrew and Richard walked the man out; when they reached the entrance hall they were greeted by a most unwelcome sight. George Wickham was demanding that Mr. Reynolds, the butler, allow him entrance.

The butler was about to summon footmen to throw the interloper out when Richard raised his hand. "Why are you here, Wickham?" Richard demanded.

"After you attended your father's funeral, did not my late uncle tell you not to set foot on his land again?" Andrew questioned.

"As I am sure my former patron did not forget me in his will, I have come to claim my due," Wickham stated wearily. Richard Fitzwilliam had always intimidated him and now he looked much stronger than he used to be. "Mr. Darcy said he would promote my interests and recommend me to the living at Kympton." Wickham closed his mouth when the younger Fitzwilliam again raised his hand.

"We should not have this discussion in a public place. Follow me to my cousin's study," Richard commanded. "Thompson, would you and another footman please follow us and remain outside the study door in case we need you?"

Thompson and an equally brawny footman followed the three men to the master's study. Andrew opened the door and entered; Richard directed Wickham to follow his brother, then entered himself, pushing the door closed behind him after confirming the footmen were in place.

Before the brazen man could speak, Richard rounded on him. "Are you delusional, Wickham? Why would you think the man who withdrew all patronage from you would remember you in his will? My brother," Richard cocked his head to the Viscount, "and I are the executors, and I can guarantee you that you were not mentioned in the will, so you will not receive a single penny. As to the church, you are the last person who should be entrusted with the spiritual welfare of others!"

"It was my intention to ask for a pecuniary advantage, as I do not intend to take orders. However, I do want to read the law and that takes money," Wickham claimed.

"Then," Andrew interjected, "I suggest you earn what you need. Do you think we do not know you are reluctant to work for your money."

"Please explain how one who was sent down from Cambridge and never graduated would be able to take orders or read the law?" Richard demanded.

Wickham flushed with anger and ignored the facts which had been pointed out to him. He would have released his vitriol had he not seen how Richard Fitzwilliam had his fists balled and ready.

"It is time for you to leave. If you *ever* return here or to any Darcy or Fitzwilliam property, you will be arrested for trespassing. You have been warned!" Richard barked at the miscreant, who shrank back in fear. "Thompson," Richard called out.

The door opened and Thompson and his fellow footman filled the frame with their bulks. "Captain?" Thompson said questioningly.

"This *man* is leaving. See him escorted off Pemberley's land and spread the word that he is never to return," Richard instructed.

Before Wickham could react, the footmen each took one of his arms and lifted him effortlessly. His feet did not touch the ground as they walked him out of the study.

"You two were absent for longer than it should take to walk someone out," Lord Matlock stated quizzically.

"Andy and I had to throw some rubbish out," Richard reported with a grin. Seeing the questioning looks—including one from his mother, who had returned from soothing Anna, Richard elucidated.

"The hubris of that wastrel!" Lord Matlock growled.

Before they could discuss Wickham further, a great screeching sound was heard in the hallway. Lady Catherine de Bourgh had arrived.

"William, you have enough on your plate; allow Andy and me, as your father's executors, to speak with our aunt," Richard suggested.

"In my role as Anne's guardian and executor of her late husband's will, I will join you," Lord Matlock stated.

The three Fitzwilliam men met with the termagant in the study. Before she could repeat her lies, Andrew read the relevant portion of his late uncle's will to her. When backed up with the threat of a serious reduction in her allowance from her brother, Lady Catherine quit the field of battle.

She was seriously displeased, something which bothered her family not at all.

CHAPTER 2

T hankfully the rest of 1804 passed without any major events affecting the family, good or bad. During the season of 1805, Richard attempted to spend as much time with his cousins as possible when he was not training his men. In March William and Anna arrived in London, after completing their mourning for their father.

Bingley was in Town as well; his sisters had convinced him he needed a house in the city. Rather than purchase in Mayfair as they had wanted, Bingley had found a moderately sized house on Curzon Street in a less fashionable area.

From what Richard had been told by Bingley, Miss Bingley, about to turn one and twenty, was becoming desperate to find a man to offer for her. She was even more of a social-climbing fortune hunter than her older sister. She demanded to be out at seventeen, and Bingley had allowed it.

No matter how often one of the sisters hinted Richard's mother, Lady Matlock, should sponsor them so they could be presented, Richard would not ask it of his mother, and she would not have done so if he had.

Their brother, who spoke of purchasing an estate, had not yet joined the ranks of the landed gentry. Hence, regardless of the Miss Bingleys' pretensions and airs, they were the daughters of a tradesman, which precluded them from being accepted at the Queen's drawing room.

In any case, Lady Matlock would have objected to sponsoring either of the sisters, due to their rudeness and vulgarity, most clearly displayed in the younger Miss Bingley, who acted as though she belonged in the highest levels of society.

Both Bingley sisters had set their caps at poor William, but he could not have been less interested in them if he had tried. Miss Louisa Bingley seemed to understand that, but her sister, told one and all how she would become the next mistress of Darcy House and Pemberley.

Although Richard did not like the arts his cousin employed to ward off those he felt were undesirable, which was almost everyone in society, with ladies like Miss Caroline chasing him, he could understand why William hid behind a mask.

When his mask was in place most self-respecting ladies would leave him be. Miss Caroline was among the small group who ignored the signals of disdain William was clearly sending. She was determined to gain access to the *Ton*. She obviously saw her brother's friend as the vehicle to achieve her desires. Her prey's feelings on the matter were completely irrelevant to her.

One afternoon, early in March, Richard had two days of leave and was spending it with his cousins at Darcy House. They would be celebrating Anna's ninth birthday on the morrow and Richard's parents and brother were to join them.

A runner from his regiment delivered a missive to Richard. It informed him he was being promoted to major and he had to report back forthwith as the regiment was about to be deployed to the Peninsula.

~~~~~~~/~~~~~~~

By the time the regiment of Dragoons Major Richard Fitzwilliam served in returned to England in June of 1806, the regiment had not seen any significant action, which was a double-edged sword.

The positive was they had lost not a single man to the war, but the negative was time plodded along slowly, making it difficult for them to keep their edge. Another positive of being posted back to England was the men would see their families, eat fresh, warm meals, and not have to sleep in cold and draughty tents.

Crossing the English Channel was not one of Richard's favourite activities; he did not fare well on ships. This was the reason he had decided against a career in the Royal Navy.

By the time the ship Richard was on sailed up the Thames and docked near Admiralty House, he was more than ready to walk on solid ground again. He knew from past experience he would walk unsteadily for a few days until his body stopped trying to anticipate the rise and fall of a ship.

On his return to England, Richard wrote to his family, informing them of his presence on English soil once again, but stated he could not find his way to them unless and until he completed his duties.

The regiment was commanded by a new colonel, since Brigadier-General Atherton now commanded the brigade. They returned to their quarters next to their training grounds. It took a few days to complete everything that needed to be done. As soon as all officers like Richard who commanded companies reported all tasks completed to the colonel, most men and officers were released and granted a month's leave.

By the time he was released, Richard had not yet heard from his family. However, he knew they would be at their estates; since he had asked them not to come to London to collect him, he decided to call on Gardiner to check on his investments—which now included his bequest from his uncle—before taking the post north.

As he alighted from the hackney which brought him to the Gardiner and Associates warehouses, Richard spied Mr. Gardiner exiting his place of business. He was accompanied by two young girls; his guess was they were ten or twelve years old.

They were both pretty little creatures. One, was slightly shorter than the other, had emerald-green eyes, and wavy raven hair. She had a vibrant glow about her. The other had lighter and straighter hair. Her eyes were hazel with flecks of green and gold.

"Gardiner, I was coming to meet with you to go over the state of my investments," Richard hailed the man. "However, if you are busy, I can stop by next time I am in London.

Before Gardiner could reply one of the girls impertinently interjected. "You are a major in the Royal Dragoons, are you not?" she enquired.

"Lizzy," Gardiner admonished her. "I am sorry, Major, I was walking my nieces back to my house. They are good with numbers and found it entertaining to help my clerks tally figures. You are welcome to join me. I have the ledger with my investors' information in my office at home."

"Gardiner, would you please introduce me to your nieces?" Richard requested. "If it is not an imposition, I will accompany you to your house."

"As to the second, it is not an intrusion for you to visit my house," Gardiner assured the Major. "Major Fitzwilliam, I present two of my five nieces. The one who questioned you about your rank and regiment is Miss Elizabeth Bennet of Longbourn in Hertfordshire; she is the second of five sisters." Richard's eyebrows raised in surprise at the mention of five sisters and no brother. "Next to her is Miss Mary Bennet, next in age after Elizabeth. Lizzy and Mary, the Honourable Major Richard Fitzwilliam, second son of the Earl of Matlock."

"How is it you were able to identify not only my rank but my regiment, Miss Bennet?" Richard queried as they began to walk along Gracechurch Street.

"Jane is Miss Bennet; I am Miss Elizabeth." Richard acknowledged his error with a grin. "My papa allows me to read the newspapers and I love to follow current events. The war with the little Corsican is big news," Elizabeth responded. "A few days ago, there was an article on the Dragoons and a drawing of their regimental insignia. Some days earlier there was a drawing of the identification of various ranks."

"You remembered that from one reading?" Richard questioned.

"Our Lizzy is a voracious reader and remembers what she has read, almost verbatim, after one reading," Gardiner explained. "Although more shy and less apt to demonstrate her abilities, Mary here," Gardiner inclined his head to his middle niece, "has a similar ability."

Mary, who was uncomfortable with praise, blushed at her uncle's kind, but true, words. Thanks to her mother's constant unkind words to both her and Lizzy, Mary had begun to think she did not merit such acknowledgement.

Thankfully, Elizabeth knew her worth. Although it caused her momentary pain when their mother denigrated her, she did not take it to heart the way Mary did. Although their father would not trouble himself to check their mother, he did send his eldest girls to the Gardiners for some months each year to allow them to thrive in a better environment.

"May I enquire as to how old your nieces are?" Richard asked.

"Jane, who is at Uncle's house, and is, by far, the prettiest girl alive, is nineteen. I am sixteen; Mary will be fifteen in two months; Kitty and Lydia, who are now at Longbourn, are thirteen and eleven," Elizabeth averred.

Richard was surprised. He supposed, due to their sizes—they were both on the petite side, Miss Elizabeth more so than Miss Mary—they were younger than had just been reported. He had underestimated their ages; he had been off by three or four years.

"Did your regiment return to England recently?" Mary enquired shyly.

"Indeed, it did, three days ago," Richard replied. "I have a month's leave now."

"Is none of your family in London?" Gardiner enquired.

"No, they left Town for their estates," Richard averred.

"If you like, we can convey you with us into Derbyshire. My wife, who you will soon meet, is the daughter of Mr. Adam Lambert, the rector at the church in Lambton. On the morrow, we will travel to Hertfordshire to deliver our two eldest nieces and our two children to Longbourn. We will depart for Derbyshire on the same day; Mary will be accompanying us," Gardiner said.

"As long as it is not an inconvenience..." Richard responded.

"Not at all. We have a second carriage as far as Longbourn as my brother, Thomas Bennet, sent his to London earlier today," Gardiner explained. "You can see we will not be cramped; with just the four of us travelling north from Longbourn, there will be more than enough room."

"In that case, I accept with thanks for your generosity, Mr. Gardiner," Richard gave a half bow as they arrived at a smart, well-built house opposite a park.

Gardiner led them into the house and to a sitting room, where Richard saw a lady who looked to be but a few years his senior, and a blond, blue-eyed, absolute beauty. Bingley would claim the blond as his newest angel if he ever beheld her. Based on Miss Elizabeth's statement about her older sister, Richard correctly assumed the beauty was the eldest Bennet sister.

Gardiner made the introductions to his wife and niece, then led the Major into his office and reviewed his investment portfolio with him. Richard was, as always, most impressed by the growth in his balance. As he had instructed, each time dividends were paid, they were folded back into the principal.

While in the study, Gardiner once again thanked the Major for sending his father, brother, and cousin to him as investors. Through them, he had gained more members of the upper ten thousand as clients.

When Mrs. Gardiner informed him her three nieces would share a bed for the night, freeing up a guest chamber, Richard demurred, claiming he would sleep on the settee. He had, after all, slept in far worse places in the army.

After being assured by all three Bennet sisters present that it was no hardship to share a bed, Richard dropped his opposition to the plan. Before going up to change for dinner, Miss Elizabeth pulled him aside.

"Major, if I were you, I would not wear your uniform on the morrow," Elizabeth suggested.

"Why would that be, Miss Elizabeth?"

"My younger sisters, and even my mother, will be much calmer if you are not wearing a scarlet coat. As young as they are, my youngest two sisters are convinced they will marry men in the army," Elizabeth related. "Also, unless you want my mother to push Jane at you relentlessly, do not mention your lineage."

"Is that a warning you issue to any man who visits your home?"

"If I were able to, I would," Elizabeth responded sardonically. "My mother is worried about the future because we have no brother and Longbourn is entailed away from the female line. She believes when Papa passes, which she imagines is imminent, she will be forced to live in, as she says, *the hedgerows.*"

"In that, Miss Elizabeth, she is not unlike most society matrons, even if they do not worry about their future. She has legitimate concerns, so do not be too hard on her," Richard stated.

Elizabeth looked at the Major thoughtfully. She had never considered things from that perspective before. "You have given me much to think on," She stated, then led the

Major upstairs and indicated the door to his chamber.

~~~~~~~/~~~~~~~

Having left London not long after sunup, the two carriages approached Meryton a little after ten o'clock. Richard rode in the Gardiner conveyance with Mr. and Mrs. Gardiner and Miss Mary. It was fitting, as the four would be together for the journey into Derbyshire.

The two eldest Bennet sisters and the two Gardiner children—Lilly and Eddy—rode in the Bennet equipage. Lilly was eight and Eddy was five. Sadly, since Eddy's birth, Madeline Gardiner had not fallen in the family way again.

When the coachmen pulled the carriages to a halt in Longbourn's drive, Richard was greeted with the sight of a medium-sized manor house on what looked like a moderate estate. After meeting the excitable matron and her equally exuberant youngest two daughters, Richard understood the wisdom of Miss Elizabeth's advice to him.

The master of the estate joined his wife to welcome his returning daughters. It did not take long for Richard to observe that Mr. Bennet, rather than check his wife or youngest daughters' vulgar effusions, made sport of them and made cutting comments, most of which went over their heads.

The mortification on the faces of the three eldest Bennet sisters was easy to see as their family displayed their inability to behave. Richard could tell the older sisters had learnt proper behaviour from the Gardiners rather than from their own parents.

Thankfully, Gardiner distracted his sister by presenting her with a bolt of fabric and a roll of lace before she could quiz the gentleman about his prospects. While she was exclaiming over the fine gifts, Gardiner and his wife kissed their children and exhorted them to behave while their parents were away. At the same time, Mary hugged her two older sisters.

Soon after he ushered his wife, the Major, and Mary

into his conveyance, they were off, making for the Great North Road.

~~~~~~~/~~~~~~~

By their third day of travel, as they approached Snowhaven, Richard had been able to draw Mary Bennet out and discovered there was so much more to the young lady than she let on. She was as intelligent as her next older sister and had a rapier sharp wit when she chose to employ it.

The occupants of the carriage had many stimulating conversations during rest stops and evenings at inns. When they arrived at the gatehouse, the keeper recognised a member of the family and informed Richard his family was at Pemberley.

As it was only another ten miles, and not far out of their way, Gardiner told his coachman to proceed to the Darcy estate. For Madeline Gardiner, it had been many years since she visited Pemberley. Her mother had been alive the last time she had been there, so many emotions roiled within her as the carriage approached the mansion.

While a Darcy footman retrieved Richard's small trunk, he thanked the Gardiners profusely for their kindness. Rather than intrude, the Gardiners elected to travel the five miles to Lambton, where a suite of chambers was waiting for them at the Rose and Crown Inn.

Richard asked Mr. Reynolds not to announce him. When he entered the drawing room, everyone expressed their surprise and pleasure at seeing him. It was good to be with family again.

~~~~~~~/~~~~~~~

The day after arriving at Pemberley, Richard took Anna, now ten, with him to visit the Gardiners at the Rose and Crown Inn in Lambton. While he thanked them once again, Mary Bennet and Georgiana Darcy spoke together, shyly at first, but then they discovered their mutual love of music, specifically music for the pianoforte.

The almost five-year age difference notwithstanding, for the fortnight the Gardiners were in Lambton, Mary and Anna, as they now addressed one another, spent a great deal of time together.

As Darcy was familiar with Gardiner through his investments, he agreed to invite them to dinner twice. One afternoon he was speaking to Richard when he opined Miss Mary was too far below her to be a good friend for Anna.

After a set-down by his co-guardian, with his Aunt, Uncle, and Andrew heartily agreeing with Richard, Darcy backed down and promised not to discourage the friendship as the two girls had agreed to correspond.

Ten days after the Gardiners and Miss Mary departed the area, Richard returned to London in his brother Andrew's coach. It was time for him to report for duty once again.

CHAPTER 3

From 1807 until May of 1808, Richard Fitzwilliam could be found training officers and men for their return to the Peninsula. In February of 1808, then Major Fitzwilliam was promoted to second in command of the regiment. It was much sooner than he should have been promoted but there were exigent circumstances.

His predecessor, Lieutenant Colonel Jackson Forster, sustained a serious injury to his leg during a training exercise. He had tripped over a rock protruding from the ground when he was leading his men in a 'charge' against an 'enemy' position.

The Lieutenant Colonel had fallen in such a way that his right leg was broken in multiple places. The surgeons had opined that, even if Lieutenant Colonel Forster did not lose his leg, he would never be fit for combat again.

Richard had been close to the man and knew how great a disappointment it was to Forster because, like himself, he had earned all his promotions. Richard was happy Major General Atherton, as he now was, saw fit to promote him due to the unforeseen circumstances; however, at the same time he wished it had not come at the expense of his friend's career in the regulars.

During the previous eighteen months, Richard had spent as much of his leave time with his family as possible. He took his duty as co-guardian very seriously, as he did all of his duties. He realised his limitations in fulfilling that particular role while he was in the army, given how little of his time was his own.

When he last had leave, he had observed William in society. His cousin's hauteur, pride, and arrogance had become more pronounced. Being away as often as he was, Richard did not see a path forward for him to help William correct his behaviour. At least his cousin spent time with Bingley, who seemed able to blunt William's taciturn outlook when they were together.

In March of 1807, the former Miss Bingley, who was terrified of being labelled as *on the shelf* accepted the hand of Mr. Harold Hurst. The man was a member of the third circle, or second circle at best. He was not from the heights of society both of the Bingley sisters wished to reach, but he *was* a gentleman and heir to Winsdale, a minor estate in Surrey.

It amused Richard when the new Miss Bingley— Caroline—railed about Mr. Hurst being of too low a social standing for her sister to marry, seeming to forget she was herself from the lowest rung of the societal ladder, being the daughter of a tradesman. At least after her marriage, the new Mrs. Hurst was considered a gentlewoman.

He could not understand why, as much as William disliked Miss Bingley—no, that was too weak a term; *detested* was more accurate—he allowed her to cling to his arm when they were in company while she denigrated any person she considered a rival for Darcy's affections. Those who she disparaged were far above her in society, yet William never objected.

When Richard asked his cousin why he allowed her abhorrent behaviour to stand without comment, William stated it was because he did not want to damage his friendship with Bingley.

Richard pointed out Bingley knew all about his sister's behaviour and that the friendship would be a weak one indeed if Bingley pulled out of it due to his harpy of a sister being told a few home truths.

As William had done since his father's death, he chose to rely on his own counsel and stated he knew best. Richard knew how obstinate his cousin could be, so he chose not to argue with him on that particular subject.

He had warned William to be on high alert because he was certain Miss Caroline Bingley was not beneath affecting a compromise to get what she wanted. William reminded Richard what his father had written in his will with respect to being entrapped into marriage, then he stated he would *never* marry the daughter of a tradesman.

Although he had invoked his father's words, he seemed to have forgotten that both of his parents had advised him to marry for love, not convenience. William had stated it was expected of a Darcy of Pemberley to make a brilliant match.

As he had with his opinions about Miss Bingley, Richard bit his tongue. A few days after that conversation, he discussed it with his parents and Andy—who had not come close to finding a woman it would not be a punishment to spend an evening with, never mind a lifetime.

They had all noted the same things Richard had, but agreed nothing would be gained by pushing William; he would only dig in his heels. They decided, instead, they would spend as much time with Anna as they could.

Anna had turned twelve in March of 1808. A few months before, she had the misfortune to meet Miss Bingley, who decided fawning over a girl not yet twelve would be an excellent way to garner William's attention. Poor Anna disliked the woman intensely but knew she could say nothing to William as long as he allowed Miss Bingley to call at Darcy House.

From that time on Anna was invited to reside at Matlock House when she was in London. Darcy knew Anna loved Aunt Elaine and Uncle Reggie, so he did not object to the arrangement. As Anna never knew her mother, Aunt Elaine happily stood in as surrogate mother for both Darcy and Anna. Thankfully for Miss Darcy, and much to the harridan's consternation, Miss Bingley never was admitted to Matlock House.

At the end of May of 1808, the Dragoons were ordered to the Peninsula. They were deployed to the Kingdom of Portugal and the Algarve and would be based near the village of Roliça, where they would join a force under the command of General Sir Arthur Wellesley.

~~~~~~~/~~~~~~~

During their first three months, there had been only a few probing skirmishes. Based on information the Secretary of War, Viscount Castlereagh, had received about the size of the French forces being sent to Roliça, he sent another fifteen thousand men and ordered General Sir John Moore from Sweden to augment the English forces in the area.

On the seventeenth day of August, Lieutenant Colonel Richard Fitzwilliam got his first taste of battle. After a hard fight against the French—commanded by General of Division Henri-François Delaborde—and after losing many of their men, including Colonel Lake of the 29th Regiment of Foot, the Dragoons were part of the final wave that chased the French from their positions and won the day.

Among the almost five hundred English soldiers lost that day was Colonel Trenton, the commander of Richard's regiment. Major General Atherton gave Richard a field promotion to Colonel and, with it, command of the regiment.

The Dragoons were sent to the rear to lick their wounds. Due to that, they were not involved in the Battle of Vimeiro four days later. A month later, Richard and his regiment were moved close to Sahagún in Spain.

The Battle of Sahagún was fought on the twenty-first of December in 1808. Richard was wounded—not seriously—when a ball fired from a French musket ricocheted off a rock and grazed his left forearm.

Thankfully, the Dragoons' losses were light in that battle. Things were quiet for the Dragoons until January of 1809. After Sahagún, the brigade encamped outside of Madrid in order to contain the French occupying that city.

Richard's arm healed quickly; luckily, there was never any sign of infection. By the first week in January, all that remained was a small, almost unnoticeable, scar. They were still encamped outside of Madrid when they learned the Battle of Corunna had been fought.

The British forces had been pursued by Marshal of the Empire Jean-de-Dieu Soult. After a fierce battle around the port of Corunna, they had managed to embark aboard Royal Navy ships under the cover of darkness; however, it had cost them the life of General Sir John Moore.

At least the General had left the mortal world knowing the bulk of his army had escaped. Although he would not have shied away from the battle, Richard was not unhappy the Dragoons' orders to join Lieutenant-General Sir John Moore had been rescinded.

They had instead been ordered to join Wellesley's forces east of Madrid before the end of April in 1809. Plans to liberate Madrid with the Spanish army under the command of General Cuesta were being made.

~~~~~~~/~~~~~~~

The Dragoons were one of the many battalions Wellesley deployed for the Battle of Talavera, which raged on July 27th and 28th of 1809. Richard led his regiment, supported by a second regiment led by another colonel, who took, at heavy cost, a strategic hill overlooking Madrid. By some miracle, Colonel Richard Fitzwilliam escaped being injured on the first day of the battle.

On the second day, the Dragoons made a bayonet charge to repulse a French attempt to retake the hill. The French were determined to regain the hill they had ceded to the Dragoons, so they unleashed a cannonade that lasted until noon.

Richard and the other colonel had kept the men of their regiments safe in trenches they had dug below the crest of the hill.

There was a two-hour armistice so both sides could collect their wounded and dead. As soon as it expired, the cannons on both sides roared again. During a skirmish on the left flank of the hill, Richard was wounded during close-quarter combat.

After disabling several French officers with his sabre, Richard was struck in his left thigh by a ball from a French rifle. It hit and broke the bone, but by pure chance missed any major blood vessel.

At almost the same moment, a French infantryman attacked Richard with his bayonet. Richard was stabbed as he fell from being shot, which was the only reason the blow only glanced his right side, by some miracle not penetrating his ribs.

As there was massive bleeding from his chest and leg, the French soldier was about to finish off the prostrate English officer when one of Richard's men shot the Frenchman in the face and ended his life.

Under the cover of darkness, while cannon balls flew in both directions, Richard and other wounded Dragoons were collected and brought to the medical tents. At first, the surgeon thought Richard was a hopeless case, but after the blood was cleaned and his wounds revealed, the man opined Richard might be saved.

~~~~~~~/~~~~~~~

He was unconscious for more than a week while his body fought a raging fever caused by infection of the long cut over his ribs. When he did awake, Richard was delirious and knew not where he was, but he had the feeling the ground under his pallet was unstable. He was not aware of it, but Richard was on a ship carrying him back to England.

Richard's parents, Andy, and William met the ship carrying the gravely wounded Colonel at Southampton, although he was unaware of it. General Atherton had sent the family a dispatch as soon as he learned the Colonel had been injured.

The letter was received in time for them to meet the transport ship. The family made the journey from Derbyshire in under two days rather than the normal three.

Lady Matlock had refused to wait in the coach and joined her husband, son, and nephew each day when they checked to see which ships had arrived. On the third day, it was Richard's ship.

When she saw her younger son, Lady Matlock almost swooned, but stopped herself by force of will alone. The three men were no less horrified when they saw the bloody bandages and Richard's ashen pallor.

Lord Matlock approached the doctor, who was directing who should go where, and introduced himself so the medical man would know his rank. "I want to take my son to London to be cared for by the best doctors and surgeons we can find," the Earl said with as much authority as he could muster under the circumstances.

"Who is your son?" the doctor asked without emotion. He had seen too many hopeless cases to show his feelings.

"Colonel Richard Fitzwilliam of the Dragoons," the Earl pointed to the stretcher being carried by Richard's batman and another dragoon.

"As long as you can transport him as he is now, I cannot stop you, My Lord," the doctor replied impassively.

"One of our coaches is ready to transport him lying down," Lord Matlock responded. They had placed a wooden board in one of the coaches, running from one bench to the other; it formed a makeshift bed for this exact purpose.

The doctor issued an order for the men to carry the Colonel to the Earl's carriage. "I will not leave my Colonel," said Brown, Richard's batman.

"It is no more than I expected. A doctor is waiting in the coach. He will ride with you and my son," Lord Matlock informed the fiercely loyal man.

Dr. Bartholomew supervised Richard's placement in the conveyance and made sure the patient was as comfortable as possible. He and Brown entered the equipage once the Colonel was situated. Brooking no argument, Lady Matlock joined them.

As it was over seventy miles to London, so as not to jostle the Colonel unnecessarily, they stopped at an inn that night. By the time they arrived at Matlock House, with the patient thankfully unconscious for most of the journey, it was the afternoon of the next day, Friday, August eighteenth, 1809.

When Richard was carried into the house, the servants looked as sombre as his family. He was much loved by all of them; not a few prayers were said for his full recovery.

The doctor summoned a surgeon, one who had been with the army previously, a Mr. Kincaid McTavish. He was not happy with the way Richard's leg had been set, opining that he would have difficulty walking—never mind riding—if things were left as they were.

In consultation with Mr. Bartholomew and the family, it was decided to permit McTavish to re-break the leg in order to reset the bone. The blessing was Richard remained unconscious throughout the procedure.

~~~~~~~/~~~~~~~

There was only one in the family who hoped her nephew would succumb to his wounds. Ever since her brother had taken away the title *Mistress of Rosings Park* from her when Anne reached the age stipulated in her late husband's disgraceful will, Lady Catherine had hoped her nephew would not return from the war alive.

The will stipulated once Anne turned three and twenty in October of 1807, and she was unmarried, the estate became Anne's property. In the event Lady Catherine's sickly daughter did not survive until that age, or passed while unmarried, Rosings Park would go to her undeserving nephew.

Lady Catherine was convinced Rosings Park should belong to her. There was no provision she knew about in Sir Lewis's will stating what would happen if Richard Fitzwilliam was killed in battle. Lady Catherine believed that, if Richard was killed, the estate, the house in London, and the de Bourgh fortune would become hers—she had told herself it would be so; therefore, it was fact to her.

A further annoyance to Lady Catherine was that the parson at Hunsford was preparing to retire. He was a man who had always shown the correct deference due one of her rank. Reggie had denied her request to appoint the clergyman's replacement.

Her interfering brother had sent notice to the Bishop of Kent that unless a man was appointed by Anne, with his approval, the preferment would be invalid! It was not to be borne, but she knew not what to do. At least she had been allowed to remain in the manor house—for now—and had not been sent to the dower house. She was determined to discover a way to reclaim her power.

~~~~~~~/~~~~~~~

Richard's recovery was slow and painful, but once the fever was beaten, he started to make steady progress. Within a month he was able to stay awake for most of the day. He had been weaned off laudanum and now only used willow bark tea for pain. The doctor had expressed concern about the addictive properties of laudanum.

In November of that year, General Atherton, now a

Lieutenant-General, visited his colonel. Based on the medical assessment that although he would walk again, and possibly ride, Richard could never be a combat soldier, he offered Richard a choice.

He could command the Dragoons' training grounds, or he could resign with his honour intact and sell his commission. Being stubborn, Richard decided to wait until he went before the Army's medical board and was ruled unfit for combat before he would consider another path forward for his life.

By December he was able to leave his bed, albeit using crutches and with Brown watching over him like a mother hen. Richard was still not used to being assisted down the stairs by Brown and a footman, but he knew it was what he must endure if he did not want to remain upstairs.

Christmastide was celebrated at Matlock House that year. The Darcys, whose house was just across the square, visited every day. Richard was impressed by how much his shared ward, now thirteen, had improved on the pianoforte, even if she was shy about playing before an audience, including before close family members.

Darcy was much as he had been, except among family he did not don his mask. He was relieved Richard was on the mend. After so much loss in his relatively short life, Darcy did not know how he could have survived losing Richard as well.

Richard's medical board was set for February of 1810.

CHAPTER 4

He had his answer now. The medical board ruled Colonel Richard Fitzwilliam would never be fit to serve in combat again. All that was left for Richard was to choose another path—teaching others to be soldiers or retiring.

Richard looked at the cane in his hand. Unlike for so many other gentlemen, this was not an affectation or a fashionable accoutrement; it was a necessity in order for him to walk. His leg had healed to the point he no longer needed a crutch; as long as he had some support on his left side, he could walk.

How far had he fallen from the vibrant, fit officer who had ridden into battle, sabre drawn, leading hundreds of men and their officers! The periods of melancholy he experienced from time to time did not come as often as they had when he first regained consciousness and began to heal.

He was slowly learning to look at all that he had—he was alive and surrounded by his family—rather than what he had lost. It was not yet a sure thing, but he was hopeful he could ride Invictus again one day.

His faithful battle charger, Harridan, had been cut down at Talavera. His charger remained on the field of battle that ended Richard's ability to fight with the Dragoons, or any other regiment, again.

There was a third option, which Richard had rejected already. The militia. Forster had visited Richard during his recuperation in an effort to convince his former comrade in arms to join him in the militia.

His friend commanded a regiment of the Derbyshire Militia and had been given the rank of colonel. For him, it was a way to remain in the army even though he was no longer fit to ride into combat.

Forster walked with a pronounced limp, but even though one leg would never be as strong as it had been, he was able to ride, something Richard was praying hard he would be able to do again.

After considering entering the militia for but a brief moment, Richard decided it would not be one of his options. He would stick with the two he was considering, if, as Bartholomew assured him, the board found him unfit for active service. The doctor had been correct.

There was no more procrastinating; he had to make a decision. He was not one to remain idle for the rest of his life; he needed to have an occupation. With that thought in mind, he hailed a hackney cab.

It was not a question of finances that he wanted an occupation. He simply needed to have a purpose. Thanks to his investments with Edward Gardiner, what he would receive for the sale of his commission, and the fact he would be placed on half pay, he could live comfortably. This was not counting on the fact that, unless Anne married—something she vowed she never would—he would inherit a prosperous estate after her passing.

Darcy had offered him the satellite estate of Rivington, in Surrey, but Richard did not want charity; he still had his pride. If he chose to resign from the Army, he would be willing to *lease* the estate from his cousin.

First Richard had to make a decision; then, he could consider his options. As he watched London's buildings slip past the window of his cab, he reached a resolution.

For the same reason he could not see himself in the

militia—he was not one to be a show soldier—he would not be able to accept a role in the Army less than the one he used to perform. He would resign and sell out. There was no dishonour in doing so; he was not one—like some cowards—to sell out as soon as the possibility of combat reared its head.

Richard grinned as the horse pulling the cab turned into Grosvenor Square. He knew his decision would result in two resignations from the Army. He was as sure as he could be that his batman, Jimmy Brown, would want to remain with him. A more fiercely loyal man Richard had never encountered.

Poor Brown would have to take lessons from William's valet, Carstens, on how to be a gentleman's man—or something approximating it. Richard would never care if his cravat had as many folds and knots as Beau Brummel and his set.

The reason his man would study with Carstens was Richard had accepted William's invitation to live with him and Anna if he resigned from the Army and until he made a decision about his next steps. He would live with his cousins until he was ready to be on his own again.

As proud as he was of being independent, Richard had no improper pride that would prevent him from acknowledging he was still months away from being able to live independently.

His parents or Andy would have been happy for him to reside with them, but he accepted William's invitation because he was Anna's co-guardian and would now, finally, be able to discharge his duty to her on an ongoing basis.

~~~~~~~/~~~~~~~

"Rich, you are not ready to ride twenty miles or so on horseback, are you?" Darcy asked his cousin.

The two were seated in the master's study at Darcy House. It was mid-April, more than a month after the day Anna turned fourteen and three weeks since the first time

Richard had ridden Invictus again.

He had only been able to ride for fifteen minutes, but it had been a start. In three weeks, Richard was able to ride comfortably for an hour, but he had ridden at the canter only once.

"I do not think I am ready for so long a ride," Richard responded. "Even with frequent rest stops, I do not believe it is wise. Why do you ask?"

"You remember that Bingley has been considering the purchase of an estate in order to join the landed gentry, do you not?"

"Yes, I remember talk of that. What has it to do with the ride you mentioned?"

"He was rushing into the purchase of an estate, something with which he has no experience, so I advised he find one to lease before he commits most of his fortune to acquire one of his own."

"That would be a good way for him to learn estate management and decide if it is something he wishes to undertake—not just what his sisters demand," Richard agreed. "Why twenty miles?" A memory stirred for Richard of the time Gardiner had invited him to join his family for their journey into Derbyshire. They had travelled about twenty miles first before they headed north.

"Richard, where did you go?" Darcy asked amusedly.

"I am sorry, William; I was lost in thought."

"A small town in Hertfordshire, Meryton, is that distance. There is an estate, Netherfield Park, being offered for lease in the neighbourhood and I am riding with Bingley on the morrow to inspect it."

"It is good you will be with him. As good a head for business as Bingley has, he would not know how to evaluate an estate, something in which you are well versed." Richard paused as he was struck by a thought which caused him to grin. "I assume the reason you two are riding is a certain shrew would have demanded to join you if you travelled by coach."

"You have the right of it, Rich. Will you join Anna at Matlock House? She is going to visit your mother on the morrow.

"I will; I owe Mother a visit. She called here only yesterday. Andy will be there as well."

"Speaking of your brother, do you know why he has been so interested in volunteering at Covenant House of late?"

Covenant House was a charity run by a board chaired by Lady Matlock for unwed and put-upon girls to recover and try to learn life skills. They were provided a place to live while they were increasing, and their children were placed in loving homes if the young mother could not, or did not want to, care for the babe.

Mrs. Gardiner was on the board as well. As far as Richard knew, her nieces volunteered there when they were in London. He remembered them fondly from four years ago when he had met them—especially Miss Mary, who had ridden with him in the carriage to Derbyshire.

"Andy has not said anything to me, so I know not why, or how often, he volunteers there."

"Rather than mixing with those below us, he should pledge funds, as I do," Darcy stated with a sniff of disdain.

"He does not tell you how to administer the charities you support, so please allow my brother the same courtesy." Richard wanted to take William to task for his arrogance, but he decided against it—for now. "Do I need to remind you the chair of the charity is someone who would not enjoy hearing of your disdain for those who are helped there?"

Darcy had the decency to look chagrined. He would not enjoy a setdown from his Aunt Elaine.

~~~~~~~/~~~~~~~

Two days after Lizzy had turned twenty, Jane Bennet had come to stay with her Aunt and Uncle Gardiner and her two cousins, on the seventh day of March. She had planned to remain for a month, but it was now going on six weeks.

The reason for Jane's lengthened stay was a man. The first Friday Jane had been in residence with the Gardiners on Gracechurch Street, she accompanied Aunt Maddie to Covenant House to volunteer—just as Lizzy and Mary did when they came to stay with the Gardiners.

Jane had a few accomplishments like embroidery, playing the harp, and compounding scents and herbal remedies in the stillroom among them. Embroidery and stillroom expertise were subjects in demand for the girls at Covenant House, so she taught classes in both on Mondays, Wednesdays, and Fridays when she was in London. With her serenity and patience, the eldest Bennet daughter was very popular among the girls and staff at Covenant House.

She could not but remember the first meeting with pleasure.

~~~~~~~/~~~~~~~

Friday, the ninth of March

Jane, who would be three and twenty early in July, was alighting from the Gardiner carriage after Aunt Maddie did, when a large coach with a coat of arms on the door pulled to a halt behind them.

A tall, sandy blond haired man, very handsome and well-built, stepped down and then turned to hand someone down from inside the cabin. From previous visits, Jane recognised the lady as the Countess of Matlock.

The Countess must have seen her and Aunt Maddie, because she said something to the man with her and then the two walked over to Jane and her aunt. As they drew near, Jane noticed the man had piercing deep-blue eyes. He was even more handsome close up.

"Mrs. Gardiner, Miss Bennet, it is good to see you again. It has been quite a while since I have seen you or your other nieces who volunteer here," Lady Matlock said in greeting. "Have either of you met my eldest son yet?"

Mrs. Gardiner and Jane Bennet both curtsied to the Countess and her son. "We have not been accorded the honour before, My Lady," Madeline replied.

Andrew Fitzwilliam had never seen a more beautiful woman. She was tall, blond, with intriguing cerulean-blue eyes that shone with intelligence. He hoped she would not be another fawning woman who saw him as a way to increase her standing, wealth, and connections—someone who would agree with anything he said, no matter how ridiculous it might be.

"Andrew, this is Mrs. Gardiner, who is on the board of Covenant House, and her eldest niece, Miss Jane Bennet of, if memory serves, Longbourn in Hertfordshire." Jane nodded to the Countess that it was so. "Madeline, Miss Bennet, my son, Lord Andrew Fitzwilliam, Viscount Hilldale."

Both ladies curtsied and Andrew bowed to them. "It is a pleasure to meet you both," Andrew stated.

While his mother spoke to her friend, Andrew approached the beauty, hoping against hope she was more than a pretty face. "Miss Bennet, is this your first time volunteering here?"

"No, My Lord; I began to volunteer when I was fifteen, about eight years ago," Jane replied.

'Impressive. She is not coy or batting her eyelashes at me as most do,' *Andrew thought silently to himself.* 'Almost every woman of my acquaintance would make some inane comment about not revealing her age while doing so anyway.'

"That is laudable. Did your sisters begin at the same age?" Andrew enquired.

"My next younger sister, Elizabeth, and the sister after her, Mary, also began when they were fifteen." Jane said, then paused. "Unfortunately, the two youngest, Catherine, who is seventeen

now, and Lydia, fifteen, do not visit the Gardiners and they claim volunteering is not fun. They have no interest in assisting those less fortunate than ourselves."

"Five sisters! Do you have any brothers?" Andrew asked.

"No, I do not." Jane decided not to mention the entail as it was not germane to their conversation. "Your brother is in the Army, is he not? I remember meeting him four years ago. He rode with the Gardiners, myself, and two of my sisters to Longbourn and then on to Derbyshire."

"I remember Richard mentioning it," Andrew recalled. "He said one sister was with them and he had interesting conversations with her."

"That would be Mary. Both she and Lizzy are highly intelligent," Jane agreed.

"You seem the same way, if I may say so, Miss Bennet," Andrew stated and found he meant it. The longer he spoke with Miss Bennet, the more he saw her depths. There had been no fawning, no coquettishness, and no batting of eyelashes. She spoke to him as he had always desired to be spoken to, as just another man.

Jane blushed. "I do not have the wit and intelligence of Lizzy and Mary. That is not false modesty, My Lord, just a fact."

Much to Andrew's chagrin, the ladies had to enter the house. If he did not have a prior appointment, he would have remained.

~~~~~~~/~~~~~~~

For the first fortnight Jane had volunteered, Andrew Fitzwilliam found a reason to be present at Covenant House almost every time she was there as well. Both his mother and Jane's aunt could see an attachment was growing between them, but they did nothing to either encourage or discourage it.

In the third week, Andrew Fitzwilliam requested permission to call on Miss Jane Bennet, which both she and her uncle granted. They had decided the calls would all be at the Gardiners' house or walking in the small park opposite. Jane understood it had nothing to do with the Viscount being embarrassed to be seen with her, but rather to escape the attention of the *Ton*. Whatever, if anything, would be allowed to develop naturally, away from the whispering and staring of polite society.

It was the same reason, something Jane explained to Andrew, why she had said not a word to her mother about his calling on her. She was open about informing him that Mrs. Bennet's mission in life was to see all of her daughters well disposed of in marriage.

It was during this discussion Jane explained her mother's fears regarding the entail to heirs male on the estate. Andrew understood the matron's fears but deferred to Jane regarding when and what to tell her mother.

It was more difficult for Jane to explain why she was happy Uncle Edward was allowed to grant or deny requests for her while she was under his care. She did, however, explain her father's penchant for making fun of everyone, especially his wife. She felt he would have teased his wife by hinting at something without telling her the truth of the matter.

Jane kept a steady correspondence with Lizzy and Mary, but due to her mother's habit of reading post addressed to others, Jane was circumspect in what she said to them. To circumvent her mother, she told all in a letter sent in care of Charlotte Lucas, a good friend to the three eldest Bennet sisters.

A few days ago, Andrew requested and had been granted an official courtship. Jane would be returning to Longbourn soon—she could not extend her visit again—and Andrew would be travelling to Hilldale in Staffordshire for the spring planting. Other than Lizzy and Mary, no one at Longbourn would be told of the courtship yet.

Jane was gratified that the Earl and the Countess were happy their son had found a lady who excited his interest. That Jane was the daughter of a minor country squire concerned them not at all.

~~~~~~~/~~~~~~~

The day Richard and Anna visited Matlock House, the same day Darcy and Bingley were on their way to Hertfordshire, Andrew confided in Richard before he began his journey to his estate.

Richard was sworn to silence until Andrew's return from Hilldale. The former could not but grin. He knew now why Andrew had been so preoccupied and could not tell William.

CHAPTER 5

E lizabeth Bennet twirled around, enjoying the warmth of the April day. It was late morning and the azure sky held nary a cloud.

Spring was one of Elizabeth Bennet's favourite seasons. There were new lambs in the field; the trees and shrubs were verdant once again; in the fallow fields and alongside paths, brightly-coloured wildflowers bloomed.

The field she was in was one that had been allowed to lie fallow, but all around were the signs of life in fields that had been ploughed and planted. The seedlings were breaking through the surface, giving the impression each planted field was covered in a mist of green.

Walking across the fields of her beloved home on such a day revived her spirits after being subjected to yet another of her mother's denigrating comments. Elizabeth was well aware that, even though her mother was of mean understanding, she was not driven by a desire to hurt, but by fear for her future, thanks to the entail under which Longbourn suffered.

How Elizabeth wished she were able to go back in time to confront her great-grandfather Bennet and make it clear to him what damage such an inflexibly-written entail could cause if, as in her parents' case, no living son was born. Being aware her wish was one that could never be granted did not prevent her from dreaming about how much better their lives would have been without the entail.

Had there been a Bennet son, the entail would have ended with him. Instead, the estate would devolve to a faceless distant cousin by the name of Collins. Elizabeth shook off her melancholic thoughts of the entail and the effect on her family's life if Papa was called home before all five of his daughters were married.

She was walking along a treeline of a field that bordered the vacant estate of Netherfield Park, Longbourn's neighbour on the west. Rumour said Netherfield Park might have a tenant soon.

That rumour emanated from Elizabeth's aunt, Hattie Philips, her mother's older sister, married to Meryton's solicitor. Uncle Frank had taken over late Grandfather Elias Gardiner's practice, when his late father-in-law's own son, Uncle Edward Gardiner, decided he did not wish to pursue the law. Uncle and Aunt Philips had never been blessed with children of their own, hence they doted on their Bennet and Gardiner nieces and nephew.

Along with Elizabeth's own mother, the youngest of the three Gardiner siblings, Aunt Hattie was one of the foremost gossips in the area. As soon as she heard there was a potential lessee for Netherfield Park, Aunt Hattie had made with all speed to Longbourn in order to inform her sister of the wonderful news.

Of course, this meant the whole neighbourhood would know it within hours. The fact it was only potential, and the man had not leased the estate yet, did not discourage the sisters from spreading the news far and wide.

When she spied two men racing across the field on the other side of the fence, Elizabeth was glad she was hidden by the trees so they would not see her walking with her bonnet in hand and her hair down.

She guessed one of them was the potential new resident of the neighbourhood. From what Elizabeth could see from her vantage point, they both wore well-tailored suits, which spoke of them being men of means. They sported highly polished riding boots.

The two men were attired in dark riding jackets and beige breeches. Their cravats seemed to be fashionably arranged, reminiscent of the style of that ridiculous peacock of a man, Beau Brummell.

Elizabeth watched as the taller of the two readjusted his beaver before the men slowed their horses and wheeled them back towards the direction of Netherfield Park's manor house.

~~~~~~~/~~~~~~~

As he and Bingley turned back towards the manor house, Darcy thought he saw a flash of colour near a stand of trees in the field of the estate across the fence. He dismissed it as an illusion.

"Well, what think you?" Bingley asked, making Darcy forget about what he thought he had seen.

"After inspecting the house, barns, and tenant cottages, I saw nothing that might cause any significant problems," Darcy reported. "The same holds true for the home farm and tenant farms we inspected. The spring planting has been completed, and by all accounts correctly. The steward who toured the fields with us seems to be competent. In short, I see nothing ill about this estate."

Thanks to its location in the north spring planting at Pemberley occurred later than in Hertfordshire. Darcy would not be returning to his estate to supervise the spring planting there; he had planned everything in advance with Chalmers and was confident in his steward's abilities. If the man needed guidance from Darcy, he would inform the master of Pemberley by courier.

"I was hoping you would say that. I will see Mr. Philips at his office and sign the lease for a year," Bingley decided.

"You do not want to ruminate on the decision for a while?" Darcy suggested.

"Since when have you known me to do that, Darce?"

Bingley reposted. "You know whatever I do is done in a hurry. Once I am residing here, if I should resolve to quit Netherfield Park, I should probably be off in five minutes. At present, however, I consider myself quite fixed here for a year after my lease begins."

"I am afraid that is an accurate sketch of your character, my friend," Darcy agreed.

"Will you be my guest and assist me in learning what I need to know about managing an estate?" Bingley requested. He saw his friend hesitate and knew why. "You are debating whether you wish to reside in the same house as my younger sister, are you not?"

"I beg your pardon, Bingley, but I am," Darcy admitted.

"Then I extend the invitation to Miss Darcy and your cousins. Fitzwilliam will be able to deflect my sister, and if your eldest cousin accepts, Caroline will be distracted by having a viscount in residence."

"I will pass the invitation on to them and let you know."

The friends rode the two miles into the small market town without further conversation. Mr. Philips received the two with pleasure. Not long afterwards, the deed was done, and Bingley had signed the lease. The date agreed upon for him to move in was the second day of July.

Soon enough, the two men were riding out of Meryton and on their way back to London.

~~~~~~~/~~~~~~~

The day after Darcy returned from Hertfordshire he told Richard and Anna about Bingley leasing an estate in that shire. When Darcy had extended an invitation for Richard and Anna to join him at Netherfield Park, Richard agreed without delay. Anna was more than happy to be one of the party, in spite of her aversion for Miss Bingley, because Mary Bennet, her friend with whom she corresponded regularly, lived close to the estate Mr. Bingley had leased.

Richard was happy to be spending time near the lady who—if his brother had anything to say about it—would become his sister one day. It was inducement enough, even without the amusement he expected to experience when Darcy discovered that particular fact.

Knowing Bingley's penchant for willowy blonds, Richard felt he should be on hand to warn the man off if he sniffed around Miss Bennet like a bloodhound catching the scent of his quarry.

"Richard, will you accompany me to Rosings Park for Easter?" Darcy asked.

"You know I have no patience for our aunt's inanities," Richard replied.

"Neither do I, but your father requested I do this for him starting last year. Also, it will give us a chance to see Anne and make sure all is well with her. As she is determined never to marry, it would behove you to become familiar with your future property."

"I cannot predict when that might happen. I certainly hope Anne will be with us for many years to come," Richard insisted. "But yes, I will join you. What of Anna?"

"There is no reason to subject her to our aunt. She will be happy to remain in London with your parents," Darcy stated. "We need to look for a companion for her when we return from Rosings Park. She no longer needs a governess; besides, Miss Huxtable informed me she has accepted another position."

"You will hear no argument from me on that," Richard agreed. "Why do you not place an advertisement? We can interview candidates after we return from Kent. Or, if you prefer, we can ask Mother to find a good candidate."

"With all due respect to Aunt Elaine, I want to manage something of this importance," Darcy replied dismissively.

"When do you want to depart for Kent?" Richard

enquired, ignoring his cousin's haughty response.

"I was thinking of arriving there on Wednesday, the eighteenth day of April. Ten days, or a fortnight at the most, will be more than enough time in Aunt Catherine's company."

The cousins agreed upon that date for departure.

~~~~~~~/~~~~~~~

Mary was sitting with her older sisters when her father handed her a letter that arrived in yesterday morning's post. It had sat on his desk since then; he only now bestirred himself to hand it to his middle daughter.

"Thank you, Papa," Mary responded. Her countenance brightened when she noticed that the neat script was her friend Anna's.

Bennet made an inaudible response and returned to his study, where he took up a book and poured a fresh glass of port. "Go ahead and read your letter, Mary; Lizzy and I will not feel slighted if you do," Jane assured their younger sister.

"You will hear no argument from me," Elizabeth agreed.

"Thank you," Mary returned excitedly as she broke the Darcy seal and began to read.

16 April 1810

Matlock House, London

Mary, my very good friend,

I will be seeing you soon! William told me that I will be joining him and Richard when we are guests of Mr. Bingley, my brother's good friend, who has signed a lease for the estate of Netherfield Park, which I believe is near Longbourn.

My brother tells me Mr. Bingley will take up residence on the 2nd of July and we will arrive a few days afterwards. The reason we will not arrive at the same time is Miss Bingley (you will remember what I told you about her), who, if we travel at the same time, will demand she ride with us in our coach.

"My friend will be here in July," Mary reported excitedly. Then she covered her mouth to stifle her laugh. "Do you remember what Mama said when Aunt Hattie told her about Mr. Bingley leasing the estate, that he is wealthy and, more importantly, single?"

"You mean: *A single man in possession of a good fortune, must be in want of a wife*, right before Mama announced he would be Jane's husband," Elizabeth giggled. "Janey, we will have to assist you in deflecting our mother until your Andrew returns to your side."

"Mayhap I will tell Mama something to make sure she does not attempt to push me at Mr. Bingley, embarrassing both of us," Jane mused.

Andrew had told her that he would return from his estate as soon as he could, as long as there were no pressing needs in Staffordshire—hopefully by the end of May. Mayhap Mama would become aware Jane was no longer available by the time Mr. Bingley arrived in the area.

Mary returned to her letter.

I look forward to meeting your older sisters. I am sure the younger ones cannot be as bad as you have described. I am close to the age of your youngest sister; mayhap we will have much in common.

When I told Richard (my co-guardian) I was writing to you, he requested I send his regards to your sisters he has met, especially the one his brother met at Covenant House.

My governess has accepted a post with another family. I will miss her sorely, but when my brother and cousin return from my Cousin Anne's estate they will employ a companion for me. I hope she will be as pleasant as Miss Huxtable was.

I look forward to seeing you again.

Your friend,

Anna

Mary folded her missive and smiled. She was looking forward to seeing Anna again. "Anna is very shy, but I am sure you will both make her feel welcome," Mary told her older sisters. "I hope Kitty and Lydia—and for that matter, Mama—do not frighten her and make her hesitate to visit us here."

"Lizzy and I will make sure Miss Darcy is well shielded from the worst of the excesses of Mama and our sisters," Jane assured Mary. "We will keep her away from Papa's sardonic comments as well. She may not understand our father's wry sense of humour."

Mary relaxed. She had no doubt her sisters would assist her in making Anna both welcome and comfortable.

~~~~~~~/~~~~~~~

William Clem Collins was a young man of five and twenty years. His mother had been called home to God when he was seven and his father had followed her to his eternal reward two years ago.

Unfortunately, even though he was educated and unlike his illiterate father, could read, Collins was a man of little sense. An aunt, his late mother's sister, had left him a legacy with the stipulation it be used to give William an education.

His late father had railed against the stipulations, claiming the money should have gone to him, but none of his attempts to change the will had been successful. Hence, over his father's objections—after all, *he* had done *perfectly* well without an education—William had attended a small school in Somerset, the county which had been home to the Collins line since its split with the Bennets over a hundred years ago.

Thereafter, Collins attended a theological seminary in Kent, having decided to make the church his profession. From his father, Collins learnt to revere those with rank and titles, while at the same time thinking himself superior to most without such rank.

About a year ago, Collins finally succeeded in taking

orders, after serving for more than two years as a curate. He had recently heard the parish of Hunsford was seeking a new rector and had put his name forward for consideration.

He did not comprehend why the patroness of the parish, Miss Anne de Bourgh, the mistress of Rosings Park, had sent him on his way scant minutes after he met with her.

Collins could not understand why she had not appreciated his prepared compliments and the grovelling and fawning he employed. Surely she was impressed with his deference for the distinctions of rank?

After having been turned down for four other livings, Collins settled for a curacy with the rector of Woburn Abbey in Bedfordshire, Mr. Lawrence Skywalker.

It was galling he was not the one to whom the Duke and Duchess of Bedford, who had preferred Mr. Skywalker to the living, paid their attentions, but he needed the work, and the position came with a small cottage.

He reasoned once the Duke and Duchess noted how much deference he was willing to pay them, the Duke would prefer him to one of the other livings in his gift. His Grace had another two livings in Bedfordshire, as well as others attached to his many satellite estates.

His other hope was his distant cousin, the one his father had disdained, Mr. Thomas Bennet, the master of Longbourn, would shuffle off the mortal coil sooner rather than later, enabling him to take his rightful place as the master of an estate.

It was gratifying to learn his future property was in Hertfordshire, less than four hours southwest of Woburn Abbey in Bedfordshire.

CHAPTER 6

Darcy was thankful his cousin assisted him in avoiding Lady Catherine—for the most part—during their stay at Rosings Park. Together, they decided everything needing to be done could be dealt with in less time than they had originally planned, so they would end their stay earlier.

Their aunt still believed the myth she had created and perpetuated that if Darcy married her daughter, he would take Anne to Pemberley, leaving her to manage Rosings Park once again. Lady Catherine was as vociferous as ever in attempting to browbeat Anne and Darcy into agreeing to her demand that they marry.

Neither agreed; they never would marry. She only retreated after Richard threatened to summon his father and have her removed from the manor house. Knowing it was no idle threat, with ill grace, she left their company with a huff and her nose high in the air.

Thankfully, without Lady Catherine's ineptitude in estate management, there had been far less to do than they originally thought. While Darcy reviewed the ledgers and met with the steward—one appointed by the Earl—Richard took a tour of the park and called on tenants to see if they needed any assistance.

Without Lady Catherine's officious interference in their lives, combined with the new parson not sharing anything told to him in confidence with her, the tenants were far more content than they had been in many years.

The Hunsford rector's parishioners sang his praises to Richard. On this visit, he and Darcy were looking forward to attending services at Hunsford, something which could not be said in the past, when the theme of sermons had always been *preserving the distinction of rank*, and the rectitude of deference to one's betters.

Attending services at Hunsford church had been pleasant. The reason being that Mr. John Deacon, the new rector Anne had appointed, was nothing like the sycophant their aunt would have preferred to the living.

As she had not been allowed to appoint the new clergyman—and had no influence over the content of his sermons—in an effort to *deprive* the man of her *wisdom*, Lady Catherine had refused to attend services since Mr. Deacon took over. If she had known how much her absence was appreciated, she would have been seriously displeased.

With everything completed and Anne assuring them she needed nothing further from them, Richard and Darcy returned to London a few days after Easter.

~~~~~~~/~~~~~~~

"Did you find out why Andy was so distracted before he departed for Hilldale?" Darcy asked not long after his coach had departed Bromley on the way back to Town.

"Yes, I did," Richard responded succinctly.

"Well? What was his sudden interest in Covenant House that took him there so often?"

"Is it so difficult for you to accept that—unlike you—Andy believes they need more than just money there?" Richard paused. "William, are you or are you not fiercely private?"

"You know I am. What are you saying?"

"That if Andy wanted to announce anything he would. Until he does, we need to respect his wishes."

"Wait, Rich, are you saying he is involved with a lady?"

"All I am saying is when it is time to inform you, or anyone else, of anything he wishes to share, he will do so."

"I am sure as the heir to the Matlock earldom, Andy will choose an appropriate woman when he does make a choice," Darcy predicted.

"And what, pray tell, do you think is *an appropriate* woman?"

"From the *Ton*, preferably titled, with impeccable breeding, and a significant dowry."

"Those sound like a list of requirements to purchase something, mayhap a horse, not looking for the woman who will share your life with you," Richard bit back. "Did not your own parents make a love match? My late Aunt Anne chose to marry your father even though he was merely what you are—a gentleman farmer."

"Yes, but my father was very wealthy!"

"What happened to you, William? Why do you choose to forget they married for love, as my parents did, as Andy and I will? Tell me something; how many of the ladies you have described have you considered making an offer to?"

Darcy had no answer. He did not like being rebuked by Richard. Rather than consider his words, he turned and looked out of the window.

~~~~~~~/~~~~~~~

After their dustup in the coach, Richard remained at Matlock House rather than return to his chamber at Darcy House. Ever since their return to London, William had been standoffish, so Richard allowed him his space.

Anna remained in his parents' house, so he was able to spend time with one Darcy who was not sulking. They would all see William at Matlock House in two nights, at a family dinner. Richard was certain his cousin would get over his pique by then.

Darcy arrived early for the family dinner, held on the first Friday in May. Richard attempted to speak with him before dinner, but he sensed Darcy was avoiding him . If he did not know better, he would have thought Darcy looked somewhat guilty. The reason for William's behaviour came into stark relief at dinner time.

"You will be pleased to know I have employed a companion for Anna," Darcy announced after the first course had been served.

"When will I meet her?" Georgiana asked enthusiastically.

Hers was the only response. There was stony silence from the three Fitzwilliams. "Mother, please excuse William and me; we need to use Father's study," Richard stated as evenly as he could as he stood and pushed his chair back before a footman could react.

"There is no need to..." Darcy began.

"NOW! I will not ask you again," a fuming Richard barked out.

"How could you?" Lady Matlock shook her head.

Darcy saw he had no support among the Fitzwilliams, so with as much dignity as he could muster, he stood and followed his cousin to his uncle's study. As soon as he entered, Richard slammed the door closed.

"Are you such a petulant child that you would make such a decision without one word to me?" Richard spat out.

"I am her brother; it was my right to..." Darcy began attempting to defend his actions.

"Yes, you are her brother, but as you well know, your late father appointed us as *co-guardians*. In addition, did you not tell me before we went into Kent that *we* would choose an appropriate candidate *together*!"

"You *chose* not to stay at Darcy House..."

"That is brown, and you know it. You were acting like a child who had been denied his favourite toy all because I called you out on the nonsense you were spouting in the coach. I stayed with my parents to allow you time to calm down. However, you—like a little child—chose not to settle things with me and went behind my back and did this, displaying a childish level of petulance. Were you incapacitated to such a degree you could not send me a note to come meet the candidates for the position?"

As his cousin had hit the nail on the head, Darcy knew not what to say. At the same time, his pride and arrogance would not allow him to admit his cousin had the right of it. He did what he always did when he did not want to engage; he turned and looked out of the window onto the square.

Richard wanted to pummel his cousin. He loved William like a brother, but he could not understand why his cousin's character had changed so much since he had entered society.

"Do you think turning your back on me and looking out of the window at nothing in particular will make things better between us?" Richard demanded.

"It is done and done for the best," Darcy stated when he turned around, unable to look his cousin in the eye.

"Who is the woman?"

"Mrs. Karen Younge."

"Did you check her characters?"

"Of course I read them," Darcy replied indignantly.

"William, you are not a simpleton. You know that is not what I meant. Did you contact the people she worked for to verify the characters are genuine?"

"They were from some of the leading families in the *Ton*! Of course they were real."

"So, you did not *lower* yourself to verify them. I want to

meet this paragon. When is she supposed to begin?"

Knowing his cousin would not recede, Darcy knew he had no alternative but to allow Richard to meet Mrs. Younge soon. "She is to begin on Monday coming; you may meet her then."

"I am of two minds whether to demand you tell this woman the position is not hers and for us to begin again," Richard mused.

"You cannot do that! You would humiliate me," Darcy insisted.

"In point of fact, I could. Further, if you forced the issue and we went to court, a judge would explain the meaning of *co-guardian* to you. Would that not be much more *humiliating*?" Richard could see by the look of horror on his cousin's face that he had made his point.

"You would take me, who has been like a brother to you, to court?"

"I would for the welfare of Anna, yes. It is convenient to forget we are like brothers when you do what you just did, is it not?"

Darcy had the decency to look embarrassed. "The companion suggested taking Anna to Ramsgate for part of the summer. She thinks the sea air will be healthy for our ward."

"William, have you forgotten Anna is to accompany us to Bingley's leased estate? I am sorry, but no. *We* can all go to Ramsgate another time. Anna was telling me earlier today how much she is looking forward to accompanying us. You must know it raises my suspicions that a new companion would propose something like that right away."

"It was because I mentioned how much Anna dislikes being around Miss Bingley. I am sure if I had not mentioned it, she would not have made the suggestion," Darcy hedged. "In that case, she will join us when we go to Netherfield Park so there will be one more person to keep Anna away from Miss

Bingley."

"Do not forget Anna's friend lives at the neighbouring estate."

Darcy was going to comment about the friend's unsuitability, but he bit his tongue. He was well aware of Richard's feelings on the matter and Anna had been corresponding with the Bennet girl for some years now.

"I am aware of that."

"If I see anything I do not like about this Mrs. Younge, I will dismiss her," Richard stated, brooking no opposition.

"I am sure you will see what I did; she is the ideal candidate. She is neither too old nor too young."

"Time will tell. Come, let us return to the dining parlour."

~~~~~~~/~~~~~~~

When Richard met Mrs. Younge on Monday morning, he found her answers too perfect; however, there was nothing specific he could call on to demand she be dismissed. She was good with Anna, who took a liking to the woman.

Richard decided he would not relax his vigilance. Regardless of what Darcy said, the desire to take Anna to Ramsgate right away had raised his hackles.

~~~~~~~/~~~~~~~

"Damn!" George Wickham exclaimed when he read the note from his paramour. Not only was Karen unable to take Georgiana Darcy to Ramsgate and away from her brother, she would be in some little town in Hertfordshire with her brother in attendance.

Even worse, Richard Fitzwilliam would be there as well. Wickham knew Darcy could thrash him in a fight if he chose to, but he suspected Darcy would not lower himself to that level.

The cousin was very different from Darcy. Wickham

had always feared Richard Fitzwilliam. He was certain Fitzwilliam would not hesitate to use lethal force to protect a loved one if he felt it necessary.

If he was to go to a town where both Darcy and Fitzwilliam were, he would have to have a good excuse to be there, or they would immediately suspect his motivation for putting himself in their path.

He was not yet sure how he would accomplish it, but Wickham was determined to find a legitimate reason to be in the nowhere town of Meryton. He would find a way soon enough.

It would be Karen's task to make sure Miss Darcy would be amenable to his overtures. She was not yet fifteen, the perfect age for Wickham to manipulate her easily. He would get his revenge on the Darcys for withdrawing their patronage through her. No one took that which was his due without consequence. Marrying the girl and claiming her dowry would be a complete revenge; it would also get him much-needed funds.

His late father had learnt the hard way one does not cross George Wickham and live to talk about it. He had avenged himself on his father for the crime of having sided with the Darcy's against him.

~~~~~~~/~~~~~~~

In the second week of June, Mary received a thick letter from her friend Anna. When she broke the seal, she discovered a second letter within; written on the outside was:

Please hand to Miss Jane Bennet

Mary found Jane in the stillroom and handed her the missive. "Thank you, Mary. I will read it soon," Jane said.

"Why do you think there would be a letter for you from Anna? Oh! It must be from your Andrew," Mary realised.

Jane completed the remedy she had been working on,

then rubbed her hands on her apron before removing it and hanging it on a peg in the stillroom. She walked out into the park and sat on a bench under an oak tree.

She broke the seal and began to read.

9 June 1810

Jane (I enjoy being able to use your familiar name),

Do not be alarmed that I am writing to you. I am well, I promise you, and this is not a letter to break our courtship. That would be the last thing in the world I would desire to do. If it were possible for me to be with you in Hertfordshire already, I would be there now.

I have sent this missive to Richard and asked him to have Anna include it in a letter to your sister, Mary.

The reason I have written to you is there will be an unavoidable delay in my returning to your side. Two nights ago, there was a fire in the tenant village which completely burnt down four houses and damaged several others.

It could have been far worse than it was. By the grace of God, only one elderly man was lost. One was still too many. However, there were many injuries, from serious to mild.

I will remain here until rebuilding is well on its way and I know all of those displaced by the fire have been placed in lodgings until their new cottages have been built.

Although I am not yet sure, I hope to be on my way to you, my wonderful Jane, in about a month.

There is much I want to say to you, but it will have to keep until we see each other again. Hopefully, soon we will be able to exchange letters with the approval of your father.

With my warmest regards,

Andrew

Knowing Andrew as she did, Jane was not surprised he would insist on remaining to see to the welfare of his tenants. Many others would have left the task to a steward, but not her

Andrew.

She missed him and hoped he would be at her side soon, but knowing he was giving succour to those in need warmed Jane's heart.

The line about being able to write to one another made her feel a tingling sensation. It was a veiled reference to his wanting to ask for her hand. As she had already fallen in love with Andrew, if and when he asked that particular question, Jane would accept with alacrity.

While she prayed all of his tenants would be well, she also hoped her Andrew would come to speak to Papa as soon as possible.

CHAPTER 7

Caroline Bingley sniffed disdainfully as she appraised the manor house of the estate her brother had leased for the Bingley family's first foray into joining the ranks of the landed gentry.

If the estate had been close to Pemberley in Derbyshire, it would have been perfect. She conveniently forgot one of the criteria she had demanded her brother meet was the estate he leased must be close to London. Netherfield Park was only twenty miles from Town.

Mr. Darcy had escorted her brother to view the estate and approved of his taking it; it was the only thing that prevented her from openly criticizing the place. The last thing she would do was publicly disagree with the man she had chosen to be her husband—as soon as she could induce him to offer for her.

She had pushed her brother to take an estate as she was certain the only thing holding Mr. Darcy back from offering for her was that he had not yet observed her performing the duties of the mistress of an estate.

Miss Bingley had been educated at one of the finest seminaries for ladies in London, so—in her mind—she was eminently qualified to be the mistress of an estate. She knew how to order servants around and she would impress him with her skills as a hostess.

As she evaluated the house, she had to admit it seemed a fine structure. She was sure the décor would not be up to her standards and was miffed her brother had told her the lease precluded her from making any substantial changes within the house.

At least Mr. Darcy had seen her decorating skills at her brother's house on Curzon Street in London. She had seen his approving looks more than once. If only Charles would allow her to redecorate every time a new fashion trend swept through the *Ton*.

It mattered not, because Miss Bingley was certain Mr. Darcy's wealth would enable her to make changes to Pemberley and Darcy house whenever she felt the need; he would not restrict her as her brother did. As leaders in the *Ton*, they would have to keep up with or fashionable trends—or set them.

The only negative with regards to Mr. Darcy was he did not have a title. She was sure once she was married to him, she could convince him to seek a title. They were of one mind on most things. Mr. Darcy always seemed to agree with her, which boded well for their future. If that was not encouragement, she knew not what was.

"Caroline," Bingley called out, not for the first time as his sister seemed lost in her own thoughts while appraising the outside of the house. "Should we go inside, or would you like to stand out here longer?"

Without responding, Miss Bingley huffed, placed her nose high in the air, and marched up the stone steps to the veranda and the double doors beyond. Bingley was grinning as he walked behind his sister; the Hursts followed him.

Bingley introduced his family to the butler and housekeeper, Mr. and Mrs. Nichols, and informed the two senior staff members Miss Bingley would be acting as his hostess. Mrs. Nichols led the Bingleys and the Hursts to the family wing on the second floor.

Miss Bingley claimed the mistress's chambers, while Bingley took the master's side. They were of a good size and had a private sitting room between them.

The Hursts selected a suite two doors down from the master suite. As they had never shared a bedchamber since they had married, both Louisa and Harold Hurst were relieved they each had their own bedchamber, bathing room, and dressing room. Like the master suite, their bedchambers were separated by a sitting room.

Bingley heard a perfunctory knock on the door leading from the sitting room into his chambers. Before he could call out, his younger sister pushed the door open and marched in. As usual, she did not seem pleased. Long ago, Bingley realised his sister was determined never to be pleased.

"Charles, why is it you failed to persuade Mr. Darcy to ride with me—us—today?" Miss Bingley demanded.

"Caroline, you are like a dog with a bone. Did we not have this discussion, *ad nauseam*, before we departed London? Darcy had business to attend to. When he travels to Hertfordshire he will do so with his cousin, the former Colonel, and his sister," Bingley repeated. "Did I not tell you his older cousin, Viscount Hilldale, may be joining us in a sennight or so?"

"But he should have come with his good friends," Miss Bingley insisted.

"You mean his good *friend*!" Bingley cried. "How many times have I told you it is he and I who are friends; you just happen to be my sister." He held up his hand to stop the vitriol she was about to unleash. "Caroline, I will tell you this one last time. Darcy will never offer for you, even if you engineer a compromise. If you lower yourself to those depths, the only result will be your ruin, not a wedding."

"You know not of what you speak. Mr. Darcy always encourages me…"

"No, Caroline, he does not. However, I know you will continue to see things as you wish them to be. You have been warned! It will be on your own head if you ruin yourself."

"When the Viscount arrives, I will attract his attention; then Mr. Darcy will see what he is missing." Miss Bingley turned on her heel and returned to their shared sitting room, pulling the door shut behind her with a slam.

Bingley could only shake his head at just how wilfully blind his sister was. He thought back to the conversation he had with Fitzwilliam on Saturday before their departure from London.

Bingley had received a note from the former Colonel to meet him at Boodle's. Although he normally saw Fitzwilliam with Darcy, he did not think it far out of the ordinary for the meeting to be requested sans Darcy.

"Please sit," Richard had stated in welcome as he pointed to an armchair opposite him. They were in a private parlour off the main room where the members of the club congregated. Richard had not stood, since he still needed his cane for support; it was too great an effort when he was to sit right down again.

"Am I here to be recruited for a secret mission to serve King and country?" Bingley had jested.

"Nothing that exciting," Richard had replied. "There is no easy way to begin this, so I will dive in headlong. Bingley, you have a look you prefer in a woman, do you not?"

Bingley had looked quizzically, his eyebrows knitted in thought. "I am not so shallow…"

"Blond, blue eyes, willowy. Should I go on?"

Bingley cogitated and realised all the angels he had fallen in love with, regardless of how fleetingly, met the criteria Fitzwilliam had enumerated. Was he truly that superficial?

"Perhaps you have a point, but what has that to do with your wanting to see me?"

"On Monday you will take up residence at your leased estate in Hertfordshire, will you not?"

"Correct," Bingley had agreed.

"Your nearest neighbours are the Bennets of Longbourn. They have five daughters, the eldest of whom meets your picture of the ideal woman, many times over."

"Are you telling me to be circumspect with her, so I do not raise expectations if I have no intention of fulfilling them?"

"No, I am warning you that she is being courted by a close friend of mine. My intention is to save both of you the mortification of her having to reject you herself. Her name is Miss Jane Bennet. When you see her your breath will be stolen by her beauty. Before you ask, Darcy is not aware she is being courted, or by whom. It will be public knowledge soon enough. Until then, I wanted you to be forewarned."

"Your warning is appreciated. I would hate to make a fool of myself. My honour would never allow me to interfere with a lady being courted by another."

Fitzwilliam stood, shook Bingley's hand, and the two men had parted company.

It was fortuitous Fitzwilliam had warned him. If she was even half as beautiful as he had been told, Bingley would, no doubt, have been pulled towards her as metal is to a magnet.

Although he knew Miss Bennet was unavailable, he was looking forward to meeting the Bennets, hoping one of the other four sisters might spark his interest.

~~~~~~~/~~~~~~~

"Our daughters will die old maids in the hedgerows because you refuse to do your duty and call on Mr. Bingley," Mrs. Bennet lamented as she flapped her lace square, fanning herself furiously.

"Are you telling me I should not have called on Mr. Bingley?" Bennet asked with put-on innocence. He ignored the reproving looks his three eldest daughters were giving him.

"Did I not tell you what a good father he is," Fanny

Bennet beamed, quite forgetting her lamentations seconds before. "Now Jane will catch Mr. Bingley and we will be saved from the hedgerows."

"Mama, I will not be catching anyone. Mr. Bingley and I may never suit," Jane objected.

At first, Fanny looked at her eldest and usually most complying daughter as if she had grown a second head. "Jane, you could not be so beautiful for no reason. Of course, you and Mr. Bingley will suit. Has Miss Lizzy been filling your head with her impertinent nonsense?"

"No, Mama, she has not. It is my own opinion and has nothing to do with Lizzy or anyone else," Jane insisted.

"No one knows what I suffer!" Fanny exclaimed as the lace square began to flap furiously once again. "Hill! Bring my salts! What flutterings and palpitations! They will be the death of me."

Without another word, Fanny Bennet stormed from the drawing room with the long-suffering housekeeper following in her wake, a vinaigrette at the ready.

"Papa, what is Mr. Bingley like? Is he handsome?" Kitty Bennet, the second youngest sister, enquired.

"What care I how he looks. He is not an officer and only a man in a scarlet coat will do for me," Lydia, the youngest Bennet, interjected.

"As I am no judge of another man's level of handsomeness, I cannot tell you that," Bennet grinned. "however, he is an amiable gentleman. At the moment it is just himself, his younger sister, who is his hostess, and his older sister and that sister's husband. The matchmaking mamas in the neighbourhood will be vastly diverted when he is joined by two friends from London on the morrow, one of which has a younger sister."

"That would be Anna—Miss Darcy," Mary said. "She wrote and told me that she was accompanying her brother and cousin, the former Colonel Fitzwilliam. Jane and Lizzy will remember meeting him in London at the Gardiners' house."

"I remember; he was a very pleasant man," Elizabeth recalled.

"Also, Anna told me that her eldest cousin," Mary turned and looked at her eldest sister, "should be joining them, perhaps in the next fortnight."

Bennet, Fanny, and their two youngest daughters did not notice the blush that suffused Jane's face when Mary mentioned Andrew. It seemed her wish to see him again would soon be granted.

"A viscount is all well and good, but only if he wears a scarlet coat," Lydia commented dreamily.

The three eldest Bennet sisters looked to their father to see if he would check his youngest and most exuberant daughter. He said nothing before standing and returning to the sanctuary of his study.

He had just received the most diverting of letters from his distant cousin, who would one day inherit Longbourn. Hearing his daughter mention Gardiner caused a pang of guilt for Bennet.

His brother-in-law Gardiner had been begging Bennet to invest for his wife's and daughters' futures for many years. Rather than take any action, Bennet had turned a deaf ear.

Until Lydia was born, after which his wife had been told she could bear no more children, Bennet had relied on the birth of a son and heir to secure his family's future. Once he accepted said heir would never be, he just could not bother any longer. Rather than make an attempt to prove or disprove the midwife's assertion, the Bennet parents had not lain together since before Lydia's birth.

As far as his cousin's drivel went, he had almost a month to reply to the nonsense. Why should he do today which could be put off for another time?

In the drawing room, Kitty addressed her older sisters. "Mary, do you think Miss Darcy will enjoy knowing me?"

"Anna is shy, and will not be fifteen until March next, so she is not out," Mary explained.

"Then she will be out soon enough," Lydia asserted.

"No Lyddie, she will not. Our mother pushing us out at fifteen is the exception, not the rule," Mary averred. "In London society, the earliest it is acceptable to come out is seventeen, but most wait until they are eighteen—or older."

"How boring!" Lydia exclaimed. "How can you have fun when you are not out?"

"Lydia, girls of your age, or even Kitty's age, do not have the maturity to be out in society yet," Elizabeth responded. "There is much more to do besides flirting with men in red coats."

"Come, Kitty, let us leave our boring sisters, who are discussing uninteresting topics," Lydia demanded as she stood and made for the door. Obediently, Kitty meekly followed her younger and more forceful sister out of the drawing room.

The three sisters remaining in the room could only shake their heads at their younger sisters' antics. All they could do was pray Lydia—with Kitty following her in all things— would not ruin herself and, by extension, her sisters.

~~~~~~~/~~~~~~~

Charles Bingley returned Mr. Bennet's call the day after the latter's visit to Netherfield Park. Much to his disappointment, he was told that Mrs. Bennet and her daughters were out making morning calls.

When he expressed his disappointment at not meeting the rest of the family, Bennet reminded him there was an assembly on Friday evening coming, where he could meet them and all the other families in the area.

On his return ride to Netherfield Park, Bingley could not

but smile when he thought about his friend Darcy's reaction to attending a local assembly the day after he arrived in the area.

Bingley was not sure if Fitzwilliam would attend; he knew he might be precluded from dancing because he still had trouble with his leg.

CHAPTER 8

The Darcy coach, accompanied by two grooms riding Zeus and Invictus, and with Phoebe—Anna's mare gifted to her on her last birthday—tied behind the carriage, arrived at Netherfield Park just after eleven on Thursday morning.

All three family members were pleased to see Bingley waiting for them in the drive but were not so pleased to see his shrew of a sister standing next to him. She seemed to be jostling her brother to get into a better position to leap forward as soon as they began to alight from the coach.

Mrs. Younge sat impassively, trying to portray the very picture of a professional companion. It was becoming more difficult to do so because Karen Younge was frustrated. George wanted her to work on Miss Darcy before he found a way to come to Meryton, but there had been no opportunity to do so.

She hoped she would soon be able to begin to prepare the girl for when George arrived. Even if her lover had to marry the mousy little girl to revenge himself on the Darcys and gain her dowry—thirty thousand pounds—he would always love her. He had promised her that.

"William, allow me to alight first. That harridan is ready to jump. If she sees me and not you, it will confuse her. Use the door on the opposite side for yourself and Anna while I distract her," Richard suggested.

"That is a good plan; thank you," Darcy agreed.

Once a footman opened the door, Richard climbed down, his back purposely to the two Bingleys, while Darcy handed Anna down on the other side of the conveyance. As he had expected, the harpy sunk her talons into his arm.

"Why, Miss Bingley, your welcome is almost as enthusiastic as it would be for my cousin," Richard stated as he turned around with his cane in hand.

Miss Bingley dropped his arm as if it were something dirty. Her beady eyes were searching for her prey, but she had not seen him yet.

Richard decided it was time to bring this woman, who was far too high in the instep, down a peg or three. "Miss Bingley, have you not told us—repeatedly—that you attended one of the most exclusive seminaries in London?" Richard asked innocently.

"Why, yes. Yes, I did," Miss Bingley preened. She liked nothing more than being able to extol her exclusive education.

"I assume it is because, as the daughter of a *tradesman,* you were not taught this from birth, but a lady never grabs a gentleman's arm without first being invited to do so," Richard stated firmly as Darcy walked up and stood next to him, Anna on his arm. "I thought that seminary you boast about would have taught you etiquette. Mayhap I was wrong about that."

If there was one thing Miss Bingley hated with a passion, it was being reminded of her roots in trade, but that paled in comparison to her antecedents being pointed out in front of Mr. Darcy, as his insouciant cousin had just done.

The woman's face turned purple, then she turned on her heel and ran up the stairs and into the house. "Pardon me, Bingley, but it is high time someone called her out for her behaviour," Richard stated contritely. He was not sorry for what he said. He was worried he might have put Bingley on the spot, which was not Richard's aim. He had done something that Darcy should have done long ago.

Richard was sure Miss Bingley took Darcy's silence as tacit approval of her actions, which she had been taking as encouragement to continue behaving most outrageously.

As he spoke, Richard eyed his cousin. He was pleased to see what he had said to Bingley had not been lost on William.

"Mayhap she will finally pay heed. You must know I have no idea how many times I have had this very conversation with her," Bingley said, shaking his head. "Before I proceed, welcome to Netherfield Park."

Bingley led them up the stairs onto the stone veranda which ran to the left and right of the front doors, then turned about and was about to relate something to his friends when Darcy interjected.

"Bingley, would you object if Mrs. Younge and my sister are shown to their chambers now?" Darcy requested. "Mrs. Younge, this is Mr. Bingley, the master of the estate. Bingley, Mrs. Younge is Anna's companion."

"Of course, how thoughtless of me." He beckoned to an older lady who was standing just inside the doors. The lady stepped out onto the veranda. "This is Mrs. Nichols, the housekeeper. She will show Miss Darcy and Mrs. Younge to their suite."

The housekeeper led Miss Darcy and her companion up the stairs to the guest wing. She showed them to a suite with two bedchambers. Once the housekeeper left, Mrs. Younge thought she had time to bring George's name up; however, when she entered her charge's rooms, Miss Darcy's maid was there, unpacking her young mistress's trunks.

~~~~~~~/~~~~~~~

Rather than speak on the veranda, Richard suggested they adjourn to Bingley's study. As they walked, Richard felt his leg telling him he had been doing too much, causing him to lean on his cane more than he had been doing of late.

Once in the study, Bingley closed the door. "Anyone for a drink?" Bingley pointed to the decanters on the sideboard.

"Not for me," Darcy replied.

"A little early for me," Richard agreed.

"If you had a sister like mine, you would find any time of the day an appropriate time to drink," Bingley stated sardonically. He slumped into a wingback chair while the cousins sat on a settee opposite. "Before you ask, I told her only yesterday evening you will never offer for her, Darce. In fact, I told her that was true even if she lowers herself to attempt to compromise you."

"Thank you, Bingley. I am glad you told her that," Darcy responded.

"The only problem is she might refuse to hear what you said," Richard pointed out.

"That is what worries me. Thanks to the way our late mother, and to a lesser extent, our late father, spoilt Caroline, she thinks she will get whatever she desires," Bingley related sadly. "Regardless of what is said to her, she hears things in a way which matches her desires." Bingley looked to Richard. "How she will turn what you said into a positive, I have no idea, but she will."

"Does she suffer from some mental malady? At the very least it sounds to me like she is delusional," Richard hypothesised. He turned to his cousin. "William, I am sure you do not want to hear this, but my belief is—as I have told you in the past—you have done her no favours by tolerating her behaviour around you.

"I know you will never marry her, as does Bingley, but you must be aware how she continues to interpret your behaviour towards her. You have never called her to account. You are silent; she takes this as your agreement, which only encourages her."

"You have given me much to think about," Darcy replied tersely.

"If you gentlemen will excuse me, I will go to my chamber and rest. My leg is barking at me," Richard stated as he was about to stand.

"Before you do, I have accepted an invitation to the local assembly on the morrow. They have a bimonthly ball in Meryton, and I feel it is a good way to meet the gently bred families in the area," Bingley related.

"You know I cannot abide such events, especially among those I do not know," Darcy stated with distaste. "Besides, I do not want to leave Anna on her own."

"Come now, William, that is codswallop," Richard said evenly. "You know Anna's companion will be here, and I predict if Miss Bingley hears you are remaining here with your sister, she will decide to stay back as well. In addition, if on the morrow my leg is as bad as it is now, I will be here to keep an eye on Anna and her companion."

"Please Darce, I am trying to establish myself in the neighbourhood. It will not help my standing if you slight the citizens of the area by not attending the assembly."

Knowing what Bingley said was true and having no legitimate excuse as his cousin did, Darcy knew he would have to attend the infernal assembly. He would not dance. He was sure, even if one of the young ladies was Anna's friend, it would be a punishment to stand up with any lady so far below him in society.

"In that case, I will attend," Darcy allowed.

~~~~~~~/~~~~~~~

Richard stood and made his way to his chamber after enquiring which was his from Mrs. Nichols. The chamber was not as large or luxuriously appointed as the ones at Snowhaven or Pemberley, but there was nothing to repine. Richard was in a suite shared with his cousin. When he entered, he found Brown unpacking his clothing. Although his former batman was still a soldier at heart, he was becoming a creditable valet under the tutelage of Darcy's man, Carstens.

Brown mentioned Miss Darcy and Mrs. Younge were in

the suite across the hall, so Richard made his way there to see how his ward was settling in. He knocked on the door and entered when he heard his young cousin bid him do so.

"Are you happy with your chambers, Sprite?" Richard enquired.

"Yes, they are very comfortable," Georgiana responded happily. "Richard, please say I may visit Mary on the morrow. I have not seen her since we met in Derbyshire."

Just as he was about to answer, Richard noticed the companion enter Anna's room from the shared sitting room. He noted the moment she saw him, which caused her to scowl. She schooled her features in an instant, but Richard knew what he had seen. Mrs. Younge turned and returned from whence she had come.

"Of course you may! As long as my leg does not object, I will accompany you in the morning," Richard promised.

Anna clapped her hands together. "Thank you, Richard. I will be happy to see Mary again and finally meet her sisters. I am looking forward to being in company with Miss Bennet and Miss Elizabeth. Mary told me that the younger two are much closer to my age, but they are a bit too lively."

"Do not forget I too have not seen them for four years, either. I got to know Miss Mary, but she was only fifteen then, just a bit older than you are now."

"I should have remembered you travelled with the Gardiners and Mary into Derbyshire. Do you think William will object to my visiting Mary and her family?"

"He has not stopped you from corresponding with her, has he?" Richard replied. He did not like to lie by omission, but in this case he decided it was better than explaining her brother's improper pride to Anna.

~~~~~~~/~~~~~~~

The next morning, just after ten, Richard and Anna were on their way to Longbourn. Mrs. Younge was given the morning to herself as her charge would be with one of her guardians.

As they made the three-mile journey to the Bennets' estate, Richard was still seething at his cousin's attitude. The previous evening, he had spoken to Darcy in their shared sitting room.

Darcy was not in a good humour as Miss Bingley had been in rare form at dinner. As her brother had predicted, she had made as if nothing unpleasant had occurred earlier in the day. Rather than deal with her behaviour, Darcy had claimed fatigue and made for his chambers, spending barely five minutes in the drawing room after dinner.

Within a minute or two Richard followed his younger cousin to their suite. He had found Darcy in a dark mood, matched by the lack of light in their shared sitting room, a snifter of brandy in hand.

Richard lit some candles. "William, until you well and truly put her in her place—not with vague hints as you do now—her behaviour will never change," Richard told his cousin. "At least after today, the shrew is wary around me."

"I am a gentleman, and as such, I cannot..." Darcy had begun to say.

*"You know that is very brown. Do you want to wait until the virago attempts to compromise you, because I promise you as she grows more desperate, she will; it is not if, but **when** she will attempt it."*

Rather than answer, Darcy took a long draw from his snifter. "I assume Anna will have her normal lessons in her suite on the morrow so she will not have to be in Miss Bingley's company."

"She will not be in that woman's company, and neither will she be at lessons. I am conveying her to Longbourn to see her friend."

"I reluctantly agreed to them exchanging letters, but I will not agree to Anna spending time with those whose condition in life

is so decidedly beneath ours."

"Did you think I was making a request? No, William, I was not! As her other guardian, I am allowing her to see her friend without regard to your arrogant and prideful nonsense. Do I need to remind you that in rank I am above you?"

Darcy had taken a deep breath. "Why did you not discuss this with me before you told Anna you would take her?"

"William, are you not the one who indicated we need not discuss unimportant things with each other? At least I did not employ a companion without consulting you."

William did not reply to that. He threw back the remainder of his brandy and made for his bedchamber.

Richard was snapped from his reverie as the coach came to a halt in front of Longbourn's manor house. It was just as he remembered it from his first brief visit in 1806.

He led Anna to the front door, which was answered almost as soon as he knocked. The butler, after relieving them of their outerwear, led them to the drawing room where the ladies of the house were to be found.

After entering the drawing room he felt Anna trying to hide herself behind him as her shyness asserted itself. Richard very gently guided his ward to stand next to him. He saw Miss Bennet, who gave him a shy smile.

"Miss Bennet, will you introduce the ladies I do not know so I may then introduce my ward to all of you?" Richard requested.

Miss Bennet introduced her mother and two youngest sisters, after which Richard introduced Anna to them and Miss Elizabeth. When he had seen them last, the Bennet ladies had been pretty, but nothing like they were now.

At the time, Miss Mary had caught his attention, but as she had been only fifteen, he had treated her as he would his young cousin. Now, however, she was nineteen or twenty, so he was interested to find out if there was the possibility of anything beyond friendship between them.

Andrew was courting the most beautiful of women, but her beauty was not the reason he was courting her. From what Andy had told him, Miss Bennet was an estimable lady—one who put the needs of others ahead of her own and cared not for Andy's title and wealth, but only for the man within.

It pleased Richard to know he would become a brother to the five Bennet sisters once Andy took Jane Bennet for his wife. He smiled to himself when he imagined William's reaction after having listed the attributes women must possess before he or Andy could consider marrying them.

He was approached by the youngest Bennet. "Is it true you were a colonel?" Lydia asked.

"It is, Miss Lydia," Richard responded.

"It is so sad you do not wear a scarlet coat any longer. You would have been ever so much more handsome," Lydia stated brashly as she batted her eyelids furiously at the former officer.

"Lydia!" Jane, Elizabeth, and Mary chorused.

"You three hush; my darling Lydia did nothing wrong," Fanny said in support of her favourite.

"As much as it pains me to say this, Mrs. Bennet, in point of fact, she did. A girl, who should be in, like my ward, should not make such bold and flirtatious statements to *any* man unless you want her to become known as the greatest of flirts, one who will make her family look ridiculous," Richard stated.

Fanny was about to retort when she remembered the man was the son of an earl. She simply began to fan herself with her lace square.

Lydia, who had expected her mother to give the man a setdown for talking about her in such a manner, could only sit and stare as her mother said not a word.

Before anything else indecorous could be said, or Lydia expose the family any further, Elizabeth suggested a walk in the park. Thankfully, her mother and Lydia decided not to join them. Lydia gave Kitty a look showing her feelings of betrayal when her sister did not remain with her but joined the group making its way outside.

It did not take long for Anna to feel comfortable with the three of Mary's sisters who joined them in the park. Soon enough she was on familiar-name terms with Mary's two older and next younger sisters. She shared a love of the pianoforte with Mary; she and Kitty liked to draw and sketch.

Richard was pleased with the way he saw the Bennet sisters draw Anna out of her shyness. They were all disappointed when he informed them that he would miss the assembly because his leg was paining him.

Before they returned to the house for tea, Richard had a quiet talk with Andrew's lady and passed on his brother's regards. He confirmed Andy hoped to arrive in Hertfordshire early the following week. Miss Bennet had smiled beatifically when he shared that titbit of news.

They planned to meet at Netherfield Park in two days. Richard decided he would speak to Bingley to make sure Miss Bingley did not insert herself and try to monopolise Anna's time while she entertained her friends.

During tea, Richard noticed Miss Lydia kept as far from him as possible while her mother, who was not rude or inhospitable, was much quieter than she had been when they arrived—as if she were trying to solve an unsolvable conundrum.

After two extremely enjoyable hours, Richard and Anna departed to allow the Bennet ladies time to prepare for the assembly that evening.

CHAPTER 9

As might be expected in a house with a mother and five daughters, preparations for a ball, even the bimonthly assembly in Meryton, created a great deal of noise. The mayhem was not lessened by a flighty and nervous mother who kept changing her advice about what each of her daughter should wear to capture a husband.

During all of this, their father locked himself in his study and inserted wads of cotton in his ears to try and lessen the noise within the walls of his home. He had a book in his hand and a glass of port close by. For Thomas Bennet, other than the noises that intruded from time to time, his world was as it should be.

The cotton he stuffed in his ears made certain he would hear no talk of lace and other womanly accoutrements, none of which interested him in the least. Even his three intelligent daughters were caught up in the melee occurring beyond the sanctuary of his study.

"Jane, Jane!" Fanny Bennet cried as she burst into her eldest daughter's chamber. "You will not attract Mr. Bingley's notice in that dress!"

"Mama, as I have already stated, I have no interest in doing so," Jane averred.

"You know not of what you speak," Fanny shrieked. "The dress needs to be lower cut and there is not nearly enough lace..."

Just then, much to Jane's delight, Lydia drew their mother's attention to herself. This was one time Jane was grateful the youngest Bennet delighted in being the centre of attention.

"Mama, is my dress low cut enough?" Lydia asked. She proudly displayed her womanly assets, which were almost escaping from their bounds.

Although Lydia was the youngest Bennet, she was the tallest, surpassing Jane's height by a fraction of an inch. She had the body of a woman, although she was still a young girl.

Fanny was about to complement Lydia when she heard the voice of the Colonel, son of a peer, in her head. "Lydia, you will not go out dressed like that. Change right this instant into a more modest dress, one that keeps your breasts hidden as they should be."

Lydia stood and gaped at her mother. She expected her mother to compliment her, not tell her to change her dress. This was something Mama would say to Lizzy or Mary, not to her. She did not like it, not one little bit.

"But Mama, you helped me choose this dress! We *borrowed* it from Kitty, do you not remember?" Lydia pleaded.

Kitty was smaller than Lydia which is why her chest had almost escaped the confines of the dress. Hearing their mother, all four older Bennet sisters breathed sighs of relief; Kitty because Lydia would not wear her dress, and the eldest three because for whatever reason their mother had decided not to allow her to leave the house dressed indecently.

"Now, Lydia! Unless, of course, you would prefer to remain at home and go back in until you are eighteen," Fanny commanded.

Lydia was so surprised; she looked as if she had been run over by a carriage. She considered pleading her case, but she did not like the determined glint in her mother's eye. She decided it was better to change than miss the assembly altogether.

Before Fanny could return to Jane and worry about

her dress not being revealing enough, Elizabeth reminded the Bennet matron she needed to ready herself. As soon as Fanny noticed the time she bolted for her chamber.

~~~~~~~/~~~~~~~

Anna and Richard joined the rest of the party in the drawing room to see them off to the assembly. As expected, when the time to depart drew near, Bingley, Darcy, and the Hursts were ready, but there was neither hide nor hair of Miss Bingley.

Miss Bingley had been warned if she was not ready to leave on time, she would be left behind. As the time to depart approached, Mrs. Hurst looked around nervously.

"Charles, surely you did not mean to depart without Caroline," Mrs. Hurst stated. "You know Caroline likes to be fashionably late so she can make an entrance."

"Mrs. Hurst, I am sorry, but even most peers do not hold by that nonsense anymore," Richard volunteered. "In fact, it is considered unfashionably rude. This, Madam, is a country assembly, not a ball at St. James, so I promise you rather than make an entrance dressed for a royal ball, as I suspect your sister will be, she—and the rest of you by extension—will become a laughingstock."

"Have I not told you the same before," Hurst, for once sober, interjected.

"You do not think I should give her a little more time?" Bingley enquired.

"No, Bingley, I am sorry, but I do not," Richard responded. "If you never stick by your word, what incentive does your sister have to amend her behaviour?" Richard paused as he looked Bingley in the eye. "Do you remember what you told us in the study about Miss Bingley thinking she will always get what she wants?" Bingley nodded. "It is not all her own fault."

"What do you mean, Fitzwilliam?" Bingley wondered.

"If your parents, then you and Mrs. Hurst, had not always given into her, or given her a hollow ultimatum of *if* and *then*, what do you expect she would think? As it is now, when the *if* occurs you never follow through with the *then*," Richard explained.

"What do you mean by *if* and *then*?" Mrs. Hurst questioned.

"Tonight is a perfect example. *If* you are not ready on time, *then* we will depart without you," Richard elucidated.

It was obvious by the looks on their faces both Mrs. Hurst and Bingley understood what Richard had been saying. Brother and sister looked at one another and nodded.

At the same time, Darcy began to consider how, like Bingley and his family, he had allowed Miss Bingley to behave in unacceptable ways, which only led to more outrageous behaviour on her part. He was not ready to admit it to Richard yet, but his cousin might have the right of it.

"Come, Darcy, it is time to depart," Bingley said firmly.

The four leaving for the assembly made their way to the entrance hall to collect their outerwear. Before he left the drawing room, Bingley extended his hand to Richard.

"Thank you, Fitzwilliam. It is high time we did this and more," Bingley told his friend. "I am only sorry we are leaving you to hear my sister voice her displeasure."

"I survived battles on the Peninsula. I will not wilt before your sister," Richard assured his host.

~~~~~~~/~~~~~~~

The Bingley coach joined the line of carriages dropping off their passengers at the assembly hall on Meryton's main street. Torches had been lit either side of the hall on the street seeing that the light of day was fading in the west.

The three men alighted, then Hurst handed down his wife. When the Netherfield Park party entered the assembly hall, it was about ten minutes before the dancing was to commence.

The level of conversation was drastically reduced when they entered, because most of the attendees had never seen them before, save for the men who had welcomed Bingley to the area.

Sir William Lucas, the self-appointed master of ceremonies, approached Bingley, who introduced the rest of his party. If Sir William was surprised the younger sister who was Mr. Bingley's hostess was absent, he never remarked on that fact.

~~~~~~~/~~~~~~~

Darcy felt uncomfortable being the object of so many stares. At least there had not yet been any mention of his purported income. The realization struck him that the one person missing from their party was the one who thought nothing of mentioning the size of her dowry and what she believed his income to be.

If he had not been in a crowded assembly room, Darcy would have slapped his own forehead at the realisation it was Miss Bingley who spread his reputed income as if that somehow increased her own consequence.

What a fool he had been! Richard had been correct. Now was not the time to think of that since he had to be careful in case someone tried to entrap him. The knight he had just been introduced to was leading their party around, making them known to the families who resided in the area.

~~~~~~~/~~~~~~~

As Sir William approached the Bennets, he was about to start the introductions when he saw the instant Mr. Bingley noticed Jane Bennet. He had seen that look on many a young man before Mr. Bingley, so all Sir William could do was smile.

Bingley thought he had died and gone to heaven. She was ethereal and by far the most beautiful woman he had ever seen. If that were not enough, she was willowy, blond, and had the most perfect cerulean-blue eyes.

"That beauty, Mr. Bingley, is the eldest Miss Bennet," Sir William leant over and told the young man who was staring at Miss Bennet.

The name stopped him in his tracks. "That is Miss Jane Bennet?" Bingley asked.

"Yes, have you met before?" Sir William raised his eyebrows quizzically.

"No, but…" Bingley remembered Fitzwilliam told him the beauty's courtship was not known abroad yet, so he stopped himself before he spoke. "I heard she was very pretty."

"As are all of her sisters," Sir William stated. He noticed his youngest daughter, Maria, was speaking to the two youngest Bennets, who were with their mother. The three eldest were with Charlotte and his eldest son Franklin, standing near his wife and just past Mrs. Bennet.

"Mrs. Bennet, may I have the honour of introducing you and your two daughters to Mr. Bingley and his party?" Sir William asked.

"Of course, Sir William. It would be my pleasure to meet them," Fanny gushed.

Sir William made the introductions and before he moved on to his wife and family standing with the three eldest Bennet daughters, Mrs. Bennet approached Mr. Darcy. She was sure Mr. Bingley would not be able to resist Jane's beauty, but Mr. Darcy looked like he needed some prompting.

"Do you not wish to dance, Sir?" Fanny asked as she batted her eyelids towards her youngest daughter, forgetting what the former colonel had said earlier.

"Not if I can help it," Darcy replied tersely. He turned on his heel and stalked to the corner farthest away from the annoying matron.

"Well, I never! What a rude, disagreeable man," Fanny said at a volume that was heard by many in the hall.

~~~~~~~/~~~~~~~

Elizabeth had been watching with interest since the tall, dark, and extremely handsome man entered the hall. He looked sombre and taciturn, but that did not negate the fact he was an Adonis.

While Jane and Mary were speaking to Charlotte, Elizabeth could not but smile as she saw the instant Mr. Bingley clapped his eyes on Jane. Sir William said something to the man, which seemed to snap him out of his beauty-induced stupor.

She watched as Sir William made the introductions to the Bingley party. Everything seemed normal until Mama spoke to the handsome man. She obviously said something he found vulgar or inappropriate if the moue of distaste on his face was anything to go by.

'Mama, please tell me you did not push Kitty or Lydia at him,' Elizabeth beseeched silently. The man turned and marched to a corner while her mother loudly exclaimed that the man was deficient in his manners.

Before she could examine what had occurred further, Sir William arrived with the other three persons in the Bingley party and introduced them to his wife, his two eldest offspring, and the three eldest Bennet sisters.

Mr. Hurst took off in the direction of the refreshment tables, while Mrs. Hurst stood awkwardly after being deserted by her husband. Franklin Lucas, seeing the woman's distress, asked her to dance the first set with him. His offer was gratefully accepted.

As much as he wanted to dance the first with Miss Bennet, Bingley turned to Miss Lucas. "If it has not already been claimed, would you do me the honour of standing up with me for the first set?" he requested.

Charlotte had been sure he would ask Jane and then the other Bennets before her, but she happily accepted. He then asked the three Bennet sisters for a set each in order of their age.

"Unfortunately, I am unable to dance the third set with you, Sir," Elizabeth responded. "If you desire it, my fifth set is open. Due to the dearth of men thanks to the Corsican tyrant's war, each lady sits out two sets to allow everyone the chance to dance."

"That is an admirable way of ensuring everyone who desires to dance may do so," Bingley stated. "I request your fifth set of dances, Miss Elizabeth."

Bingley then led Miss Lucas to the floor and joined the line for the first set.

~~~~~~~/~~~~~~~

About the time the first set was concluding, Miss Bingley exited her chambers and began her glide down the stairs. She expected to hear Mr. Darcy exclaim over her fashionable burnt orange ensemble, which included a turban and ostrich feathers dyed to match.

As soon as she had heard Lady Susan Vernon had proclaimed the colour the most fashionable one, Miss Bingley had ordered a new wardrobe built around this shade of orange.

She had no doubt she would outshine everyone. Not only was she dressed in the height of fashion, but she was dripping with jewels and had applied a liberal amount of her expensive French scent.

She was surprised no one, especially Mr. Darcy, was waiting to admire her as she descended the stairs. She assumed they were in the drawing room having an aperitif.

As she was the mistress, they should have waited for her, but she supposed she could be magnanimous and forgive them. When she entered the drawing room she came to an abrupt halt.

The only one within was Mr. Darcy's rude cousin, who had tried to draw her attention to himself. As if she would be interested in a mere second son!

"Welcome, Miss Bingley; have you come to keep this old soldier company?" Richard drawled.

"Where is everyone?" Miss Bingley shrieked.

"As you see, I am here. Miss Darcy is in her chambers, and everyone else is at the assembly," Richard informed the outraged woman.

"**How dare they leave without me**!" she screamed.

"How dare you, madam? Who do you think you are that four people who have the manners to be ready on time should wait because you, the puffed-up daughter of a tradesman, wearing a hideous outfit, *chose* to be late and ignored the departure time. Your brother clearly told you he would leave on time," Richard barked.

Miss Bingley stood and glared at Richard before turning on her heel and screeching at the butler to have a carriage made ready for her. Her screams continued when she was told the master's coach was in use.

After the shrew stomped up the stairs, Richard followed slowly so as to not over-exert his leg.

~~~~~~~/~~~~~~~

Mrs. Younge was happy that, at last, she had Miss Darcy alone without either of her guardians observing her. For the first half hour, she allowed her charge to read. She listened as the mistress of the estate was screaming from downstairs. She heard the woman stomp her way upstairs and then a door slammed closed with much force. Seconds later there was the sound of items being broken.

With the noise being made, Mrs. Younge decided it was time to begin preparing Miss Darcy. "You are at such a mature age now, Miss Darcy," Mrs. Younge cooed.

Anna, who had been reading, looked up at her companion with surprise and no little pleasure. "You think I am mature? I am not yet fifteen," Georgiana stated.

"You know many girls marry at fifteen, so it is obviously not..." Mrs. Younge suddenly closed her mouth as the door from the hallway was pushed open and the former colonel limped into the room.

"You may go to bed, Mrs. Younge. I will spend the time with my cousin until she turns in for the night," Richard commanded.

At first, Mrs. Younge was nervous. She was worried the man had overheard what she had said to Miss Darcy, but he did not call her out for it so he must not have heard her.

Mrs. Younge bade her charge and her guardian a good night, then made her way to her bedchamber to prepare for her going to bed. As soon as she was gone, Richard asked Anna to follow him to his and William's sitting room.

"Anna, Mrs. Younge was mistaken. You are growing up, just as you should, but you are not nearly ready for marriage. Further, it is not something you should be thinking of yet," Richard told his ward gently.

"Why is that?" Georgiana asked with wide eyes.

"When you marry, you will no longer be able to live with William. Also, you will have many duties and responsibilities —those of an adult," Richard explained. "At the age you are now, you have the freedom to grow up and enjoy your girlhood. If you marry that would all be gone. In my opinion, the earliest a girl should marry is when she is nineteen or twenty. So you can see, Sprite, you have at least four or five years. Besides, could you see both William and me giving our consent for you to marry before you are out?"

"Why do I need both of your permissions?"

"The way your late father wrote the terms of your dowry, if some blackguard convinces you to elope, your dowry would be forfeit. That way, unless the man is wealthy in his own right, you and he would live in poverty. Anna dear," Richard caused his ward to look up at him, her eyes wide as she processed what he was telling her. "I need you to promise me if *anyone* tries to convince you to do things you know William and I would disapprove of, and especially if they tell you not to tell us, you will do exactly that as soon as may be."

"You have my word of honour, Richard. I am not ready to be matched with anyone yet. I want to enjoy my time and then come out as I should. Based on what you have told me, I can see playing with matches could get a girl burned."

"If your companion starts talking about it being acceptable for you to marry so young, just nod or say yes now and again and make sure you tell me as soon as you are able."

"I promise I will do that," Georgiana vowed.

They spoke for an hour more until Anna tired and took herself to her chambers, where her maid was waiting for her.

Richard knew he needed to be extra vigilant. He would need more proof before he sacked Mrs. Younge. He wanted to be able to show William irrefutable proof of his folly in employing her without verifying her characters.

CHAPTER 10

Dancing the first set with Miss Lucas had been enjoyable. Even though he knew Miss Bennet was being courted, he greatly enjoyed the second set of dances. If only the angel did not already have an understanding with another man…but there was nothing to do but be honourable.

"Colonel Fitzwilliam made me aware you are being courted," Bingley shared during the first dance of the set. "He did not reveal the name of the gentleman."

"I appreciate the Colonel's discretion," Jane replied as she inclined her head towards Mr. Bingley. "I am of age, so technically the courtship is official, but as the man in question has not…" They were separated by the dance as Jane circled around another dancer while that man's partner did the same, circling around Mr. Bingley.

When they came back together, Jane picked up where she had left off, "As I was saying, he has not had a chance to speak to my father yet. However, I do not think it will be much longer and then it will become known publicly. I would appreciate your being discreet until then."

They danced apart again. "I will be the soul of discretion until I hear word it is official," Bingley promised when he rejoined his partner.

"It puzzles me why the Colonel would feel the need to inform you of my courtship," Jane stated.

Thankfully for Bingley, whose colour deepened, he was not required to give an immediate reply, due to the steps of the dance. Before he was able to think of a cogent response, the first dance of the set came to an end.

Bingley led Miss Bennet to the side away from others so he would not be overheard. "The Colonel's reason will not do me credit, but I cannot be less than honest," Bingley admitted. "It seems I have a *type* in the ladies I favour..." He gave a brief explanation, his colour heightening as he did. "Thanks to Fitzwilliam pointing that out to me, I will be able to correct my course and look for more than superficial qualities in a lady, and to be more circumspect in my attentions."

"That you are able to admit it was something you needed to fix is an admirable quality," Jane responded sincerely. He was not the man for her, but she was sure he would be a good man for someone.

Before Bingley could answer Miss Bennet, the line formed for the second dance of their set.

~~~~~~~/~~~~~~~

At the end of Elizabeth's second set, which she danced with Jeremy Goulding, the heir to Haye Park, she took a seat, one of the few open along the wall. She would wait there during the third set, which was the first of two she planned to sit out.

After seating herself, Elizabeth noticed she was near the corner where the tall, handsome man—he would be more handsome if he did not scowl so much—had hidden himself away.

Jane was dancing with Jeremy and Mary with John Lucas, the second Lucas son. As the dancers moved about, she noticed Mr. Bingley was standing up with Maria Lucas. Kitty and Lydia were also enjoying the dance. Knowing Lydia, Elizabeth was sure if she had not been asked to dance, she would have demanded a man stand up with her.

She could only shake her head and hope Lydia would not ruin all of them one day. If only their mother and their father would take the time to check Lydia! It was a dream that would not be realised as her mother saw nothing wrong in the way her youngest and favourite daughter behaved. Her father only noticed her as an object to provide amusement for himself.

The first dance of the set ended, and Elizabeth watched as Mr. Bingley approached his distant, but handsome, friend. He seemed to have a purposeful gleam in his eye; what it was, Elizabeth had no notion.

"Come, Darcy," Bingley demanded, "I must have you dance. I hate to see you standing about in this stupid manner. The next set will begin after the upcoming dance. You had much better dance."

"I certainly shall not. You know how I detest it unless I am particularly acquainted with my partner. At an assembly such as this, it would be insupportable. Your older sister is engaged, and there is not another woman in the room with whom it would not be a punishment for me to stand up with."

"I would not be so fastidious as you are," cried Bingley, "for a kingdom! Upon my honour, I never met with so many pleasant girls in my life as I have this evening; there are several of them who are uncommonly pretty."

"*You* danced the previous set with the only handsome girl in the room," said Mr. Darcy, looking at the eldest Miss Bennet.

Not that she was trying to eavesdrop, but Elizabeth could not help but hear the two men given their proximity and the fact neither moderated his voice. With Mr. Darcy's assertion regarding Jane, Elizabeth could not argue.

"Oh! She is the most beautiful woman I ever beheld!" Bingley responded with a certain level of sadness showing on his mien, knowing Miss Bennet could never be his. Remembering his purpose, he shook off his momentary melancholy. "But there is one of her sisters sitting down just behind you who is very pretty too, and I dare say very agreeable. I have met her so allow me to make the introduction."

"Which do you mean?" Turning around, he looked at Elizabeth for a moment until, catching her eye, he turned back to his friend and coldly said, "She is tolerable, but not handsome enough to tempt *me*. I am in no humour at present to give consequence to young ladies who are slighted by other men. You had better return to your partner and enjoy the rest of your dance, for you are wasting your time with me."

If it were not the start of the second dance, Bingley would have taken his friend to task for his rudeness, but he would not allow Miss Maria to stand in the middle of the dancefloor without him.

Elizabeth was outraged. She stood with more force than she intended to, causing the chair to slam against the wall. She came to a halt in front of the man who had uttered the slight against her, gave him the gimlet eye, then walked quickly around the perimeter of the dancefloor until she reached Charlotte.

For a moment Darcy, who was not proud he had insulted an unknown woman to deter Bingley, worried the woman was about to slap him. He saw unmistakeable rage shooting out of her emerald-green eyes directed squarely at himself.

As he watched her walk, he had to admit she was not just tolerable, she was quite handsome. Then, to assuage his conscience, he tried to rationalise his actions. '*It is her fault for listening to a conversation she should not have!*' Darcy thought. '*Besides, I was correct. Why should I dance with one who is ignored by others?*'

His indignation grew as he watched the lady in question, her head together with the lady Bingley had danced the first with. There was no mistaking he was the subject of the discussion, given the way both ladies were looking at him and…how dare they laugh at him!

Did they not know he was a Darcy of Pemberley! Who were they to make sport of him, a member of the top echelon of the first circles? His family traced its roots back to the Conqueror and had relations who were members of the nobility.

Who were they? The daughters of a country squire or a puffed-up knight! It was unconscionable they were laughing at him. Outraged, Darcy stubbornly ignored the inner voice telling him he deserved this and more because it was his words which had caused the situation in the first place.

Darcy was, at that moment, thankful Richard was not present. He had no doubt it would have led to a setdown and lecture, not necessarily in that order.

~~~~~~~/~~~~~~~

At Netherfield Park, the tantrum Miss Bingley unleashed raged for the better part of an hour. Richard was sure not a single piece of bric-a-brac, or anything breakable, in her chambers had survived the storm, given the sounds of breakage he had heard.

When he had a chance to speak to Bingley he would recommend Miss Bingley be made to pay for all of the destruction. Richard was sure financial consequences would be the hardest-hitting thing Bingley could do to demonstrate his rejection of his sister's behaviour.

He was relaxing in the sitting room he shared with Darcy with his leg on a footstool, cushioned by a pillow Brown had brought for him. When his leg ached, for whatever reason, elevating it gave him the most relief. Richard had long since ceased taking willow bark tea except for the most extreme pain; it had been almost a year since he had last imbibed laudanum.

Knowing his cousin had been a reluctant participant at the assembly in Meryton, Richard could only hope Darcy would not cause Bingley's standing in the neighbourhood to be impacted if he asserted his improper pride against any of the locals.

Richard could not fathom how Darcy failed to see incongruity between his treatment of the residents of Lambton versus those of other market towns in England, including Meryton.

His cousin treated the residents of Lambton with respect, not disdain. Although Richard knew Darcy did not do well among strangers, he was no pup wet behind the ears. He was a man who had lived in the world for some years, who should be able to go into new company without giving offence.

Without telling them why, Richard had posted two Darcy footmen in the hallway between the suite he and his cousin were sharing and the one where Anna and her companion were staying. They were told to be particularly vigilant.

Now that his suspicions were fully aroused, Richard would do everything he could to ensure his ward's safety.

~~~~~~~/~~~~~~~

"Miss Elizabeth, you must allow me to apologise for my friend's intemperate words," Bingley stated shortly after he had commenced the fifth set with the lady.

"If anyone should apologise it is Mr. Darcy himself, not you, Sir. You have behaved as a gentleman the entirety of the time you have been here," Elizabeth responded.

"It is I who provoked Darcy when I well knew he did not intend to dance, so I am afraid I do bear some of the responsibility," Bingley insisted.

"Given neither of you lowered your voices and my position right behind Mr. Darcy, I overheard what was said. Did you attempt to goad him into dancing? You did. That being said, it was he and he alone who chose to use the words he did. If they were not thoughts he was having anyway, he would never have voiced them," Elizabeth opined. "Like you, he is a man fully grown and he must take responsibility for his own choices."

"Rather than dispute who shares the greater part of the blame, I choose to speak of more pleasant subjects," Bingley decided.

"As I am not one built for melancholy and because I dearly love to laugh, you will hear no objection to that from me," Elizabeth agreed.

From his corner where he had spent the ball so far, Darcy closely observed the young lady he had insulted as she danced with his friend. She was light on her feet and seemed to be highly proficient at the steps.

Darcy could not detect any fawning on her part. She seemed oblivious to the fact Bingley was reputed to have five thousand per annum, the number that had been bandied about. Of his purported income there was not a whisper, proving his supposition that Miss Caroline Bingley was the one who generated speculation about his wealth when they were in company together.

Another thing which shocked Darcy was that Bingley had only danced once with arguably the most beautiful woman in the room. She was, in looks, exactly the type of woman with whom Bingley often would become infatuated. For some unfathomable reason, after dancing a single set with her, Bingley had not approached the willowy blond again. It was far from how Darcy was accustomed to seeing his friend act.

Even more puzzling was why the same woman, who obviously could have danced every set if she so chose, was sitting out a set. Only then did he notice that almost all of the young ladies present seemed to be refusing men for certain sets.

Darcy turned his thoughts from that conundrum to

another. Subsequent to learning the name of the woman he had slighted—Elizabeth Bennet—he may have been wrong about far more than thinking her merely tolerable.

For the rest of the assembly, Darcy avoided Bingley as he was sure his friend would tell him what he wanted to at the time of the insult. He did his duty and danced with Mrs. Hurst who, he discovered, was a more interesting person in the absence of her younger sister.

By the end of the evening, although he had not resolved to apologise for his unwarranted insult, Darcy had come to the realisation that every lady had sat out one or two sets because there were many more ladies than gentlemen.

To himself at least, he acknowledged that made his refusal to dance with anyone except Mrs. Hurst rather ungentlemanly. That was something which troubled Darcy because he always sought to act as a true gentleman. No matter what he tried to tell himself in justification, at heart he knew there was no way to rehabilitate his behaviour that night.

~~~~~~~/~~~~~~~

In the coach on the return to Netherfield Park, Bingley resisted the urge to take Darcy to task there and then. He decided it would be a conversation better held with Fitzwilliam present.

"Charles, I am all amazement," Louisa Hurst stated not long after the carriage was pulled into motion. "As soon as I saw Miss Jane Bennet, I thought you would attach yourself to her side and not move from it for the rest of the night."

"It was recently pointed out to me that I have, although unwittingly, been raising expectations among my *angels* and then not fulfilling them. It was also pointed out to me that all my *angels* share similar physical appearances," Bingley owned. "With Miss Bennet, I sat back and allowed her to lead the way, and I am confident she was not interested in me as anything but a new neighbour. I have resolved to be more open to learning what others think and feel, not only my own selfish desires."

"I am proud of you," Mrs. Hurst said, looking at her loudly-snoring husband. "I spoke with Miss Bennet during one of the sets she voluntarily sat out. Did you know the local ladies sit out two sets each due to the dearth of young men thanks to the war?"

"Yes, *Miss Elizabeth* told me as much when I requested a set from her, one of the two she *planned* to sit out," Bingley was looking directly at Darcy as he said the last.

For his part, Darcy did not miss the rebuke in his friend's words and looked everywhere except at his friend.

~~~~~~~/~~~~~~~

The mood in the Bennet carriage was festive as the two youngest Bennets extolled the fun they had dancing every set. Knowing their mother would not support them if they pointed out Kitty and Lydia should have sat out two sets, the three older sisters chose not to mention that fact.

"Miss Lizzy, did I hear correctly that the rude and disagreeable man from Derbyshire slighted you?" Fanny demanded to know. Elizabeth was her least favourite daughter, but woe betide anyone—other than herself—who denigrated one of her daughters.

"He did, Mama. It did not affect me; he means nothing to me, after all," Elizabeth claimed.

The truth was the insult had cut her to the quick. She would usually laugh off something like this; she could not understand why she had not in this case. It was a problem to solve another time.

Thankfully, the mile-long return to Longbourn passed quickly. Before their mother could interrogate Jane regarding her dancing with Mr. Bingley, they had arrived home.

CHAPTER 11

Richard's leg felt much better the morning after the assembly. He had breakfasted with the two Darcy's and his ward's companion before Miss Bingley arrived downstairs—thankfully.

Darcy and Bingley had gone riding with Anna first. They had returned with her and then gone on a longer ride so his ward was at her lessons when Richard, who had taken a walk in the park to exercise and strengthen his leg, returned to the house.

He thought about entering the dining parlour for another cup of coffee when he heard the sound of Miss Bingley's grating voice.

"How could you allow Charles to depart without me? What must Mr. Darcy have thought of the incivility to his future wife?" Miss Bingley demanded.

"Caroline, Mr. Darcy agreed we should depart on time. I promise you he did not utter a word in opposition to us leaving at the time we said we would," Mrs. Hurst replied.

"The poor man! He was subjected to those far below him without my being there to console him," Miss Bingley tutted.

Richard found himself diverted at Miss Bingley's ability to ignore anything which did not fit the narrative she was telling herself. He should not have remained where he was. As a gentleman, he should have announced his presence or continued on his way. That being said, he decided to listen for a little longer.

"We met the principal families of the neighbourhood.

One lady was by far the prettiest I have ever beheld, one whom Charles would normally name *an angel*. For whatever reason, though, he did not. Her name is Miss Jane Bennet," Mrs. Hurst related.

'*Good*,' Richard told himself silently. '*Bingley took my information Miss Bennet is being courted to heart.*'

"I am sure all of the people hereabout are savage, with no sense of fashion or style," Miss Bingley sniffed disdainfully. "Did my Mr. Darcy have to fend off any fortune hunters discussing his income last night?"

'*No, because you were not there and you were not able to spread word of his income*,' Richard thought as he shook his head.

"He only danced with me, even though more than one young lady was in want of a partner," Mrs. Hurst told her sister. "Charles tried to convince him to dance, and Mr. Darcy insulted one of the Bennet sisters."

"I am sure she deserved it. At his level of society, what would he care of a country mushroom's feelings?" Miss Bingley sneered. "What did she do to raise his ire?"

"Caroline, she did nothing; Charles was importuning Mr. Darcy. It did Mr. Darcy no credit when he said something about Miss Elizabeth Bennet being tolerable but not handsome enough to tempt him and not giving consequence to ladies slighted by other men."

At that point, Richard almost burst into the dining parlour, but he restrained himself. '*I will have words with my arrogant cousin! I care not what Bingley may have said to him! How dare he insult one who will more than likely become my sister! Does he truly think he is above the rules of polite discourse?*' Richard fumed to himself.

"I am sure this Miss Eliza deserved it," Miss Bingley opined.

Richard had heard enough. He walked into the dining

parlour. He could see Mrs. Hurst was chagrined because she was certain he had overheard her account of his cousin's behaviour. Miss Bingley, on the other hand, had a supercilious look on her mien.

"Miss Bingley, it seems you did not learn very much at that seminary you constantly harp about," Richard barked. "If I were your brother, I would try to recover the money spent on your education. Do you not understand as the newest and lowest members of the local society, if my cousin did what Mrs. Hurst just related, then you may find your family being shunned."

"What care I if some lowly country nobodies..." Miss Bingley began but stopped after seeing the glare the Colonel was shooting her.

"It seems you have the attention span of a gadfly, Miss Bingley. If the landed gentry hereabout are, according to you, lowborn, and you as the daughter of a tradesman are below *them*, where does that place you?" Richard demanded.

"I have a dowry of twenty thousand pounds; my family is wealthy; and I am connected to many members of the first circles. I am *far* above anyone in this benighted neighbourhood!" Miss Bingley screeched.

"Do you know how gauche you are?" Miss Bingley gasped and held her hand to her chest. "It seems how to avoid vulgarity by not speaking of your family's wealth or the amount of your dowry was another lesson you missed at the seminary you boast of attending. Additionally, I am sure they taught, but you elected to ignore, the fact it is not dowry or wealth which determines your place in society, but birth."

Seeing Miss Bingley was about to disagree, Richard continued speaking before she could do so. "You, Miss Bingley, do not have a single connection to the first circles; your *brother*, who is mine and my cousin's friend, does. That you consider any invitation to him as one extended to you as well does not change that fact. I have never met one so high in the instep as you in all of my days in society."

It was then Miss Bingley noticed Mr. Darcy and her brother, who had returned from their ride. The two had been on their way up to change when they heard raised voices coming from the dining parlour and had stopped and stood in the doorway.

"Mr. Darcy, please correct your rude cousin. Did you hear what he said about my not being your friend?" Miss Bingley cooed and batted her eyelids at Mr. Darcy.

"What my cousin said is the absolute truth," Darcy confirmed. "You, Miss Bingley, are no more than my friend's sister. Until now, I have not wished to embarrass your brother by pointing out you were not included in his invitations, but that will not be the case going forward."

"Mr. Darcy, you cannot be serious!" Miss Bingley exclaimed in a high-pitched, grating, and panicky voice.

"My cousin has the right of it," Darcy admitted. "I have remained silent and allowed you to behave in a reprehensible, most unladylike fashion without making my opinion known for far too long. Your brother and the Hursts will still be welcome in my homes, but unless you are specifically invited, you will not be."

Caroline Bingley was reeling as she saw her dreams of becoming Mrs. Darcy being blown away like wisps of smoke on the wind. "But surely I will be able to call on dear Georgiana at..." she began, only to be cut off again.

"Miss Bingley, when did my cousin or I ever give you leave to address *Miss Darcy* so familiarly?" Richard barked. "Do you think any of us are unaware, my ward included, that your only motivation for your so-called *friendship* with my young cousin is thinking it would recommend you to her brother? If you were any more transparent you would be a window."

Seeing no support for her in the room, Miss Bingley

bolted up the stairs and into her bedchamber. There was no sound of breaking porcelain or glass after the door was slammed; she had destroyed anything breakable the previous night.

"Please pardon me, Bingley, but I could not remain silent when I heard your younger sister speaking the way she did," Richard stated contritely.

"You have nothing for which to apologise," Bingley granted. "I am only sorry we," he indicated his sister and himself, "did not put our feet down years ago while there was a chance to correct her."

"Charles, even then it would have been a monumental task after the way our late mother spoilt Caroline and put ideas about rising to the top of society in her head," Mrs. Hurst stated calmly. "I used to think that way as well; thankfully, I no longer do. Also, do not forget that Father allowed Mother and Caroline free rein and gave our sister anything she asked for."

"If you will excuse me, I will bathe and change now," Darcy requested.

"Not so fast, William," Richard stated firmly. "You and I need to have a discussion."

"Allow me to bathe and dress, then I will meet you in our sitting room," Darcy offered. Richard nodded tersely.

"Charles, before you do the same as Mr. Darcy, do you know our sister had a tantrum of epic proportions last night? She broke every single glass or porcelain item in her bedchamber," Louisa said.

"It sounded like there was a battle being fought in there," Richard added.

"That will cost me a pretty penny; the landlord will insist I replace everything, Bingley sighed.

"Why should it cost you anything? Does not your younger sister have her own money?" Richard prodded.

"Yes, she does, even though she overspends each quarter —and that is before I receive invoices from the modistes, cobblers, jewellers, and others," Bingley related, shaking his head.

"Think of what I told you regarding how you allow her to dictate the time you will depart for an event—regardless of the time you planned to arrive. Apply that principle to her overspending," Richard suggested.

Bingley cogitated for some moments. "If she is financially responsible for the damage she causes, and I refuse to pay her excesses, she will learn," Bingley realised.

"That would be my opinion," Richard agreed. "Bingley, may we speak in private before you go to bathe?"

"Come to my study," Bingley invited.

"Tell me about last night and my cousin's insult of Miss Elizabeth," Richard requested once the study door had been closed.

"How did you learn about that? I intended to address it with Darce, with you in the room," Bingley revealed.

"I am not proud of it, but I overheard a conversation between your sisters," Richard acknowledged. "Mrs. Hurst mentioned something about William's insult. As you were the one speaking to my cousin, I wanted to hear from you directly before I take William to task."

Bingley related the whole of the conversation, making sure to accept the bulk of the blame because he was the one who had provoked Darcy into responding.

"Yes, you pushed him, but you did not force him to behave in such an ungentlemanly fashion," Richard said, none too happy the story Mrs. Hurst related had been confirmed as truthful. "Thank you for revealing all to me. When my cousin is dressed, he and I will be having a discussion."

~~~~~~~/~~~~~~~

George Wickham entered a bar in a seedy part of London, where he believed he would be anonymous. Much to his chagrin, he spied a man he knew from Lambton wearing the scarlet coat of the army. It was...Wickham had to dig deep into his recollections. Denny, that was it. His father owned a haberdashery in Lambton so it would not be a shop where he would have incurred debt.

Before Wickham approached the man, he tried to remember if Denny had any sisters and if the man had, had he meddled with them. Before Wickham could recall, he was recognised.

"Wickham, you reprobate you, I have not seen you for more than five years," Denny said, extending his hand in greeting.

Denny's welcome told Wickham if the man had a sister, she had not been one from whom he had taken her virtue. "Denny, is that you?" Wickham feigned surprise. "Since when have you been in the army?"

"I am not in the regulars. I serve in Colonel Forster's regiment of the Derbyshire Militia. If, like me, you are from Derbyshire, and you have had a gentleman's education, you can receive a free lieutenant's commission in the regiment."

The last thing Wickham wanted was to serve in anything, especially not a military unit. He hated being told what to do and when to do it. He decided to continue speaking to Denny because perhaps the man would buy him a drink.

"Where is your unit now? Why are you not with them?" Wickham asked to pass the time.

"We are in Leicestershire for another month, less to be honest. Our encampment is not a mile outside of Leicester," Denny responded. "We move to Hertfordshire on the seventeenth of August."

Wickham felt a surge of excitement. Hertfordshire! This could be his excuse to be in the area so he could enact his plan against the Darcys and Fitzwilliams! He schooled his features and calmed himself. "Where in Hertfordshire?" he asked as evenly as he was able to.

"If memory serves, a small market town called Meryton," Denny supplied.

As he fought to keep himself under regulation, Wickham tried to project nonchalance. He knew he would find a way to be in the area without raising the suspicions of Miss Darcy's guardians!

"What is the process if a man like me wanted to join the militia? You are aware I am from Derbyshire. I am not sure if you know or not, but I did graduate from Cambridge." Wickham knew he was stretching the truth; he never took his final exams due to being sent down, and without the Darcys' patronage he could not induce the administration of the school to accept him back or change his records.

"Are you saying you will join us?" Denny enquired.

"I am. When do we depart for Leicestershire?" Wickham queried while trying to keep his features even.

"In five days. Meet me at this inn no later than ten in the morning, then you and the other recruits will join me and Captain Hamilton and make for the Leicestershire encampment," Denny related.

Now that he had a plan, Wickham needed to send a letter to Karen. She would make sure Darcy's sister would welcome his approach when he arrived in Meryton. He knew how it would be; he could not be so very intelligent for no reason.

He would soon revenge himself on Darcy and his extended family and have thirty thousand pounds in hand, according to what his paramour had learnt about Miss Darcy's dowry. A month in the militia would be nothing compared to the funds that would be his.

CHAPTER 12

Darcy huffed impatiently as he waited for his cousin. He suspected Richard had heard about what had happened at the assembly, more precisely his own behaviour at said ball. Darcy was aware that his behaviour had been lacking, although is pride kept him from acknowledging it aloud.

Richard entered the sitting room and made sure the door was pulled securely closed as a precaution. To ensure a certain shrew did not attempt to eavesdrop, he had stationed Thompson in the hall outside the sitting room door.

"William, do you have a mental deficiency?" Richard attacked.

"How can you ask me that?" Darcy responded haughtily. "You know I do not!"

"It is what I *used* to believe. However, I am no longer certain," Richard shook his head sadly.

Darcy was at sixes and sevens on how to respond. He had expected Richard to continue on as he had begun, not despondently as he was now.

"Are you questioning my honour?" Darcy blustered.

"No William, I am aware you are an honourable man. It is your character and behaviour I am questioning." Seeing William was about to respond, Richard continued, giving him no chance to do so. "What do you believe my parents, who are far above you in rank, would think of your reprehensible conduct at the assembly? Do you think Andy would agree with you? Even worse, do you not think my late Aunt and Uncle

Darcy would have been ashamed and heartily disappointed by your behaviour? What has happened to you to cause you to become a social pariah?"

He was about to ring a peal over his cousin's head for calling him on the carpet like an errant schoolboy when what Richard said about his beloved late parents pierced Darcy's consciousness.

Rather than his indignant pacing, Darcy fell back into the armchair behind him. As he thought about his parents and their wishes for him, not what he had convinced himself they meant, but what they had actually said, he began to feel like the worst kind of cad. He sat forward, his elbows on his knees and head in his hands.

The question Richard asked was a poignant one. What had occurred to drive him so far from the path on which his parents had guided him? As a child, he had been taught what was right and to correct his temper. His parents had given him the best of principles. Why had he now chosen to follow them in pride and conceit?

As an only son, and for many years an only child, Darcy realised he had been spoilt by the attention and deference he had received from everyone—first, from the servants and tenants at Pemberley, and then by the *Ton* after he ventured into society.

His parents were the best of people, especially his father. They were all that was benevolent and amiable. They never taught him to be selfish and overbearing, nor did they teach him to care for no one other than those in his family circle. They never meant for him to think meanly of the sense and worth of others compared to his own. They had, in fact, taught him quite the opposite.

So, what was the reason? He could try to blame it on being hunted for years in society, but Andy and many others had suffered the same without behaving as he did. Darcy knew it was a conundrum he would not solve now, but it was a beginning. He was finally willing to admit his behaviour had been sorely lacking.

Richard sat silently, watching the emotions play over his cousin's face. He was well aware invoking William's parents was the one thing that might break through the mask of indifference William had created.

Of one thing he was certain, he had forced William into a state of introspection. His cousin would need time to ruminate and come to a conclusion on his own; however, before he allowed William to seek solitude, he had a few more things to say.

"William, if it were Anna at the dance last night, and someone said that about her, within her hearing..." Richard stopped as Darcy interjected.

"The Bennet girl should not have been listening to a private conversation," Darcy claimed. As he said the words he knew how weak of an excuse that was.

"Did you moderate your voice before speaking words that should never have crossed the lips of a gentleman?" Darcy blanched when his cousin spoke of his ungentlemanlike conduct. "Did you first see if anyone was close to you? Did you think you and Bingley should move to somewhere which guaranteed your privacy?"

"No. No, I did not."

"Then, as I was saying, what would you have done had someone said what you did about your sister in her hearing? Did you know all the young ladies *chose* to sit out two sets due to the number of young men who have enlisted in the army leaving an unequal number? Miss Elizabeth was not slighted by any men, except for you, as she *chose* to sit out."

"Bingley was pushing me..."

"Yes, he was. Mayhap he should have left you alone to stew and glare at everyone, but he did not. That is not an excuse for your reprehensible behaviour." Richard paused. "A true gentleman would own his error and apologise forthwith, and I mean a *sincere* apology."

He was about to object he should not have to apologise to one so far below him in society when in his mind's eye Darcy saw the spectre of his parents' disapproving looks. "Allow me time to think and I will do what I have to do."

"At some point, you may discover the Bennets have connections to rival your own," Richard stated cryptically.

'That family have good connections? I think not. You do not always have the right of it, Cousin,' Darcy told himself silently. He had been wrong in his insulting statement, but in this, he was sure he was not.

"Before you sit there thinking I know not of what I speak, they are already connected to the Darcys of Pemberley," Richard reminded his cousin smugly. "You cannot deny Miss Mary, and it seems the other two older Bennet sisters also have been a good influence on our ward."

"I suppose that is true," Darcy admitted.

Richard stood and clapped his cousin on the back. "You know, when you are not being an arrogant horse's arse, you can be a rather pleasant fellow." Richard made his way out of the sitting room before his indignant cousin could respond. He dismissed the footman as he exited the room.

~~~~~~~/~~~~~~~

"Lizzy, mayhap it is not the best idea to repeat the story of Mr. Darcy's slight to one and all. If things progress with Andrew, he will be our cousin one day," Jane told her younger sister.

"I do not excuse his words, but I am sure he is not so very bad, Anna calls him the best of brothers," Mary pointed out.

"Mayhap he is mercurial," Elizabeth suggested. "I will not speak of what happened to anyone outside of our immediate family, but how will you stop Mama? You know as soon as she is ready to go, she will be on her way to see Aunt Hattie. Not long afterwards, the story will be all over Meryton and the surrounding area." Elizabeth paused as she cogitated. "Unless you tell Mama that Mr. Bingley might be put off if he hears negative gossip being spread about his friend."

"Lizzy, you are brilliant! That will work," Jane agreed. "I will tell her just that, and no more. I will not prevaricate to our mother and tell her I have an interest in Mr. Bingley which does not exist." Jane paused as her colour heightened. "The truth is, if I had not met and fallen in love with Andrew, Mr. Bingley would not have been a man to whom I would have been attracted. He seems like a estimable man, just not for me. As it is, I am well pleased to have met Andrew when I did making it much easier to put Mama off."

"Is he as handsome as Mr. Bingley?" Elizabeth asked.

"More so," Jane replied. "Andrew is everything a man should be. He owns my heart, and I am confident his is in my keeping as well. I cannot wait until he arrives."

"His brother has mentioned nothing about a further delay, has he?" Mary enquired.

"Thankfully, no," Jane averred.

"Mary, you and the Colonel seem to get along very well," Elizabeth observed.

Mary did something she did not often do, she blushed. "He is no more than Anna's guardian. Most of the time we speak of her," Mary claimed.

Jane shook her head when Elizabeth looked at her. If there was something developing between Mary and Richard, it needed to be left to percolate on its own, at a pace comfortable to both Mary and her brother-to-be.

Elizabeth nodded her understanding. "When will Anna call on us again, or are we a visit in her debt?" Elizabeth asked to change the subject to a more neutral one.

"She will be calling early this afternoon. We need to

discuss the ball, after all," Mary informed her sisters.

"I know, I know," Elizabeth raised her hands. "Not a word will cross my lips of the insult in Anna's presence. Jane, you need to speak to Mama before she comes, and I will make sure Kitty and Lydia are forewarned."

So agreed, Jane made for her mother's chamber while Elizabeth went to seek out the two youngest Bennets.

~~~~~~~/~~~~~~~

"Richard, where are you and Anna going?" Darcy asked, although he was almost certain he knew what the answer would be.

"We are visiting the Bennets. I promised our ward she could call on them today. You know how young ladies like to discuss a ball the day after." Richard looked at his cousin pointedly as he said the last.

"In that case, may I accompany you so I may make my apologies?" Darcy requested.

"For what does William have to apologise?" Georgiana enquired.

"That, Anna, is not my story to tell," Richard stated.

"It is however mine," Darcy owned. "Anna, I was not in the best of moods last evening when we departed…"

Darcy told his sister the truth of what had occurred at the assembly, and he did not make light of or gloss over his bad behaviour. The more Anna listened the more shocked she became. When Darcy had completed his recitation, there was silence for some moments after.

"William! How could you have said that about Lizzy?" Georgiana asked censoriously. "I had always thought you the perfect brother and gentleman."

"Anna, I am as fallible as the next man—and often more so," Darcy stated. He went on to admit to his much younger sister how far he had strayed from the teachings of their parents. "There is much for which I must make amends. For too long, in my arrogance and pride, I have relied only on my own counsel. It will not be easy, but your brother needs to change." Darcy looked over at his cousin. "That does not mean I will not err from time to time, or that it will not take me time to make the needed amendments to my character."

"Nothing worthwhile is easy. You know that, William," Richard stated.

He was glad William had taken this first step. His willingness to accompany them to Longbourn and make his apologies, coupled with wanting to admit his deficiencies before his sister, were positive signs.

Darcy inclined his head to acknowledge the rectitude of Richard's words. "What time are we to depart, and will Mrs. Younge be ready?"

"There is no need for the companion to join us," Richard insisted. "We will both be with Anna, also she will be with young ladies at their home, I have told Mrs. Younge she may have the time to herself."

Darcy could not fault his cousin's logic, so he did not raise any objections to Mrs. Younge not joining them.

~~~~~~~/~~~~~~~

Mrs. Younge was at her wit's end. Because she had not been summarily sacked—or worse, she was sure the dratted Colonel had not heard what she had been saying to Miss Darcy yesterday. However, since then she had not been alone with her charge. Miss Darcy's maid had been sitting in the room with her during lessons this morning. When she took Miss Darcy for a walk, one of the huge Darcy footmen was close by, just as he was near any room in which they were situated.

If all of that were not bad enough, now she was again being left behind when Miss Darcy called on her friends. Mrs. Younge had met the friends when they called on Miss Darcy at Netherfield Park. However, other than having heard the name of the estate she knew not where it was.

She was afraid of what George would say if she reported her lack of progress. She had not heard from him of late, so she had no way of knowing if her paramour had found a creditable excuse to be in the area.

She could post a letter to her boarding house on Edward Street where George would be residing until he had a reason to travel to Hertfordshire. However, she did not want to lie to George, so it was better to wait until he wrote to her. Then she would answer.

By that time, she hoped she would have some intelligence on the friends and others in the neighbourhood to pass on to George. What would she ultimately be able to report about the younger Darcy being amenable to seeing him? To that end, she needed to find a way to have Miss Darcy with her where no one was close enough to overhear them. It was a puzzle without a solution; Mrs. Younge had not yet come close to solving it.

The companion stood at the window in her bedchamber watching as the Darcy coach carrying her charge disappeared down Netherfield's drive in a cloud of dust.

CHAPTER 13

"Colonel, Miss Darcy, welcome to Longbourn. I suppose you are welcome as well, Mr. Darcy," Fanny Bennet stated peevishly as the visitors were being shown into the drawing room.

Although she had no charitable feelings towards Mr. Darcy, Elizabeth cringed at her mother's display of ill-breeding. Whatever level of disdain Mr. Darcy held them in was sure to be magnified by her mother's crass welcome.

"Mrs. Bennet, I completely understand your less than enthusiastic welcome; I deserve no less after my performance at the assembly. My aim in coming to your home today is to apologise to Miss Elizabeth, and to everyone else I slighted with my ungentlemanlike behaviour," Darcy stated contritely.

Both Fanny Bennet and her second daughter had a similar reaction—utter incomprehension. Neither thought that the proud and disagreeable man (Elizabeth would add *insufferable* to that description) would lower himself to acknowledge his poor behaviour—or apologise as well.

Richard did not miss the incredulity with which his cousin's statement was met. 'You have many amends to make,' he thought to himself as he watched William squirm.

Elizabeth was the first to recover her equanimity. "It is gracious of you to apologise, Mr. Darcy," Elizabeth managed.

"As yet, I have not begged your pardons; however, please allow me to begin with you, Miss Elizabeth." Darcy paused as the woman who was, as plainly as the nose on his face, very pretty, nodded her assent. She was, in fact, beautiful. "There was no excuse for my uncharitable, and completely inaccurate, characterisation of your person at the assembly.

"The fact my words were not even close to reality is beside the point. I should never have spoken so. The truth was I looked in your direction but was too angry to take in your person properly. I was annoyed at Bingley for importuning me and said something I was sure would cause him to desist. That is no excuse, of course. I am a man who prides himself on always acting as a gentleman should. Last evening I did not. I humbly beg for your forgiveness and ask that we may begin again."

"I forgive you, Mr. Darcy," Elizabeth granted, "and yes, we may begin our association anew."

Darcy bowed to Miss Elizabeth and then turned to face the Bennet matron. "Even though I would not have asked a girl who, if my guess is correct, is no older than my *much* younger sister, to dance, I should not have stalked off while you were still speaking to me. For my lack of manners and common decency, I beg your pardon."

Listening to the sincere apologies William was making, Richard nodded his approval. William's current behaviour showed what his parents hoped regarding the type of man he would become. Richard was sure Aunt Anne and Uncle Robert were smiling down on them after watching their son beginning to amend his character.

Although she was mean of understanding, of one thing Fanny was sure. It would do no good for herself and her family if she refused to accept Mr. Darcy's apologies. Lizzy had the right of it when she granted him her pardon. After all, he might be the girls' entrée into London society. He could possibly put her girls into the paths of other rich men.

"All is forgiven, Mr. Darcy," Fanny allowed magnanimously. "Kitty, please ring for tea."

While her mother was waiting for tea, Elizabeth

knocked on her father's study door. When bade enter, she related the happenings in the drawing room and urged her father to take tea with his family and their guests. Fortunately, it did not take much cajoling to bestir her father from his book.

Bennet had considered the story of Mr. Darcy's behaviour at the assembly quite diverting, so he did not object to meeting the man. Like his second daughter, he would not have expected an apology from a man of Mr. Darcy's status.

~~~~~~~/~~~~~~~

Since Netherfield Park's cook was being driven to Meryton to make some purchases for the kitchen, at least Mrs. Younge did not have to walk the two miles to the small nowhere market town.

The cart came to a halt outside the general store. Mrs. Younge was helped down by the lad driving it. She made her way to the Red Lion Inn where she had asked for any post addressed to her to be held.

George had advised her not to have letters from him delivered to the same house where Darcy and Fitzwilliam were residing. He had told her it was critical the cousins not become aware of his plans.

"Are there any letters for Mrs. Karen Younge?" Karen asked the landlord.

"One," the man informed her. "Tuppence, please."

Mrs. Younge handed over the two coins and was provided with the missive. She returned to where the cart was waiting to be loaded and the lad assisted her up to the bench. While she waited, Karen Younge broke the seal and opened the page.

6 July 1810

My darling Karen,

My apologies for asking you to remain in those dishonourable men's company. We will not be apart much longer.

Soon everything we wanted for each other will be ours.

It was good news for us when you informed me your charge's dowry is £30,000. We will make a good life for ourselves once we abandon Miss Darcy, which we will as soon as we have her dowry in hand.

Mrs. Younge could imagine what a wonderful life she would have with the man she loved, who had professed his undying love for her. She could not wait to be free of her employment so she and George could be together again. She picked up the page again.

I think we should leave England, but you and I will have time to decide such things soon enough.

In the meantime, as I said I would, I have found a way to come to Meryton without being questioned as to why I am there.

When you next see me you will have to address me as Lieutenant Wickham. I joined a regiment of the Derbyshire Militia. It will be encamped near Meryton on or around the 17th day of August.

As long as you have Miss Darcy prepared, it will be the work of but a few minutes for me to convince her to elope with me. Of course, we will tell her we have to bring you along to ensure the proprieties are observed.

In just over a month, all of our dreams will come true.

In the meanwhile, as I am to depart the boarding house rather soon, do not write your report to me in London, please send it to:

Lt. George Wickham
Derbyshire Militia
Encamped outside of Leicester, Leicestershire
Thank you my one and only true love,
Your George.

Karen enjoyed receiving letters from her lover, but she

was somewhat fearful about what to write in response to this one. She could delay replying for a few days, but respond she must.

~~~~~~~/~~~~~~~

Bennet returned to his study and picked up the letter he had been ignoring for close to a fortnight. He decided it was time to read it. He broke the seal and opened the pages.

26 June 1810

Curate Cottage

On the great estate of Woburn Abbey, Bedfordshire

Dear Sir,

The disagreement subsisting between yourself and my late honoured father always gave me much uneasiness, and since I have had the misfortune to lose him, I have frequently wished to heal the breach. For some time, however, I was prevented by my own doubts, fearing it might seem disrespectful to his memory for me to be on good terms with anyone with whom it had always pleased him to be at variance.

My mind, however, is now made up on the subject. Having received ordination at Easter, I have been so fortunate as to be distinguished by the patronage of Mr. Lawrence Skywalker, rector to their Graces the Duke and Duchess of Bedford.

He has generously selected me to be the curate of this parish, where it shall be my earnest endeavour to demean myself with grateful respect towards him and their graces, and be ever ready to perform those rites and ceremonies which are instituted by the Church of England whenever my patron requires me to lead a service.

Bennet could only shake his head. The man was pompous and obsequious at the same time. Did he not realise, as a curate, he was the lowest rank in the church? Bennet doubted very seriously if the man ever came in contact with the Duke and Duchess, but his letter tried to give the impression of a connection that Bennet believed existed only in the man's head.

As a clergyman, moreover, I feel it my duty to promote and establish the blessing of peace in all families within the reach of my influence. On these grounds, I flatter myself that my present overtures are highly commendable, and the circumstance of my being next in the entail of Longbourn estate will be kindly overlooked on your side, and not lead you to reject the offered olive branch.

I cannot be otherwise than concerned at being the means of injuring your amiable daughters, and beg leave to apologise for it, as well as to assure you of my readiness to make them every possible amends, but of this hereafter.

If you should have no objection to receive me into your house, I propose myself the satisfaction of waiting on you and your family, on Monday the 30th day of July, by four o'clock, and shall probably trespass on your hospitality till the Saturday sennight following, which I can do without any inconvenience, as Mr. Skywalker is far from objecting to my occasional absence on a Sunday, provided some other clergyman is engaged to do my duties, such as they are.

I remain, dear sir, with respectful compliments to your lady and daughters, your well-wisher and friend,

William Collins

Bennet debated replying in the negative but the opportunity to laugh at the man who would write such a letter was too much for him. He placed the missive in the pile of those needing a response.

He would send a positive reply as soon as he got around to it.

~~~~~~~/~~~~~~~

Not long after her father returned to his study, Elizabeth suggested a walk for those who desired exercise. Lydia cried off but all the others, save Fanny, decided the day was fine and a walk was a welcome suggestion.

Given the warmth of the day, the five young ladies felt no outerwear was required, so soon seven walkers were strolling around the park. It did not take long for Anna and Kitty to seat themselves on the swing suspended from the very thick bough of an ancient oak tree in the centre of Longbourn's park.

The two soon had their heads together discussing whatever young ladies of their age usually did. Anna, with her longer legs, pushed against the ground to move the swing gently back and forth.

Jane and Elizabeth walked with Mr. Darcy, leaving Mary and the Colonel to pair up. Neither of the latter two objected to that circumstance. There was no question of propriety, given the number of individuals in the park; none of them were out of sight of the others at any time.

"Miss Mary, if I remember correctly, during our journey north four years past, you did not wear spectacles, how is it that you now do?" Richard enquired.

Mary blushed. "The truth is I do not need them," Mary admitted.

"If you are willing to share with me, why do you wear them?" Richard queried.

"You have seen how my mother is, have you not?" Richard nodded. "In her mind, the only pretty daughters she has are Jane and Lydia, who are her favourites. She has told me I am plain for so many years I suppose I began to dress accordingly. Spectacles fit that persona."

Richard stopped dead in his tracks. It took Mary a few steps before she realised he was no longer walking next to her. She turned to face him and did not miss the thunderous scowl he was sporting. At first, she thought she had displeased him in some way.

He closed the distance between himself and the middle Bennet daughter. Richard stood close to her. To calm himself, he counted to ten and took deep breaths.

"Miss Mary, excuse me for being indecorous, but does your mother have a problem with her sight?"

Again, Mary blushed, this time much deeper. "As far as I know, Mama sees very well."

"Then please explain how your mother can say you are plain when you are anything but?" Richard paused. "Why do you think she denigrates your looks, and if I were to guess Miss Elizabeth's as well?"

"You are correct, Lizzy is her least favourite daughter. Part of it is she cannot understand us. We both love to read and have been educated in subjects usually reserved for men. In addition, Lizzy loves to walk—she can walk for miles at a time. Our mother finds that objectionable.

"She always tells us no man wants a wife who reads too much and is more clever than him. In Lizzy's case, she adds men do not want a wife who runs around the countryside like a hoyden."

"Your mother could not be more wrong. There are men who would appreciate you for the gifts you have and would never expect you to hide who you are. I assume the way you do your hair and the gowns you wear are also part of this persona?"

"You are rather forthright, are you not Colonel?" Mary deflected. It discomposed her that this man seemed to be able to see the real Mary Bennet.

"If I spoke out of turn, then I beg your pardon," Richard responded contritely. "However, one of the many things I learnt in the army is you do not always have time for society's polite games, which often end with nothing of consequence ever being said. I am very direct, and it seems to me you were attempting to change the subject."

"You have the right of it, Colonel. Yes, the way I dress is part of the persona I have created, one which matches what my mother says of me."

"I think she has the power to influence—something you have granted her—how you feel about yourself, which is the only reason you would cede to her. If I were to speculate, I would say, because your eldest and youngest sisters look like your mother, she favours them. She thinks the way *she* looks is the epitome of beauty. In my humble opinion, you should follow Miss Elizabeth's example. You said your mother denigrates her even more than you, did you not?"

"I did say that," Mary confirmed.

"Yet Miss Elizabeth has not changed who she is to fit what your mother thinks she is, has she?" Mary shook her head. "Then why do you allow her to turn you into someone you are not?"

"You have given me much to think on. Thank you, Colonel."

Richard inclined his head to the young lady with whom he was hoping to further a friendship. He was impressed that other than a blush or two, she had held her own and not backed down.

All too soon it was time to return to Netherfield Park. The Darcys and the Colonel took their leave of Mrs. Bennet and her daughters and sent their compliments to the master of the estate before they entered their coach.

The four eldest Bennet sisters accepted an invitation to visit Anna on Monday, but they would all see one another at church on the morrow because Richard had suggested he and the Darcys worship in the church at Longbourn.

Darcy was feeling something unexpected—an attraction to Miss Elizabeth. Given his ideas regarding the class of lady he should marry, he was flummoxed by his unexpected feelings.

CHAPTER 14

Elizabeth, who was normally so sure her character sketches were unfailingly accurate, was overset by confusion following Mr. Darcy's apology. Not only had the man begged her pardon, but he had humbled himself before her mother as well.

Nothing in her sketch of his character had matched up with the contrition he had displayed that afternoon. If she had been so wrong about Mr. Darcy, could it be she had erred in other character sketches?

The question plagued her as she lay awake in her bed. Her confidence in her conclusions, which she had never doubted before, had been shaken severely.

When he had asked for them, for all of the Bennets, to begin again, Elizabeth had answered in the affirmative. The truth was she was pleased to do so as she admitted she had been drawn to Mr. Darcy from the first time she saw him. That is, before he opened his mouth to insult her.

She realised that was the reason she had reacted to his words in the way she did. Had she not cared for his opinion of her, the words would have rolled off her back like water off a duck's.

It was humbling to admit her prejudices against Mr. Darcy had been enflamed because her vanity had been injured by the first man she had ever been attracted to.

Her epiphany regarding her motivations rendered the fact they were to start over even more fortuitous. Yes, the man was still proud; that had not changed. Because of the difference in their social status, Elizabeth's rational mind was certain there would never be anything between them other than an acquaintance. At the same time, her traitorous heart whispered there could be more.

It was after midnight before Elizabeth eventually fell into a fitful sleep. Given the direction of her thoughts before she succumbed to Morpheus, her dreams of a certain tall, proud man from Derbyshire were no great surprise.

~~~~~~~/~~~~~~~

Still fuming over what the Colonel had said to her, and worse, Mr. Darcy's agreeing with him, Caroline Bingley had remained in her chambers since she was embarrassed in front of the man she intended to marry.

On Sunday, Miss Bingley elected to remain abed while the rest of the Netherfield Park party attended services. She required time to think about how she could convince Mr. Darcy that she was more than just his friend's sister.

She had told too many of her *friends* in London she would become Mrs. Darcy by the end of the year to returned to London without—at the least—an official courtship with the man.

She considered a public compromise, but her brother's warning rang in her ears. She knew Mr. Darcy did not say things he did not mean—although she knew that did not apply to her wishes for a future together; however, it meant he would refuse to marry her if entrapped. Charles had already told her he would support Mr. Darcy in such a case.

An idea struck her. She would suggest a ball to her brother. When Mr. Darcy saw how adept a hostess she was and the quality of the ball she would organise, he would be convinced she would be the perfect choice for his wife.

All she had to do was present her idea to her brother. She was sure, given how sociable Charles was, he would agree. To make him happy she would befriend the eldest Bennet daughter. She did not believe for a moment that Charles was not interested in the chit, as Louisa had asserted.

She would never allow a lowborn country nobody to marry her brother, but she would be a useful distraction while they resided in the wilds of Hertfordshire. Unless Charles married a lady from the first circles, her marriageability would be adversely impacted, and Miss Caroline Bingley was not about to allow that to occur—ever.

~~~~~~~/~~~~~~~

On Monday morning, Richard stood in the drive with Anna and Mrs. Hurst to welcome the Bennet sisters to Netherfield Park. Unsurprisingly, Miss Bingley had not felt the need to wait on those *so far below* herself.

Knowing she would refuse to hear what he said, Richard had held his peace when she made her nonsensical utterings. Besides, it was far more pleasant without her company as they waited for Anna's friends to arrive.

As soon as the footman opened the door of the Bennet carriage, Richard stepped forward to hand the sisters out. When it was Miss Mary's turn, Richard gifted her with a broad, welcoming smile and kept her hand in his own a little longer than propriety allowed.

He was pleased to see the blush contact with her hand produced on Miss Mary's cheeks, even though she wore gloves. Even more pleasing was the fact she was not wearing her spectacles, her hair was not in a severe bun, and she was wearing a becoming cream gown. It was modest, but it suited her well. Her bonnet had a yellow rim, an olive green ribbon, and a pink fabric flower affixed to one side; the crown was light green.

That she had taken his words so seriously and was no longer hiding her true looks warmed Richard's heart. He suspected it must have been his conversation with her which sparked her decision to make the changes he now was seeing.

Her mother must be blind. Miss Mary was the furthest thing from plain there was. If he decided to pursue her, it would not be predicated on her looks. However, it was a positive sign that she would no longer allow her mother's nonsensical statements about her looks to hold sway over her.

Richard smiled to himself when Mrs. Younge had attempted to hide the moue of distaste on her face when she had been informed her charge would be spending the time the Miss Bennets visited with one of her guardians—himself.

Her reaction to once again not having time alone with Anna heightened his already aroused suspicions. Any other governess or companion would have relished additional time off.

Because he was sure she was up to no good, he began to formulate a plan. He was happy to put his strategic thinking to a use in a manner that would not end in the death of anyone.

The four arriving ladies curtsied to those waiting to welcome them. In return, there were two curtsies and a half bow from Richard, who could not yet execute a full bow without feeling pain in his injured leg.

"Miss Lydia did not want to join you?" Richard asked when he noted who was missing.

"She chose to remain at Longbourn," Jane replied for the sisters.

"I hope Miss Bingley is well again," Elizabeth stated.

When that lady had not been seen at church, the Bennets had been told she was under the weather. Elizabeth's question was not because she missed Miss Bingley's company —none of the sisters missed her, not even Jane, after what they had been told about the lady by Anna and the Colonel. She had asked to be polite.

"She is much improved," Mrs. Hurst averred. "In fact, she and my husband are in the drawing room waiting to welcome all of you." Louisa knew the last thing her sister wanted was to welcome, or spend time with, anyone from the neighbourhood.

"Where is your cousin, Colonel?" Mary enquired.

"He had business to transact and correspondence to write, so he is in the library. He said he would join us for tea, however," Richard explained.

Mrs. Hurst led the guests into the drawing room where her husband and sister were to be found. "Would you introduce us to your sister, Mrs. Hurst," Jane requested on behalf of her sisters.

Miss Bingley was about to make a caustic remark about the temerity of a country mushroom usurping her prerogative to request an introduction. The words died in her throat when she saw the glower the Colonel was directing at her.

As the introductions were made, each Bennet sister curtsied to the youngest Bingley when her name was spoken; in return, Miss Bingley barely inclined her head to the Bennets.

There was no denying Miss Bennet was beautiful. If she were to be honest with herself, Miss Bingley would admit all of the Bennet sisters were pretty. At last, she met the one Mr. Darcy had seen fit to put in her place at the assembly. If she looked at Mr. Darcy in a way Miss Bingley did not approve of, she would know how to act.

The Bennet sisters were surprised to see someone overdressed for a morning call in the country. To them, Miss Bingley looked as if she were ready to dine with members of the nobility in London.

Before Miss Bingley could say anything insulting, Anna requested Kitty accompany her to look at her sketches, while the other three Bennet sisters joined the Colonel for a walk in the park. Mrs. Hurst demurred. Miss Bingley had not been asked to join either group.

"No fashion or style," Miss Bingley pronounced when their guests had left the drawing room. "Those dowdy gowns!

Really, Louisa, they must be far below us."

Richard, who had returned for his gloves—which he had forgotten—heard the ungenerous comment.

"Need I remind you *again*, you are the lowest-born person here, Miss Bingley," Richard drawled. "Also, another lesson you seem to have missed at that oft-boasted-about seminary of yours was the appropriate dress for various situations. You are dressed for a London formal soirée while the rest of us are dressed for morning calls in the country. The Bennets are dressed appropriately. You, I am afraid, are not." Without looking at the outraged woman, Richard retrieved his gloves and left the drawing room.

"I am sure Mr. Darcy appreciates the sophistication of my attire," Miss Bingley said, attempting to soothe her bruised feelings.

Unfortunately for her, that man entered the drawing room just then. "Miss Bingley, I am sorry for any pain I may give you, but I do not agree with you. I think you are far too overdressed for morning calls in the country," Darcy stated.

He retrieved the book next to the chair where he had been seated yesterday evening, then made his way back to the library to avoid hearing Miss Bingley's lamentations.

~~~~~~~/~~~~~~~

Karen Younge sought out her charge and found her poring over artwork with one of her friends. "Miss Darcy, it is time for a lesson," Mrs. Younge asserted in an attempt to get the girl on her own.

"Should we ask the Colonel?" Georgiana responded. "He told me I was free to spend time with my friends today; did he not tell you that?"

"You are correct, I forgot. Please excuse me, Miss Darcy," Mrs. Younge replied through gritted teeth as she tamped down her growing fury.

It would be more than three weeks before George should

arrive; however, before she replied to his letter, she needed some progress to report. Mayhap this one time she would dissemble to George.

By the time he and the militia arrived, it would not be a lie. She would find a way to achieve the task George had given her.

~~~~~~~/~~~~~~~

Jane and Elizabeth walked into the formal gardens, while Mary and the Colonel followed a gravel path cutting through the middle of the park. As they were all visible to each other, there was no issue with the two groups walking apart.

"Lizzy, I am so happy. Richard told me that Andrew will be here on Wednesday," Jane gushed.

Elizabeth loosed one of her tinkling laughs. It was very unlike Jane to show so much emotion, but she could understand why. Jane had shared how much she loved Andrew.

For Jane to love him, the Viscount had to be a good person. Jane would never allow herself to love anyone who was unworthy. As happy as she was for Jane, Elizabeth felt a tinge of sadness, because she had never felt a fraction of what Jane did for her suitor.

'*You have, for Mr. Darcy,*' her conscience screamed in her head.

"You know this means our mother will become aware of your courtship, then you will no longer be able to protect Andrew from Mama's effusions. Do not forget Papa will want to make sport of him," Elizabeth pointed out.

"My Andrew is made of stern stuff; he will not bolt because of our parents," Jane stated confidently.

"I am sure he is, Janey dearest. You know I could never have lost you to anyone less worthy."

The sisters found a bench that gave them a clear view of the pair who were slowly walking along the path. Jane reached across, placed her arm around her younger sister's shoulders, and gave her a hug.

~~~~~~~/~~~~~~~

"Miss Mary, you look beautiful today," Richard stated as he offered her his arm.

At first, Miss Mary rested her left hand on his right arm gently. Richard held the cane in his left hand; he still needed a little support on his left side as he walked. Thankfully, each day his leg seemed to be growing stronger.

He looked forward to the day when he would not need the cane for anything other than an accoutrement. At least his limp was barely noticeable now.

"Thank you, Colonel," Mary blushed as she replied. "I must admit my mother stared at me today when we left Longbourn. She was so surprised at the difference in my look she made no comment before my sisters and I boarded the carriage."

"Based on your mother's obvious issues with her eyesight, I believe she is the one who needs spectacles," Richard said boldly.

"As that is not something I would ever say to her, I leave it up to someone else," Mary shared. She decided to change the subject before she became too discomposed. "Jane will be pleased when your brother arrives. I heard you tell her he will be here in two days."

"You heard correctly," Richard confirmed. "As we will be brother and sister one day, would you call me Richard?"

'If things go as I desire, we will be much more than in-laws,' Richard told himself silently.

"In that case, please call me Mary," she granted.

They walked until Richard's leg started to object. At that point, they returned to where Jane and Elizabeth were seated and sat on a bench opposite them.

Richard asked Elizabeth to address him informally when in private, until the understanding between Jane and his brother became publicly known. She agreed and requested the same of him.

Soon enough they returned to the house for tea. They noted, but did not comment on, the fact that Miss Bingley was absent. Soon enough, Darcy, Kitty, and Anna joined them in the drawing room.

About half an hour after tea, the four Bennet sisters were on their way back to Longbourn.

CHAPTER 15

Andrew Fitzwilliam was in great anticipation as his coach pulled to a halt in front of Bingley's estate on Wednesday, just after midday. He had hoped to be in Hertfordshire a month earlier, but his duty to his estate and the wellbeing of his tenants had taken precedence.

Now that he was sure everyone was well situated and repairs and rebuilding had commenced, he felt able to depart without feeling guilt that he had placed his own felicity before the needs of those who depended on Hilldale for their ability to provide for their families. The needs of those who worked on his estate and depended on him were paramount.

He had travelled to Hertfordshire with a clear conscience. Truth be told, his steward had opined the Viscount could have departed a sennight earlier; however, Andrew had chosen to err on the side of caution.

He would—finally—now be able to speak to Mr. Bennet and then declare to the world the wonderful Miss Jane Bennet had agreed to a courtship with him. He was hoping it would not be long before he proposed to his Jane.

In his letters, Richard had intimated Jane's feelings matched his own. Hence, Andrew had resolved to ask Jane if it was too soon for him to offer for her. The worst she could say was she needed more time.

His parents had visited Hilldale a few days before he departed, and Andrew mentioned his intention to propose as soon as he sensed Jane was open to it. His mother and father had given him their unreserved blessing.

Richard, Darcy, and Anna stood on the bottom step as the Hilldale coach came to a stop. Miss Bingley had wanted to join them to welcome *her* guest, but thankfully Bingley had ordered her, on pain of losing a quarter's allowance, to remain in the drawing room with the rest of her family. She had acquiesced, but with no good grace.

"Andy, it is good to see you again," Richard boomed as he slapped his brother on the back.

"Everything is well at Hilldale?" Darcy asked.

"Welcome Andy," Georgiana added.

"It is *very* good to be here and see all of you," Andrew responded. "Thank you, Sprite. My you have grown since I last saw you and you seem much more confident." He turned to his cousin, who extended his hand in greeting. "Yes, William, everything is well, or soon will be."

"I believe Anna here has gained confidence from spending time with the Bennet sisters," Richard opined. "She has been much in their company."

"Was not Miss Mary her good friend for some years?" Andrew enquired.

"How do you know her name?" Darcy asked suspiciously.

"it is not some conundrum for you to solve, William. Richard and Anna have both mentioned her name more than once," Andrew drawled.

"Did you eat already?" Richard queried.

"Yes, at the last stop in Hatfield," Andrew averred.

"In that case, go to your room and change, then Anna and I will take you on a tour of the neighbourhood. Hatfield is close, so your horses should not be taxed," Richard suggested with a wink to his brother.

"That is a good idea," Andrew replied.

Darcy was sure he was missing something, but he could not for the life of him divine what it was. He had letters to write, so it was not as if he were free to join his cousins and his sister anyway, but it would have been agreeable to be invited.

As they entered the house, Richard briefly informed his brother about Miss Bingley's unacceptable behaviour and warned him that he would be a target of her machinations as much as William was.

The instant they entered the drawing room, before a word could be spoken by anyone else, Miss Bingley pounced. "It is gratifying to be joined by another one of our friends and be in company with people at our level of society," she cooed as she batted her eyelids at the Viscount.

"Andy, have you ever met this *lady* before? She is claiming a friendship with you," Richard questioned his brother.

"No, Rich, I have never been in her company until today. If you will recall, like our parents, I have refused to know her," Andrew responded. "Unfortunately, I have no choice but to meet her today."

"Miss Bingley I am confused about something," Richard intoned. "Are you under the impression that the Fitzwilliams and Darcys are tradesmen?"

Caroline Bingley clutched her chest as she plastered an aggrieved look on her face. "Of course not! I never said that..."

"But you surely did, Miss Bingley. Did you not just now say we are at your level of society?" Richard enquired.

"Yes, but how is that..." Miss Bingley began trying to dig herself out of the morass into which she was sinking, all thanks to her own statement.

"Miss Bingley, your total lack of knowledge on how society works, and the rank structure within it, leads me to the conclusion you never attended the seminary about which you have boasted. Even the most basic education should have taught you that you, the daughter of a tradesman, are at the bottom of the social structure. Darcy is close to the top, and my family is close to the pinnacle. Please explain how we are at the *same level*?"

She looked around for support from her sister but found no support there. Mrs. Hurst looked away, fidgeting with her bracelets as she watched her sister dig her own societal grave.

"Charles, say something! How can you allow this man to talk to me in this fashion," Miss Bingley screeched in desperation.

"I cannot but wholeheartedly agree with every word the Colonel spoke," Bingley stated evenly.

Bingley did not like to see his sister experiencing this level of pain—and rejection of all she held dear. However, he was convinced until she was shocked to the extent she began to see reality, Caroline would never mend her ways.

He had restricted her finances, taken money from her allowance to pay for her breakages, and sent letters (written by Louisa) to all the shops his younger sister patronised—and others she might patronise in the future—informing them he would no longer pay for her purchases. She would have to fund her wardrobe using her allowance—or what was left of it at the end of each quarter.

Mayhap Caroline believed he was not serious, because none of that had curbed her. It did not help that in the past he was unable to hold to his resolve, but she would soon confront an ugly truth—now he was resolved and would not waver.

Miss Bingley did the only thing left to her, she ran out of the room and up to her chambers. She slammed the door closed and then collapsed on her bed crying tears of frustration.

She could not understand how it seemed nothing she had desired would come to pass—ever. She *had known* what her level in society was, but the seminary had taught her that she must behave at the level at which she wished to become known as a member.

At least, that was the lesson Caroline Bingley had chosen to learn while being the butt of nastiness directed towards her because of her father's occupation. It was the reason she did whatever she could to distance herself from the stink of trade.

Rather than ignore her roots, since arriving at Netherfield Park Colonel Fitzwilliam had used every opportunity to remind her of her true station in life. If that were not bad enough, he usually rang a peal over her head, never allowing her to escape her damned roots when witnesses like Mr. Darcy were present.

There was no way to sanitise the words which had just been spoken. How many times had Charles and Louisa told her the Earl, Countess, and Viscount eschewed a connection with her.

However, she had insisted she knew better. Miss Bingley now acknowledged she had been deluding herself. She still had to take the chance Mr. Darcy would be impressed by her skills, so she would discuss the possibility of a ball with Charles later, once she was fit for company once again.

For the first time in many years, Caroline Bingley shed genuine tears. Unless she could convince Mr. Darcy to offer for her, her dreams of rising in society were dead.

~~~~~~~/~~~~~~~

"This is not a tour of the neighbourhood. We are riding directly to Longbourn," Georgiana exclaimed as soon as she recognised the route they were travelling.

"Yes, Sprite, that is true," Andrew admitted. "There is something you do not know, which I have not yet shared, purposefully."

"What is it?" Georgiana questioned with eyes wide.

"You like the Miss Bennets, at least the four eldest, do

you not?" Andrew probed.

"Yes, very much. I only hoped Miss Lydia was...calmer," Georgiana replied diplomatically.

"I met Miss Jane Bennet in London..." Andrew told his young cousin the story of meeting Jane and their courtship.

"Was Mr. Bingley aware of the courtship? I had thought based on what you and William have told he would have been attracted to her," Georgiana asked Richard.

"Correct," Richard acknowledged. "I informed him and warned him off."

"And William is unaware?" she enquired. The brothers both nodded.

"We are telling you now because Andy is on his way to speak to Mr. Bennet," Richard explained.

"But is not Jane of age?" Georgiana queried.

"She is, but we decided not to mention it to anyone except our closest confidants, which for Jane was her next two younger sisters and for me, my parents and Rich," Andrew informed his young cousin.

"Do Aunt Elaine and Uncle Reggie approve of Jane?" Georgiana wondered.

"Absolutely! They know she came to admire and love me —not my wealth, my title, or that I will become the Earl of Matlock, which I pray will be many, many years in the future," Andrew replied.

"I am so happy! I will have five new cousins," Georgiana clapped her hands in excitement and pleasure at the news.

The coach slowed as the coachman guided his matched team past Longbourn's gateposts.

~~~~~~~/~~~~~~~

George Wickham had to keep reminding himself why he joined this regiment of the Derbyshire Militia. It was in furtherance of his aim of taking revenge on the Darcys while enriching himself at the same time.

The only problem was he had not banked on the Colonel of the regiment being formerly of the regulars. This meant the regiment drilled regularly. He and the other officers were expected to be turned out properly at all times, and there was no shirking duty unless one wanted to test out Colonel Forster's resolve to punish, up to and including, flogging the offending officer or soldier.

He had thought all he would have to do was to strut around the city of Leicester, acquire debts, and enjoy young ladies swooning over a man in the scarlet coat of the army.

That bastard of a colonel had warned all the merchants not to issue credit to his soldiers and officers. He had made it plain if they did, and those debts were not paid, then he and his regiment would not be responsible for what was owing because he had warned them.

Not one shop in Leicester or its surrounding area would allow one penny of credit. Much to Wickham's disgust, he had to pay for anything he wished to purchase with his own blunt. No matter how much charm he used, no one would yield.

If that were not bad enough, the populace had been warned to watch over their daughters. Not only could he not acquire goods on credit, but other than the odd serving wench or two—who were much older than he preferred—no dalliances were to be had.

To make matters worse, he had yet to receive a letter from Karen. He could only hope the annoying woman had done what he asked. He was certain she was in his thrall and could have no way of knowing as soon as he had Miss Darcy's dowry in hand she would never see hide nor hair of him again. She most certainly would not see any of the money he had promised her.

Just when his worry was increasing that Mrs. Younge was not going to reply to his letter, he was handed one by the adjutant, Captain Carter. Wickham placed the missive into one of his jacket pockets. He would read it after he had been dismissed and had returned to his sparse quarters. He had learnt his lesson—thankfully it was not flogging—already regarding not performing his required duties.

After dinner with fellow officers, Wickham made directly for his room. He demurred when asked to join a game of cards. Even if he did not have a letter to read, gambling debts —like everything else—were required to be satisfied at the end of each night. The damned colonel would not even allow men to accrue debts of honour among themselves.

He lit two candles, took his uniform jacket off, and retrieved the letter. Wickham fell back into the rickety bed with a too-thin mattress. The letter was in Karen's handwriting, so at least one thing was going as it should. He quickly broke the seal.

10 July 1810

Post Drop, Red Lion Inn

Meryton, Hertfordshire

My dearest one and only love, George,

Wickham barked out derisive laughter as he read the salutation. Karen was not as young as he preferred his women, but she was easily manipulated and seemed to believe anything he said without question. She was always willing to lift her skirts for him, so she was useful for now.

I will be happy to see you in a month in this little speck of a town. I have been aching for you, my love.

My charge will be primed and ready for you. All you need do is to turn on your charm and she will be eating out of your hand. I have started the process and will keep at it, slowly and steadily.

The last thing we need is to rouse the suspicions of either of her guardians. Thankfully, they are busy with their own concerns. When the time comes, separating her from them will not be difficult.

I hate being around the men who did you so much wrong, but my love for you and my desire to assist you to get your due makes it bearable.

I cannot wait until we are on our way to a new life, flush with the money we will take from your enemy.

With all of my love,

Karen

After reading Karen's letter, Wickham's spirits were restored. His plan was on its way to being a resounding success. It was worth having to suffer under Colonel Forster for another month or so.

His sweet revenge would be achieved indeed soon enough. If only he had been able to arrange dispatching Darcy senior, as he had his own father. The old man's heart had given out before he could arrange to kill him.

If Fitzwilliam were not around, he might have sent Fitzwilliam Darcy to hell once he paid out Georgiana's dowry. However, he would rather escape with the money than have Fitzwilliam hunt him down. Mayhap if he had someone else do it for him…

That night, his uncomfortable bed did not bother Wickham.

CHAPTER 16

Fanny Bennet could not contain her curiosity. A large coach, one she did not recognise, had pulled to a stop at Longbourn. Its door was emblazoned with a coat of arms.

Desiring to learn more, she rushed to the window overlooking the drive and watched as the Colonel alighted, then turned to hand his ward out. Next, a man Fanny had never seen in the whole of her life exited the cabin.

He was as tall as Mr. Darcy and had wavy hair like his, but his hair was sandy blond, like the Colonel's. From what she could see from the window, his eyes were deep blue. As she was staring out at the arriving guests in a most vulgar fashion, she did not notice the mortification of her eldest daughter, and how Jane was being comforted by Elizabeth and Mary.

The Bennet matron rushed back to her chair. "Girls," she screeched, "a man is accompanying the Colonel and Miss Darcy, and it is neither Mr. Darcy nor Mr. Bingley. From his clothes, I can see he is rich. Jane, you will have Mr. Bingley so this man will be for Lydia."

Before Jane could retort, Hill showed the Colonel and Miss Darcy into the drawing room. Fanny wanted to greet her guests, but she could not understand why the unknown man was not with the two who stood before her.

Richard guessed what Mrs. Bennet was about to ask so he pre-empted her. "It is very kind of you to welcome us to your home again, Mrs. Bennet. The man who arrived with us is my older brother; he is currently with your husband," Richard intoned.

There was no reason Fanny could divine why the unknown man would be meeting with her husband. It was then the Colonel's words seeped into her understanding. His *older* brother!

"You said your brother, did you not?" Fanny cooed. "Is he a viscount?"

"He is Lord Andrew Fitzwilliam, Viscount Hilldale," Richard confirmed.

"Lydia, my dearest girl, you will be a viscountess!" Fanny squealed.

"But he does not wear a scarlet coat," Lydia pouted.

The other four Bennet sisters cringed at their mother's display of vulgarity, while Anna stood with her mouth hanging open, having never experienced such behaviour before.

"Excuse me for occasioning you pain, Mrs. Bennet, but why do you think my brother, who is one and thirty, would be interested in a young child like Miss Lydia? Like me, and all other men of honour, he would never look at a girl who should not be out of the schoolroom as a possible partner of his future life, or anything else which would occur between unrelated men and women," Richard stated bluntly.

"Why would he not want a wife as lively and pretty as I am?" Lydia demanded, quite forgetting the Viscount's lack of a red coat.

"What accomplishments do you have, Miss Lydia?" Richard asked the youngest Bennet.

"Mama told me as long as I am lively and know how to flirt, a girl does not need more," Lydia claimed.

"So, Mrs. Bennet, is it your aim to have your daughter become a lightskirt?" Richard did not fail to see the outrage on Mrs. Bennet's face. "I may sound ruthless in asking this question, but I was in the army for many years before I retired. Girls who behave as Miss Lydia does, as you have taught her, are very popular with officers and soldiers."

"But that is exactly what I want," Lydia gloated triumphantly as her mother nodded in agreement.

"Their popularity is because those girls are known as ones who will surrender their virtue quickly and easily." There were gasps all around the drawing room and Richard noticed Mrs. Bennet was fanning herself furiously with her lace square. "I apologise for being blunt, but what I told you is nothing but the truth. I tried to indicate this to you once before, but the path you have set Miss Lydia on is one which will end in her ruin—and that of her sisters."

Fanny fainted. Lydia was in tears while the other four Bennet sisters and Anna stared at the goings-on around them. As shocked as the three eldest Bennet sisters were at what Richard had said, they could not be sorry for his words; they hoped their mother would—finally—realise she had set Lydia on a path to sure disgrace.

The tension was relieved when Mr. Hill entered the room. "Miss Bennet, the master requests your presence in his study," the butler conveyed.

~~~~~~~/~~~~~~~

Jane entered her father's domain to find Andrew looking out of the window, his hands behind his back. From the way he held himself, Jane was sure he was not pleased. What had her father said to perturb him so?

"You desired my presence, Papa," Jane stated as calmly as she was able to.

"Jane, I know you are of age, but is this some joke that a member of the nobility is courting you?" Bennet demanded. "If it is, I will admit you aimed your arrow well. I am greatly diverted."

"Papa!" Jane exclaimed. "This is not something which

was done to entertain you. Andrew is courting me, and I am in earnest. Please tell me you were decorous in what you said to my suitor."

"If what I said makes him run off, he does not deserve you and all will be well. It is good for a young lady to be crossed in love once or twice," Bennet stated dismissively.

"It would take more than what you have said here today to make me turn my back on your eldest daughter," Andrew stated stiffly. "The only thing which would drive me away is if Jane told me that was what she desired."

"That is something I will never do," Jane responded meaningfully.

His beloved's words were a balm to his soul and caused Andrew to beam with pleasure. He knew he had not mistaken her meaning. She was ready to move beyond a courtship.

"Then why did you not speak of this courtship before today, Jane?" Bennet asked incredulously.

"Andrew wanted to honour your position as my father and speak to you before the courtship was made known to anyone," Jane explained. "For my part, I was more than happy to avoid your special brand of *sport* until Andrew returned to me. In addition, I was sure you would tell my mother, regardless of my asking you not to; my life would have been made unbearable until Andrew arrived."

Bennet was about to respond in a cutting way when he allowed his daughter's words to wash over him. She had said nothing that was not the truth.

"My Lord, allow me to apologise, I treated what you said as a joke," Bennet drawled contritely.

"Thank you, Mr. Bennet; it is appreciated." Andrew looked toward the woman he had been aching to see again since he left London many weeks ago—far too long ago. Jane nodded. "May I address your daughter in private, please."

"As long as Jane does not object," Bennet granted.

"I have no objection, Papa," Jane averred with anticipation.

"You may use my study. I will be back in ten minutes and the door will remain partially open," Bennet stated, then left his study, pulling the door mostly closed behind him.

"Jane, did I understand you correctly? Would you welcome my asking for more than a courtship?" Andrew enquired hopefully.

"Yes, I would," Jane replied simply.

Taking her hands into his own, Andrew dropped onto one knee in front of his beloved. He looked up into her eyes and saw love shining down on him.

"Until I met you, I thought I would never find someone with whom it would not be a duty to spend my life. During the time I was forced to be separated from you, I found myself missing you more every day. The maxim *distance makes the heart grow fonder* is true. Not long after you accepted my courtship, I knew I was in love with you.

"I could give you a long and flowery speech, but the truth is I cannot imagine my life without you walking beside me into the future. Jane, will you do me the greatest of honours and make me the happiest of men by agreeing to marry me?"

At first, as happiness and her feelings of love for Andrew overwhelmed her, Jane lost the power of speech; all she could do was nod most vigorously. After a few moments, she found her voice again.

"I love you with all that I am. I could never marry anyone else. Yes, Andrew, absolutely yes. I will marry you," Jane agreed with the utmost pleasure.

Andrew rose, still holding his fiancée's hands. With gentle pressure, he pulled Jane towards himself; she came to him without any resistance. She turned her head up to him, her eyes closed. Andrew lowered his head until his lips brushed hers very softly.

Each subsequent kiss deepened until Jane felt Andrew's tongue enter her mouth. The sensation was blissful; Jane's breath became ragged, and her heart rate increased significantly.

Bennet decided he was not averse to some entertainment at his eldest daughter's and her suitor's expense, so he did not clear his throat before pushing the door open. Rather, he entered his study and cleared his throat once inside. The spell broken; the couple jumped apart.

"I assume the position I discovered you in means Jane has accepted your hand?" Bennet asked.

As soon as his embarrassment at being caught by her father kissing his fiancée passed, Andrew looked Bennet squarely in the eye. "Yes, I asked for Jane's hand. Much to my delight, she has bestowed it on me."

"The rest of her as well, I trust?" Bennet stated drolly.

"Papa!" Jane admonished.

"Mr. Bennet, I ask for you to bestow your permission and blessing on our engagement," Andrew stated as seriously as he was able.

"It is yours, My Lord," Bennet stated as he extended his hand to shake his future son-in-law's hand. "As I am to be your father-in-law, I suggest you call me Bennet."

"Thank you, Bennet. I will make it my life's work to ensure Jane's happiness and comfort. Such will always be my first priority." Andrew paused. "Please call me Andrew or Hilldale."

"Papa, I am well aware you would revel in Mama's reaction and Andrew's discomposure when you announce our engagement," Jane said. "However, may I beg we inform my mother once Andrew, Richard, and Miss Darcy have left Longbourn."

Bennet felt ashamed Jane had to make such a request.

He nodded his agreement. "Hilldale, your parents are an earl and countess, are they not?"

"That is correct," Andrew confirmed.

"Will they accept Jane as your wife, a practically undowered daughter of a minor country squire, with ties to trade and no connections of note?" Bennet enquired.

"My parents, who have met Jane, approve unreservedly. They believe Jane is the perfect woman for me, as I do," Andrew assured Bennet.

"In that case, I hope the two of you will be very happy together. Yes, Jane dear, I will neither mention nor hint at anything to your mother and your youngest—and silliest—sisters," Bennet promised.

"You have not yet noticed it, but Kitty no longer follows Lydia blindly. You may be reduced to having only one silly daughter," Jane informed her father.

Bennet raised his eyebrows in surprise. "Off you go now; I have a book to read," Bennet stated dismissively.

~~~~~~~/~~~~~~~

Jane need not have worried. By the time she and Andrew returned to the drawing room, both her mother and youngest sister were no longer present. Jane looked at Lizzy and Mary quizzically. When she left the drawing room, both had still been within.

"Mama and Lydia have much to cogitate on," Elizabeth stated. "When she recovered from her faint and found you gone, she made for her bedchamber. Lydia followed her."

"I may have expressed my opinion too freely," Richard shared.

"From what I recall before I joined my father and Andrew, you said nothing which was not the truth. The hearing of it was long overdue for both Mama and Lydia. Coming from you—someone outside of our family—perhaps it will have more of an effect on their behaviour." Jane asserted.

Richard relaxed when he saw the nods of agreement from Elizabeth and Mary. He looked from his brother to Jane, then back to Andy. "Is there something you need to share with us?"

"Jane has granted me her hand in marriage and Bennet gave us his permission and blessing. He will make an announcement at dinner," Andrew stated.

The three younger Bennet sisters in the room understood why their father would wait until dinner time. They were happy their father would not force Andrew to bear witness to their mother's vulgar effusions, preventing his mortification.

As can be imagined, joyous congratulations were bestowed on the engaged couple. Many hugs and not a few kisses ensued. Thankfully, the muted celebration did not draw their mother's or youngest sister's attention to the drawing room.

Richard pulled his brother to one side. "Andy, be forewarned William may not react with the joy the rest of us have expressed," Richard notified his brother. Seeing Andy's questioning look, Richard discreetly described their cousin's opinions on what he termed an *appropriate* match for himself and Andrew.

"If William thinks his prideful and arrogant opinion will influence my marrying Jane, then he is a fool. I require neither his consent nor his blessing and will not seek it. He had better take care what he says about my fiancée. I will not tolerate his—or anyone else for that matter—denigrating her in any way," Andrew bit out softly, so only Richard would hear him.

"It is my solemn promise I will not allow William to put a damper on your time of celebration," Richard vowed.

Although Anna was happy for Andrew, she was happier

for herself, now it was certain she was to gain five new female cousins.

Not much later, the three from Netherfield Park took their leave. They were all reluctant to do so, none more so than Andrew.

CHAPTER 17

During dinner, his four eldest daughters looked at Bennet expectantly. Although he had stated he would announce Jane's engagement at dinner, he had not said *when* during the meal.

It was fortuitous he had not said anything at the start of the meal. Gooseberry fool, one of Bennet's favourite desserts, was on the menu; he wished to sate his appetite on the gooseberries folded into sweet custard—Cook made it so very well—before his wife's effusions and flutterings could affect his enjoyment of it.

After a second large helping, Bennet looked around the table and noted his family had all eaten their desserts and were only waiting for him before they stood and made for the drawing room.

Bennet stood and cleared his throat. He noticed his wife and youngest daughter start to stand. "Mrs. Bennet and Lydia, please take your seats; I have an announcement to make," Bennet commanded.

With no good cheer, mother and daughter reseated themselves. "What is it, Mr. Bennet? I have had a very trying day today. That colonel, who means nothing to us, said rude things about my Lydia," Fanny lamented. "I never want to see that man again!"

"That would be a great pity, and quite awkward, as he is to become a brother to our daughters," Bennet stated.

"Of what are you talking..." Suddenly, Fanny stopped speaking as the wheels began to grind in her head. "But if he were to be a brother to *all* of our daughters, that would mean one of them is engaged to the *Viscount!*" Fanny squealed the last. "Lydia, did I not tell you he would be attracted to your liveliness, regardless of what the Colonel said! I just knew how it would be!"

"But Mama, I never saw him today, or ever before, nor has he seen me," Lydia stated.

"Then it means one of my other daughters..." Fanny was at a loss. Jane was for Mr. Bingley. Surely Lizzy, Mary or Kitty could not have attracted a future earl.

"Papa," Jane admonished.

"It is our eldest. Jane is engaged to Lord Hilldale. You are to be mother-in-law to a viscount, my dear," Bennet explained.

For some moments Fanny attempted to speak but not a word issued forth from her mouth. Bennet watched his wife with amusement, sure she was about to make a spectacle of herself.

"What of Mr. Bingley? Did I not say he would be Jane's husband?" It was at that moment the relative wealth and rank of the two men became clear to the Bennet matron. "Hang Mr. Bingley! You have lost nothing, Jane. He is nothing to a viscount..."

"Mama, Andrew and I began to court in London. As I attempted to point out to you on numerous occasions, I was never attracted to Mr. Bingley. Thanks to my future brother informing him I was being courted; Mr. Bingley never showed any preference for me," Jane stipulated.

"This is not fair!" Lydia blurted out. She sat with her arms akimbo looking aggrieved. She wanted to be the first of her sisters to marry. Her mood darkened when not even her mother paid her any heed.

"Why did you not tell me before now?" Fanny enquired.

"Andrew was called to his estate in Staffordshire before he could speak with Papa," Jane reported. "Even though I am of age, both of us wanted to speak to Papa and receive his permission and blessing before we told anyone." As she preferred not to prevaricate, Jane hoped her mother would not ask if she had told any of her sisters. "Due to a fire at his estate, his journey into Hertfordshire was delayed. He proposed this afternoon, I accepted him, and Papa blessed the engagement."

"This is too much, I will go distracted," Fanny said as she began to fan herself furiously. "You will be a viscountess. What clothes, jewels, carriages, and pin money you will have! Your husband will save us from the hedgerows. In the morning I must visit all of my friends."

Jane was relieved Andrew was not present to hear her mother's crass pronouncements, although she knew he would have taken it in stride. Nevertheless, she still preferred it this way. Her fiancé had been spared the worst of her mother's exclamations, although Jane was sure Mama would have her say as soon as she saw Andrew again.

"Mrs. Bennet, you mentioned the Colonel's *rude* comments to Lydia," Bennet reminded his wife.

"That is all forgot now; I am sure he did not mean what he said," Fanny gushed.

Bennet made a mental note to invite the younger Fitzwilliam brother into his study. As much as he hated stirring himself to action, seeing Lydia's reaction to the engagement gave him pause.

It would be interesting to hear firsthand what the Colonel had said, but then he remembered Lizzy was more than likely aware of what had occurred. "Lizzy, please join me in my study," Bennet ordered as he stood to leave the table.

Elizabeth shot Jane an apologetic look as she was leaving. She knew her sister and was sure Jane would not be able to deflect her mother's assertions and exclamations on her own. Mary would be able to redirect their mother, at least to a certain extent. However, Elizabeth would have preferred to remain with Jane. That was not a possibility at the moment.

"Yours will be the biggest and grandest wedding ever seen hereabouts..." Bennet and Elizabeth heard Mrs. Bennet say as they retreated from the dining parlour.

He did not miss the troubled look on his second daughter's countenance. "Jane will be well, Lizzy," Bennet assured her. "Your mother will tire of the subject soon enough and then be onto the next one."

Their mother did such normally; however, given whom Jane was marrying, Elizabeth doubted it would be the same this time. As soon as it was visiting hours on the morrow, her mother would drag Jane around the neighbourhood to crow about the Bennets' good fortune.

Troubled by those thoughts, Elizabeth followed her father into his study. Bennet closed the door and indicated a chair facing his desk for Elizabeth to sit.

"Lizzy, what was your mother on about regarding Colonel Fitzwilliam and Lydia?" Bennet enquired.

"The Colonel pointed out the ills of Lydia being out in society and her inappropriate behaviour and flirtatiousness —not for the first time. It began today when Mama claimed..." Elizabeth, who had an excellent memory, related the conversation to her father up until her mother fainted and Jane was summoned to the study.

"Excuse me, for I must speak plainly. If you, my dear Papa, will not take the trouble to check both my mother and Lydia by following the Colonel's advice, our respectability in the world will be affected by the wild volatility, the assurance, and the disdain of all restraint which mark Lydia's character.

"You need to teach her that her present pursuits are not to be the business of her life. If you are unwilling to do so, she will soon be beyond the reach of amendment. Her character will be fixed, and she will, at not yet sixteen, be the most determined flirt that ever made herself or her family ridiculous; a flirt, too, in the worst and meanest degree of flirtation, without any attraction beyond youth and a tolerable person. And, from the ignorance and emptiness of her mind, she is wholly unable to ward off any portion of that universal contempt which her rage for admiration will excite.

"All I can say is thank goodness Kitty no longer follows Lydia blindly or it would have been two such girls to correct. I have heard a company of militia will be arriving in a few weeks. With Lydia's foolish fixation on officers, what think you will happen once there are scarlet coats aplenty in Meryton?"

Bennet could not help but recognise Lizzy's whole heart was in the subject. However, he was not willing to expend energy if he did not have to do so. "Do not make yourself uneasy, my love. Wherever you, Jane, and Mary are known, you must be respected and valued; you will not appear to less advantage for having a very silly sister.

"When the officers arrive, Lydia will see they will find women better worth their notice. Let us hope, therefore, her seeing that may teach her of her own insignificance. At any rate, she cannot grow many degrees worse. What would you have me do? Lock her up for the rest of her life?"

Knowing her father would ignore her concerns, Elizabeth asked her father, "Papa, you will speak to Richard about this, will you not?"

"If it will make you feel easier, please ask him to see me the next time he visits Longbourn," Bennet said as he waved his hand in dismissal. He wanted to speak to the Colonel and now he would accomplish that end with out expending any effort.

Before Elizabeth closed the door, Bennet had poured a glass of port and opened his book to where he left off before dinner, conveniently pushing the conversation he had with Lizzy out of his conscious mind.

~~~~~~~/~~~~~~~

After returning to Netherfield Park, the brothers sought out their cousin. His valet told them his master had sequestered himself in the sitting room between his and the Colonel's bedchambers.

As soon as Richard made sure Anna's maid was with her, he and Andrew made for the sitting room in the suite opposite their young cousin's. When they entered, they found William engrossed in a book.

"When did you complete your business?" Richard enquired.

"An hour ago," Darcy responded. "I decided not to join the Bingleys and Hursts in the drawing room until you and Anna joined us again."

"William, I have some, from your perspective, unexpected news," Andrew began.

Darcy inserted a bookmark, closed his book, and placed it on the table next to him. He wanted to give his cousin his undivided attention. "I am all in anticipation of you news. Are you going to tell me you have found a woman worthy of becoming your wife?"

"Yes, I am," Andrew averred. There was no missing Darcy's surprise at his jest being accurate. "I have been courting her, but we became engaged today."

"Today! Please do not tell me you have engaged yourself to some country miss with no connections or wealth. You must be ribbing me; next you will tell me it is one of the Miss Bennets," Darcy returned incredulously. He missed the warning look Richard was shooting at him.

"William, Richard told me you saw the error of your ways, but now I find you as proud and arrogant as ever," Andrew bit back. "Yes, I am engaged to Miss Jane Bennet. A better woman for me I have never found."

"The Bennet ladies are pleasant, but you are supposed to make a brilliant match, as am I," Darcy protested.

"Says who?" Richard interjected. "Since when did the *great* Fitzwilliam Darcy become the arbiter of what a brilliant match is?"

Darcy recoiled at Richard's rebuke. Was he the only one in the family who cared about family pride and honour?

"What do you think your parents will say about a match with one so far below you?" Darcy was sure he had played a trump card.

"Mother and Father have known Jane from the time she came to London," Andrew shot back. "Not only do they approve of her, they already love her as a daughter."

This was not what Darcy expected to hear. "How did you meet her in London? She does not move in the same circles as you do."

"My soon-to-be sister, and her sisters, volunteer at Covenant House when they are in town," Richard filled in.

The conversation with Richard regarding the inordinate time Andrew spent at Covenant House came flooding back to Darcy. Suddenly he understood why Andy spent so much time there.

"Were you trapped by a fortune hunter and are now honour-bound..." Darcy stopped when he saw the looks of disgust from both of his cousins.

Their disdain was directed at him! He could see, as he had at the assembly, he had allowed his mouth to run away with him before properly considering his words. He blanched as Richard had to restrain Andrew.

"William, have you lost your good sense?" Richard barked. "When you made your sincere apologies to the Bennets, I thought you were becoming the man your parents hoped you would become. But I was wrong; you are as arrogant, prideful, and haughty as you ever were. If you continue down this path, you will alienate everyone who loves you and will live a very lonely existence.

"I suggest you take a tray for dinner, as you are not fit to be in company. Anna is so pleased to gain the Bennet sisters as cousins, it would break her heart to see this side of you."

Before he gave into his urge to attack his cousin physically, Andrew turned, marched from the sitting room, and made for his suite, which was across the hall and next to the one Anna and her companion were sharing. Richard shook his head at his cousin, then turned on his heel and departed the room as well, pulling the door closed behind him.

Darcy sat in a stupor. Richard's words that he was on a path to being alone in the world ran through his head again and again. Why could he not control himself? Just like at the assembly, he knew the words should not have crossed his lips even as he spoke them.

Was it possible his reaction was part of the battle being waged between his head and his heart? His heart told him he was falling in love with Miss Elizabeth Bennet while his head insisted she was unsuitable.

The truth he had to acknowledge was he had never seen any of the tendencies he accused Miss Bennet of in the Bennet sisters with whom he was familiar. Neither Miss Bennet nor her other sisters had attempted to ingratiate themselves with him—or with Bingley. If any of them were fortune hunters, they would have considered him and Bingley prime targets.

Next, he considered the damage he had just wrought between himself and his cousins, especially Andrew. Would they inform his aunt and uncle of his words? Would that cost him his relationship with the Matlocks?

One thing he was certain of was Andrew never dissembled. If he said Aunt Elaine and Uncle Reggie approved of Miss Bennet, then it was true. What had he done?

Richard invoking the memory of his parents set Darcy thinking about them and what they had *actually* said about marriage, not what he had interpreted them as saying about it over the years.

What they had *actually* said was they hoped he would make a brilliant *love match*, without concern for connections and wealth. All they had asked was the lady be the daughter of a gentleman, at least

The question of why he had corrupted their words was something for which he would have to seek the answer. He had much soul-searching to do.

~~~~~~~/~~~~~~~

Miss Bingley was disappointed when the Colonel informed those in the dining parlour Mr. Darcy had decided to take a tray in his suite that evening. Each time she missed a chance to impress him was a wasted opportunity.

At least the Viscount was in residence. If she could kindle his interest, that would make up for not being able to attract Mr. Darcy. He was just as wealthy, had a title, and would one day become an earl.

"If I may have your attention before we begin the meal," Andrew requested once everyone else had taken their seats. "It is my pleasure to announce I offered for Miss Jane Bennet this afternoon and she has done me the supreme honour of accepting my proposal."

Bingley had known Miss Bennet was being courted, but not by whom. Now it was certain she was never to be his, which was just as well, as he had begun to be interested in another woman. Miss Bingley had a pinched look on her face and was about to make a cutting remark about the Bennets when she looked over and saw the look of warning on the Colonel's countenance.

She bit her tongue. She had learnt to hold her peace around the man because he always managed to work her being the daughter of a tradesman into the conversation whenever she tried to point out what she believed was her superiority.

To her it was a degradation that one as low as Miss Jane

Bennet was to be a viscount's wife. Miss Bingley was sure the Earl and Countess would object vociferously as soon as they became aware of the travesty.

Hurst raised his wine glass once the Viscount took his seat. "On behalf of my wife and myself, we wish you and Miss Bennet happy."

"And we, the Bingleys, do as well," Bingley stated, finding he meant it.

"Andy, I am overjoyed at your gifting me five new cousins," Georgiana added happily.

Miss Bingley stewed in silence. She had lost the Viscount to a country mushroom before she had begun to attract his attention. All that was left was to make sure Mr. Darcy was convinced to offer for her.

She had been unable to talk to Charles about a ball yet. It became imperative to do so immediately, and not waste any more time. "Charles, I have been thinking," Miss Bingley tutted. "We have done no entertaining and we need a way to thank all of your neighbours for their warm welcome. What say you to a ball?"

Bingley was taken aback that his youngest sister would make a suggestion to entertain those she had termed *savage*. Whatever her motivation, Bingley thought it a grand idea. He was a very social man, and a ball would be just the thing to enjoy the society of the neighbourhood.

"Netherfield Park will hold a ball. As soon as I am told how long it will take to make enough white soup, we will select the date," Bingley enthused.

In Richard's opinion, Miss Bingley had an ulterior motive, more than likely tied to William. She would need to be watched. He decided he needed to enlist the aid of some of his former soldiers and officers who were seeking employment.

He would send Brown to London on the morrow.

CHAPTER 18

Darcy had hardly slept the previous night. The spectre of life alone, his behaviour possibly pushing Anna away, had haunted him. When he slept, it had been fitfully; each time he awoke he had been in a cold sweat.

He had a recurring dream of wandering the halls of Pemberly, very much alone. There were cobwebs, dirt, and dust all around him. In his dream, he had even pushed the staff and servants away, so he was alone in his sprawling, empty mansion.

The image in the dream—more a nightmare than a dream—struck fear into his heart. Life would not be worth living if that ever became his future. Darcy was not sure how yet, but he was certain of one thing—he had to begin to make significant changes in his character.

The first step would be to make a heartfelt apology—it seemed he was often doing that—to Andy. Knowing his older cousin would more than likely not wish to see him, Darcy decided he would speak to Richard first and request him to inform Andrew, when he was ready to hear it, that his apology would be forthcoming.

Resolved he had much for which to atone, Darcy rang for Carstens and asked his man to lay out his riding clothes. A long, hard ride on Zeus was what he needed to centre himself.

~~~~~~~/~~~~~~~

Not long after he woke, Richard saw Brown off on his way to London on Invictus. He had made sure to give his valet

—former batman—explicit instructions. So his horse would not have to make the ride there and back on the same day, Richard gave his man coin to spend the night at an inn in Town so he could return tomorrow with his stallion well rested.

Richard was not surprised when he found William was not breaking his fast with him and his brother. He was well versed with his cousin's need for solitude to think, especially after he had inserted his Hessian into his mouth and had been called out for it.

There was no denying his words to William the previous afternoon had been brutal, but Richard believed it was what his cousin needed to hear to make him see the possible consequences of his behaviour.

"Are you ready to brave Mrs. Bennet?" Richard enquired jokingly.

"If I am able to suffer Aunt Catherine's company, I can survive Mrs. Bennet's," Andrew responded. He would bear much more than their aunt for his Jane. "By the way, where did your valet go so early this morning? I saw him ride out on Invictus."

"I will inform you when there is no chance of someone *inadvertently* eavesdropping. What time would you like to visit our soon-to-be family?" Richard questioned.

Andrew felt there was a reason beyond seeing Jane driving Richard's desire to be at Longbourn. He would observe and ask his brother once he was more sure of his suspicions.

"I sent an express to Snowhaven to inform our parents Jane accepted me and a note to the papers in London for the betrothal announcement to be printed," Andrew told his brother. "Had I known you were sending Brown to Town, I would have sent the note for the *Times of London* with him."

"My prediction is our parents will follow the missive within days," Richard guessed.

Just then, Bingley joined them. "No Darce this morning?

Is he still not feeling well?" Bingley wondered.

"I believe our cousin is taking a ride this morning," Richard responded. "You know how much he likes an early morning gallop."

"Yes, I suppose I do," Bingley stated. "Hilldale, I assume you are for Longbourn soon?"

"Yes, I am. Richard, Anna, and I will be calling on the Bennets," Andrew confirmed.

"How is your younger sister?" Richard enquired.

"Caroline does not stir from her chambers before eleven, unless she knows Darce will be here." Bingley shook his head. "Although she seems to accept what I have told her regarding the consequences if she compromises him, I think she still believes he will offer for her one day."

"If I were to wager, I would put money on her *believing* she will impress him with her skill at organising the ball," Richard opined. "Your sister never understood the things she holds dear—society, London, the *Ton*—are all things my cousin finds objectionable in other than very small doses."

"As I have stated previously, Caroline only sees what she wishes to see," Bingley shook his head. "Where is Miss Darcy?"

"My ward likes to break her fast in her chambers," Richard replied. "She will be ready by the time we need to depart." He paused. "Just before you arrived to break your fast, we were discussing that our parents will probably wish to join us in Hertfordshire to express their approbation of Andrew's engagement. Would it be an imposition for you to host them here?"

"It would be a pleasure to have Lord and Lady Matlock as guests in my home," Bingley assured the brothers. "If they come, I will have to make sure Caroline does not fawn over them. You must know how long she has desired to be known to them."

"It would not be the first time our parents have had to

fend off social climbers and sycophants," Andrew pointed out.

"In that case, I will send an express to them after our meal," Richard decided. "Bingley, do you desire to accompany us to Longbourn?"

"No, thank you. I have an appointment," Bingley responded cryptically.

The Hursts joined the men. After Hurst made sure his wife was comfortably seated, he made her a plate before doing the same for himself.

~~~~~~~/~~~~~~~

Miss Darcy was going to be in the company of her cousins and the Bennets yet another day. Mrs. Younge was fit to be tied. She had not been alone with Miss Darcy since coming to this benighted estate.

She was in a quandary. On one hand, she wanted to complain to Mr. Darcy that she never had time alone with his sister. However, she was sure that would lead to uncomfortable questions—ones she did not want to answer.

How would she explain to George when he arrived that she had failed in the tasks he had set for her? She remembered her prevarication in the letter she had sent him and realised it would not endear her to the man she loved.

Karen Younge was at a loss as to what to do. She finally arrived at a way to change things. She would tell Mr. Darcy she did not think his sister had enough time to take her lessons and ask how he wanted her to adjust the schedule due to that fact.

It would be different from demanding time alone with Miss Darcy. Once he stepped in—something she was sure he would do given how much he valued education—then she would find a way to have the young girl alone with her.

She would not fail her George! Her future with him was within her grasp and she would not lose that chance for any reason.

~~~~~~~/~~~~~~~

For the first few moments after her future son-in-law was shown into Longbourn's drawing room, accompanied by his brother and young cousin, Fanny Bennet was in awe of him, which meant she said nothing, other than a clipped greeting.

That did not last long. "You are very welcome, Your Lordship," Fanny gushed. "What an honour to have you offer for my Jane. Oh, I knew she could not be so beautiful for nothing."

"As I will be your son-in-law, please call me Andrew," Andrew allowed. "As far as the honour goes, it is entirely on my side. Yes, Jane is pretty, but I was attracted to much more than her beauty."

Fanny did not know how to respond to that statement. Was beauty not the most important thing to a man? It was what had brought her to the attention of Thomas Bennet all those years ago.

As this was going on, Elizabeth approached her brother-to-be. "Colo...Richard, my father asks that you see him in his study when you are able."

Richard was about to excuse himself when the youngest Bennet proved once again she should be in the nursery under the care of the strictest of governesses.

Lydia, who had never learnt when to keep her thoughts to herself, batted her eyelids at Jane's handsome fiancé. "Would you not have liked to be engaged to a more lively woman?"

She still believed he was lacking because he did not wear a red coat, but she wanted to prove she could have any man she desired and the nonsense the Colonel had spewed was just that —nonsense—at the same time.

Andrew looked the brash girl up and down. He did not miss the looks of mortification on his fiancée's face and on the faces of her other three sisters. The Bennet matron was smiling indulgently at her youngest. No wonder the little chit thought she could be so forward.

"You must be Miss Lydia." Lydia nodded and smiled at him in what she considered her most coquettish fashion. "Have you not already been informed by my brother that even were I not irrevocably in love with Jane, I would not have the slightest bit of interest in a flirtatious child with nothing but fluff between her ears?"

"Lydia dear, mayhap you should not flirt with an engaged man," Fanny stated as she began to turn red with mortification that her youngest had been set down two days in a row and for the same thing.

"Mrs. Bennet, the problem is *not* your youngest flirting with my brother, who is engaged—to her sister, by the way—but her behaving in such a manner at all. When the militia arrives in a few weeks, if you allow Miss Lydia to behave in this fashion, it will not be long before her virtue, and with it, the respectability of your family, is surrendered," Richard warned.

At long last, the Colonel had said something that Fanny could understand. She looked around and noticed the censorious way everyone was looking at Lydia. Had she set her daughter on the path to ruin?

"Mama!" Lydia screeched, "How can you allow them to speak to me so?"

"Lydia, please go to your bedchamber," a very shaken Fanny Bennet ordered.

After looking at her mother as though she had sprouted an extra head, Lydia stormed out of the room, up the stairs, and slammed the door to her chamber so hard the sound reverberated through the whole of the house.

"Excuse me, Mr. Bennet has requested my presence," Richard stated.

He walked to the master's study and knocked on the door. When he was bidden to enter, he opened the door and entered Mr. Bennet's sanctuary. Other than Darcy's enormous library, Richard had never seen so many books crammed into a room before.

Every wall, except for the door and the windows, was covered in bookcases, all of which were filled to capacity, in fact, some books had been placed horizontally on top of those standing vertically on the shelves.

If that were not enough, there were several stacks of books on the floor. Richard surmised if Mr. Bennet ever saw William's library the man would never leave it again. It was no secret the man behind the desk spent his time in this room rather than managing his estate and family.

"You asked to see me," Richard stated after he had seated himself in a chair in front of Mr. Bennet's broad oak desk.

The man wore half-lens spectacles so he could read but could look up and see longer distances without removing them. A half-empty glass of port was to his left, and an open book, face down, on his desk.

"What gives you the right to pass judgement on my family?" Bennet demanded. "It has come to my notice that more than once you have taken my youngest and—to a lesser extent—my wife to task over issues which are not your concern."

Bennet knew he was being peevish, but he felt embarrassed a man had come into his home and pointed out glaring deficiencies with the way he had failed to manage and educate members of his family.

He was the master here and it was his decision how to protect his family. As he always did, he ignored the voice which screamed in his head: *'You do not protect them, you only laugh at their foibles and ignore their improprieties!'*

"The question, *Sir*, is why have you not taken charge of your family?" Before Mr. Bennet could give an indignant reply, Richard forged ahead. "Are you so enamoured with hiding yourself in this room with a book and a glass of port that you care not if your family is on the road to ruin?"

"You exaggerate," Bennet claimed, with much less confidence than he had when the man entered his study.

"Do I? Your youngest has flirted with me no matter how much she is told of my disinterest. She tried the same with my brother just before I joined you, trying to convince him to leave Jane for her. She has nothing but officers in her head, and a regiment of militia is joining the neighbourhood in the near future. How long do you think it will be before one of the officers accepts what she is offering so freely? When that happens—and as she is now it *will* happen—will you still hide yourself away after your family has been ruined?"

This was a reaction for which Bennet had not allowed. He had thought the Colonel would back off as soon as he expressed his displeasure, but if anything, he had only hardened the Colonel's resolve. In a way, he was like Lizzy, whose courage always rose at any attempt to intimidate her.

Richard continued as soon as he saw that Mr. Bennet was considering his words. "The fact I am soon to be your daughters' brother gives me every right to be concerned for their futures, something—correct me if I misspeak here— with which you have not concerned yourself. As it is now, all they have are themselves, which are powerful inducements to attract a man to some of them, but what chance of any marriage will they have if you allow your wife to continue to guide your youngest daughter on the sure path to ruin?"

Bennet was reeling, almost as if he were in Gentleman Jack's being pummelled from all sides. Once the birth of a son seemed impossible, he admitted he had given up on the estate, and along with it his daughters' futures.

He had convinced himself—quite easily—there was no reason to make the estate more prosperous only for one of the hated Collinses to inherit the result of his hard work. As he sat now, with the former colonel before him, Bennet had to admit it had just been an excuse to do as little as possible.

He acknowledged he had always been of an indolent bent, so it was convenient he had a logical reason not to exert himself. Not only had he failed to make improvements Collins might benefit from, he also had sacrificed his daughters' future well-being.

If he had listened to Gardiner when he first married Fanny and invested with him, his daughters would all have respectable dowries, and he would have been able to add to his wife's jointure. Doing so would have assuaged her fears for the future.

Rather than providing for, and protecting, his family, which were the primary duties of a husband, he had sat back and made sport of them, none more so than his wife. His shame burnt deeply as Bennet came to admit his inaction and disinterest in his family's future had led to this point. He had berated the man for telling the truth.

"There is truth in what you have been saying," Bennet stated stoically. "I realise now your highlighting my failure to parent my daughters was to help them. An attempt of one who will soon be connected to this family." Bennet closed his book and slotted it between two others on a shelf behind his desk. "Thank you for waking me up from my twenty-year stupor. I have much over which to cogitate."

Richard inclined his head, then withdrew from the study. All he could do was pray Mr. Bennet had not paid lip service and was going to make genuine changes.

CHAPTER 19

As much as he pushed to be part of the advance team Colonel Forster was sending to Meryton, Lieutenant George Wickham was denied—much to his chagrin. Knowing how much the Colonel disliked being questioned once he had given an order, Wickham, with no good grace, accepted he would not be gratified.

His hope had been to join the group travelling to Hertfordshire so he could shorten the time he was languishing in the damned militia. Denied his usual pursuits, Wickham's time since accepting the commission was thoroughly unenjoyable and hence seemed to drag on interminably.

He had not heard from Karen of late but, based on her previous letter, he was confident by now Miss Darcy was primed and ready for him to sweep her off her feet. It was his calculation of how well his paramour was doing that prompted his desire to join the group seeking out an area for their encampment in the new location.

He had needed to borrow money from some of his fellow officers. In order to explain why he was short of funds; Wickham had spun a tale of how he had been cheated of his rightful inheritance by his patron's son. He also told them he had been meant for the church, but that, too, had been denied him.

Given his belief he would be on his way to Gretna Green with Miss Darcy before anyone came in contact with Darcy, he had used the man's real name when he blamed him for all his supposed woes.

Colonel Forster was leading the men who would depart on the morrow; Denny would be one of them. Wickham had tried to convince his *friend* to swap with him, but Denny had demurred, stating the Colonel had made it plain there would be no switching with other men.

With a little more than three weeks to go before the regiment's move, Wickham knew he would have to make the best of the situation as it was. There was far too much at stake to disappear before his arrival in Meryton.

On his days off, when he was allowed to use one of the regiment's horses, Wickham had ridden farther afield to see if he could gain some much-needed credit, but word had reached all of the towns he visited about not extending credit to members of the militia.

Playing cards was no longer an option. His brother officers knew he had no spare funds, so thanks to the Colonel's rule about no debts of honour, Wickham had been denied the ability to participate in games of chance.

Five and twenty more days. He only had to endure that much longer and then he would have a massive reward and could finally free himself from the cloying and annoying Karen Younge.

In order to make sure she stuck to his plans, he wrote her a letter and asked Denny to drop it off at the Red Lion Inn in Meryton. His friend took the letter without question.

His plan was well formed. As far as Wickham was concerned, it had no chance of failure.

~~~~~~~/~~~~~~~

Fanny Bennet was troubled as she walked to her husband's study. She could not remember the last time her husband had invited her to meet with him, never mind in his study.

She had barely knocked when her husband opened the door for her rather than just calling for her to enter. Fanny looked around the room as if seeing it for the first time—it had been a few years since she had been inside, after all.

"Please sit, Mrs. Bennet," Bennet pointed to the settee between the two windows that looked out onto the park. Once his wife took her seat, Bennet sat on the other end of the settee facing his nervous-looking wife. He could see she was worried; this was not a put-on attack of her infamous nerves.

Rather than babbling, Fanny sat silently with her hands crossed in her lap, waiting for her husband to tell her why he had summoned her hither.

"Fanny, am I correct Richard, the Colonel, has been blunt in making certain points about what you have taught Lydia in general, and her behaviour towards members of the opposite sex in particular?" Bennet began, as gently as he could, not wanting his voice to sound accusatory.

Rather than speak, Fanny nodded first. "It seems rather than prepare her to catch a husband, I have put her on the road to ruin," Fanny stated as tears began to roll down her cheeks. These were not the crocodile tears Bennet was used to seeing from his wife and youngest daughter when they wanted to get their way, but rather they were as real as could be, driven by what Bennet could see was deep sorrow.

He knew he needed to allow his wife to have her say before he spoke, so Bennet reached out and took one of his wife's hands and gently patted it as a show of support.

Her husband showing her compassion was not something Fanny had experienced in almost twenty years. The tenderness of her husband's action caught her completely off guard. He was not mocking her but sitting and quietly listening to what she had to say.

Fanny took a deep breath and continued with what she desired to impart. "At first, I refused to hear what the Colonel was telling me. I told myself he was just being rude and haughty, like his cousin was before he apologised to us.

The truth was that I realised there was much to what he was saying."

For once her lace square was being used to dry her tears rather than to flap to show her level of nervousness. Tears were still falling, so Bennet extracted his much larger handkerchief from his jacket pocket and proffered it to his wife, who took it gratefully.

With her eyes and cheeks dried Fanny gripped the piece of fabric her husband had handed her tightly in her hands, which she placed back in her lap.

"What I taught the youngest two, and attempted to show the three eldest, was the same thing I learnt from my mother, which I finally realise is not the way to catch a man. When I attracted you and you offered for me, I believed what my mother had taught me was correct.

"It always flummoxed me that no matter what I tried to teach them, Jane, Lizzy, and Mary never seemed to learn my lessons. I never wanted to acknowledge it, but Maddie is a gentlewoman, and the three eldest girls took their lessons on how to behave from her. I always resented Maddie's influence over them, but I should have been thanking her for making them the ladies they are today.

"I am aware I denigrated Lizzy and Mary because they look like the Bennets and not like me. In that, I did my daughters a great disservice. It has not escaped me that Mary has blossomed of late and no longer hides her light under a bushel. I am not sure what changed, but whatever it is, it is positive."

Fanny dabbed her eyes again. They were still moist even though the stream of tears had ceased. "I have never learnt how to be a gentlewoman. I knew nothing about propriety, regardless of what I claimed to the contrary. I now see the way I was telling our daughters to catch a husband would do the opposite. From what Jane's fiancé and the Colonel have said, I see now no man of character would want the type of woman I was moulding Lydia to become."

She paused and took a deep breath. "That being said, since I recognise how I was and am still, why did you offer for me?"

"Before I answer you, allow me to state we have both made mistakes. My own are too numerous to enumerate this day, not merely the ones to which you are referring but many more, particularly my hiding in this study and sticking my head in the sand," Bennet owned. "I thought if I did not see the problems it meant they did not exist. I was wrong. Allow me to answer your final question before I say anything else."

Bennet took a deep breath as he considered his words with care. "Fanny, I offered for you because I fell in love with you. It was that simple. I was aware you were not raised a gentlewoman. I did, however, see you for who you truly were, but I thought my love would be enough. I know now without respect; love will not endure.

"As much as it shames me to recall this, at some point I forgot about my love as we had daughter after daughter. I withdrew into this study and, rather than teach and support you, I mocked and made sport of you.

"Jane and Lizzy begged me not to agree to your putting them out at fifteen. They knew from what they had learnt from Maddie and seen in London it was far too young, but I ignored them. Even worse, I laughed at their fears.

"Thankfully, Mary benefited a little from instruction by our sister in Town, but the rest she acquired from Jane and Lizzy. Here again, I erred greatly. I should have employed a governess. It was not as if our income could not support one, but I did not want to bother. When the older three proposed teaching Kitty and Lydia what they learnt, I left it to the younger ones to choose whether they wanted to learn or not. I should have insisted on it. If nothing else, I hope you can see the fault does not lie with you alone but is shared by both of us.

"If I had not been so indolent, it would have been easy to save for your and the girls futures in the event the worst happened to me. Even though you would have never been *thrown into the hedgerows,* you have a legitimate concern and, rather than laugh, I should have done something to remedy the situation."

Bennet remembered the letter lying in the *to-be-dealt-with* pile. He reached over and retrieved it. "I was going to wait until the day before this man's coming, or even worse, the day of his arrival. Please read this letter." Bennet handed the missive from the heir presumptive to his wife.

"It is barely a sennight!" Fanny exclaimed once she read the words on the page. "Did you respond to him?"

"To my shame, I told him to proceed with his planned visit in order to further my amusement," Bennet admitted. "Not just to laugh at him, but to see your reaction as well." Bennet hung his head.

"This olive branch—do you think he means to offer for one of our girls?" Fanny enquired.

"Yes, but I cannot see any of our girls accepting him. Mr. Collins is unintelligent, sycophantic, and pompous at the same time. I would never force one of our girls to marry where they have no inclination."

"Thankfully, Jane is engaged. Neither Lizzy nor Mary would respect a man so far less than them in intelligence; that would leave Kitty and Lydia, who I now understand are too young to be out, never mind old enough to be a man's wife."

"When he arrives, I will inform him he will not be allowed to address any of our daughters regarding matrimony. If he importunes any of the girls I will send him on his way immediately. By the way, from what Jane and Lizzy have told me, Kitty no longer follows Lydia and has been exhibiting more good sense of late," Bennet remembered.

"I agree regarding Mr. Collins. Now that you mention it, our two eldest daughters have the right of it. Kitty has been changing and I refused to acknowledge the fact. Lydia is none too happy to lose Kitty as an acolyte." Fanny paused as she looked out one of the windows at nothing in particular. "We will have to put them back in, will we not?"

"Yes, I am afraid so. From what you observed, and the girls mentioned, I believe Kitty will accept it with equanimity; Lydia, however, will not."

"She will respond vociferously and with much vitriol, but it must be. We cannot keep making the same mistakes that we have in the past just for peace and quiet at home."

Bennet thought back to his conversation with Lizzy, where he had placed quiet in the home above all else. He shook his head at his hubris. "The nursery is on the top floor, just below the attics. Hopefully, we will not hear her caterwauling from there. Regardless of whether we are able to hear her or not, it must be done."

"At the time I did not think so, but I will always be thankful the Colonel spoke as he did," Fanny stated.

Her husband related his initial statement to the former Colonel and the way the man had taken charge of the conversation, seeing through his bluster. "He will be a valuable addition to the family, and a very good brother to our girls," Bennet opined.

"Do you want me to inform Kitty and Lydia of our decision?" Fanny enquired.

"As you stated, it is *our* decision, so it is something we will do together. That way, Lydia will see no daylight between us to exploit," Bennet responded.

When they stood, Fanny was taken aback with a pleasant surprise as her husband pulled her into a hug.

~~~~~~~/~~~~~~~

"You **CANNOT** put me back in!" Lydia insisted.

As surprised as Lydia was, her three eldest sisters thought they must be living in an alternate reality. Never had they seen their parents stand shoulder to shoulder supporting one another.

As predicted, Kitty had accepted the decision with nary a complaint. Due to her burgeoning friendship with Anna, she was aware that the normal age to come out in polite society was eighteen. In addition, all three of her older sisters had shared their opinions that none of them felt ready to come out at fifteen.

"Lydia, unless you want to receive no allowance for the foreseeable future, you will speak to your mother and me with respect," Bennet demanded.

"*You* never speak to Mama with respect," Lydia spat out in an attempt to sow discord between her parents, who had been most unreasonable in their demands.

"For which I have apologised to your mother in private," Bennet owned.

Not only was Lydia shocked, but the other four Bennet sisters were as well. Surely the earth had begun to spin in the opposite direction!

"How we proceed from here will depend on your behaviour. If we see the need, you will be sent to the nursery and there you will remain until we are sure you are able to behave as a young lady should," Fanny said with steel in her voice. "If it means you will be locked in the nursery, so be it. If you choose to misbehave even after you are back in, then you will be sent to a school for wayward girls. The choice is yours."

"I hate all of you!" Lydia bellowed.

"We are doing this because we love you," Bennet stated. "If we did not care we would allow you to ruin yourself, and by extension any of your unmarried sisters."

"This is all that damned Colonel's fault…" Whatever else Lydia was about to say died in her throat as an angry father took a step towards her, causing her to shrink back in fear.

"This is exactly why you are back in. You are no lady. As long as you are under my care, you will not use such language again. Unless and until you learn propriety and how to behave as a gentlewoman, you will remain in, until your majority if that is what it takes!" Bennet boomed.

"You do not realise it yet, but the Colonel did us the greatest of favours. Do you have any idea what sort of life you would have if you carried on as you were and ended up being ruined?" Fanny held up her hand. "Before you say it, I am well aware the way I was teaching you was wrong. I have to learn," Fanny looked at her three eldest daughters, "and my hope is you girls will help me." All three nodded happily. "None of that changes the fact you need to learn how to act with propriety."

Lydia pouted in the worst way and would have run out of the room had her father not skewered her with a look of warning, causing her to remain seated.

"If you were ruined, we would have to cast you out with nothing," Bennet related to his horrified daughter. "You would have been set loose in the world with no one and nothing to assist you. I promise you that a poor officer, if that was who took your virtue, can barely afford to live on his own, never mind support a wife."

Lydia was angry and frightened at the same time. How could this be? "I am sure I will get an officer to marry me. I should be the first of my sisters to marry," she asserted, forgetting everything which she had just been told.

Bennet and Fanny looked at one another and nodded. "Hill," Bennet called. "Have two footmen escort Miss Lydia to the nursery. The door is to be locked and a footman on duty outside it at all times." Bennet then turned to his youngest. "If you think you can escape via the window, it is the highest point in the house, well over thirty feet, and there is nothing to hold onto. You would fall to your death."

"**NO! NO! NO!**" Lydia screamed as the men took an arm each. They lifted Lydia clear of the floor as if holding nothing and, with Mrs. Hill holding her chatelaine following them, up the stairs they marched.

It took a few minutes until the nursery door was locked before the noise Lydia was making faded. With relative quiet once more, Fanny addressed her daughters.

"Lizzy and Mary, I pray you can see it in your hearts to forgive me for all of the times I treated you as less than my other daughters. I cannot change the past, but I will swear not to repeat that behaviour," Fanny asked contritely.

Mary nodded to Elizabeth. "Of course, we forgive you, Mama," Elizabeth stated.

Bennet then took his turn begging his family's pardon for his past sins. Except for Lydia, who was still caterwauling in the nursery, it was a much happier Bennet family after the meeting than before.

CHAPTER 20

Richard Fitzwilliam saw the last man he ever expected to see in Meryton standing with a group of militia officers. He had heard a regiment of the Derbyshire Militia was to encamp near Meryton, but he had not known it was the one commanded by his old comrade in arms.

"Fitzwilliam!" Forster boomed. "Of all of the market towns in the realm, fancy seeing you in this one. Are you trying to follow me around?" Forster jested.

"As I was here before you, if there was any following being done, it is not by me. How are you doing? I see you still limp," Richard responded as he extended his hand to his friend.

"As do you, and you use a cane," Forster observed. "I was sad to read about your injuries and subsequent medical boards. You know, they are looking for good men to command militia regiments. A man such as you, who was a Colonel, may be promoted to command a battalion."

"Although becoming your commanding officer would be an attraction, as I told you when you came to see me after Talavera, the militia is not for me. It seems to have been good for you, however," Richard said. "I assume yours will be the regiment gracing the neighbourhood with its company."

"Aye, that is the truth." Forster turned to the two officers waiting patiently for him. "Sanderson and Denny, come meet one of the heroes of Talavera. May I?" Forster inclined his head to his two officers.

Neither of the two had ever seen their Colonel so jovial before. They were used to his businesslike, gruff, and stern persona.

Richard nodded his assent. "Captain Sanderson, Lieutenant Denny, it is your honour to meet the Honourable Colonel Richard Fitzwilliam, retired. He almost lost his life at Talavera," Forster drawled.

"Fitzwilliam? Are you related to one Fitzwilliam Darcy?" Denny enquired, with a certain level of distaste when he spoke.

"Yes, he is my cousin," Richard responded. "How would you know his name; I have never heard him mention a Denny before."

Forster turned to his officer. "Is your attitude due to the tales Wickham has been telling?" he barked, causing his lieutenant to shrink back. "Did I not tell you unless there was proof, or we heard the other side of the story, it is but a fanciful yarn told by a man about whom we know little?"

"How do you know that blackguard?" Richard demanded.

"He has been a lieutenant in my regiment for some weeks now," Forster reported. "Denny here," Forster inclined his head to the uncomfortable-looking man, "recruited him in London."

"Do we have somewhere to talk privately?" Richard enquired.

Forster inclined his head towards the Red Lion Inn. "We have a private parlour at the inn for our use. Sanderson, join the other officers and men and report back regarding a location for an encampment. Denny," Forster glowered at his officer, "you will join us."

The Captain saluted smartly, much crisper than Richard would have expected from an officer in the militia, but he reminded himself Forster would never accept anything less from his men.

With that, Sanderson turned on his heel and went to find the other men from his regiment who had accompanied them to Meryton. Denny followed the two colonels like an errant schoolboy who had been called on the carpet to see the headmaster. He knew he would not be caned, but he was prepared for the verbal equivalent of it. Had he missed something about Wickham?

~~~~~~~/~~~~~~~

If Wickham thought the rules would be relaxed with Major Montgomery in temporary command, he had been sorely disappointed. If anything, the Major adhered to the rules even more closely than the Colonel.

He was perturbed he had not heard from Karen of late. He craved to know how she was proceeding in laying the groundwork for him to convince Miss Darcy to elope with him.

He had written her another letter, demanding to know how she was proceeding with her preparation of the prig's sister. Knowing how much Karen believed herself in love with him, Wickham knew he needed to play up his disappointment with her not sending him regular updates. This way, she would think she was in jeopardy of losing his good opinion. It was the letter he had handed Denny to leave for Karen at the inn in Meryton.

Adding to his frustration was the fact he was out of funds. It would be two more days before he would receive his meagre monthly wages. At least that would allow him to buy some grog and play a few hands of cards. Mayhap this time he would have better luck and earn some serious coin from his fellow officers—one could never tell.

He was already imagining spending the thirty thousand pounds he would receive on handing proof of his marriage to Darcy. That of course, would not be enough, he had a plan to demand more. He could not wait to see his enemy's face after learning he had been bested by the son of his father's late steward.

With happy thoughts of revenge dancing in his head, Wickham fell asleep with a smile on his face.

~~~~~~~/~~~~~~~

As soon as Forster pushed the door closed, Richard rounded on the Lieutenant. "Let me guess. Wickham told you a tale of woe about being cheated out of a clerical living by my cousin and denied the inheritance left for him by my uncle."

The Colonel's injury did not make him any less imposing and Denny would not look the man in the eye. He simply nodded.

"And he has used this lie of his to borrow money from you and other officers, swearing he would soon be receiving his *due*?" Again, Denny nodded.

"Did I not make it clear there would be no debts of honour among my officers?" Forster barked.

"You did, Colonel, and none of us have any such debts," Denny averred. "You never mentioned it was outside of the rules to make personal loans."

"How much does Wickham owe you?" Forster demanded.

"Twenty pounds," Denny admitted.

"Let me tell you the truth about George Wickham. By the way, I have proof to support my assertions. How much proof did he give you to bear out his tales?" Richard enquired.

"None," Denny acknowledged as he hung his head. He would have a few choice words with Wickham when the forward party returned to their current encampment.

"I do not need any," Forster insisted. "I have long known you as a completely honest man. I know what you tell us will be nothing less than the truth."

"This is the truth of the relationship between that libertine and my family. George Wickham did spend a good portion of his childhood at Pemberley, the Darcys' estate, as his father was my late Uncle Robert's steward.

"At some point, due to Mr. Wickham having saved his life—the need to save his life we are sure George caused—my Uncle Robert agreed to become godfather to George Wickham. My uncle's attachment to him was so steady he never saw the defects of character my brother, my cousin, and I witnessed in his unguarded moments when he displayed his vicious propensities and want of principles. His licentiousness at Cambridge was common knowledge to his fellow students, but unknown at home.

"At the end of his first year at Cambridge, my cousin and I presented my uncle with irrefutable proof of his debts, the young girls he had seduced, and the debauchery in which he engaged. My late uncle's eyes were opened and, with Wickham's father's support, he withdrew all patronage of his former godson.

"His father did not have much money saved, but he used what he had so his son could complete his university education. Wickham was sent down in his final year and never graduated. About a year later, Mr. Wickham was dead due to a suspicious riding accident."

Colonel Forster gave Denny a pointed look. He had unwittingly supported Wickham's claims he had completed his gentleman's education and had graduated with honours. By this time, Denny, who was sure he had been hoodwinked, knew not which way to look.

"After his father's death—which he is suspected of having caused—we know not how or where Wickham lived. We believed it was in London," Richard continued. "My Uncle Robert succumbed to a weak heart. The day the will was to be read, none other than George Wickham, who had been previously run off Pemberley's lands, showed up displaying his brazen best and demanding the inheritance he was sure he had been left, as well as the value of the living his *godfather* had *promised* him.

"He claimed he did not want to enter the church, but desired to read the law. He stated he needed the money he was sure he was due to further his scholastic endeavours. He must have thought us simpletons to think a man who had not graduated would be able to do any of the things he claimed.

"My brother and I, as executors of our late uncle's will, had him thrown out of Pemberley with unambiguous orders to arrest him if he set foot on the estate's land, or any Darcy property, again. What presumption to claim an inheritance when he knew there would be nothing for him!

"Since that last imposition at Pemberley, there has been no contact between himself and the Darcy or Fitzwilliam families. We suspect his life has been, since his father's death, free from restraint and one of idleness and dissipation."

"One thing I am aware of," Denny stated in an attempt to redeem himself in his Colonel's eyes. "He has been writing to a lady here in Meryton. I am in possession of a letter for her to be delivered to the Red Lion Inn."

"Is it with you, and who is it directed to?" Richard demanded with urgency.

"It is in my room; I forgot to give it to the landlord earlier. It is directed to a Mrs. K. Yo...something."

"Younge ," Richard prompted.

"Yes! That is it," Denny confirmed.

Suddenly all of his premonitions and the bits and pieces he had heard from Mrs. Younge coalesced in his mind. She was Wickham's accomplice! The bastard was planning something and... Richard stopped and remembered her words about Anna being old enough to marry. Wickham was planning to elope with Anna, thinking it would gain him her dowry!

"That useless man has violated the code of honour I make each and every officer sign. He will be flogged and cashiered out of the militia as soon as I return to

Leicestershire!" Forster boomed angrily.

"No, Forster, do not do that. Denny, as soon as your Colonel dismisses you, bring that letter to me." Denny nodded his agreement. "Here is what I suggest..." His strategic mind fully engaged; Richard laid out a plan. The more he spoke, the more Forster nodded his agreement.

Denny was pleased he would be part of the plan to punish the man who had played him for a fool. He was especially gratified when Colonel Fitzwilliam had pledged between his brother, cousin, and himself, they would make whole any soldiers and officers who had been duped into lending the profligate money.

Denny was freed to retrieve the letter for Colonel Fitzwilliam; he delivered it into his hand shortly thereafter. He was then sent to join Captain Sanderson and the rest of his officers and soldiers. Richard placed the letter in his pocket to read later.

Forster told Richard he intended to hold a dinner for all of the men in the neighbourhood on Thursday, the second day of August. He would send a formal invitation to the men at Netherfield Park, but he wanted to issue one to Richard personally.

Before he left the inn, Richard met with the landlord and convinced the man to hold any further letters for Mrs. Younge and notify him when, or if, they arrived.

~~~~~~~/~~~~~~~

That afternoon, Richard accompanied Anna and Andrew to Longbourn. He wanted William present when he opened the letter, but Darcy and Bingley had been out riding when he had returned from Meryton.

At Longbourn, after greeting the four older Bennet sisters in the drawing room, he was invited to join the master of the estate in his study. When Richard entered, he noticed Mrs. Bennet was also present.

"You have been rather forthright in pointing out certain deficiencies in our parenting of our youngest daughters, and our behaviour in general," Bennet began.

Richard was taken aback at the direct frontal assault and was girding his loins to back up what he had previously said to both Mr. and Mrs. Bennet. Before he could reply, Bennet raised his hand to stay him.

"Do not make yourself uneasy; if you think our aim in asking to speak to you is to rake you over the coals, you are wrong. In fact, it is quite the opposite. My wife and I would like to thank you for saying what you did. Your words caused the scales to fall from our eyes," Bennet continued.

"You could not have been more correct regarding Lydia and how my permissiveness set her on the road to ruin," Fanny acknowledged. "She is not pleased, but she is back in and will remain in the nursery until such time as she learns to behave as a lady. My husband and I agree we should employ a governess for her. Catherine is back in as well, but she will be eighteen in a matter of months and did not object in the least."

"The same cannot be said for our youngest," Bennet stated wryly.

By now Richard was beyond surprised. He had expected many things but not this. He had hoped some positive changes would come from him not sugarcoating his words. Even though Bennet had made a little apology the other day, it was still a shock. Given the personalities of the Bennet parents, as he understood them, he had not foreseen this reaction.

"If my words, which I know could have been seen as rude and interfering, have assisted you even in a small way, then I am most gratified. Your daughters are to be my sisters; we are all to be family. If I did not care for your family, I would never have presumed to speak as I did," Richard explained. "I will admit I hoped against hope I would shock you into action."

"Unless I am blind," Fanny said with a smile, "you hope

to be far more than a brother to my middle daughter. Since you came into the neighbourhood, our Mary has cast off her severe look and has looked prettier than at any time in my memory."

"As yet, I have not spoken to Miss Mary, but it is my hope, with your permission to approach her today and request a formal courtship," Richard revealed.

Bennet looked to his wife, who nodded. He looked back to the Colonel. "We have no objection to your addressing Mary, but the decision will be hers. We will not force any of our daughters to marry where they do not have the inclination to do so."

"I can ask for no more than that," Richard averred as he inclined his head to the Bennet parents. "If you will excuse me, I have a young lady to find."

"Just follow the sounds of the pianoforte," Fanny smiled.

"It seems our eldest and middle daughters will be marrying brothers unless we are both wrong," Bennet shook his head after the door had been pulled closed.

He pulled his wife to himself and demonstrated she was still a desirable woman, even after so many years of marriage.

CHAPTER 21

Following the sounds of a pianoforte being played, Richard found Mary in a parlour just off the drawing room. He stood at the door and watched as her body swayed with the feeling she was infusing into a piece from Beethoven's *Symphony number six*.

Watching her play, he thought back to the three days he had spent in the Gardiner carriage with Mary. Then, she had been too young to think of as the partner of his future life, but she had intrigued him.

When he met her again in Hertfordshire, two things had occurred. He was attracted to her, and he had detected that Miss Mary was hiding her true self from everyone. She was still the beautiful, compassionate, intelligent young lady he had met more than four years ago, but she was no longer allowing anyone to see who she truly was.

Now he was in love with Mary Bennet. He knew not how she felt about him; however, he was certain she was not indifferent to him. Although Richard felt ready to offer for her, he decided a courtship would be prudent; it would allow her feelings to catch up to his.

Mary played the last stanza of the piece and was thinking of launching into another when she heard applause behind her. She had been lost in the music and suddenly realised she was no longer alone in the parlour.

She turned to see who was applauding her playing. She was pleased to see it was Richard, who was standing at the door. She had fallen in love with the former officer, and hoped he felt some degree of the same emotion for her.

Believing she was worthy of the love of a good man was something new for Mary. At times, however, she still allowed her old doubts to creep in. When she was around Richard —it had been some weeks since she called him Richard in her thoughts—those doubts were driven completely from her head.

"I was unaware I was not alone," Mary stated shyly as her cheeks bloomed in a becoming blush.

"Your playing was far too enjoyable to disturb you before you completed the piece. You imbue the music with your soul," Richard responded.

His praise caused Mary's blush to deepen until her cheeks were nearly scarlet. "I decided to practice on the instrument after you greeted us in the drawing room," Mary explained. "Seeing Lizzy, Kitty, and Anna are with Jane and Andrew, I felt they did not need a fourth chaperone."

"I am glad to find you alone. I have permission from your parents to address you in private," Richard revealed as he pushed the door three-quarters closed. "Will you join me on the settee, Miss Mary?"

Mary slid off the pianoforte bench, moved to the settee, and sat close to the man she loved. "I am ready to listen to whatever you have to say," Mary stated, her voice just above a whisper. She was filled with anticipation.

"My purpose today is to request that you accept a courtship with me so you can learn if your feelings can grow to equal my own," Richard stated as he looked deeply into her hazel eyes. The flecks of green and gold in them seemed to sparkle like diamonds struck by the sunlight.

"Unless I know your feelings, I cannot tell you if mine do or do not match yours," Mary stated, looking back into Richard Fitzwilliam's blue eyes.

"I found myself falling in love with you not long after

seeing you again. The more I came to know you, the depths of you, the more I have fallen irrevocably in love with you. I know you are a beauty, but it is who you are inside to which I am attracted. I am offering you a courtship because I do not want to pressure you in any way. I want to give you all the time you need to determine your feelings." Richard waited for her response.

Mary's face broke into a smile and, at that moment, Richard saw love reflected in her eyes. "I do not need time to know how I feel. I am already in love with you—head over heels and lost to you. My heart beats for you alone. So, *Richard*, I do not need a courtship to discover how I feel about you."

Even had she not spoken the words, seeing the look in her eyes, and hearing the way she caressed his familiar name as she spoke, it was more than enough for Richard. There was no doubt in his mind their feelings were attuned.

As soon as she stated she did not need time to decide, he felt a frisson of pleasure travel up his spine. He slipped off the settee onto one knee in front of the woman who was dearer to him than any other. He took each of her dainty hands in his own.

"Mary, I am not one for long flowery speeches, so let me say plainly, I love you with my all and would be more than honoured if you agreed to join your life with mine and become my wife. Will you marry me, my beloved Mary?"

"A short proposal deserves an in-kind reply. Yes, Richard, I will marry you," Mary replied as tears of happiness fell from her eyes.

Richard used his handkerchief to dry Mary's happy tears before he stood and gently pulled her up to stand opposite him. The movement of their heads was mutual and soon their lips met.

Mary felt the most wonderful feeling of joy the instant their lips brushed. It was just right; this man was her match in every way. Her heart sped up as it beat its approval of the man who would protect her for the rest of her days.

Their first kiss was no more than a faint touch of their lips, but the next ones were much deeper. Mary placed a hand on each of Richard's strong shoulders to steady herself as the passion of their kisses made her unsteady on her feet.

Regardless of his desire not to end their passionate interlude, Richard stepped back. His breathing was ragged. He had kissed non-family women before, but none had ever evoked the depths of feeling—or any feelings at all—that Mary's kisses engendered in him.

"I think I need to speak to your father," Richard stated as soon as his breath returned to normal. "Your parents are under the impression I would request only a courtship."

"You did," Mary averred playfully. "Except I wanted more, and you complied."

"In that case, mayhap you should join me for my interview with your father and assure him I did not pressure you into something for which you were not ready."

Mary nodded and after one more very welcome kiss, she led Richard out of the parlour.

~~~~~~~/~~~~~~~

"Have you received a response from your parents yet?" Elizabeth asked Andrew.

"A Matlock courier arrived this morning. My parents will arrive on the morrow. They are excited to be gaining Jane as a daughter," Andrew related.

"Were all of your family pleased for you?" Elizabeth asked. She suspected, even though he had apologised for his behaviour when they first met, Mr. Darcy's pride would not allow him to accept his cousin's marriage to Jane and the Bennets' connections to those in trade.

Thankfully, Richard had informed Andrew about

William wanting to beg his pardon for his initial reaction to the news of the engagement. Richard had also urged restraint in sharing William's response with any of the Bennets, given how poor an impression their cousin had made when he first arrived in Hertfordshire.

"I have been wished well by all of my family whose opinions I care for," Andrew replied circumspectly. He had phrased his response in such a way that he did not tell an outright lie.

It was a good thing Elizabeth did not notice the way Anna rolled her eyes. Like Andrew, Richard had impressed on his ward the need for discretion in this matter. Anna had agreed to remain quiet about the incident.

Elizabeth knew she would not receive a different response, so she dropped the subject. As long as Mr. Darcy kept his improper pride under regulation, she would accept things were as they should be.

~~~~~~~/~~~~~~~

Fanny was still discussing something with her husband when there was a knock on the study door. It was Richard, along with Mary. There was no missing the glow of happiness which enveloped the couple.

"Mrs. Bennet, Bennet, I must apologise. The question I sought to ask—although I did ask it—was not the one to which Ma...Miss Mary gave her approval," Richard stated.

The eyebrows of both Bennet parents shot up in surprise. Combined with the look of supreme pleasure pouring from Mary and Richard in waves and the latter's statement, it was safe to assume Richard had proposed and been accepted.

"Speak plainly. What is it you are here to request?" Bennet insisted.

"I requested a courtship but was informed in no uncertain terms it was not necessary, because Mary is as much in love with me as I am with her. Hence, I proposed marriage to her. To my supreme pleasure, she accepted me," Richard reported.

"Mary, this is what you want?" Fanny asked as she took her middle daughter's hands in her own.

Tenderness from her mother was not something Mary ever remembered experiencing before; however, it was a feeling she enjoyed and hoped it was not a one-time happening.

"Mama, Papa, Richard did not try to convince me to accept his hand rather than a courtship," Mary assured her parents. "Just as he said, I was the one who stated a courtship would be superfluous, given I already knew who the only man in the world I could be prevailed upon to marry was. Hence, it was my absolute joy to agree to marry Richard."

Bennet looked to his wife who, with a wide smile, nodded her head. "In that case, we can do nothing other than bestow our consent and blessing for your union," Bennet granted.

"Then it is good timing my parents will arrive on the morrow," Richard revealed. "They were overjoyed at the prospect of seeing Jane as their future daughter-in-law. To know I have chosen the perfect woman for myself as well will bring them further joy—and surprise. I have not yet shared my hopes regarding Mary with them."

With a supreme effort, Fanny controlled her reaction. She would meet a peer of the realm and his countess on the morrow!

"It will be our pleasure to meet your and Andrew's parents," Fanny said calmly. "Please extend our invitation for a family dinner on the morrow to all the Fitzwilliams and Darcys."

Richard was hopeful, especially with his parents as part of the party, William would not say or do anything to offend their hosts. He had a feeling once he presented William with proof of the true character of Anna's companion, he would be far too preoccupied to deliver any slights to their hosts.

Now was not the time to think of the contents of Wickham's letter in his pocket. It was a time for celebration. Bennet stood and shook his future son-in-law's hand. "I think we have an announcement to make." With that, Bennet led his wife and the newly-engaged couple out of the study.

~~~~~~~/~~~~~~~

As soon as Bennet's announcement had been completed, the sound of congratulations rose from those in the drawing room. They were not a large group but a raucous one.

"Mary, dearest Mary," Elizabeth said, hugging her next younger sister, the one most like her in intelligence and wit. "I am so very happy for you. You could not have accepted a better man!"

"You will hear no argument from me," Mary responded as she hugged Elizabeth in return.

"So much for requesting a courtship," Andrew stated, grinning as he slapped his brother's back.

"It is what I intended; Mary had other ideas," Richard replied with a huge grin plastered on his face. "Brothers marrying sisters! How I enjoy the sound of that."

Jane was the next to pull Mary into an embrace. "Mary, such news! I knew how it would be," Jane enthused. "There was no missing the way the two of you looked at one another."

Anna replaced Jane. "We were already to be cousins, and now we will be so all over again. I am so very happy for you and Richard."

"Thank you, Anna. I am rather pleased myself," Mary smiled as she looked over at her fiancé, who was accepting wishes for happiness from Jane and Elizabeth.

Kitty was the final Bennet sister present to embrace her

older sister. "It is good that Lydia is in the nursery," Kitty said quietly next to Mary's ear. "She will not be sanguine with your marrying a colonel, even if he has retired from the army. Two sisters will be married before her. As one who wanted to be married first, Lyddie will not be pleased."

Richard, who had come to stand next to his fiancée after hugging Anna, interjected, "Apparently Miss Lydia wants to be displeased with the world. When she decides to look for the positive, her life will improve. If she sees what is occurring as a punishment and not an opportunity to improve her lot in life, nothing will change."

Given the truth of Richard's words, Kitty could not but agree with his conclusion. She thanked God every day that she no longer followed where Lydia led.

Fanny looked at the brothers who would be her sons in the future and asked, "Will you two remain with us for dinner?"

"Thank you, but no," Richard spoke before his brother could accept. "I have some business I need to go over with my cousin, and we did not let our hosts know we might miss dinner."

Not long after, the brothers and Anna were on their way back to Netherfield Park. Richard wanted to share his reasons with Andrew, but Anna's presence in the coach prevented him from speaking.

CHAPTER 22

Brown had done well. He had returned that afternoon with half a dozen men. Two of them, former sergeants, were mountainous and aptly named Biggs and Johns. Given what Richard had learnt that day, the new men would all be guarding Anna.

His cousin had been rather self-absorbed and had not yet noticed the additional men. William was not at dinner; he had taken a tray in their shared sitting room. His absence rendered Miss Bingley almost quiet. Richard was pleased he did not have to listen to the inane and cutting remarks she considered witticisms.

Before the meal, he had found time to inform Andrew of the goings-on and the letter. As soon as dinner had been eaten, he excused himself and bounded up the stairs.

Striding into their shared sitting room, Richard was presented with the sight of a dejected cousin. "Why the long face?" Richard asked before he raised the subject he needed to with William.

"Thanks in no small part to you, I have been taking a long look at myself in the mirror. I am not sanguine with the reflection I find staring back at me." Darcy paused as he contemplated the question he wanted to ask. "Am I really such a proud, arrogant prig?"

"When you choose to be, William, you are insufferable," Richard averred. He did not want to tone down his reply, knowing William needed to hear the unvarnished truth. "Yes, you apologised, but think of the unmitigated gall of one such as yourself, a visitor in this community, not only insulting a beloved resident, but thinking you could give her consequence where she had all she will ever need hereabouts."

"That was rather presumptuous of me, was it not?" Darcy owned.

"At the level of Lady Catherine! Again, I will preface this with you have indicated your willingness to apologise for the unwise words you spoke at the news of Andy's engagement. He will listen to you, but if you are insincere or ever insult Jane or a member of her family again, you will be in jeopardy of Andy cutting off his association with you." Richard looked his cousin squarely in the eye. "It is not your place to approve or disapprove of any of our choices of the ladies who best suit us. Only our parents may object. As I have attempted to tell you, but you would not listen, they do not. You will see on the morrow how pleased they are to gain Jane as a daughter."

"They are truly in love with one another, are they not?"

"Yes, they are. William, I am engaged as well," Richard revealed.

Rather than insult his cousin, Darcy cogitated for some moments without reacting. "It is Miss Mary, is it not?"

"Correct! You have more perspicacity than I thought if you have divined that. You were wise to think of your words before you spoke. I would be even less tolerant than Andy should you denigrate the woman I love. Mary thinks I am a poor soldier and she accepted me regardless. She does not know I received a bequest from your father or that I have saved my allowance from Father and most of my wages." Richard looked off into space and grinned as he thought of his beloved fiancée. "As soon as we decide on a wedding date, I will disclose all to her, including that I plan to lease Rivington from you."

"As long as you are happy, I will be so for you," Darcy pledged.

"Now we need to discuss a more unpleasant subject.

William, in employing Mrs. Younge you have invited a turncoat into your household."

"Rich, I know you were correct about my attitude and interactions with those I deemed below me but think of the characters she provided. You have been set against her from the beginning."

"Characters you thought it below you to verify," Richard pointed out. Seeing his cousin was about to object, Richard thrust the letter he previously had read at William. "Read this, then we will speak.

Although he was feeling indignant because the issue he thought long settled was being canvassed again, Darcy accepted the letter. He read the direction. "How would you be in possession of a letter addressed to Mrs. Younge?" Darcy demanded. "It is not right to breach her privacy in this fashion." Darcy began to fold the letter.

"Even when Anna's safety is at stake?" Richard challenged.

Darcy froze. Surely not. *'Please tell me I have not made a critical error in judgement regarding Anna's care and safety,'* Darcy beseeched the heavens while he unfolded the letter again. His sister's safety trumped any hesitation he felt about reading a letter addressed to another without the person's expressed permission.

28 July 1810

My darling Karen,

I am perturbed, my dearest love, that you have not posted another letter updating me on your progress laying the groundwork with your mousy charge for when I arrive in Meryton with the militia.

As he read the first paragraph, Darcy felt like casting up his accounts. Richard had been correct. He had brought a viper into contact with his sister—one who was scheming with another to harm Anna. His eyes dropped to see who had signed the missive. Wickham! It was a near thing he managed to keep the contents of his stomach where they were supposed to be. He needed to read the rest of the despicable letter, then he owed his cousin another huge apology.

With my enemy who cheated me out of my due present along with that brute of a cousin of his, it is imperative Miss Darcy be primed for my addresses so we will be able to make for Gretna Green within two days of my arrival.

Can you not see it, my dear, the life we will lead as soon as that cheater pays me his sister's dowry of £30,000? I have decided I will demand another £30,000 from him to return his sister to him before we leave the country. If he refuses, we will sell her to a brothel.

Post me a letter as soon as may be. I will be bereft without hearing news from you. I am counting the days until I see you again. Remembering the times we have lain together gets me through the drudgery I must endure in order to succeed for both of us.

Thank you, my one and only love,

Your George

"I will kill that bastard if he even approaches Anna!" Darcy proclaimed as he jumped up, throwing the offending letter to the floor.

"There is a plan in place, but we will need to see if Mrs. Younge is a co-conspirator or one of Wickham's unwitting dupes," Richard stated.

"She is to be thrown out of this house!" Darcy demanded as he paced back and forth.

"Allow me to summon her first. If she is, as I suspect, one whom Wickham has manipulated, she may be useful."

Darcy gave a tight nod, then threw himself into a leather wingback chair. First picking up the letter, Richard turned on his heel and exited the sitting room. He returned shortly with a nervous Mrs. Younge in tow.

The companion was not offered a seat. She waited, beads of sweat forming on her brow, as the Colonel pushed the door closed and sat next to his cousin who, was not impassive as was his custom—he seemed angry. Her feeling of trepidation increased.

"Mrs. Younge, who forged the characters you showed my cousin?" Richard demanded.

"I know not of what you speak." Karen turned to Mr. Darcy, whose mood looked thunderous, but she had to try and extricate herself. Why would they ask this now? "Mr. Darcy saw my characters."

"So, if I write to the families you named, they will reply that they know you?" Richard pushed.

The sweat which had been beading began to roll down Mrs. Younge's face. She could not answer. She looked around quickly for a means of escape, but the Colonel was seated between her and the hallway door. She recalled that Thompson and one of the new men—even bigger than Thompson—was posted in the hallway.

"How do you know George Wickham and why are you conspiring with him against my ward, a young lady who has never harmed you—or anyone else—in her life?"

Mrs. Younge's pallor turned an almost grey colour. Knowing she had been discovered, she decided it could not get worse, so she held her head up. "You cheated my love out of his inheritance and the living old Mr. Darcy left him. Why are you surprised he would seek to get what was his by other means?"

"Do you think you are the first woman Wickham has manipulated into doing his bidding?" Richard said with a flinty edge to his voice that gave Mrs. Younge a chill all over as if someone walked on her grave. "Wickham was never in my late uncle's will because his licentious and dishonourable behaviour caused Darcy's father to withdraw his patronage more than a year before his passing."

"You lie," Karen claimed, although she did not feel as certain as she had been.

"We have letters written by my late uncle. As an executor, I have a copy of his will. Unlike Wickham, who I am sure gave you no more proof than his honeyed words, we do have proof—a great deal of it." Richard looked at the cringing woman. "Do you know your lover was almost certainly responsible for his own father's death and attempted the same on both my cousin and my uncle before the latter's death from a disease of the heart?" Richard went on to lay out the true character of George Wickham for his paramour.

She wanted to scream *her* George could not be the man the Colonel was describing, but she had to own she had seen parts of the man being described. Her desire for him to be the man she believed she loved had won out, causing Karen to ignore her rational mind.

Far more troubling was that these men had proof they were more than willing to show her—unlike George. Without an invitation to seat herself, Mrs. Younge fell back onto the settee at the instant she realised George had used her to further his dishonest aims, her legs refusing to support her.

How is it she did not see how dishonourable he was? A man in his late twenties was willing to compromise and bed a girl of not yet fifteen and she had been so blind she had been willing to stand by and allow him to do so.

Suddenly it struck her such a man would not be apt to share any ill-gotten gains with her or anyone else. To her very great shame she had been used by a forked-tongued devil.

"What will happen to me?" Karen enquired dejectedly.

"That, Mrs. Younge, if that is your true name, is entirely up to you," Richard stated.

As much as he wanted to rant and rave at the woman

who would have placed Anna in harm's way, Darcy had thus far been able to honour Richard's request that he not speak to the woman.

"How so?" she asked timidly.

"You have two possible paths. One is prosecution for forgery and other crimes." Richard gave the woman a few moments to understand that option and its ramifications before he continued. "The other is cooperation. If you choose that option, you will not be arrested, and you will be paid until you leave my cousin's employ, which will be immediately after we apprehend your lover."

"I do not want to go to gaol. What do you require from me?" Karen would act the way the man she though loved her had behaved—she would look out for herself.

Richard laid out what was needed. When he had finished, he looked to his cousin. "Do you have aught to add?"

"My cousin's plan is sound. As long as you do not cross us and perform all the tasks he laid out for you, I agree not to turn you over to the magistrate. That being said, I do not want you around my sister ever again!" Darcy growled.

He was still extremely angry, mainly at himself for not heeding Richard's words. He knew Richard's plan would be an effective one. Better yet, Anna would never be in danger at any point while they apprehended Wickham.

Here was yet another example of his pride and his unwillingness to listen to anyone's counsel save his own. Darcy was well aware he had to learn no man was an island, least of all himself. He had amends to make.

Per the Colonel's instructions, Karen Younge sat down at the escritoire in the sitting room and wrote a letter dictated by him to Lieutenant George Wickham.

After, with two huge footmen looking on, she was moved to a bedchamber on another floor, as far from Miss Darcy as possible.

~~~~~~~/~~~~~~~

Darcy sought out his older cousin and found him in the billiards room playing a game against himself. He waited silently until Andrew completed his current shot before he cleared his throat to announce his presence.

"William," Andrew greeted his cousin coolly.

"Do you mind if I close the door so we may speak in private?" Darcy requested.

"I have no objection," Andrew returned.

After closing the door, Darcy took a few moments to collect his thoughts. The last thing he wanted was to be hasty and say the wrong thing—again!

"You see before you a penitent man. For too long I have allowed my pride and my belief in my own infallibility to guide my speech to others when I should have held my peace. I would have continued in that vein had it not been for Rich calling me to account; he pointed out the deficiencies and ungentlemanlike quality of my behaviour. Had Richard not taken charge and called me to account, I know not if I would have seen the error of my ways. See them I have, and I owe you amends. My only reaction when you shared your news—the proper reaction I had when Richard told me of his engagement to Miss Mary—should have been to wish you and Miss Bennet happy and to welcome her to the family.

"Andrew, can you forgive this imperfect man, one who has on occasion inserted his Hessian in his mouth? Of late, I have only opened my mouth to change feet." Darcy gave a ghost of a smile when he saw Andrew's lips curve up slightly. It was a start.

"It does not mean I will not err again, but I will address the reproofs which have been made and do my best to become the man my parents wanted me to be."

"It is a good thing you are able to own your faults. Yes, William, I forgive you," Andrew granted.

Darcy felt a weight lift from his shoulders, then cogitated for a second. "Did Richard tell you about my lack of judgement regarding Mrs. Younge?"

"He showed me the letter before he spoke to you. Will Mrs. Younge assist with Richard's plan to call that bastard to account?" Andrew enquired.

"Yes, she will. Richard will have her watched anytime she is awake and she will be restricted to her new chamber unless escorted by one of his new footmen. Have you seen the new footmen-guards Brown found in London for Richard?"

"I have; they are hard to miss."

"You know a man is big when he makes Thompson look small." Darcy had a grin on his face.

"Rather than matching myself, would you like to play against me?"

"Very much so." Darcy felt relief knowing Andrew had forgiven him. On the morrow, he would make his way to Longbourn and congratulate his future cousins.

CHAPTER 23

"You are all welcome," Fanny stated after the three men and Miss Darcy had been shown into her drawing room. "Are not your parents to arrive today?" she enquired of the Fitzwilliam brothers.

"They are, Mother Bennet," Richard responded. Fanny was pleased at being so addressed by one of her future sons. "They are not expected before this afternoon. As long as you approve, they will accompany us on our morning call on the morrow."

"Your parents are welcome at Longbourn any time," Fanny enthused.

Darcy stepped forward. "Until today, I did not have the opportunity to congratulate Miss Bennet and Miss Mary on their engagements and welcome them to the family as my future cousins."

"On behalf of Mary and myself, I thank you. We are happy to soon become part of your family," Jane responded.

If Elizabeth had any residual suspicion Mr. Darcy disapproved of his cousins' choices of brides, it was dispelled. She could hear sincerity in his voice and saw no disapproval in his looks.

"As we are to be cousins, as soon as these two," Darcy cocked his head towards his cousins, "marry the two fair Miss Bennets. Starting now, would you *all* please address me as William, as the rest of my family do."

"All of us except one," Andrew quipped. Seeing the

quizzical looks on the Bennets' faces, Andrew explained. "You have heard Rich and me speak of our father's sister, Lady Catherine de Bourgh?" Three of the four Bennet sisters present nodded. "She refuses to call him William when he has such a *noble* name like Fitzwilliam."

"Does Lady Catherine not realise there have been kings named William but none named Fitzwilliam?" Elizabeth wondered.

"Facts never caused my aunt to change her opinions. Her opinions are, in her mind, facts," Darcy averred.

"Speaking of our aunt reminds me that I posted a letter to our cousin, Anne, informing her of our engagements," Richard informed his brother and cousin.

Mentioning the name de Bourgh reminded Richard of how his aunt had attempted to locate a man to kill him in her erroneous idea it would cause Rosings Park to devolve to her somehow.

Her plot had been reported to the Earl by a footman. Richard's father had cut his sister's allowance to nothing, after which he explained to her that—no matter *who* she tried to have murdered, the estate would never be hers. Then she had been sent to live in a cottage on the remotest part of the estate, under constant guard.

His father had considered it a better option than the scandal that might have arisen had she been sent to Bedlam or a private asylum. The last of her teeth had been pulled. She had no money, no jewellery, and no authority, not even over herself. She had consigned herself to a very lonely prison. Richard snapped out of his reverie after noticing Jane communicating silently with her sisters.

Jane looked to each of her sisters as she nodded her agreement, even if Lizzy's nod was tentative. "As long as you call me Jane," Jane inclined her head to her next younger sister, "Elizabeth or Lizzy, Mary, and Catherine or Kitty, we would be happy to address you as William."

"William, you may address me as Aunt Fanny as Anna does," Fanny granted. Darcy gave the Bennet ladies a bow in acceptance.

"Is Miss Lydia still in the nursery?" Richard queried.

"My husband and I will not allow her to rejoin the family until she begins to amend her behaviour," Fanny stated firmly.

Bennet, who had been working with his ledgers, not reading a book as he used to do, entered the drawing room, and greeted those from Netherfield Park. "Do I need to remind you we will be receiving our distant cousin, the heir presumptive of this estate, at exactly—in his words—four this afternoon?'" Bennet enquired as he looked at his wife and daughters.

"Papa, may we visit Anna at Netherfield Park this afternoon?" Mary requested.

"That is a capital idea," Fanny agreed. "Based on his letter stating he is here to *admire* our daughters; it will be just as well if they are not here to witness his arrival."

"Is this man so objectionable?" Richard questioned.

After a brief description of the contents and tone of his letter, the men understood why the Bennet sisters were so keen to be away from Longbourn that afternoon.

"William, Richard, may I invite my friends to visit me?" Georgiana asked keenly.

"I see no reason why not," Richard responded. "In fact, it will be fortuitous because you will all be present when our parents arrive. They know about Jane, but they will be just as excited to meet their newest daughter-to-be."

It was decided the four sisters would return to Netherfield Park when the four cousins departed. Bennet ordered his carriage readied. No matter how large the Darcy coach was, it could not accommodate eight, even if some of them were petite women.

Elizabeth was watching Mr. Darcy—William—carefully. Not only was there no sign of the disdain for her family he formerly displayed, but he seemed much happier than he had been in the past.

'Oh my, how handsome he is when he does not scowl with disapproval of the world around him. This version, if it is the true man, is one I would like to come to know better.' Elizabeth told herself silently.

At the same time, Darcy was looking towards Elizabeth —to him she was an Elizabeth, not a Lizzy. *'Yes, Mother and Father, I have heard you. If Elizabeth is the one for me, you would approve of her wholeheartedly, and not only because two of her sisters are to marry Andy and Rich.'* Darcy raised his eyes to the heavens where he was sure his parents were ever vigilant and were smiling down on him because their son was finally becoming the man they wanted him to be.

He looked to his cousin who was lovingly talking to his fiancée, *'Thank you Rich. You woke me up, for who knows how empty and devoid of love my future would have been without your intervention.'* At last, he could openly admit to himself he was attracted to Elizabeth and, if she was amenable, do something about it.

Fanny called for tea and after everyone enjoyed their refreshments, the four Bennet sisters who were to travel to Netherfield Park called for their outerwear. Soon, the mistress and master of the estate watched the two conveyances leave Longbourn's drive.

~~~~~~~/~~~~~~~

Miss Bingley was annoyed that two of the Bennet chits were engaged to the sons of an earl, and that four of the lowly country sisters were visiting *her* house. She had been told in no uncertain terms she was not welcome to join those welcoming the Earl and his Countess to Netherfield Park. What made the

SHANA GRANDERSON A LADY

slight worse was that the Bennets had been invited to greet them in the drive.

She would bide her time. She was wagering that the upcoming ball would be the impetus for Mr. Darcy to offer for her—finally. Once she was married to him, it would make her a cousin of the Bennets, but she was certain she could convince her husband to sever his connection with *that* family. That he would never do such a thing to his cousins who were marrying Bennet sisters did not enter her head.

She was resolved to point out the degradation of the connection to the Bennets to the Earl and countess. She was as sure as she had ever been they would agree with her, and laud her for her concerns of their family's honour. Miss Bingley enviously watched through the drawing room window as the Matlock travelling coach came to a halt in the drive.

Lord Matlock alighted from his conveyance and then handed out his beloved wife. As soon as he was sure she was steady on her feet, he turned towards those waiting to greet him and Lady Matlock.

"Jane," the Earl boomed, "how pleased I am to see you again, even more so because you have decided to accept Andrew."

Before Jane could react, her future father-in-law pulled her into a warm hug and kissed each of her cheeks. "Is Papa what you call your father?" Lord Matlock enquired. Jane nodded. "In that case, please address me as Father."

No one else had a chance to speak before the Earl was replaced by his countess. "Jane, dear Jane! You know not how long I have waited to have a daughter." Jane was treated to another hug and more kisses on her cheeks.

"In that case, what would you say to gaining *two* daughters?" Richard asked with a wide grin.

"Richard! Are you engaged?" Lady Matlock almost squealed as she allowed her excitement to override her innate calmness. She looked at the three Bennet sisters she had not met. They were all very pretty but one seemed too young. She turned to her second son with raised eyebrows.

"Mother, Father, it is my pleasure to introduce you to my fiancée, Miss Mary Bennet. She is the third of five Bennet sisters, but first in my heart," Richard stated as he took Mary's hand and gently brought her forward to his parents.

Mary was treated to hugs and kisses just like Jane before her, except that her future mother-in-law pulled her into an embrace before her husband could.

"Please call me Mother, if you call your own mother Mama, that is," Lady Matlock looked to both of her future daughters, who nodded their agreement.

"Call me Father," please," the Earl insisted after hugging and kissing Mary on the cheeks. He turned to his sons and nephew. "Will one of you introduce my soon-to-be nieces?"

"Mother and Father, it is my pleasure to introduce Miss Elizabeth Bennet, the second eldest sister, and Miss Catherine Bennet, second to the youngest. Lizzy and Kitty, my parents, the Earl and Countess of Matlock, Lord Reginald and Lady Elaine Fitzwilliam." Andrew looked to where Bingley was standing a few feet away and watching the tableau. "This gentleman is Mr. Charles Bingley, the master of this estate and your host."

Bingley bowed to his noble guests. "You are most welcome Your Lordship, Your Ladyship."

"Aunt and Uncle, it is a pleasure to see you again," Georgiana spoke evenly as she stepped up and hugged her relations.

"It is good to see you again too, Anna," the Earl said, hugging his niece while looking at Richard and William in question.

The last time they had seen her, Anna was painfully shy, but something had coaxed her out of her shell. They suspected the change was due to her association with the Bennet sisters. Their niece was displaying confidence she had never had before. If it was as they supposed, they owed a great debt of gratitude to the sisters.

After greeting her niece, Lady Matlock addressed her younger son and nephew. "It seems we have much to talk about regarding Anna." She looked around. "Where is her companion?"

"We have much to tell you," Darcy admitted. "We will meet later when you have washed and changed."

Lady Elaine nodded to her nephew with a look that said: *I will wait, but not very long.* One did not gainsay Lady Elaine Fitzwilliam. The Countess turned back towards the Bennet sisters.

"Before we enter the house, we would like you two," Lady Matlock inclined her head to Elizabeth and Kitty, "to call us Aunt Elaine and Uncle Reggie."

"As long as you call us Lizzy and Kitty," Elizabeth accepted for her sister and herself. "As Catherine may not have positive connotations, I am sure you will prefer Kitty."

"Kate is a good alternative," Lady Matlock suggested as she smiled at what the second Bennet sister had said.

"Thank you Your La...Aunt Elaine. I think I prefer Kate; it is far more dignified than Kitty," Kate averred.

"Then from now on, Kate it will be," Jane stated to the nods of those around them.

~~~~~~~/~~~~~~~

On arriving in the drawing room, at the Earl's request, Bingley introduced the Hursts and his youngest sister. He could see Caroline was ready to pounce but in the setting they were in—welcoming guests to the estate—there was little he could do to make her hold her tongue.

"Welcome to *my* home," Miss Bingley gave a deep

curtsey to the Earl and Countess the instant Charles had completed the introductions. "As one of your same circle, I am so sorry I was not there to greet you when you arrived."

Richard shook his head. *'This woman has the memory of a gadfly!'* he told himself. He looked to his parents and silently gained their permission.

"Mother and Father, did your social status descend to that of tradespeople? Miss Bingley has just claimed we are in her circle," Richard asked.

Miss Bingley's face went from pale, to red, and then purple with rage. How could she forget the Colonel would mention her status as soon as she said something of which he did not approve.

"I-I-I m-meant…" Miss Bingley began to explain.

"That you are the pretentious daughter of a tradesman who has no understanding of her place in society," Richard interjected.

The Earl turned to his host. "I think we should either seek accommodation with our future family or stay at the local inn," Lord Matlock said. "We are unwilling to remain in a house with one like your younger sister."

"As of this moment, my older sister," Bingley indicated Mrs. Hurst with his head, "will be my hostess and my younger sister who, regardless of how many times she has been warned her delusions of grandeur are no more than that, will be leaving this very afternoon to visit our Aunt Hildebrand Bingley in Scarborough."

"**Noooo!**" Miss Bingley screeched at the top of her grating voice. "You cannot send me away. Mr. Darcy will propose to me as soon as he sees how well I organised the ball in his honour! I *will not* go! I am your hostess, not Louisa! I refuse to go anywhere until Mr. Darcy offers for me!"

"Miss Bingley, other than doing everything possible to be *out* of your company, what have I ever done to give you the impression I would propose to you? That is something I will *never* do under *any* circumstances," Darcy intoned.

"My sister-in-law sees nothing but what she wants to see," the normally quiet Hurst stated. "Her delusions are not restricted to ones of grandeur."

"Why would you not want me as your wife?" Miss Bingley whined ignoring her brother-in-law's words. "I have a huge dowry; I was trained at the best seminary; I am a consummate hostess…"

"Those are not the important attributes I am seeking in my future wife," Darcy stated bluntly. "I do not need your dowry. As my cousin has pointed out, *ad nauseam*, you may have attended a seminary but you learnt nothing of value there. A *consummate* hostess is not rude to her neighbours or her guests. I am not interested in spending my life in society; I am at heart, a gentleman farmer. We have never suited, and never will. It is time for you to forget this dream of yours; it will never—ever—become reality."

Miss Bingley, her eyes blinking rapidly, heard his words, but could not comprehend them at first, as she stood staring at Mr. Darcy. No one else spoke as she slowly began to hear and understand the words he had spoken.

As realisation dawned that her dreams had turned to ash, Miss Bingley spun on her heel and left the drawing room without a word. She made her way up to her chambers, where she ordered her maid to pack her trunks.

An hour later, the Bingley carriage departed Netherfield Park. Miss Bingley and her maid were the lone occupants. There were two footmen on the rear bench who, along with the coachman, would ensure Miss Bingley's safety until she reached her aunt's house in Scarborough.

When they farewelled their sister, Bingley had also arranged to have an express dispatched to his aunt—written by Mrs. Hurst for legibility—so when Caroline arrived at her house she would not be taken unawares.

Besides her brief words of goodbye to her brother and sister, Caroline Bingley said nothing else.

CHAPTER 24

Collins was more than pleased with what he saw as his hired gig rolled down Longbourn's drive. His future estate seemed to be everything he and the Collinses before him had imagined.

Ever since the split four generations ago, when the first Collins shed the name Bennet and took on the proud name he now bore, the men of his line had been waiting to reclaim the estate they believed was their birthright.

The entail had given them hope of recovering what they deemed to be theirs. Until the current master of Longbourn, every Bennet generation had at least one son. To this Mr. Collins's delight, his distant cousin had produced only five daughters.

He hoped they were comely. A man of his status, a clergyman who served at the pleasure of the parson of the Duke of Bedford and the future owner of a thriving estate, would not agree to marry a homely woman. He deserved much more than that.

When at exactly four in the afternoon the driver of the gig pulled back on the reins and brought his equipage to a halt in front of the manor house, Collins was not pleased to see only the master and mistress of the estate waiting to welcome him.

Where were the daughters he intended to admire and then choose the prettiest as his wife? Did they not know they were welcoming the man who would one day hold their collective futures in the palm of his hand? A slight like this would not stand! He would make sure his cousin and family would be under no misapprehension as to the level of his displeasure.

The Bennet parents watched as Bennet's cousin fought to alight from the gig. From what they could see, William Collins was rather rotund, which was hampering his efforts.

When he eventually succeeded in reaching the ground, he was sweating profusely and had to use his handkerchief to mop the sweat dripping from his face. He wore the dark garb of a clergyman with a white shirt. His hat was black with a rounded top and broad brim.

There was no missing the way the man was looking around for others to greet him. It was obvious he was not well pleased no one else was there to meet him. He lumbered before them and gave an exaggerated bow, removing his hat and sweeping it to the side. His doing so revealed a few strands of greasy hair plastered to the crown of an almost-bald head. The odour emanating from the man was horrendous.

His odour was so offensive both Bennets took a few steps back. Unfortunately, the difference was minimal. "Unless he bathes, I do not want him in my house," Fanny whispered to her husband, who nodded his agreement.

"William Collins at your service," Collins greeted as he stood and replaced his hat after mopping his face once again.

"Thomas and Frances Bennet," Bennet replied tersely.

"I expected my cousins to be here to meet their future guardian and master of this estate," Collins began, but he closed his mouth when his cousin raised his hand.

"Fanny, please go into the house," Bennet requested gently.

Due to the offensive odour wafting from the man, Fanny did not need to be asked a second time. She nodded and entered the house, pushing the door closed behind her.

"You there, do not depart yet," Bennet called to the driver of the gig who had just unlashed his passenger's trunk from the back of the small carriage.

"Why did you tell the coachman to wait?" Collins enquired.

"Because, Mr. Collins, there is a better than good chance you will not be remaining," Bennet barked back.

"Why would you turn your heir away?" Collins demanded, raising himself to his full height, only making his oversized belly protrude more. "I am here to extend an olive branch and heal the rift between our families. I intend to make amends for the harm to your daughters, who will be injured by the entail. If I do not marry one and pledge to take care of the rest, what will happen to your five poor daughters after you pass on?"

"You are *not* my heir. You are my heir *presumptive*. If my wife bears me a son, then he would become the heir apparent and be ahead of you in the line of succession," Bennet explained.

"A son!" Collins exclaimed. "Your wife is past her childbearing years."

There was no way Bennet would tell this buffoon that since Lydia's birth he had not lain with his wife—until recently. "My wife is not past bearing a child. That is neither here nor there. First, two of my daughters are engaged to the sons of an earl. Second, you will *never* be the guardian of any of them. If any of my girls are unmarried when I am called home, my will names who will stand in that role. It is not you; it never will be you."

Collins looked scandalised but Bennet cared not. He continued. "Even had two of my daughters not had understandings with men of character and worth, you would not be allowed to marry any of them under any circumstances. Do you think I dislike any of my daughters so much I would sentence her to a life with one such as you? Lastly, your odour is repulsive. *If* I allow you to remain here for the sennight you requested to be hosted, then you will bathe immediately and will do so every day you are in my house. Do I make myself clear?"

"My father taught me it is unhealthy to bathe above once a month," Collins claimed.

"If you refuse to comply with my non-negotiable demand, then climb back aboard your gig and return to whence you came," Bennet commanded.

Since he was sure his cousin would not deny him when one of his daughters accepted him, and feeling that his wife was well past giving birth to another child, Collins decided to submit himself to the humiliation of bathing daily in order to remain at Longbourn.

His cousin seemed adamant about this cleanliness thing, so he would comply. When Mr. Bennet died, which Collins was certain was close at hand, he would force the wife and daughters to submit to his will.

"I will bathe," Collins agreed peevishly.

"Every day, and you *will not* importune my daughters. Contravene either and you will be out of my house faster than your legs can carry you," Bennet threatened.

Collins nodded, knowing how things would really be. Bennet opened the front door and spoke to Mr. Hill. A footman exited the house and led the hapless curate around the house to the servants' entrance and up the servants' stairs to the bathing room, where a bath would be readied for him.

Entering the house which *would* be his one day via the same entrance the servants used angered Collins. His cousin had refused to pay him the deference a clergyman was due.

All Bennet could do was watch in wonder. He was sure the man was telling himself he would gain all his desires as he followed the footman to the back of the manor house.

He had no doubt he would be evicting Mr. Collins before the sennight was up. Good manners dictated he not rescind the invitation once the man had agreed to his terms.

~~~~~~~/~~~~~~~

George Wickham could not have been more pleased. Denny had delivered a letter from Karen to him; it was now in the pocket of his uniform coat. He would read it as soon as he was off duty and in the privacy of his meagre quarters.

Wickham was sure his implied threat he would not want to be with her any longer had spurred Karen into replying to his letter with alacrity. His revenge and a huge amount of money were within his grasp.

Once his onerous duty was complete, Wickham made for his room. As soon as the door was closed, he extracted the missive from his pocket, then shrugged off his uniform jacket and let it fall to the floor. He sat on the single rickety chair in front of a small wobbly table. He broke the seal and began to read.

29 July 1810

Post Drop, Red Lion Inn

Meryton, Hertfordshire

My dearest one and only love, George,

Wickham scoffed. He still had her. It would not be much longer before he would leave her behind forever.

You have my abject apologies I did not write to you sooner. I have been busy with Miss Darcy. You will be happy to learn I have had a great deal of time alone with my charge.

She now believes you are the epitome of a man she wishes to marry. Just as you predicted, she had fond memories of you. Your enemy was too proud to share anything about you to change those memories.

As you want me to do, I will keep working on her. By the time you arrive she will be more than ready to elope with you as soon as you greet her.

I am looking forward to our life together, my clever George. Your idea to demand double the dowry to return Miss Darcy to her brother is a stroke of genius! You are the most intelligent man I have ever met.

Even though Wickham cared not a whit for Karen Younge, her praise was welcome and no less than his due. He preened at her words agreeing with them without reservation. Soon Darcy and Fitzwilliam would discover just how he had outwitted them.

Do not be surprised if I do not write again. I do not have as much time to myself any longer and when I delivered this letter, I almost ran into Colonel Fitzwilliam. I managed to evade him, but I am sure you would rather not receive a letter than have your brilliant plan discovered.

With all of my love, and looking forward to being with you again soon,

Karen.

She was correct. He would forego letters from her if it meant keeping his plan from being discovered by the prig and his cousin.

In a little more than a fortnight, everything he wanted would be his. Thanks to getting paid, if one could call the pittance of his wages that, and in a good mood after reading Karen's letter, Wickham made his way to the taproom near the encampment to treat himself to some well-deserved grog.

~~~~~~~/~~~~~~~

Sitting in the drawing room before dinner, the Bennet sisters felt dirty as their cousin ogled them. Once he discovered Jane and Mary were engaged, the focus of his attention seemed to be Elizabeth.

Their parents had shared the man's state when their cousin had arrived at Longbourn. His odour was less offensive after he had bathed; unfortunately, it still clung to his clothing.

Hill announced dinner and the lecherous man made a beeline for Elizabeth. Her father stepped in before Collins reached her, offered his arm to his daughter, and led her into the dining parlour.

Collins was caught flat-footed because the other three Miss Bennets were gone before he could move. He entered the dining parlour to find no seat open next to Miss Elizabeth. He was about to ask Miss Bennet to move when he was addressed by his cousin's wife.

"As a guest in our home, your place is at my right hand," Fanny said, sacrificing her own comfort for her daughters.

Collins, who felt the pleasure of being seated in a place of honour keenly, preened as he strutted to take the seat next to the estate's mistress. At first, he did not notice he was as far from the Bennet sisters as possible. When he noticed that fact, he supposed it was a good sacrifice to be so revered as to be seated in a place of honour.

"Did I not hear you have five daughters, Mrs. Bennet?" Collins asked while Hill dished up the soup.

"That is true, but my youngest two are not out yet. Kitty —I mean Kate," Mrs. Bennet inclined her head to the named daughter, "will be out in a few months, but our youngest, Lydia, is but fifteen and still in the nursery."

Collins was too busy slurping the soup to ask a follow-up question. His eyes grew large when he noted the variety of dishes and the quantity of food being served. His future estate seemed to be doing very well indeed.

He piled his plate high with the plentiful bounty on the table. If he noticed looks of disgust from the Bennets, he showed no evidence of it. Soon he was shovelling food into his mouth. He was impressed by both the quantity and quality of the food.

"To which of my fair cousins is the excellency of the

meal's cooking owed?" Collins enquired, his mouth full of partially masticated food, some of which was sprayed onto the tablecloth as he spoke with his mouth full.

"Mr. Collins," Fanny bristled, "my daughters were raised as gentlewomen and none of them do housework of *any* sort. We employ a cook and a full complement of servants."

"Please pardon me for giving offence, my dear Mrs. Bennet," Collins cowered slightly at the matron's barely concealed anger. "I meant no slight to my fair cousins; I merely intended to compliment the quality of the food." By now Collins was sweating.

Having never been educated in the finer points of table manners, he used his serviette to dry his sweat. The linen was already smeared with food and gravy resulting in said food being spread across the witless man's face.

It took all of their self-control for everyone else at the table not to burst into raucous laughter. As soon as Bennet managed to regulate his mirth, he asked Hill to give Mr. Collins a clean serviette.

At first, the man knew not why he was being presented with clean linen. Mrs. Bennet leaned over and whispered in the man's ear, informing him of the reason the butler had provided him with a clean one.

It was then Collins noted the mirth bubbling out from those around the table. He wiped his face and managed to remove most of the food residue, except for a small drop of beef gravy on the end of his nose.

Mr. Collins excused himself to wash his face after dinner. After returning to the parlour, he volunteered to read to the Bennets from Fordyce's Sermons. He did not understand why all of his cousins became so tired they retired for the night before he had read more than two sentences.

~~~~~~~/~~~~~~~

The four sisters congregated in Jane's bedchamber. "If

that man stares at me in that lecherous fashion again, I will run screaming from the house," Elizabeth insisted with a huff.

"Papa has told him he will not be granted the hand of any of us," Mary reminded her sister.

"His being informed of such, and comprehending it are, I am afraid, two very different propositions," Elizabeth opined.

"The party from Netherfield Park will be here on the morrow. Given the excessive deference he displayed in his letter for those of rank, he will be too awed to bother you," Jane suggested.

"That could be true. Also, on the way up the stairs, Papa told me on the landing if Mr. Collins continues to ply me with his brand of attention and it is too much for me, he will remove the problem," Elizabeth informed her sisters.

"You see how much Papa has changed," Mary stated proudly. "Before Richard caused Papa to open his eyes, he would have sat back, laughed, and done nothing to protect you." None of the other three sisters in the room could deny what Mary said was the truth.

"I have never seen Mama and Papa so affectionate to one another. Rather than make sport of Mama, he explains things to her and supports her," Kate pointed out.

"As soon as Papa orders Mr. Collins away, all will be as it should be," Elizabeth stated.

She received three nods. The sisters spoke for another hour or so before they made their way to their own chambers to settle for the night. They each made sure to lock their doors.

CHAPTER 25

Lydia Bennet did not like the direction her life had taken ever since that damned Colonel had interfered in the harmonious running of her family. Had they not all been happy with the way things used to be?

It had been a great shock to Lydia that her mother no longer folded at her first manipulation. Mama was unmoved by her fake tears. Equally as vexing was her Papa's resolve. In the past, all she needed to do was make noise and Papa would give in to keep her quiet so he could continue to read in peace.

What had her tactics gained her now? She had been locked in the infernal nursery for days! She had ignored what Papa told her regarding how high the window was from the ground, believing he only said it to scare her.

The first evening of her unjust imprisonment Lydia had opened the window and planned to climb out until she stuck her head out to seek a way to the ground. Much to her chagrin, everything her father had told her was true.

If she attempted to climb out, she was certain to fall to her death. For a few short moments, she considered punishing her family with her end. She dismissed the idea as quickly as it entered her head.

She would not be there to see her family's suffering. There would be no more balls or fun. Most importantly, she would never be able to flirt with officers or other men again. No, she would live and show her family how wrong they were to mistreat her in this infamous fashion.

With the window ruled out as an avenue for escape, Lydia had tried to push her way out of the nursery when food was delivered. Unfortunately, there had always been a footman at the ready who caught her in his arms. No matter how much she screamed, kicked, or scratched, he returned her to the room before the door was locked again.

The only thing which had resulted from her attempts to escape when the door had been opened was food was delivered only once a day now. She had to make it last through the day. She learnt that the first time, when she had eaten everything in one sitting. No matter how much she banged on the door, no more food was forthcoming until the following day.

Her mother came to visit once a day, but she left as soon as Lydia started to berate her and her father for their inhumane treatment. On her mother's last visit, Lydia had been informed a governess was to be employed to teach her how to behave like a lady.

What did she need to know besides how to flirt with a handsome man in a scarlet coat so she would be the next to marry after Jane.

~~~~~~~/~~~~~~~

Unlike what it would have been before she and her husband realised they needed to make serious changes, Fanny Bennet was all that was grace when she welcomed the Fitzwilliams and Darcys to her home.

Bennet was standing shoulder to shoulder with his wife; he too greeted his daughters' future in-laws with no trace of his former sportive manner. At his father's request, Andrew introduced the Bennet parents to his own.

As much as Bennet would have preferred not to, he requested permission from the Earl to introduce his cousin to him. Collins practically pushed his Cousin Bennet out of his path in order to show the highborn persons his deference.

Collins was beyond awed to be in the presence of so

many members of the *Ton*. One of his cousins was engaged to a viscount and another to the second son of an earl. He could not comprehend how members of the first circles would attach themselves to ones as lowly as the Bennets, but at least there would be an advantage to himself—he too would be connected to an earl and countess.

He had just had the supreme honour of meeting said Earl and his lady wife. How rapturous it was being introduced to a peer of the realm! He was sure his adulation of their persons would assist him further in his aim to become a parson, not a curate. Mayhap the Earl would offer him a living.

The Bennets cringed when they saw the way Collins fawned over their future family members. Mr. Darcy and Anna were not spared from his effusions once he discovered they were the nephew and niece of Lord and Lady Matlock.

Elizabeth saw the moment William's mask slipped into place thanks to her cousin's sycophantic behaviour. By now she understood it was not pride or arrogance, but a means of protecting himself from unwanted attention.

At least for a short time, her cousin was distracted and not paying her his slimy attention while staring at her chest in a most lecherous manner. Unfortunately, the interlude was brief and Mr. Collins soon made his way back to Elizabeth's side.

There was no mistaking Elizabeth's abhorrence of the man and his pursuit of her. Bennet did not miss his second daughter's discomfort and resolved to end Mr. Collins's residence in his house first thing in the morning. He did not want to create a scene while guests were present.

"What is that buffoon about?" Richard asked so only Mary could hear.

"Even though Papa has told him in no uncertain terms he may not offer for any of us..." Mary quickly and quietly explained he was the heir presumptive who had decided to marry one of his *poor* cousins.

"I think a walk in the park is called for," Richard responded. Seeing Mary about to agree, Richard placed his hand on her own. "It will be a walk for some of us men only." As he spoke he looked pointedly at Collins.

Mary smiled and nodded her agreement. How she enjoyed it when Richard took charge, especially when his protective instincts were aroused. She understood, even though they were not married yet, in Richard's mind her sisters were already his sisters.

A few steps took him to where Andrew and William were standing and glaring at the clueless simpleton. "Join me for a walk in the park. I will invite that," Richard cocked his head at Collins, who was attempting to get closer to Elizabeth —who moved away each time, "to join us. in fact, I will *insist*."

"Count me in," Andrew, who also felt brotherly affection for Lizzy agreed.

"Me too," Darcy added. He would not countenance the man undressing Elizabeth with his eyes. The fact he was hoping to gain a courtship with her made the clergyman's offences much worse.

"Collins, you are taking a walk outside with my brother, cousin, and me," Richard commanded.

Even had Collins felt like refusing, he would not have. The look from the Earl's second son told him it was not a request. Besides, it would only enhance his status to be known to a viscount and two other members of the first circles.

"Please lead the way, my good sir," Collins responded as he gave a low bow.

Bennet started to move towards the men leading his idiotic cousin out of the drawing room, but Mary arrived at his side and shook her head. Bennet did not follow.

Richard led the way outside; Collins walked behind him, while Andrew and Darcy brought up the rear. They made for the little wilderness hidden from anyone in the house.

"What an honour that you want to know me; I will be your brother one day..." Collins began obsequiously as he bowed to the men again.

"Are you insane?" Richard boomed. "Or are you so simple you did not understand my future father-in-law when he told you none of his daughters would be your wife? Do you really think that Miss Elizabeth, who has more intelligence in the tip of her finger than you possess, would ever accept one such as you?"

"My cousin was only jesting with me," Collins asserted as he puffed out his chest like a cock about to crow. "I am the heir to this estate and as such I will have power over my unmarried cousins."

"How in heaven's name did you ever pass university and manage to take orders?" Darcy asked, shaking his head at the abject stupidity he was witnessing.

"It seems you do not understand the difference between an *heir presumptive* and an *heir apparent*," Richard barked. "That being said, with my brother marrying Miss Bennet and me marrying Miss Mary, why would you think my future sisters would ever be under your power?"

"B-b-but I-I a-a-am their n-n-nearest r-r-relation; it m-m-must b-be m-me..." Collins tried to splutter.

"You know, William, I think you asked the correct question. How did one with this lack of intelligence ever graduate from a seminary or university?" Richard rounded on the now quaking man. "As soon as we marry, we will be their nearest relations outside of their immediate family. Even were that not true, it is Bennet's will, not *yours*, which will determine who is named guardian of any daughters who have not yet reached their majority at his passing."

Collins only stared, not daring to speak any more. He thought if he said the wrong thing, this man or one of the others, would strike him. Unlike him, they were all well-built and looked strong. He was a coward. Just as he had cowered before his father, who used to beat him, he cowered before the men he knew were far more powerful, physically and societally, than himself.

"Even had Bennet not abjured you from addressing his daughters, in what world do you think any of them, least of all Miss Elizabeth, would desire you for her husband?" Richard demanded.

"T-t-to b-b-e m-mistress of t-this e-estate one d-d-day," Collins stuttered.

"You will *never* be master here. I will suggest Bennet pursue a simple recovery, and all of us," Richard indicated his brother and cousin, "and my parents will support that application. Then you will have nothing, unless..."

"U-u-unless?" Collins managed.

"As I understand it, the entail may be broken if the current lifetime tenant and the heir presumptive agree to break it and sign a document jointly to that effect," Richard explained, speaking in a calmer tone without any implied threats. "If you agree and we meet with Mr. Philips on the morrow to end the entail, you will receive five thousand pounds from me. If you refuse, the entail will be broken via simple recovery, and you will not receive a single penny while spending more money than I am sure you have to fight a losing battle in the Court of Chancery."

As much as he had dreamt of one day becoming the master of Longbourn and restoring the Collins line to the place he believed it rightfully belonged, Collins was not so myopic as to not be able to understand that five thousand pounds now was a much better proposition than losing the estate and receiving nothing. He knew he would not be able to pay any solicitor's bill.

"I agree to break the entail," a defeated Collins hissed.

"In that case, you will pack now and one of us will accompany you to the Red Lion Inn, where we will acquire a room for you. On the morrow, we will meet at Mr. Philips's offices at ten in the morning," Richard laid out. "One or two of my *small* footmen will be on duty to make sure you do not have a change of heart and run."

Collins nodded. The men escorted him back to the house. "Mr. Hill, Mr. Collins has decided to leave us. Please make sure he has assistance in packing and then have my brother summoned when he is ready to depart. He will be spending the night at the Red Lion," Andrew informed Longbourn's butler.

"Aye, My Lord," Hill replied. The normally stoic man could not stop the sides of his mouth from turning up at the news they were to be rid of the unwanted guest.

As soon as Collins was up the stairs, Darcy placed a restraining hand on Richard's arm. "Rich, you know that sum is nothing to me, so please allow me to cover the five thousand pounds to him."

"I want to pay half," Andrew insisted.

"It may be difficult for you two to believe, but thanks to my savings and investing all with Gardiner, I have far more wealth than you think." Richard saw Andrew and William were about to object. "However, I will agree that we split the amount to be paid to that buffoon in thirds."

Andrew and Darcy both nodded their agreement. It was a cheap price to pay for the future security of the Bennets.

~~~~~~~/~~~~~~~

Dinner was announced soon after the three men returned. Much to Elizabeth's relief, they were sans Mr. Collins. However, there was no chance to discuss what had occurred with anyone.

After the meal, which everyone enjoyed—Mrs. Bennet did set a wonderful table—the ladies made for the drawing room while Hill delivered a tray to the men with glasses and decanters of port and brandy.

No one chose to smoke. As soon as libations had been poured, Bennet could no longer hold back his curiosity. "Where is my idiot of a cousin?" he demanded to know. "I intended to evict the man in the morning."

"We had a little *chat* with Mr. Collins," Richard grinned. Seeing the raised eyebrows from both patriarchs, he clarified. "No violence was employed, regardless of our desire to pummel him after the lecherous way he was leering at Lizzy."

"That is all well, but where is the man? I could swear I heard a cart leaving the estate during dinner," Bennet enquired.

"He has agreed to break the entail..." The three younger men who had been in the little wilderness area with Collins related their conversation and offer to the man.

For some moments Bennet sat frozen in place as he processed what the men had told him and the enormity of what they had done. Slowly it pierced his realisation he would no longer be merely a lifetime tenant; he would now own the estate—or at least he would as soon as the papers were filed with the court.

"What you have done for me and my family cannot be adequately put into words. A simple thank you will never suffice," Bennet managed once he recovered his ability to speak. "However, I *will* be paying that worthless man, even if I have to take a mortgage on my estate."

"Bennet, do not fall into the trap of pride I used to fall prey to before Richard kicked me in the arse and set me straight," Darcy stated. "We are all to be family and it is what family does—we help each other."

"As the highest-ranking man here, *I* will pay that useless man," Lord Matlock decided. "You boys know the Matlock Earldom has far more money than I know what to do with and this will be a small engagement gift to my two new daughters."

The Earl knew he had trumped all objections as he saw each man nod resignedly. "Matlock, I thank you on behalf of ourselves and the generations of Bennets to come," Bennet raised his glass to the man he had already begun to feel a kinship for before his generous gift in his daughters' names.

"We need to rejoin the ladies," Bennet stated. "Will one of you ask my wife to join me in the study for a brief meeting?"

~~~~~~~/~~~~~~~

Fanny was worried when she entered her husband's study, but that worry dissipated when he pulled her into a hug and kissed her soundly. "My dear wife, the entail ends on the morrow..." Bennet related a short version of what had happened to his shocked wife.

"The estate is ours now? We will no longer have to leave it for a Collins?" Fanny verified.

"It most certainly is, or very soon will be," Bennet confirmed.

Once the guests departed, the Bennet sisters were informed of what had occurred to cause their mother to return to the drawing room glowing with happiness.

When the tale had been told, Elizabeth had a strange thought. *'Was William willing to pay a part for me? Could it be he has tender feelings for me?'* She asked herself silently. Even more surprising, she found she would not object if her supposition proved to be true.

~~~~~~~/~~~~~~~

In the end, it was anticlimactic. Philips prepared the required document and Collins and Bennet both signed it, followed by those who acted as witnesses. Collins was then warned never to approach Bennet or one of their family without an invitation, or he would be dealt with severely.

Collins agreed and was handed a draft for the agreed

upon sum and was soon on his way to Bedfordshire in a hired gig.

Philips would make sure the papers were filed with the court as expeditiously as possible. As soon as that was done the entail would be a thing of the past.

CHAPTER 26

"**H**ave you girls discussed a wedding date with your fiancés yet?" Fanny asked the day after the papers to break the entail had been signed.

"No, Mama, we have not," Jane spoke for herself and Mary. "However, we intend to do so today."

"Good. They must be the grandest weddings ever seen in..." Fanny stopped as she caught herself. "Forgive me, I momentarily forgot whose weddings they will be. Whatever you and your respective Fitzwilliam brother decide is what it will be."

Both Jane and Mary let out a breath each had not realised she was holding. For a moment their mother of old had reared her head. It was gratifying to see how Mama regulated herself, stopping before saying anything vulgar or embarrassing.

As if talking about them made them appear, the crunch of gravel told them the party from Netherfield Park was arriving as the wheels of a coach were heard from the drive. Jane and Mary did not notice, but Elizabeth was almost as excited to see the arriving party as her two engaged sisters were.

There was no use denying it any longer. She was attracted to William, and she hoped his feelings tended towards her. Elizabeth was beyond grateful William was one of those arriving from Netherfield Park.

Richard was first to enter the drawing room and,

after kissing Fanny on the cheek, made directly for Mary before remembering to greet the other Bennet sisters. Andrew followed suit, giving Fanny a peck on the cheek. Unlike his younger brother, he remembered to greet his future sisters before making a beeline for Jane.

Darcy and Anna brought up the rear, both understanding it was safer not to delay the brothers from the objects of their love. Both greeted those in the drawing room, even though Jane and Mary were lost in their worlds of love already.

Elizabeth watched in wonder as William leaned over and kissed her mother's cheek. Her mother blushed like a schoolgirl. Looking pleased with himself, William walked over and seated himself on the chair closest to Elizabeth.

Before Elizabeth could comment to the man sitting next to her, Mary commanded all their attention.

"Mama, we are going to request the use of Papa's calendar so we can consider dates for our weddings," Mary informed the Bennet matron. Still somewhat discomposed by William kissing her cheek, Fanny merely waved her consent. Once the two engaged couples exited the drawing room, Elizabeth lost her chance to make an impertinent comment because William spoke first.

"It is a pleasant day outside," he turned to face Mrs. Bennet, "would you object if we were to take a turn in the park?"

"It is a good day to walk outdoors," Fanny granted.

Darcy stood and assisted Elizabeth to stand. When their hands touched, she felt a frisson of pleasure radiating from where her bare hand touched William's own ungloved one.

Kate and Anna followed them out. With the warm temperature, all the young ladies needed were bonnets, not pelisses or other outerwear.

~~~~~~~/~~~~~~~

With the calendar her father happily provided in hand, Jane led their way into the parlour opposite the drawing room.

"Before we select dates for our weddings, I have a suggestion," Richard declared.

"Go ahead, little brother," Andrew drawled after their two fiancées nodded their agreement.

"What say you to a double wedding? It is not every day brothers marry sisters, especially when the brothers and sisters actually like being with one another," Richard recommended. "What think you, Mary and Jane?"

"I have no objection," Jane agreed. "It had always been a dream of Lizzy's and mine to marry at the same time, but as she is not being courted, never mind engaged, she will not object."

"The same holds true for me, I think it would be perfect for Jane and me to marry our respective Fitzwilliam brother in the same ceremony," Mary added.

"Do you think Mother Bennet will be sanguine with one wedding and not two?" Andrew checked.

Jane and Mary looked at one another and smiled simultaneously. "Mama will do whatever we prefer, as long as we make no extreme demands," Jane related.

"As we have resolved to have a double wedding, what do you ladies think about the date?" Richard enquired.

"What about Friday, the seventeenth of August?" Mary suggested.

Andrew and Richard looked at one another. Andrew nodded to his brother. "That date will not work..." He told Mary and Jane about Mrs. Younge's deception, Wickham's plan, and their plan to take care of the issue.

"That one man can be so evil!" Jane shook her head. "To murder anyone is bad enough, but his own father!"

"Lizzy and Kate need to be told, and our parents as well,"

Mary pointed out.

"Now that we have told you two, we intend to," Richard assured the sisters. "We believe knowledge is power; hiding the truth protects no one."

"Back to the more pleasant business at hand, what of the Monday following, the twentieth of August?" Jane proposed.

"Yes, that will work," Richard stated. Mary and Andrew nodded their agreement.

~~~~~~~/~~~~~~~

Kate and Anna made directly for the swing in the shade of the huge oak in the centre of the park. They sat there with their heads together, sharing confidences and giggling from time to time.

"You have no idea how it warms my heart to see Anna feeling free to be a young lady with others she loves to be around and who want no more than friendship from her," Darcy told Elizabeth as he watched their sisters pushing themselves gently with their legs.

"She is such a sweet girl," Elizabeth responded. "I cannot imagine anyone not able to love her or wanting to hurt her.

She did not miss the look of pain which crossed William's face as soon as she said the last. Elizabeth wondered what engendered such obvious pain in him when until then he had looked so happy.

"William, what is it?" she enquired.

"Am I that easy for you to read?" Darcy wondered.

"I know hurt when I see it."

"In my pride and arrogance, I almost harmed Anna in the worst way..." William related all from his employing Mrs. Younge without consulting Richard, his reasons for doing so, not verifying her characters, to Richard's discovery of the despicable plan.

"William, I have not known you very long, but even I

can see you are not now the man who chose Anna's companion in arrogance and spite. The evil intentions have been revealed, a plan is in place, and as you told me, Mrs. Younge was a victim of that despicable man's machinations and is now assisting you to bring him to heel.

"You need to learn part of my philosophy: *Only remember the past as that remembrance gives you pleasure.*" Elizabeth paused as she squeezed William's arm in sympathy. "You have learnt from your past errors. I am sure you will not repeat them again, so there is no further need to allow the past to weigh you down."

As he sat there listening to Elizabeth's compassion, Darcy remembered how close he had come to giving up this magnificent woman. He owed Richard a debt for forcing him to reevaluate his life, a debt he would not be able to repay in two lifetimes.

It was time to leave the past in the past and move forward with his life. Of one thing he was certain, if Elizabeth would have him, he intended to make her a permanent part of his life.

Before Elizabeth could say anything more, Sarah, one of the maids, told them Mrs. Bennet was requesting everyone join her in the drawing room for tea and Cook's famous lemon biscuits.

~~~~~~~/~~~~~~~

After tea had been drunk, the lemon biscuits consumed, and the tea service cleared away, Andrew stood and cleared his throat. "Along with Jane, Mary, and Richard, it has been decided we will have a double wedding, to be solemnised on Monday the twentieth day of this month," Andrew reported.

Keeping to her previous resolve, Fanny said not a word in opposition to either the fact it was a double wedding and it would take place less than three weeks hence. It was what the couples had chosen, and she would do everything to make sure it occurred just as her daughters wished.

"No banns have been read," Bennet pointed out, "however, if we have Mr. Pierce begin this Sunday, the final ones will be read the day before the wedding. You can send an express to your home parish to have them read there as well."

"I will dispatch one with a courier, who will arrive by Saturday," Andrew responded. "The banns will begin to be called in Matlock and Hilldale on Sunday as well."

"With that pleasant business out of the way, I need to discuss something decidedly less tasteful..." Richard, with the assistance of Andrew and William, revealed all regarding Wickham's dastardly plans to the Bennets.

Mary looked at Elizabeth, who was not reacting as she suspected she would. Elizabeth leaned towards her younger sister.

"William revealed all to me when we were in the park," Elizabeth explained.

Mary was happy William had spoken to Lizzy about this; it showed a heretofore unknown level of intimacy between them. As she looked from one to the other, she began to wonder if Lizzy had not perhaps found her match.

"At no time will Anna be at risk, or anywhere close to that miscreant. For that matter, none of us will be in harm's way," Richard assured everyone.

Fanny sat there thanking her lucky stars she had woken up when she did. If things still were as they had been, would she have encouraged Lydia towards a blackguard like this Wickham?

As Lizzy liked to say, there was no profit in looking to the past. Things were not as they used to be, and that was the salient point. Fanny would say a prayer of thanks for the positive changes in the life of her family.

With all the news imparted and discussed, Richard returned to Mary's side and did not miss the way she was watching Lizzy and William. "You also noticed, have you not?"

"So it seems," Mary said, smiling at her beloved Richard. "Do not tease them; allow them to come together in their own time."

"Yes, General Mary, I will obey your commands," Richard jested as he gave his fiancée an impertinent salute.

"See that you do," Mary teased back.

~~~~~~~/~~~~~~~

After their return to Netherfield Park, Richard conveyed an invitation from Mrs. Bennet to the Matlocks, Bingley, and the Hursts to an engagement dinner on Saturday upcoming at Longbourn, where a few families would be present, including the Lucases, the Longs, and the Gouldings.

Being a man who enjoyed society, Bingley accepted happily for his sister and brother-in-law. He was secretly pleased those families had been invited as well.

That evening at dinner, Bingley commanded the attention of those around the table. "As most of you know, my younger sister was working to organise a ball, for which no date had been set before she left us," Bingley reminded those who had heard of the plan. "What say you if we still hold it, but as a ball to celebrate the two engagements?"

"What an excellent idea, Mr. Bingley!" Lady Matlock exclaimed. "If Mrs. Hurst will allow me, I would be happy to see to the arrangements with her."

"It would be an honour to do so with you, Your Ladyship," Mrs. Hurst stated sincerely.

"When we are in private, please address me as Lady Elaine," Lady Matlock granted.

"Then it is settled. All we have to decide is a date now," Bingley enthused.

He was looking forward to the ball. He had started to fall for a local lady, one who was nothing like the *angels* with whom he used to fall in and out of love with. He would request at least two sets from her, and if he was bold, a third one as well. As yet, he had said not a word to anyone. Everything was too new and the last thing he wanted was to be seen as capricious with a woman again, just in case nothing came of it.

Before Bingley could suggest the Friday before the double wedding, Richard offered a date of his own. "What say you to Tuesday, the fourteenth of August? That allows almost a fortnight to organise everything, and will allow time for all of us to recover before the twentieth."

"That is as good a day as any," Bingley agreed, looking at his older sister.

"Yes, Charles, there will be more than enough white soup ready for the ball," Mrs. Hurst assured her brother, who believed no ball could be held without serving that soup.

After dinner, once all the residents were alone in the drawing room, the door was closed. Biggs was stationed outside the doors to make sure no one could hear what was being discussed. At the same time, Johns stood guard in the servants' passageway leading to the drawing room.

Darcy stood. "I am sure you have noticed Mrs. Younge has not been seen out of her chambers for some days now..." He shared a synopsis of why and what was soon to occur.

"Now I understand why you chose a date which excluded Friday," Bingley realised.

Richard nodded his head. "That, and I believe there should be more time between a wedding and the celebratory ball before it."

"If you need any assistance, you have only to ask," Bingley volunteered.

"That is the same for me," Hurst added.

It had not escaped those who knew Hurst that since Miss Bingley's eviction from Netherfield Park, he partook in many more activities and did not seem to sleep his time away in a stupor from too much drink.

Hurst had shared the truth with his wife. He was almost never in his cups, but he had feigned such as a way of avoiding his virago of a sister-in-law. Louisa Hurst found she could not condemn her husband for avoiding her younger sister. Caroline should have arrived in Scarborough by now. The letter confirming her arrival had not yet reached Hertfordshire, however.

With the discussion of possible unpleasantness over, Mrs. Hurst and Anna entertained the residents on the pianoforte. Lord and Lady Matlock were well pleased Anna had overcome her aversion to exhibit before more than her brother.

CHAPTER 27

Receiving a letter from Anne was not a usual occurrence. Nichols had just brought one to Richard on his silver salver. Rather than allow his imagination to take flight, Richard broke the seal, opened the missive, and began to read.

2 August 1810

Richard, I am as happy to hear your news as I was to hear about Andrew being engaged to his own Miss Bennet. Please convey my heartiest congratulations to all.

Allow me to express my outrage and apologise for my mother's (I hesitate to call her that) unconscionable plan to have you murdered in a futile attempt to regain control of my property.

Although I knew her avarice had driven her beyond the edge of reason, I never imagined she would plan something so despicable. All I can do is thank God her plan was discovered before she could harm you, or any other.

"You have nothing for which to beg my pardon, Annie," Richard spoke aloud. "We have all known for some time your mother is as insane as any resident of Bedlam. You are blameless! You are as much a victim of her machinations as anyone else she has victimised." He continued reading Anne's words.

With Lady Catherine defanged and under constant guard in her cottage, it is now safe for you to be here. I must ask for your indulgence. Will you, Andrew, William, and your fiancées wait on me here at my estate as soon as may be?

If it were not for my indifferent health I would travel to Hertfordshire, but I am sure you know the maladies which befall me when I attempt to travel any distance in a coach.

As I do not know your commitments, if it is inconvenient to come away now, I will understand.

With cousinly regard,

Anne

Richard could not imagine why Anne wanted to see all of them now, but he was not of a mind to deny her request. There was talk of travelling to London to shop for trousseaus, so mayhap they could go to Kent first.

Unsurprisingly, his parents decided to join the party. Andrew and William agreed as well. After they arrived at Longbourn, Jane and Mary received their parents' permission as long as Elizabeth joined them as an additional chaperone.

Anna would be hosted at Longbourn. She was more than pleased with the arrangement. As much as she enjoyed spending time with the three older Bennet sisters—especially Mary, she and Kate had developed a deep bond; any excuse to spend more time with her new best friend was welcome.

With all decided for a departure, Anne's courier was sent back to Rosings Park with a letter telling his mistress who would be arriving to visit her on the morrow.

~~~~~~~/~~~~~~~

Thanks to a departure at first light, with only two rest stops along the way, the two coaches arrived at Rosings Park in the early afternoon. The arriving guests were informed the mistress was resting but had requested the Colonel join her as soon as he had washed and changed.

Once ready, Richard made for the private sitting room attached to the master suite. "Anne, you wanted to meet with me," he stated.

"Thank you for attending me, Richard," Anne

responded.

"Are you sure you do not want the rest of the family here as well?" Richard asked.

"No, I requested you alone by design. It is about the future of the estate," Anne said. "After I have rested, I will take pleasure in welcoming the family and meeting your and Andy's fiancées."

He sat in a wingback chair across a low tea table from his cousin. "What about the estate?" Richard enquired.

"My mother was correct about one thing—regardless of her insanity. It is true I am not strong enough to manage my inheritance." Seeing Richard was about to protest, Anne lifted her dainty hand. "Rich, I have been examined by a cadre of doctors—real doctors, not the quacks my mother foisted on me. I was lucky not to join Papa in death when we both took ill, but it most certainly shortened my life.

"I could live a few more years, but it may be for only a few months. Both my heart and lungs were damaged by the scarlet fever." Richard allowed it was so. "It is for that reason I have signed the estate, house in London, and the de Bourgh fortune over to you. You are to marry soon; you and your wife will need a home of your own."

"Anne, I, we, cannot take that which is yours," Richard objected.

"Accepting Rosings Park is yours will enable me to live in peace and likely allow me to live longer than I would if you did not," Anne insisted. "Talk to Uncle Reggie, Andy, or William; they will confirm managing an estate, making decisions that do not impact the estate's dependants negatively, and so much more, are all very stressful. Stress is not something that is my friend. Will you refuse to do that which will allow me to live without the weight of the estate on my shoulders?"

"As unfair as it is, when you put it like that, I suppose I

must accept that which you have gifted Mary and me." Richard shook his head. He knew he was well and truly trapped. It seemed he was to become an estate owner sooner than he had thought possible. He would no longer need to lease Rivington from William. "I do have some terms. Unless they are met, I will not accept your gift."

"What are they?" Anne queried.

"You will live here for the rest of your days, as if the estate still belongs to you. Any time you desire to travel—if you are able—you will do so without having to request the use of one of the coaches, and the phaeton and pony will remain yours to use whenever you desire," Richard said.

"All items I expected you would demand of me," Anne smiled. "You already know I do not travel—which was why I requested you join me here, but I thank you for your solicitousness. What I want to make sure of is that Mrs. Jenkinson will be well taken care of after I am no more. My dowry has never been touched and I would like her to receive half of the principal. She has been more of a mother to me than the lady who bore me. She has a daughter and grandchildren who otherwise would not be able to afford an extra mouth to feed."

"It will be as you say," Richard vowed. He paused as he went over some things in his head. "Do you want me to tell the family, or would you like to tell them yourself when you join us later?"

"Richard, you are technically the master of Rosings Park now, so I would be happy for you to share the news with everyone before I join you," Anne stated. "When you depart the estate, travel via London and see my solicitor. He is waiting for you with documents for you to sign. I have already signed them. As soon as they are filed with the courts, everything will be legally yours"

"You were that sure I would accept?" Richard grinned.

"Was I wrong?" Anne bantered. "Did I not tell you the estate is already yours?"

"No, you were not," Richard admitted. Suddenly he remembered he had told Mary all about Rivington. "It seems I will have to inform my fiancée we will no longer need to plan to live in Surrey at Rivington." He explained about their cousin's offer and his own stipulation it would be a lease, not a gift.

"When my mother hears you are the new owner of Rosings Park, you know she will come close to having an apoplexy. I am sure even now, under constant guard, she is still trying to formulate a way she can regain control of the estate," Anne revealed. "She does not know if she makes any attempt to escape she will be committed to an asylum on the Isle of Wight."

"Let us hope her mania does not drive her to make an attempt. She will not like the results," Richard asserted. "There are worse places to reside than in a cottage."

"My mother has only added to the pressure I feel in managing the estate. She will be seriously displeased once the change of ownership is made public."

"You look tired, Annie. I will leave now and allow you to rest."

"I am rather fatigued. Thank you for relieving me of this burden, Rich."

While Anne made her way to her bedchamber, the new master of Rosings Park—as he would legally become once he visited Mr. Spencer in London—made his way downstairs to find Mary and his family.

~~~~~~~/~~~~~~~

After he entered the drawing room, before saying anything to the family, Richard requested Mary join him for a private interview. They had made for the study, with the door left partly open and a maid seated outside.

"Richard, I can scarcely believe this news," Mary exclaimed. "I cannot fully comprehend your cousin Anne has done this, although I do understand her reasons. As soon as may be I will thank her in person."

"We would have enjoyed managing Rivington, but I have to admit the prospect of looking after *our* very own estate has gotten me excited about the possibilities," Richard admitted.

He pulled his beloved Mary into a warm hug. The couple shared a few kisses before they returned to the family waiting for them in the drawing room.

After Richard relayed what Anne had decided, there was silence for some moments as everyone digested the news. "Mary, you are to be mistress of all of this!" Elizabeth managed in wonder. "I understand there is an advantage to Miss de Bourgh, but what generosity of spirit to do this for the two of you."

"I could not say it better than Lizzy," Lord Matlock boomed. "As the executor of the late Sir Lewis's will, I can tell you what Anne has done is well within her rights. Mary, you and Richard will do very well here."

"Then you will no longer need the lease on Rivington," Darcy stated. "I suppose I will let you out of it without penalty."

Elizabeth was pleased to see the wry humour William displayed. The more she came to know him, the more she came to believe he would be her perfect match. *'If only...'* Elizabeth wished silently. It was up to him to speak; all she could do was accept or reject any offer she would ever receive.

"Richard, Mary, I could not be happier for you two," Andrew drawled.

"All I can do is agree with my fiancé," Jane added.

Lady Matlock sat still with tears in her eyes. Her son's future was set, and she could not have thought of another more deserving than her Richard. She remembered the dark days when they did not know if he would survive the infection after being wounded.

By the Grace of God, he had survived and recovered. He still walked with a limp, but of late Lady Matlock had noticed Richard needed his cane for support less and less often.

She had been beyond pleased when she met Mary as Richard's betrothed. Lady Elaine knew they would have done well together at the estate they were to lease from William. However, it had always been her dream Richard would become master of his own property.

Not only did he—or he would as soon as the papers were signed—own Rosings Park, but there was de Bourgh House in London, and the rather substantial de Bourgh fortune. Mary and Richard, and any children they would be blessed with, would be secure.

Once the congratulations abated, Lady Matlock stood and pulled first Mary and then Richard into extended hugs. "I could not be happier for you," she said next to his ear so only Richard could hear.

"What say you we remain here for the weekend and then depart for London on Monday?" Richard suggested. "While Mother and the ladies go shopping, I can meet with Mr. H. Spencer and sign the papers."

No one objected to the plan. "May we have one of the couriers carry a letter to the Gardiners?" Jane requested. "That way Uncle will be ready for us to look for fabric in his warehouse and Aunt Maddie will be informed of our coming to London so she may join us as we shop."

With the agreement of the party to the plan, Jane sat and wrote the letter to their family to be handed to a courier who would be sent to London. While she was writing, Darcy approached Miss Elizabeth.

"Unless I am mistaken, you like to take early morning rambles while you commune with nature, do you not?" he enquired.

"Yes, I most certainly do," Elizabeth responded with a welcoming smile.

"In that case, may I show you the groves and the glade on the morrow? We will take a footman with us to preserve propriety," Darcy proposed.

"As long as you do not object to walking out with the sun, I would love to see the groves and the glade," Elizabeth replied with another beaming smile, causing Darcy's heart to speed up.

"If it meets with your approval, we will meet in the entranceway just before sunup," Darcy suggested.

"In that case, I look forward to seeing *you* then," Elizabeth stated boldly. She looked directly at William when she spoke, hoping he would understand her meaning.

Darcy was thrilled. He hoped he had not misread the signals Elizabeth was sending. He thought she was indicating she looked forward to his company more than she looked forward to exploring the walking paths around the estate.

"When will we be able to express our gratitude to Anne?" Lord Matlock asked.

"Once she has rested, she will join us in the drawing room," Richard reported. "Do any of you remember how gaudy the décor was when our *dear* aunt reigned here?" There were nods from those who had visited the estate when Lady Catherine was its mistress. He turned to Mary and her sisters. "Lady Catherine used to have the estate decorated to display her status and wealth. It was ostentatious and gauche, and only displayed her lack of taste. Thankfully, as soon as Anne assumed her rightful place, the first thing she did was to redecorate completely."

"I hope she has done the same at de Bourgh House," Lady Matlock expressed.

"You mean *Fitzwilliam* House, do you not Mother?"

Richard intoned.

"Yes, I most certainly do. How well that sounds, Son. How convenient that your house in London is on Grosvenor Square as well," Lady Matlock agreed.

Richard pulled the bell and had the housekeeper assemble the staff and servants in the entrance hall, after which he announced to them that the next time he visited he would be the master of the estate and his new wife the mistress.

The senior staff and servants were pleased by the announcement. As long as Lady Catherine was never given dominion over their lives again, they would be happy.

~~~~~~~/~~~~~~~

As soon as Anne was seated, with Mrs. Jenkinson's aid, Richard introduced Mary and her next older sister. Andrew then had the pleasure of introducing Jane to his cousin.

"Miss de Bourgh," Mary began after taking a seat on the settee next to Anne. The latter placed a thin hand on Mary's arm to halt her words.

"Miss Mary, I would very much like it if you and your sisters, who will soon be my cousins, were to call me Anne," she requested.

Mary looked to her sisters, both of whom nodded. "In that case, Anne, please call us by our given names as well." Anne nodded her agreement. "As I was about to say, I do not know how to adequately thank you for what you have gifted Richard and me. I second Richard's assertion you will always be a most valued part of our household. I know the words do not match the gift, but thank you, Anne, from the bottom of my heart, thank you."

The rest of her family and soon-to-be family expressed their approbation and gratitude for Anne's generosity. Anne felt waves of genuine love and appreciation wash over her. For far too long she had been alone with only Jenki as company.

Thanks to her mother's machinations in the past, she could never get close to her cousins, or they to her, under Lady Catherine's watchful eye. Now there was no impediment to interacting with them or the rest of the family.

Anne de Bourgh knew from this day onwards; she would never again be a family of one—which had nothing to do with her signing the estate over to Richard. She would be part of a large, extended, and loving family.

She knew, for however much time she would be granted in the mortal world, her life would be a pleasurable one.

CHAPTER 28

Saturday morning, Elizabeth was waiting in the entrance hall with a footman standing off to the side. She thought William had the right of it; the distance and speed at which she preferred to walk would have been a hardship for a maid not used to such exertion.

Darcy made his way down the grand stairs and into the hall. There stood Elizabeth. How well she looked! She was by far the most handsome woman of his acquaintance.

"Good morning, William. It was good of you to join me," Elizabeth teased.

The tease produced a dimple-revealing smile from Darcy. He was so handsome when he smiled it took Elizabeth's breath away. '*He should smile far more*,' Elizabeth told herself silently as she admired his handsome face and noble mien.

"Please pardon me for making you wait for me for *so many hours*," Darcy jested in return.

The fact he was willing to laugh at himself was another point in William's favour. "As you have the knowledge of the area, I am in your hands," Elizabeth managed breathlessly.

"Shall we," Darcy said, offering his arm to Elizabeth, who rested her hand on his forearm. They proceeded out the double doors of the manor house.

They crossed the circular drive in front of the house and entered the formal gardens, which, even though summer was waning, were full of colourful blooms.

"You prefer more natural gardens to formal gardens, if I am not mistaken," Darcy guessed.

"You are correct. I prefer it when nature is given free rein and not counteracted by the awkward tastes of man," Elizabeth confirmed.

'*You will love Pemberley in that case,*' was on the tip of his tongue. Instead, he said, "Then you would have hated the way the formal gardens looked when my aunt was mistress here."

She arched one eyebrow in question, which made Elizabeth look even more attractive to him.

"You have heard my cousins and me relate how Lady Catherine believed she could control everything, have you not?"

"Yes, I have. William, please tell me she did not think she could command nature?"

"She did. The flower beds," William pointed to the beds ahead of them which had an attractive mix of various plants and colours, "had to be ordered and arranged by type of plant and colour. The blades of grass had to be the same length; she would sack a gardener if she judged a single blade longer than others." All Elizabeth could do was shake her head. "Do you see the topiary there?" He pointed to shaped shrubs on one side of the gardens. Elizabeth nodded. "In her wisdom, my aunt decided each shrub had to be exactly the same, down to the number of leaves."

"Did she not realise that would have rendered the topiary boring?"

"One would think so, but the *great lady,* as she considered herself, never cared about the thoughts and opinions of others," Darcy explained.

Elizabeth could but shake her head as they followed a path through the gardens away from the house. They walked for almost ten minutes until she thought the groves and glade were a figment of William's imaginings. Then they passed a line of ordered trees and came to the end of the manicured lawn.

There before her, Elizabeth saw the beginning of a grove, wonderfully unspoilt by man, or in this case, by Lady Catherine. "How is it Lady Catherine allowed this wilderness?" Elizabeth enquired.

"Her husband would not allow her to cut down all the trees she desired and wrote that into his will. He did agree to have the row of trees we just passed planted so his wife would not have to see the blight—the *jungle*, as she termed it—when she walked in the gardens."

"How often did Lady Catherine walk in the gardens?"

"That is just it," William smiled, his dimples making themselves known again, "as far as any of us know, she never did."

The last revelation caused Elizabeth to allow one of her tinkling laughs to escape. She covered her mouth in embarrassment. "I should not laugh at your aunt, regardless of what she planned to do to Richard."

"It is no less than the rest of us do. You will not offend me or any member of the family if you find her antics amusing." To himself, Darcy thought, *'What would I not give to hear that laughter as much as possible for the rest of my days.'*

By now they had reached the entrance to the grove. Without noticing, Elizabeth had wrapped her hand around William's arm rather than rest it lightly on his forearm, as she had when they had commenced their walk.

The path they were on was shaded by a verdant tree canopy on each side of it. The birds were out in full force, their song serenading them as the two walked in contented companionship with the footman following at a respectful distance.

Some birds were flitting from branch to branch. Others took wing above their heads. One cheeky robin did not care they were walking close by as he wrestled a worm from the ground.

By now the sun had risen and shone down wherever there was a break in the natural canopy above their heads. In the middle of the path, and on the ground on either side of it, wildflowers showed their colours, especially in sunlit areas.

They walked for about a half-mile until they reached a point where a much narrower path branched off to the left.

"That leads to the glade. I assume you would like to see it?"

"Yes, very much so," Elizabeth enthused.

By now her hand was holding tightly onto his arm, almost possessively. Darcy had no complaints; in fact, he felt quite the opposite.

It felt right to be close to this man. Elizabeth felt like she was home. She suspected in William she had found the other half of her heart. Her thoughts were brought back to the more mundane as William led her along the path towards the sounds of croaking toads and frogs, which grew louder the further they walked. The distinctive hum of insects could be heard around them.

They reached the end of the path, and a tree-ringed clearing was revealed before them. Roughly in the centre was a small pond with a large boulder in the middle.

Two frogs sunning themselves on the rock launched themselves into the water as soon as they heard the crunch of footsteps. The splash they made disturbed the pink and yellow water lilies on the surface of the pond.

Another tinkling laugh escaped from Elizabeth before she covered her mouth with her hand. "It seems the frogs did not appreciate our intrusion."

"I do not feel badly about it," William stated with an affected haughty air. "It is very seldom humans intrude on their domain here."

Darcy led Elizabeth to a flattened boulder that served as

269

a bench. Elizabeth untied her bonnet and allowed her errant curls to fall down around her neck on the sides and in the back. Darcy had to exert all his self-control not to take one of those curls and rub it between his fingers. He was sure it would feel silky and soft to his touch. If things went his way, it would be his pleasure to be allowed to do so one day.

"Did you come play here as a little boy?" Elizabeth asked as she rested with her arms behind her, her face pointing up to the opening in the trees surrounding the glade that allowed them to see the sky.

"Yes. Mother and Father would bring me to join the Fitzwilliams here each Easter. While Uncle Lewis was alive, and before Anne became ill, we spent hours in this place. I may have gifted Anne a frog here when I was seven and she was perhaps four or five."

Elizabeth sat up and looked at Darcy with an arched eyebrow. "Mr. Fastidious William Darcy used to gift frogs to little girls?"

"Only that one time. Father was not impressed, especially with my Aunt Catherine screeching about Anne's dirtied dress. It was one of the few times Father administered corporal punishment to me," Darcy revealed.

"Poor Anne," Elizabeth giggled.

"She did not seem to mind as much. Unfortunately, my aunt would not let it go." Darcy paused as he searched his memories. "Come to think on it, I suspect Lady Catherine was upset about the fact my parents had rebuffed her attempt to get them to agree to engage me to Anne—not for the first time. That Uncle Lewis did not agree seemed to not enter into the equation for my aunt at the time."

Elizabeth related a time she had taken a dare from Johnny Lucas that she could not walk across slippery stepping stones to cross a large, muddy pond. She had been more than halfway when the younger Lucas son, seeing she would succeed, threw stones at her, causing her to fall into the muddy water.

She had William guffawing at the picture of a seven-year-old Elizabeth arriving home covered in muck from head to foot to face her mother's extreme displeasure. She related how she had refused to tell the real reason for her falling into the pond, so Johnny Lucas had escaped punishment.

From that day on, Elizabeth had a faithful protector in the form of the younger Lucas son. "Given that my mother thought I was a hoyden, I am not sure she would have believed me had I told her the truth about Johnny."

Darcy felt a tinge of jealousy regarding the closeness between the second Lucas son and Elizabeth. He pushed it aside, remembering the day Elizabeth had been talking about him and how she could never marry him as he felt too much like a brother.

Knowing they would be expected to break their fasts with the rest of the residents of Rosings Park, they reluctantly left the rock and informed the footman they were to move on. Elizabeth fixed her bonnet back in place and managed to hide most of the tempting curls which had been freed.

Rather than retrace their steps, they walked in the same direction they had to arrive at the glade. About ten minutes later, they exited the grove, and before them the Hunsford parsonage appeared. It abutted one side of Rosings Park, near the entrance gates and the drive leading to the mansion.

The rector was checking on his hives as they passed the parsonage. Darcy remembered him from the previous Easter. "Good morning, Mr. Deacon. Elizabeth, may I introduce Mr. John Deacon, the rector of the church at Hunsford. Mr. Deacon, Miss Elizabeth Bennet of Longbourn in Hertfordshire."

During the introduction, the clergyman's wife, heavy with child, joined her husband. Her youngest, a boy, was holding her hand while his other thumb was being sucked happily. Four other children, three boys and a girl, brought up the rear.

"May I introduce my family?" Deacon asked proudly. Darcy and Elizabeth nodded. "My devoted wife, Mrs. Veronica Deacon; my eldest Robert, twelve; Micheal, who is ten; the one rose among the thorns, Laura, seven; Joshua, who is five; and Luke is not yet three. Family, Mr. Fitzwilliam Darcy of Pemberley in Derbyshire and Miss Elizabeth Bennet of Longbourn in Herefordshire."

"Hertfordshire," Elizabeth corrected.

Mrs. Deacon invited them in to break their fasts, but Darcy and Elizabeth politely declined and explained their family was expecting them to eat the morning meal with them. After a few minutes more conversation with the pleasant family, the two struck out across the park for the half-mile walk back to the manor house.

~~~~~~~/~~~~~~~

On Sunday morning everyone, including Anne, attended services at Hunsford. As it had been since Mr. Deacon's being preferred to the living, the church was full. Being a man who wrote his own sermons, this one, like all he delivered, was well worth listening to and did not cause any of the parishioners to nod off during its recitation.

Mr. Deacon and his wife stood and greeted each of the congregants and said a few words to all as they exited the church. After the last man, a sycophant appointed by Lady Catherine, the parishioners thanked their lucky stars that lady had not been allowed to appoint his replacement.

Once the last of those who desired a word or two with the rector had left, Richard conveyed an invitation to the Deacons, including the children, to join the family for the after services meal. Mrs. Deacon happily accepted the invitation on behalf of her family.

~~~~~~~/~~~~~~~

When the Deacons arrived, they were introduced to the Earl, the Countess, and the members of the party they had not yet met. Although the children were awed to meet a peer, it soon became evident the Fitzwilliam parents were very down to earth.

After the meal, at which all of the Deacon children behaved well, the change in ownership of Rosings Park was revealed to the Deacons. The reverend understood why the invitation had been proffered by Mr. Fitzwilliam and not by, or on behalf of, Miss de Bourgh.

"Like my cousin before me, I will refrain from interfering in parish business unless you request my assistance, and I will never ask you to reveal confidential information to me which has been shared with you by your parishioners," Richard assured Deacon.

"In that case, Mr. Fitzwilliam…" the clergyman began to reply.

"Call me Fitzwilliam," Richard corrected him.

"…Fitzwilliam, then you and I will get along famously. I would never compromise my parishioners regardless of a patron's demands," Deacon completed.

"The mark of a good clergyman," Richard insisted.

"Once we are married and living here, I look forward to assisting you with charitable endeavours, or in any other capacity you feel my help will be beneficial," Mary told Mrs. Deacon.

Both ladies felt they would become good friends after Mary came to live at the estate as Mrs. Fitzwilliam.

As if she had not been impressed with William already, seeing him talking to the three older Deacon boys and not dismissing them simply because they were children gave Elizabeth a window onto how William would be as a father. She very much liked what she was seeing.

She knew it was premature to think about children, but it was still gratifying to see this side of him.

An hour after the meal, the Deacons left to make the half-mile walk back to their home. On Monday morning, the two coaches departed before the sun was up.

~~~~~~~/~~~~~~~

Richard made directly for Anne's solicitor on arriving in London. He was there for about an hour. On Tuesday, as planned, the three Bennet sisters and Lady Matlock made for Gardiner's warehouse to select fabrics for various gowns and dresses.

The four men spent time at White's and catching up on correspondence. On Wednesday morning, after the ladies had left to collect Madeline Gardiner and make for the modiste on Bond Street, the Earl summoned his second son to his study at Matlock House.

"Did Mr. Specter tell you when the transfer of the deed will be official?" Lord Matlock enquired.

"The documents have been filed in the Court of Chancery already, so it will be on the morrow, or the next day at the latest," Richard responded. "Once it is official, I will take Mary to see Fitzwilliam House. Thankfully, it is only five doors down on William's side of the square so we can walk there. If Anne has not had it redecorated, we will have our work cut out for us."

The Earl dismissed his son with a wave and returned to his correspondence.

Richard was missing Mary. It was almost worth suffering the shopping to be near her. Almost. At least that evening they were to use the Matlock and Darcy boxes at Drury Lane to see a production of *A Midsummer Night's Dream*.

He would be able to sit next to Mary and hold her hand when the lights went down. Darcy, who supposedly was reading the *Times of London*, was instead imagining how wonderful it would be to be able to hold Elizabeth's hand during their time at the theatre that night.

Andrew was counting the days remaining until he made Jane his partner for the rest of his days.

CHAPTER 29

With all the shopping completed, the final day in London had nothing particular scheduled for the morning. There would be a tour of Fitzwilliam House in the afternoon, and the Gardiners and their two children would join the residents of Matlock House for dinner that evening.

As predicted, the documents conveying the former de Bourgh properties to Richard had been filed and the new deeds were issued by the court on Wednesday. Rosings Park and the house on Grosvenor Square now belonged to Richard by law.

The former de Bourgh fortune had become his as soon as he signed the documents at the solicitor's office. The next day, while the ladies were visiting Bond Street again, he and the solicitor had gone to the bank and transferred all de Bourgh accounts to Richard's name.

A large portion of the liquid funds were added to his investment account with his soon-to-be uncle, Edward Gardiner. Richard then retained Mr. Specter as his lawyer and instructed the man to craft a generous marriage settlement for Mary.

When he had shown the draft to Mary, she had objected he was settling too large an amount on her. Richard would not be moved for any reason. He told her he could not rest easy unless he knew her future would be secure if the worst happened to him. That argument had won the day.

Thanks to no scheduled activities for the morning, it allowed the three couples (two engaged and one unofficially courting) to walk in Hyde Park. They departed from the Fitzwilliams' house not long after sunrise and entered the park via the Grosvenor Gate.

Elizabeth and Darcy walked ahead of the other two couples; Mary and Richard followed them; and Jane and Andrew brought up the rear. They would act as chaperones for one another, so no maids or footmen followed them.

It was a warm August day. Many members of the *Ton* had sought their estates for the summer and had not yet returned to Town. Additionally, it was not the fashionable hour, so the only people in the park were those who were taking exercise or enjoying the pleasant day. There were none of the *see or be seen* crowd.

As the three couples walked along the Serpentine, they were passed by men on horseback who doffed their hats when they noted acquaintances of theirs, but none stopped to seek an introduction to the unknown ladies.

The ladies walking with the Fitzwilliam brothers were obviously their fiancées—the notices had appeared in the papers weeks ago—however, none who saw Darcy with the raven-haired beauty on his arm stopped to ask him about her, knowing how closely he guarded his privacy.

For their part, neither Elizabeth nor Darcy noticed the questioning looks of those who passed them by. They were lost in their thoughts of the person with whom they were walking.

'*Will he speak soon?*' Elizabeth asked herself silently as they strolled along the wide gravel way which was known as Rotten Row. '*I Think he will, at least my hope is he will. What a difference from not long after I knew him when I told myself he was the last man in the world I could be prevailed upon to marry. If I am being honest with myself, I must own I was dissembling to myself then. It was due to the fact I had felt an instant attraction to William that my reaction to his words at the assembly was so severe.*'

'*I need to ask her for a courtship, I need her in my life like I need air to breathe. I am sure Elizabeth is not indifferent to me so why am I waiting?*' Darcy berated himself as he looked at the woman he loved with a sideways glance. He stiffened his back. Delaying would not make it more or less likely she would agree to his application.

"Elizabeth, when we return to Matlock House, may I have a private interview with you?" Darcy requested.

"Yes, William, it is my pleasure to grant your request," Elizabeth averred as her whole countenance lit up with pleasure. '*Did he hear my thoughts?*' she wondered in awe of the timing.

There was no missing the way Elizabeth glowed with pleasure right after she granted her permission for him to address her. '*You see how pleased she is, you could have asked her this question at Rosings Park!*' he told himself silently as he shook his head at the nonsensical delay, if only by about a sennight.

"Are you shaking your thoughts so they become ordered?" Elizabeth teased.

"Is that what you do whenever you shake your head?" Darcy deflected.

Behind them, Richard had been watching the interaction between his formerly staid cousin and his soon-to-be sister. He could see something significant had passed between them; he did not know what, although he had a strong suspicion.

If he was correct, Andy, William, and he would be brothers one day, just as they used to imagine they were when they played together as young boys. Until he began to change and his mercenary and vicious propensities came to the fore, for a short time, George Wickham used to be counted as part of the band of brothers.

Thoughts of Wickham made Richard contemplate the

confrontation to come in a little more than a sennight. He shook the musings from his head. No one forced George Wickham to make the choices he did, or to murder his own father. Finally, Wickham would have to face the consequences of his criminal actions.

A much happier thought was that in ten days he would be married to his Mary. That was something Richard could anticipate! The final banns would be published the Sunday before the wedding and the next day they would be united in holy matrimony, and never have to separate again.

"Richard, where did you go?" Mary asked ,having noted the faraway look in her fiancé's eyes.

"Please accept my apologies for my inattentiveness; I was wool-gathering," Richard responded.

"I could tell," Mary smiled. "Is there anything about which I should be concerned?"

"Mostly good things. Did you notice Lizzy and William? I have a feeling it will not be long before they move from an unofficial to an official courtship," Richard predicted.

"Regarding that, you will hear no disagreement from me," Mary averred. "Those two have been dancing around the issue for weeks without coming to any resolution."

"I am looking forward to seeing Fitzwilliam House with you later. From what Anne shared with me, she did not redecorate as she has not come to London in many years, but she did have the housekeeper and butler collect all of Lady Catherine's worst excesses and send them out for sale," Richard related.

"It pleases me that your house in London..." Mary began to reply.

"You mean *our house* in Town," Richard corrected.

"It is a happy circumstance that *our* abode is a few doors away from Darcy and Matlock Houses, and Hilldale House is barely a mile distant on Portman Square," Mary completed her thought. "Who could have imagined the possibility of three Bennet sisters being mistresses of grand houses in London, or of estates of consequence for that matter."

"It is well known to me that wealth, rank, and connections are not motivating factors for any of you in choosing your partners," Richard returned. "My brother and I, and I suspect William, have been fortunate to have found women who love us for who we are, not what we have."

Mary squeezed Richard's arm to indicate her agreement with his statement. Not long after, the three couples turned and made their way back towards the Grosvenor Gate.

~~~~~~~/~~~~~~~

Elizabeth and William were granted the use of a small parlour by Lady Matlock. She positioned a maid outside the door and her husband admonished his nephew not to close the door completely. He allowed them no more than ten minutes in private.

He pushed the door three-quarters closed, then William turned and took a seat in a wingback chair facing Elizabeth on a settee.

"When we first met, I was not adept at making a good impression on any of the Bennets, least of all you," Darcy began self-deprecatingly. "As Richard pointed out, I was a rather arrogant horse's ar...hindquarters...full of improper pride. What you may not know is in his own way, Richard made me see just how far I had strayed from my parents' teachings. I had become a man of whom they would not have approved.

"When I began to see everything clearly and remembered what it was my parents desired for me, I was able to admit I had felt an attraction to you from almost the very beginning." Darcy paused as he went over what he wanted to say next. He thought about how he would say it so as not to give offence. "Although I believed it at the time, part of my reason for that despicable utterance at the assembly was because when I turned and looked at you, I felt something I had never felt before and it frightened me.

"In my misplaced pride and wrongheaded beliefs, I thought an alliance with you, or anyone of your social status, would be a degradation to all I held dear and the death knell to Anna's chances of making a splendid match."

It was essential Elizabeth understand how he used to think and how differently he did now. "When Andrew announced his engagement, I am ashamed to admit I was not complementary to him or your eldest sister. Richard issued a set-down such as he had never done before. It was after I started to consider his words I had the epiphany which showed me how wrong I had been and made me remember what my parents had demanded of me, not the words I had corrupted in my own head.

"From that moment on, besides making amends where I needed to, I allowed the war between my head and my heart to come to an end, finally accepting my heart had been right all along. It was then I admitted to myself what my heart already knew. You were the only woman for me, and I needed to do whatever I could to secure your good opinion and please a woman who deserves to be pleased." Darcy stopped talking to allow Elizabeth time to assimilate what he had said so far. "After you think, inform me whether you wish me to continue or if you wish to end this."

Elizabeth sat impassively. Much of what he was telling her she had intuited on her own. She had suspected he was not sanguine with Jane's engagement to Andrew, but by the time she saw him, he had decided to change.

That was the crux of the matter. He had changed. He was still changing for the better. How many would never admit their faults and blindly continue on the path they had set for themselves rather than, show weakness—for that is what they would see it as—and correct themselves. William had recognised his errors and was working assiduously to fix them.

It took a man of the highest moral fibre and character to both admit to, and then work to change his faults. No, there was nothing he had done in the *past* that would change her regard for William. The man she was falling in love with was the one he was deep down, not the one he had portrayed when they first met.

Darcy hardly breathed as Elizabeth considered her answer. "It would please me greatly if you continue on to the purpose of this interview you requested," Elizabeth stated firmly.

Feeling a great weight lift from his shoulders, Darcy stood and made his way around the low table between them and, after wordlessly asking permission from Elizabeth and having it granted, he sat next to her on the settee.

"Elizabeth, in vain I have struggled. It will not do. My feelings will not be repressed. You must allow me to tell you how ardently I admire and love you," Darcy managed to say that which he had wanted to say for some weeks now. "Do not ask me when or why I fell in love with you, because I was in the middle before I admitted to myself I had begun. How could I not fall in love with the most intelligent, compassionate, and handsome woman of my acquaintance? I know this is all new for you, so I am requesting an official courtship...for now. If... when you are ready and have come to love me, then there will be another question I need to ask you."

"I will not claim feelings I do not yet possess. At this time, I have tender—very tender—feelings for you. If I did not believe I would be in love with you in the near future then my answer would not be a resounding yes. I will grant you an official courtship. That being said, I have come to believe you are the only man in the world I could be prevailed upon to marry."

His handsome face lit up with pleasure as he reached for

Elizabeth's hands and took one in each of his own. He bestowed a lingering kiss on the top of each hand before gently turning each over in its turn and kissing the pulse of each wrist. His lips remained in contact with her skin for even longer than they had on the other side of each hand.

At the first kiss on the top of her left hand, Elizabeth's heart began to race. With each successive kiss, it sped up and her breathing became ragged. Her eyes slipped shut and for some moments after his lips left her right wrist's pulse, Elizabeth did not open her eyes.

When she did, she had the dreamiest of looks in her eyes. She could still feel his lips on her skin even though they were no longer there. Elizabeth could only imagine what it would be like to receive her first romantic kiss from the man when they arrived at that point.

"There is no point riding into Hertfordshire to see your father today as we will be there on the morrow," Darcy reasoned. "You have not reached your majority yet, have you?"

"N-no, I will be one and twenty in March," Elizabeth reported.

"What date in March?" Darcy enquired.

"The fifth," Elizabeth revealed.

"It is proper that we say nothing to our family here until your father has granted his permission and blessing," Darcy stated regretfully. He would have preferred to shout the fact Elizabeth had granted him a courtship from every rooftop in London.

"We will manage to keep our counsel for one day," Elizabeth opined.

With smiles wreathing their faces, they rejoined the rest of the residents in the drawing room, but could not be induced to reveal anything.

~~~~~~~/~~~~~~~

"I can only imagine what this house looked like before Anne had her mother's hideous style of décor removed and sold," Mary stated as they viewed the main drawing room in the house.

They were accompanied by the residents of Matlock House as well as the Gardiners. Mary was referring to the decidedly uncomfortable looking furniture in the room.

She sat on one of the settees and it was worse than she had imagined. "Mary, if you and Fitzwilliam so desire, I can instruct one of my clerks to inventory anything you want to dispose of," Gardiner offered when he saw the moue of distaste on Mary's face as soon as she sat on the lumpy piece of furniture. "You will not believe the tastes of some who will buy things just because they used to belong to Lord and Lady whatnot. We will tell the truth and the card will list *previously owned by the Honourable Lady Catherine de Bourgh*.

"A woman of no class and less taste," Richard interjected.

"As I said, there is no accounting for tastes," Gardiner reiterated.

"Thank you, Uncle," Mary responded happily. "I will make lists as we go from room to room."

The housekeeper led the party and there was no mistaking the low esteem in which she, the butler, and the servants felt for Lady Catherine. Richard had a quiet conversation with the butler, who revealed Lady Catherine had underpaid them for many years. Knowing Miss de Bourgh was not of a strong constitution, they had written nothing on the subject to her.

Richard immediately raised the wages of all those working at Fitzwilliam House to better than most paid in London. In addition, he committed to pay a bonus to each and every man and woman employed for the last few years at the house to mitigate the effects of his aunt's mismanagement in some way.

Word travelled like wildfire and soon the senior staff and servants were walking about with a spring in their steps and smiles on their faces.

In the end, other than the master's chambers, which were the only rooms on which Lady Catherine had not exercised her brand of decorating, Mary tore up her list and told her Uncle to take everything not in Richard's chambers.

Gardiner promised his clerk would be put to work on the morrow and as soon as the items sold, he would inform his niece and Richard.

The next morning at first light, after a most enjoyable dinner with the Fitzwilliams, more than three carriages departed for Hertfordshire. The Gardiners were coming to Hertfordshire so they would be able to spend the last sennight or so of their nieces' being single with them.

Before he departed, Gardiner left detailed instructions for one of his clerks regarding the removal of practically all of Fitzwilliam House's furnishings.

The carriages arrived at Longbourn before eleven that morning.

CHAPTER 30

George Wickham felt the anticipation building within himself. The group that, along with Colonel Forster, had scouted for, and found, an area for the encampment in Meryton, had returned.

On his return, Denny told Wickham about the dinner with the gentlemen of the area. Wickham pretended to pay Denny heed, but he heard mayhap one word in ten.

There was some talk, not only from Denny, but the other officers who had been part of the advance party, about very pretty young ladies in the area. This would have normally been something of interest to Wickham, but he did not intend to be there above a day or two at the most.

Soon, less than four days now, he would move with the regiment to Hertfordshire from the wilds of Leicestershire and finally get his due while taking his revenge on Darcy and his infernal family. His plan had evolved in his head.

His new plan was to have the bloody prig killed as soon as he received the funds and he had dispatched the no longer useful Karen Younge. He was sure Pemberley would then devolve to the sister, who would be his wife by then. Why should he settle for sixty thousand pounds when he could have it all?

As soon as he became master of Pemberley, he would have more than enough money to pay others to kill off the Fitzwilliams. They were like the Darcys, a very wealthy family. Mayhap he would inherit all of their wealth and land if his then-wife was the only living family member.

Of course, once he had used the former Miss Darcy for his own pleasure, until he finally felt like he had taken enough revenge on that blasted family, then she too would have to go, and the last drop of Darcy blood would die with her.

With so much wealth he would be untouchable and then he would live the life of a gentleman at ease for the rest of his life. That vast wealth would allow him to take revenge on anyone who had ever slighted him.

He rubbed his hands at the prospect. He was as sure as he had ever been that his plan was flawless.

~~~~~~~/~~~~~~~

It was very telling to all those who were to continue on to Netherfield Park that Darcy elected to remain at Longbourn. The Bennet sisters alighted and the four Fitzwilliams rode back to Bingley's estate sans Darcy.

He had given some weak excuse about checking on Anna, but none of the Fitzwilliams doubted the true reason was he desired to speak to Bennet about something rather important.

Darcy greeted his sister and the rest of the Bennets before requesting of Mr. Bennet if they could meet in his study. The three returning sisters were heartily surprised to see Lydia in the drawing room, as well as a lady they had never met before.

"Girls and Edward, this is Mrs. McPhee, companion and governess to Kate and Lydia. Mrs. McPhee, my three eldest, Miss Jane Bennet, Miss Elizabeth, and Miss Mary. This gentleman is my brother, Mr. Edward Gardiner of London." Bows and curtsies were exchanged.

Seeing the transformation in Lydia since they departed just over ten days ago, the three eldest Bennet sisters knew there was a story to be told. None of them were indecorous and would not ask in front of Lydia or the companion.

"We brought you girls some ribbons and fabric from my

warehouse," Gardiner informed his youngest two nieces.

"Thank you, Uncle Edward, where is Aunt Maddie and our cousins?" Kate enquired.

Lydia looked to Mrs. McPhee who nodded. "Thank you for your generous gifts, Uncle Edward," Lydia stated in a moderated voice.

"You are both very welcome," Gardiner responded. "To your question Kate, your aunt is with your cousins in the park; they needed to stretch their legs after being confined to the carriage."

She looked to the companion again and then Lydia turned to her three eldest sisters. "Jane and Mary please allow me to wish you happy in finding such good men to whom you are engaged. At the same time, would all of you please pardon me for all of my past offences against you."

"Thank you Lyddie, and of course, you are forgiven," Jane granted.

"The same for me and thank you for apologising," Elizabeth responded.

"Richard and I appreciate your good wishes and I too pardon you," Mary added.

Lydia looked relieved and she received a look of approval from the companion which resulted in a ghost of a smile from the youngest Bennet.

"Mrs. McPhee, may we go see our aunt and cousins in the park?" Kate requested after checking with Anna if she wanted to join them.

"As long as your mother does not object, I do not," Mrs. McPhee replied in a heavily accented Scottish brogue.

"Please go ahead, Mrs. McPhee, I see no reason for the girls to remain indoors at present," Fanny allowed.

Without a word of complaint she would not be included in the conversations between her mother and older sisters as had been her wont in the past, Lydia followed Kate, Anna, and the companion out of the drawing room.

All three remaining Bennet sisters looked to their mother. "What?" Fanny questioned innocently. "Is there something you three want to know or are you ready to tell me about your time in Kent and London?"

"Mama!" they all chorused exasperatedly. They were not used to their mother teasing them.

"You want to know what occurred for the change you see in Lydia, do you not?" The sisters nodded vigorously. "It was all by chance. The day after you three departed for Kent," Fanny began, "Mrs. McPhee came to Longbourn. She said she had been travelling from Scotland to London and the way she had travelled on the post brought her to Meryton. She was walking about, as she had a few hours before the next post to London, and heard Lady Lucas and Mrs. Long talking about our search for a companion and governess in one.

"Seeing that she was on her way to London to seek exactly that kind of employment, she asked for directions to Longbourn and arrived at our door. She had glowing characters, and what attracted us more than anything was her experience with children who did not behave as they should. Your father sent expresses to two of her characters he selected randomly, and the answers reiterated what they had written."

"You and Papa obviously employed her, but how did she get Lydia to change to the degree she evidently has?" Elizabeth pressed.

"Your father and I were about to ask the lady to call again once we had heard from those to whom we wrote. She had another suggestion," Fanny revealed. "Mrs. McPhee requested to be allowed to spend two hours with Lydia. Now, I will never know what was said in the nursery, but just before the time was up, Mrs. McPhee followed Lydia into the drawing room where your youngest sister proceeded to give detailed apologies to your father and me." Fanny paused. "We employed the woman on the spot. Her only condition was we were not to try and force a confidence regarding what was said in the nursery. She said if Lydia chose to tell, then she would have no objection. Lydia has not and we have kept our word and not pressed her on the subject."

"If I believed in magic, I would ascribe that to the change I saw, but magic does not exist," Elizabeth asserted.

"Not magic, but luck which brought Mrs. McPhee to us. I need not know what she told Lydia, all I know is my brash flirtatious girl who was on the road to ruin is now a much more demure young lady," Fanny insisted. "Do you girls know what business William has with your father?"

"I know not, Mama," Jane replied honestly.

Thankfully for Elizabeth, her mother did not ask her that question as she would not have lied to her.

~~~~~~~/~~~~~~~

"When young men in your family request to see me in private it is to ask for the hand of one of my daughters," Bennet drawled. "Are you here to tell me Lizzy has accepted your hand in marriage?"

"She has indeed accepted…" Darcy paused amusedly as he watched Bennet's eyebrows shoot up in concern. It was nice to make sport of Bennet for once rather than be the target of his humour. "…a request to enter into an official courtship," Darcy completed.

He almost guffawed watching Bennet visibly relax. "You will do for her," Bennet admitted, "I used to think you devoid of a sense of humour, but I see now just how wrong I was. You have my consent and blessing for your courtship with Lizzy."

"Thank you, Bennet, it is most appreciated," Darcy stood and extended his hand.

"If you eventually win her hand, just treat her as she deserves to be treated," Bennet stated as he shook the hand of the man who he was sure would be his son one day—and apparently in the not too far distant future if Lizzy's looks towards Darcy were anything to go by.

In intellect and interests, they were extremely well matched, and Bennet knew Lizzy would never accept a man she felt she could not love and respect.

"Come. Let us go make this official," Bennet stated as he came around the desk and led the way out of his study.

As the two men entered the drawing room, they heard the Bennet matron exclaim. "Well bless me. You are to be the mistress of a huge estate, are you not?" Fanny questioned.

"Yes, Mama, I am," Mary confirmed.

"What is this about?" Bennet enquired.

Mary related the news about Anne's gifts and the fact all was registered with the court. She told how they had visited Fitzwilliam House in London and how everything except the furniture in the master's chamber was to be sold by their Uncle Edward.

"I assume the changes will be reflected in the new settlement." Bennet cogitated for a moment or two. "So that is why Fitzwilliam wants to replace the one Philips drew up for him."

Mary nodded her agreement. "Richard will be present at Longbourn in a few short hours, and I know he has a copy for you to review."

Somehow, his three eldest daughters were destined to one day be mistresses of three great estates. In addition, Jane would be a countess at some point in the future. Bennet knew Fanny hoped, as he did, that would come to pass many years, decades, from now. Ever since meeting the Matlocks, he and his wife had grown very close to them.

"While we digest Mary's and Fitzwilliam's good fortune, I have an announcement. Mr. Darcy has offered Lizzy a courtship and she has accepted," Bennet revealed.

For some moments, Fanny was struck dumb. As she was sitting and grasping the enormity of the news, the group from the park entered the drawing room. Lilly and Eddy, twelve and nine respectively, greeted their Aunt and Uncle Bennet.

"What has Mama so shocked?" Kate enquired. Bennet repeated the news he had just shared with everyone in the drawing room.

"But I should be next after Mary..." Lydia, displaying a little of her old self, interjected before she clamped her hands over her mouth. She looked around the room her eyes settling on Mrs. McPhee who gave her a warning look. "Please grant me your pardon, I spoke out of turn."

"My goodness!" Fanny exclaimed. "Lizzy and William, who would have thought it?"

"I knew it!" Jane and Mary said at the same time. They giggled at saying the same thing simultaneously.

"Richard and I saw something occurred when we all walked along Rotten Row yesterday," Mary shared.

"Andrew and I saw that as well," Jane added, "and then they would say nothing at Matlock House yester-evening after William spoke to Lizzy in the parlour."

"We did not want to be presumptuous and say something before William spoke to Papa," Elizabeth explained apologetically.

"Of course, we understand, silly," Jane responded as she drew Elizabeth into a hug.

Mary soon replaced their eldest sister. "I am so happy for you Lizzy," she stated. "Richard told me some time back he believed you two would be ideal for each other."

"If you marry Mr. Darcy you will live only five miles from where I grew up, in Lambton," Madeline informed her second eldest niece when she took her turn to hug Lizzy.

"You grew up in Lambton?" Anna enquired keenly.

"Have you ever been to Pemberley, Mrs. Gardiner?"

"Yes, I used to accompany my mother on occasion when she would visit your mother, Lady Anne," Madeline revealed.

It did not take long for the two Darcys to be seated next to Madeline as she related her memories and impressions of their mother. For William, it was a welcome reminder of a time when his mother was with him. Anna was thrilled, as she always was to hear stories about her mother who she had been far too young to remember.

An hour later, the two Darcys were on their way back to Netherfield Park, but not before William had secured the first and supper sets with Elizabeth. He also reserved a set with Aunt Fanny, Jane, and Mary.

For once he intended to enjoy a ball like he had never before.

~~~~~~~/~~~~~~~

"I am told Wickham has not written any more letters to you in the time we were in Kent and London, as far as I know, you have not attempted to warn him, have you?" Richard asked as he sat opposite Mrs. Younge in the small sitting room opposite her bedchamber.

"No I have not," Karen insisted. "I was played for a fool by that man, but never again. If it were not to see him because you have demanded it, I would never want to be in his company again."

"Wickham has always had the ability to make friends, however keeping them has never been something he is able to do," Richard stated almost wistfully.

Everything was in place for the militia's arrival. He was convinced Mrs. Younge would play her part and then he could forget about the miscreant and think only of Mary and his upcoming wedding.

As he left the sitting room, he nodded to the maid who had been Mrs. Younge's constant companion since all had been revealed as well as the footmen on duty in the hallway outside of the bedchamber.

He made his way down to the main drawing room to join Bingley, the Hursts, his parents, and Andrew for tea. He was looking forward to the ball on the morrow. Especially as he finally felt there was enough strength in his leg to dance.

Mary had granted him the first, supper, and final sets. He could only hope his leg would support him for all three sets of dances. He had heard Andy secure the same sets with Jane as well.

From the conversation between his mother and Mrs. Hurst it seemed all the arrangements for the ball were in place, and much to Bingley's pleasure, more than enough white soup had been made.

One thing Richard could not puzzle was who Bingley would open the ball with, but he did inform the residents of his leased estate he had secured a partner for the first, in addition to other sets. As he was being coy regarding who the lady was, all the rest of the party could do was guess.

CHAPTER 31

As Richard and Mary took the position just below Jane and Andrew in the line, and above Lizzy and William, he was still wondering with whom Bingley would open the ball. Neither Andrew nor William had a clue as to the identity of the woman given how tight-lipped Bingley had been.

He had to admit they had been much distracted with their own business and had not been able to spend very much time with Bingley. Richard wondered if she was another blond-haired, willowy, blue-eyed angel or if Bingley had taken his words to heart and had begun to look past a lady's external looks to how she was within.

The musicians played a few bars of music to signal the imminent start of the first dance of the opening set. The six members of the three couples all looked on in surprise as Bingley led Miss Charlotte Lucas to stand opposite him at the head of the line. The Hursts were next to them.

Charlotte was glowing with happiness as she lined up opposite Mr. Bingley. Her three friends were lined up just past Mrs. Hurst, all looking at her questioningly. Miss Lucas gave them a nod of acknowledgement as they would all have much to speak about on the morrow.

Richard was impressed. Not only had Bingley looked beyond the superficial outside of a person, that is not to say Miss Lucas was homely, she was not, but he had seemed to have chosen a woman of good sense and intelligence. They were practically the same age, but that did not seem to be an impediment between them. There was no missing the tender looks being exchanged between the two.

Mrs. Hurst nodded to the leader of the group of local musicians, and they began to play. The ball had commenced. With the first bar of the Boulanger, the line of dancers, who had formed the requisite circles, came alive.

Given the nature of the dance, there was no chance to have any conversation during the first dance. After a short break, the second dance of the first set was Mr. Beveridge's Maggot, which did lend itself to opportunities for speaking to one's partner.

For the first few moments of the dance, Richard said nothing to his beloved Mary. "My mother and Mrs. Hurst decorated the ballroom very well, did they not?" Richard asked when the steps brought him together with Mary.

"They did," Mary responded succinctly. Thereafter, they were quiet the next few times the dance brought them together.

"It is *your* turn to say something now, Mary dearest. I talked about the decorations, and *you* ought to make some sort of remark on the size of the room, or the number of couples."

She smiled, "I assure you Richard, whatever you wish me to say will be said. I am yours to command, Colonel my Colonel."

"Very well. That reply will do for the present. Perhaps by and by I may observe that private balls are much pleasanter than public ones. But *now* we may be silent," Richard teased his beloved.

"Do you talk by rule while you are dancing?" Mary teased back.

"Sometimes. One must speak a little, you know. It would look odd for an engaged couple to be entirely silent for half an hour together; and yet for the advantage of *some*, conversation ought to be so arranged that they may have the trouble of saying as little as possible."

"Are you consulting your own feelings in the present case, or do you imagine you are gratifying mine?" Mary enquired archly.

"Both," replied Richard with a wide smile; "for I have always seen a great similarity in the turn of our minds. We are both of a social, open disposition, willing to speak, even if we do not expect to say something that will amaze the whole room." They were separated by the steps of the dance again.

"This is a very striking resemblance of your own character, I am sure," said she. "How near it may be to *mine*, I cannot pretend to say. *You* think it a faithful portrait undoubtedly."

For some steps, they moved around others in the line and then came back together. Mary continued. "I have never been as social as you are, but that is one of the things in which we complement one another well."

"Like William and Lizzy do," Richard opined. "With them, the roles are reversed. Lizzy being the one to bring humour and society to my taciturn cousin." Mary nodded her agreement.

For the second set, Richard and Andrew exchanged partners while Darcy danced with Mrs. Hurst and her husband partnered Elizabeth. Bingley paired with one of the Long sisters.

The supper set saw the same pairings for those who had made up the first five couples of the first set. If eyebrows had been raised when Bingley had danced the first set with Miss Lucas, seeing him stand up with her for the supper set caused the eyebrows of most in attendance to disappear under their hairlines.

There was no missing the smug look on Lady Lucas's countenance as she watched her eldest dance with an extremely eligible man. Charlotte and Mr. Bingley had begged her indulgence in not broadcasting their connection abroad to allow them to get to know one another without the staring and questions that would follow public knowledge of Miss Lucas having a suitor.

Fanny Bennet was very pleased for her friend as she had known how worried Sarah Lucas was that Charlotte was on the shelf. She looked over and saw Maria Lucas dancing with the Goulding heir. As she watched she thought about her two youngest daughters who were at home.

It was the right thing to put them back in. They, along with Anna, were at home with Mrs. McPhee and although Lydia had looked a little disappointed she would not be attending the ball, not a word of protest had been uttered when those attending the ball had departed.

Sitting down for supper, the three Bennet sisters looked at Charlotte quizzically while the men were making plates for their partners. "This is neither the time nor the place," Charlotte stated quietly. "As I am after any ball, I will be at Longbourn to see you in the morning."

The three Bennet sisters nodded their understanding and the conversation turned to how each of them was enjoying the night. Also discussed was the fact the Bennet parents had danced both the first and supper sets with one another. None in attendance could remember the last time they had seen the mistress and master of Longbourn dance with each other, even a single time.

While Bingley was filling the two plates, Richard came and stood next to him. "I am very proud of you, Bingley, you have chosen a woman of substance and not based on some superficial criteria," Richard said so only Bingley could hear.

"If you had not made me look at the shallowness of my prior behaviour with regards to women, I may have missed seeing the gem which is Charlotte. Thank you for that Fitzwilliam," Bingley replied, "I forgot to mention, Caroline arrived safely in Scarborough and seems to have accepted her residence there with good cheer, according to my aunt." Bingley then picked up the two plates and made his way back to the table where his lady was seated.

"William, did my mother tell you she has an excellent candidate for Anna's companion, a Mrs. Annesley," Richard stated after those at their table had completed their meals.

"No, I have not been able to speak to Aunt Elaine about the topic yet," Darcy responded. He gave a look of contrition. "Unlike the previous time, I am more than willing to accept her assistance in finding an appropriate companion for Anna."

"We all make mistakes, William," Elizabeth soothed quietly next to his ear as she placed her hand on William's arm. "Lord knows, I have made my share of them."

Darcy smiled as he felt himself relax. He knew not how Elizabeth had the uncanny ability to say or do the thing he needed at exactly the right time, but she did, and he would forever be grateful for that.

When it was time for young ladies to exhibit before the post-supper dancing commenced, some young ladies from the neighbourhood did so, then Mrs. Hurst played Beethoven's Andante in F, rather masterfully.

Once Mrs. Hurst had completed her selection, Mary sat at the instrument with Jane and Elizabeth standing next to her. Mary began to play *Ask If Yon Damask Rose* while Jane and Elizabeth sang the words beautifully. Jane's mezzo-soprano blended perfectly with Elizabeth's contralto.

The two fiancés and one suitor were mesmerized by the artistry of their respective ladies. Mary's playing was masterful, infused full of feelings, and Andrew and Darcy could not remember hearing better singing, even in London.

At the end of the rendition, the applause was thunderous and even though there were many calls of encore, the ladies demurred while expressing their gratitude for the appreciation shown by those at the ball.

~~~~~~~/~~~~~~~

As tempting as it had been to request the final set from Elizabeth, Darcy did not. They were not engaged—yet. Something he hoped would not be long in coming. As much as he desired to dance with Elizabeth again, especially as the final dance of the set would be a waltz, he knew propriety dictated he not request a third set from her.

While she understood why William could not engage her for the final set, it did not lessen Elizabeth's desire to have him stand up with her for those two dances. How she would have revelled in the closeness between them had they danced the waltz.

She was able to smooth over her disappointment with two consolations. William would sit and talk to her during the set so although not dancing, Elizabeth would not be bereft of his company. The other was once he offered for her, something she found herself anticipating, they would be able to dance three sets together.

Jane and Mary had no such restrictions, and both were most pleased to be lining up opposite her respective fiancé when the final set was called. Seeing Jane opposite her viscount and Mary standing across from the former Colonel was expected.

What was completely unexpected to the denizens of Meryton was seeing Thomas Bennet lead his wife to the floor for the final dances. He looked happy to be with his wife and she was blushing like the Fanny Gardiner from years past when she had first danced with the man who would become her husband.

"Mary, have I told you how gorgeous you look?" Richard asked while they waited for the musicians to begin playing.

"Once or twice," Mary returned with an arched eyebrow.

"I am the luckiest man in the world to be marrying you in but a few days," Richard stated as he looked into Mary's eyes.

"Which fact makes me the most fortunate woman in the world who will have you as her husband soon enough," Mary responded, love shining from her eyes as she looked at the man she loved with all she was.

Before any more words could be uttered between the engaged couple, the music began, and the dancers took their first steps of the minuet.

"If only we had known Richard earlier and he had shocked my parents out of their respective malaises years ago," Elizabeth sighed as she watched her mother and father dancing. "Better still if they had been always as they are now."

"My cousin has been waking many up to the folly of their ways," Darcy stated introspectively, "I count myself among them."

"In a few days he will be my brother," Elizabeth pointed out. "For so long I have dreamt of having a brother and now it will become a reality, except rather than one I will have two of them."

'Hopefully, Andrew, Richard, and I will be brothers before too much time has passed,' Darcy mused silently.

He had no way of knowing it, but Elizabeth was having the identical thought regarding William and her soon-to-be brothers.

For the rest of the final set, they spoke of inconsequential things. When the waltz had been completed, the guests were complimentary in the extreme regarding the quality of the ball, as they began to depart.

The Bennets were not the first people to depart but were somewhere in the middle. It should have come as no surprise to discover the final ones to leave Netherfield Park that night was the Lucas family.

~~~~~~~/~~~~~~~

When Charlotte and Maria Lucas arrived at Longbourn,

a little after eleven the next morning, they found the five Bennet sisters and Miss Darcy in the park. The youngest three were taking turns pushing one another on the swing while the older three sat on some benches in the shade of the trees.

Maria, who was close to Kate and Lydia, made for the swing and Charlotte joined her three friends. She sat down on the bench with Elizabeth. Charlotte looked at each of her friends and was greeted with arched eyebrows, all gifting her their questioning looks.

"Have we been so busy with our own concerns we did not notice you and Mr. Bingley had become close?" Jane enquired.

"While that may be partially true, the major portion of your not knowing falls to decisions Charl...Mr. Bingley and I took," Charlotte began and then stopped herself. "You three know I met him at the assembly where he opened the dancing with me. At the time he chose me because he was aware Jane was beyond his reach—something he only told me once your engagement to Lord Hilldale became public knowledge."

The three Bennet sisters nodded as they knew of what Charlotte spoke. "The dinner we missed at Lucas Lodge!" Elizabeth exclaimed. "That is when you saw him next, was it not?"

"Eliza has the right of it," Charlotte agreed. "We ended up speaking for most of the evening, except for when we had the meal. He told me what Mr. Fitzwilliam said to open his eyes to his shallow requirements for a lady. The more we spoke the more we discovered that our characters aligned.

"Not too many days later he asked to call on me and I requested we do so in private. After my disappointment with Mr. Kincaid, I was determined not to be ridiculed again for being jilted, hence my request to keep our relationship to ourselves."

"You also said you would never allow yourself to fall in

love again, but I see an unmistakable glow of happiness about your person," Jane observed.

"I did say that, did I not? Along with claims that I am not a romantic. Against all of the odds, we fell in love with each other," Charlotte revealed. "The more we got to know one another, the more we discovered how well we fit together. Charles requested a courtship from me a few weeks ago, right around the time the Colonel and Mary became engaged."

"Charlotte are you being courted or are you now engaged?" Mary queried.

"We became engaged at the ball," Charlotte revealed as her colour heightened greatly. "During the final set, which neither of us wanted to dance as we could not dance it with each other, Charles proposed to me, and I agreed. My parents agreed to remain until the last of the guests left so Charles could address Papa. He did and Papa granted his blessing. We did not want to announce it at the ball celebrating your engagements."

"Now I remember, I did not see you dancing the final set, yet neither did I see you on the sides of the dancefloor," Elizabeth recalled.

"We—we were on one of the balconies," Charlotte admitted with a deep blush.

Before Charlotte knew what she was about, she had been pulled into a four-way hug between herself and the three eldest Bennet sisters.

Once all of the wishes for happiness had been conveyed the four friends took their places on the benches. "When will you marry?" Jane questioned.

"We have not discussed that yet," Charlotte averred.

While the new engagement was being discussed, Elizabeth spied the Lucas carriage arriving and Lady Lucas alighted. "Mama and Papa are about to find out what we just did." Elizabeth cocked her head towards Lady Lucas.

After discussing the ball and how much each of them enjoyed it, the sisters and Charlotte collected the four younger girls and they all made their way into the house for tea. Charlotte received hearty and sincere congratulations from Mrs. Bennet and the two younger Bennets.

CHAPTER 32

Friday morning Colonel Forster's regiment of the Derbyshire Militia marched smartly down Meryton's main street. The way his regiment was seen was a point of pride for the Colonel who commanded them.

Lieutenant George Wickham could not remember feeling more excited seeing that he was on the cusp of all his plans coming to fruition. He would need to exercise a modicum of patience before he took himself to the inn to collect the letter he was sure would be there telling him where and when to meet Karen and her charge.

By this time on the morrow, he would be on his way to Gretna Green. Karen would have some coin which would be used to rent a carriage to take them thither.

Poor fool that she was, she thought she would be accompanying him all the way. Once they were more than a day away from Meryton and in the middle of the countryside, he would push her out of the moving conveyance. If she happened to die when she hit the ground, so much the better. Dead people tell no tales.

Before he did that, he would make sure Miss Darcy had been administered a laudanum-laced drink. When she awoke the next morning, she would be told Mrs. Younge had decided to visit family rather than travel all the way to Scotland.

As Wickham marched next to the soldiers in his company, he eyed the shops with regret. It was just as well he would be leaving on the morrow because he was certain the infernal Colonel would warn the merchants here against issuing credit the same way he had in Leicestershire, so there would be no credit extended.

As soon as he in remembered all the money to which he would have access, his regret over not being able to purchase on credit lessened, however, gaining things without having to pay for them was still superior in his mind.

There was no mistaking how many pretty girls lived in the area who would have been ripe for the plucking had he intended to remain here. One night was not enough time for him to convince one she was in love with him. Then again, Wickham scowled, the bastard of a colonel would start spreading his warnings if he had not done so already.

Denny had told of all the pleasant people at the dinner the Colonel had given for the gentlemen of the area while they had been scouting for a location for the encampment. At first, he had not being paying attention, but later, he had heard another officer talking about the dinner.

Wickham had felt momentarily panicked and returned to his friend to ask who was at the dinner. He had relaxed when Denny related that none of the men from Netherfield Park, which Wickham knew was where Karen was with the prig and his cousin, had been able to attend.

At last, the Colonel marched them into the new encampment. As soon as Wickham was able, he told his sergeant to get the men situated in their tents and he made his way back into the town and directly to the Red Lion Inn.

On asking, the landlord was pointed out to him. "Do you have a letter for George Wickham?" he asked trying his best to mask his excitement.

"Aye, the lady dropped it off this morning," the landlord replied. He reached below the counter and handed the letter to the officer.

As it had never been carried by the post, there was no

postage due, which made Wickham happy. The more of his dwindling coin he could retain, the better. He smiled thinking about how he would be able to sell the jewellery he was sure the young Miss Darcy would have with her in order to give him some money until he was handed her dowry.

Rather than the taproom for an ale, Wickham made all speed to return to his tent. Thank goodness he was to leave on the morrow. In the last encampment, the officers' quarters were in a structure. Here, however, he would have to suffer the degradation of sleeping in a tent for the one night he would be in this nowhere town. At least as an officer he had a tent to himself and did not have to share the space like the soldiers.

He closed the tent flap and sat on the chair. Thankfully one had been placed in the tent of each officer. First, he lit a candle and then he hungrily broke the seal and began to read.

17 August 1810

My dearest George,

As you are reading this it means you are finally here! I cannot wait to see you again my one and only true love.

As he always did, Wickham scoffed when he read the sentiments Karen expressed. He had well and truly fooled the silly woman. He went back to the note.

My charge is being hosted at a neighbouring estate, which is but 1 mile from the town. I convinced your enemies it was good for her to be with young ladies her own age.

She is fully prepared for your arrival so there will be little for you to do to have your plan succeed. She has been extremely malleable which means she will not give us any trouble as we travel to Scotland.

Each morning I have walked with Miss Darcy, so when we do so on the morrow, no one will think it is anything out of the ordinary. The young ladies who live at the estate do not rise at the time we walk out; hence, it will be only the two of us you will see.

We will leave the Longbourn estate at 8 in the morning. We walk to Oakham Mount (you can get directions from anyone in Meryton) and arrive there by half after the hour. On the Meryton side of the hill there is a stand of trees with a clearing. We will be within.

__A warning__: Your enemy and his cousin often ride in the morning, and they return to Netherfield Park at about the time my charge and I depart. Do not come early! If you do there will be a good chance they will see you and then everything we have worked towards so assiduously will be for naught.

Thank goodness Karen had told him about the prig's and his cousin's habit of riding in the morning. She had the right of it. Imagine after all his meticulous planning to be thwarted by being seen by one of them on the very day his revenge would begin to be extracted. Even though he would cast her aside, there was no arguing that Karen did have her uses.

Just as an aside, I do not know when you saw Miss Darcy last, but she is much taller than you remember her. In fact, she is a little taller than I am.

I will see you in the morning my George and you will finally receive your due.

With all the love you deserve from me,

Karen

He could not wait for the nighttime hours to pass until time to depart in the morning. Once he was married, he would claim his money and then as soon as he had employed men for the purpose, Darcy would die. It would be poetic justice—his death would be funded by money from his own coffers. This way his hands would be clean.

Wickham left his tent; the letter secured in an inside pocket of his uniform jacket. It was important he be seen to be following his normal routine. Part of that routine was eating with his fellow officers.

It was the final time he would have to lower himself to eat the slop they served. He made sure outwardly he behaved in the same way he had since joining the regiment.

Later that evening, he forced himself to lie down on the cot in his tent. He needed his wits about him in the morning so he had to manage as much sleep as possible.

~~~~~~~/~~~~~~~

Sleeping past sunrise was not a possibility for George Wickham. Normally he was one who hated rising early—one of his biggest complaints in the militia—but this morning, he could not be up early enough.

As much as he wanted to rush to the meeting spot, he knew he needed to be careful and patient. Karen's words of warning still swam before his eyes. To be safe, he would plan to be at the meeting place just after the time Karen had indicated.

Although the time for the officers to break their fasts was at nine, the cook did have coffee and some baked goods available for officers who had duty overnight. Wickham made his way into the officers' mess tent and helped himself to a cup of coffee and a roll which he slathered with butter.

He kept an eye on his fob watch—one which had been stolen from some unsuspecting man at an inn in London—as the hands inched closer and closer to eight.

He calculated if he left at that hour, it would give him time to get directions from someone in the town and then arrive at the desired time. To him, it seemed time had slowed and the second and minute hands were moving far slower than normal.

At long last the hour hand was on the mark for the eight and the minute hand had finally reached the twelve. Wickham took a last bite of his roll, a final swig of the coffee, and then wiped his hands clean on a serviette. He stood and walked out of the tent relishing in the knowledge he would never be returning to the damned militia camp again.

The encampment was a half mile south of the town which did not take Wickham long to walk. He walked to the smithy and asked for directions to Oakham Mount. The man happily pointed to an eminence a little over a mile to the northeast of the town. With a cheerful thank you to the blacksmith, Wickham set out for the hill.

Wickham arrived not long after half after the hour and quickly saw the stand of trees Karen had described in her letter. He cocked his head to one side as he stood and listened. There were no sounds of riders on horses, and then for good measure, he looked around and saw no one.

All the while looking around him, just in case, Wickham walked until he reached the treeline. He looked ahead and could see the stand was a few trees deep. Beyond them was the clearing which had been described in Karen's letter. He saw a flash of colour within.

He was about to advance to the clearing when he felt a hand on his arm. His free hand instinctively reached for the pistol he had secured in his waistband.

"George, it is me," Karen assured him.

Identifying her voice and then turning to see her, Wickham withdrew his arm and left the pistol where it was. "It is so good to see you, my dear," Wickham drawled. "Why are you not in the clearing?"

"We have a problem; Miss Darcy heard her brother and cousin talking about a time you placed a thorn under old Mr. Darcy's saddle and then there was something about your killing your own father. She is scared to meet you now," Karen reported.

Karen Younge saw the moment the charming façade was dropped, and a flinty hard look replaced it on his face. "Yes, I killed my own father because he betrayed me, part of his crimes against me was saving old Mr. Darcy. That man should have died by my hand as well," Wickham hissed. "You need to convince her all is well. If I was willing to kill my own father, what do you think I would do to you if you failed me?"

"Give me two minutes to talk to her and I will assuage her fears," Karen said timidly.

"Go," Wickham commanded.

He watched as she slipped past the trees and into the clearing. She approached where he had seen the colours within, and it seemed she had an earnest conversation with her charge. Wickham could hear the hum of voices, but not what was being said.

After what seemed an interminable time, which was in fact less than two minutes, he heard Karen call him. '*Good,*' he told himself, '*she took my threat seriously.*' Wickham made his way towards the clearing.

While he walked, he could see Karen and the tall, blonde Miss Darcy next to her as he got closer. Just before he entered the clearing, he had to go around two trees causing him to lose visual contact with his paramour and her charge. He cleared the trees, entered the clearing, and froze as his blood turned to ice in his veins.

Rather than Karen and Miss Darcy, before him stood Darcy, the two Fitzwilliam brothers, Colonel Forster, and a half dozen other officers and soldiers. The militiamen all had their weapons trained on him.

Escape was his only option, so Wickham turned on his heel and tried to run back the way he had come. He could not understand how he ran into a tree, until he realised it was not a tree but a huge mountain of a man.

There were two of them and before he could try to run in a different direction, each of the enormous men grabbed one of his arms. One of them reached in and removed the pistol from Wickham's waistband, made a thorough search to make sure he had no more weapons secreted on his person, and then the two dragged him back towards those in the clearing.

"Why are you detaining me? All I did was take a walk to see the views from Oakham Mount," Wickham claimed. How could they prove otherwise? Karen would never talk.

"You are to be tried for at least two crimes—so far," Richard drawled.

"What crimes?" Wickham asked innocently.

"We all," Richard made a sweeping motion with his arm to indicate all of the men present, "heard you admit to murdering your father and for the attempted murder of my late Uncle Robert," Richard listed.

"Of course, the attempted kidnapping of a gentlewoman could be a third charge if it were needed," Darcy growled.

"And before you are transferred to the Old Bailey, I will be taking some skin off your back with forty lashes for wilfully lying to gain a free commission, breaking the pledge of honour you signed, and conduct unbecoming of an officer," Forster barked.

He stepped forward and ripped the insignia of Wickham's rank from the epaulets of the former Lieutenant's uniform jacket.

"Wickham meet my ward," Richard spat out derisively.

A lad of twelve stepped forward in his becoming gown, shawl, and blond wig. He was the son of the smithy who had directed Wickham to the mount. A thousand pounds and a promise his son would never be in harm's way had convinced the blacksmith to agree to allow his son to be the bait in the net.

By this point, Wickham's knees were growing weak and he would have had a hard time standing on his own legs had he not been held up by the giant men on either side of him.

Everything had been planned! He had manipulated Karen perfectly! How was it he was in such dire straits now?

"If you are wondering how you came to be caught so easily, mayhap I will tell you later when we come and speak to the magistrate at the gaol." Richard turned to his friend. "Forster, do you think you can hold off flogging him until the morrow?"

Colonel Forster made a show of having to consider the request carefully. "Until the morning, yes." Forster closed the distance to the shaking man until his face was inches away from Wickham's. "Under normal circumstances, I detest having to flog any of my men, but in your case, you are no longer one of my men and I have never met a man who deserves his due more than you." Forster turned and began to tell Captain Carter to get the men ready to return to the encampment.

"You wanted your due, now you will receive it," Richard told the reeling miscreant.

They were going to have him hung! Wickham almost soiled himself at that thought. He was supposed to be the one who ended them!

The men who he had heard Fitzwilliam call Biggs and Johns, lifted his feet clear of the ground while another clapped manacles onto each of his ankles. Next irons were fitted to his wrists and the two big men lifted him and walked out of the clearing with his feet dangling uselessly below him.

He was roughly tossed into the back of a donkey drawn cart. Before it moved, the two enormous men slipped onto the cart—one on the bench the other in the bed next to Wickham. One of them nodded to the driver and they were off.

A ten-minute ride later, Wickham was thrown into his temporary new home, a cell in the Meryton town gaol.

CHAPTER 33

The instant Wickham had been locked in his temporary home, the men had dropped off the lad along with the draft with the blacksmith and his wife, who were beyond pleased young Jim had not a scratch on him just like the Colonel had promised them. The money was welcome, but nothing was worth their son being harmed.

From there they rode most of the one mile at a gallop, slowing down to a walk before passing the gateposts indicating Longbourn's land, giving their three stallions a walk along the quarter mile drive so they could cool down after the gallop.

"As you can see we are all unharmed, and young Jim, the smithy's son, was never closer than ten yards to the criminal," Richard reported when he and the other men arrived back at Longbourn.

"Nevertheless, it is gratifying to see you are well with our own eyes," Mary told her fiancé. "Mother and Father are with Anna in the drawing room visiting our parents and younger sisters."

"Did the blackguard put up any resistance?" Elizabeth questioned.

"No, Biggs disarmed him before he knew what was happening," Darcy related. Then he grinned. "I have never seen him look so terrified as he did when he was grabbed by Biggs and Johns. Those two can strike the fear of God into anyone they choose."

"Do you ladies mind of we join those in the drawing room to tell all?" Andrew suggested. "That way we will not need to repeat the story."

The three Bennet sisters, who had met their respective men on Longbourn's drive, nodded their agreement. The men followed the sisters into the drawing room.

"Yes Mother, as you see we are all unharmed," Richard assured his mother seeing her questioning look as soon as he, Andrew, and William entered the room. "And the lad as well, we returned him to his parents without so much as a scratch on his person."

"Well, what occurred?" Lord Matlock demanded.

"It was all according to plan..." Richard began but the other two who had been present for Wickham's capture added parts as they felt it was needed.

The Earl whistled with incredulity. "That depraved man willingly admitted to attempting to hurt my late brother and to the murder of his father?"

"He did. After my friend has taken a piece of Wickham's flesh and as soon as he has healed, he will be moved to the Old Bailey. Unfortunately, the next assizes in Hertford is more than two months distant, hence the choice to send him to London," Richard explained.

"Can he not be court martialled so he will not be able to try and tarnish Anna's reputation?" Bennet asked.

"No, he cannot be, unfortunately," Richard responded. "The degenerate never broke any military laws which would warrant one. Anna's name will not be mentioned though. There is more than enough with the murder and attempted murder to end his preying on innocents across the realm. There will be no mention of an attempted kidnapping."

"We all agree with Richard that there is no need to mention what he intended for Anna," Darcy stated in support.

"How could someone Papa used to support want to harm me in that way?" Anna asked despondently.

Darcy had wanted to protect his sister from the knowledge of the plot against her, but Richard had disagreed stating she needed to know there was evil like this in the world which would only assist in protecting her in the future.

It did not take Darcy long to realise Richard had the right of it. Hence, he had withdrawn any opposition to Anna being told all.

"Because Anna dear," Fanny took the distressed girl's hand, "there are unfortunately men, and women, in the world who are innately evil and try to gain what they desire by any means, usually foul and never fair. In future, you will know to question motivations of those who befriend you so you may determine if their motives are pure."

Bennet was beyond proud of his wife. Fanny had given a well-reasoned and cogent explanation to their adopted niece. Since they had both woken up and had begun to change, they also began sleeping in the same bed again. Bennet smiled as he thought of this fact. They should have never stopped being together since before Lydia was born. They had denied themselves the pleasures of the flesh for fifteen years. No more!

"Thank you, Aunt Fanny, that makes me feel somewhat better," Georgiana replied. "In that case, he deserves whatever punishment he receives."

Not long after, the soon-to-be extended family enjoyed the midday meal in Longbourn's dining parlour. After the meal, the three men who had been at Wickham's capture mounted their horses for the ride back into Meryton.

~~~~~~~/~~~~~~~

"Are you here to gloat?" Wickham spat out when he saw the three hated men standing on the other side of his gaol cell door.

"No Wickham. That is something in which you would

engage. Unlike you, we are men of honour," Richard bit back. "Only you would concoct a plan which involved using a girl of only fourteen years."

"You owe me," Wickham asserted sullenly.

"For what?" Darcy asked.

"You stole my inheritance..." Wickham began before he was cut off by derisive laughter emanating from all three men looking at him scornfully through the bars which separated them.

"Are you such a simpleton that you have begun to believe your own lies?" Andrew derided.

"Old man Darcy would have left me an estate had you not tittle tattled on me!" Wickham claimed.

"If you believed that, why did you try and murder my uncle with that stunt of placing a thorn under his saddle?" Richard challenged.

Wickham looked away and would not turn towards any of the cousins who were standing and staring at him with disdain.

"Had you convinced yourself you were in his old will and thought killing him would be a quick way to gain what you believed you would be bequeathed? That is the reason you tried the same with William's mount." Richard paused as he cogitated. "You thought you would gain Pemberley that way."

"You fool, all Uncle Robert left you in his previous will was five hundred pounds and the recommendation *if* you graduated and took orders, for the preferment of one of the livings within Pemberley's gift. Killing him and William would have made you a murderer even before you ended your father's life, but it would have gained nothing, except the noose," Andrew stated.

"What did you think marrying Anna would have done for you?" Darcy demanded.

Knowing there was no reason to hold anything back, Wickham turned towards the smug prigs. "If you had not stopped me, after wedding her and claiming her dowry, I would have had all of you killed. Then as Miss Darcy's husband I would have commanded the wealth of the Darcys and Fitzwilliams!"

"You think by marrying Anna, you would have been in line for all of that. You poor delusional fool, you would have received not a penny!" Richard shook his head. The man's avarice had driven all reason from his head. The sad thing was he seemed to believe what he was spouting was fact.

"What do you mean, I would have had her dowry, and then..." Wickham was cut off again.

"You would have had nothing..." Richard explained the terms of his late uncle's will, which would have come into effect the instant Anna married without her guardians' permission and the added sin of an elopement. "Where would you have had the money to employ your assassins? We all know you are far too much of a coward to have done the deeds yourself unless you could sneak into the stables like a thief in the night. You would never have got close enough to any of us to tamper with our tack or horses. Besides you would have been dead."

"How so?" Wickham was reeling. Even had he not been arrested this day; his plans would have come to naught.

"Do you not think we would not have hunted you down and ended you for harming our Anna?" Richard asked menacingly.

Even though there were the bars between them, Wickham shrank back in fear. He situated himself on the corner of the cot furthest from where the three glaring men stood. "You said you would tell me how you anticipated my plan. Did that wench Karen Younge betray me?"

"No, she did not. Your hubris and inability not to tell

tall tales to garner sympathy did," Richard began. "When Lieutenant Denny heard my name..." He told of all which had occurred with Denny up to the letter being turned over to him. "Forster wanted you demoted, flogged, and cashiered out of the regiment, but I explained that would only make you someone else's problem. I asked my *friend* to have you watched at all times. The reason was I wanted you to confess to murdering your father and trying the same with Uncle Robert. Forster's way would only have engendered you pain, as you will discover on the morrow at dawn."

Wickham felt a cold shiver travel the length of his spine as he imagined the Colonel with a cat-o-nine tails in his hand. He could only hope he would faint away after a few stroke so he would not feel all of the pain.

"I wanted to make sure you could never again impose yourself on a young girl, cheat another tradesman of his hard earned money, or harm any more innocents. Mrs. Younge willingly wrote the final two letters to you once she was shown proof of your true self and became convinced she was just one more dupe you were using. What did you plan Wicky? I am sure had you managed to abscond with Anna, Mrs. Younge would not have lived to tell the tale."

Given how close Fitzwilliam was to the truth, Wickham simply looked away, unable to look his former friends in their eyes.

"I thought so. It has always been the same with you. You do not see people as friends, all they are to you are things to be used, abused, and discarded." Richard paused as he felt the growing disgust he had for the man rise in his throat. "You were given the rope to hang yourself and you took it willingly. Who do you think selected the place you were captured earlier today?"

George Wickham did not need to answer the rhetorical question as it was plain Fitzwilliam had been the architect of his doom. He should have known. When they used to play together as boys, more than ninety percent of the time, plans were formed by Fitzwilliam, and his plans were usually flawless. *'Unlike mine!'* he admitted silently to himself.

"You were so unaware of your surroundings; we had more than a dozen men hidden in the trees. Some of them the size of Biggs and Johns, the two who apprehended you, yet you noticed only what we wanted you to notice—Mrs. Younge and the lad who was playing the role of my ward. Our horses were being held on the far side of Oakham Mount so you would not hear any of them nickering." Richard looked at the man in the cell and saw the moment realisation dawned his plans had never had even a small chance of success.

"Surely you will not allow me to hang, Darcy," Wickham used his last card. "Your father did count me as his godson, after all."

"Only because your father rescued him after your stunt with the thorn," Darcy barked. "You should have been hung for attempted murder then. So no, *Wickham*, there will be no pleas for leniency on your behalf. You have made your bed, and now you are the one who must lie in it."

"You always thought what we have came to us easily, but you never understood with privilege and wealth comes great responsibility," Andrew stated. "You could have been so much more than you have become, but you *chose* the path of evil and now you are about to experience the consequences of your bad decisions and criminal actions."

"Miss Darcy's reputation will..." Wickham attempted out of pure desperation.

"My ward's reputation will be untarnished. You will be tried for murder and attempted murder, nothing else," Richard informed the wastrel. "Any mention of Anna will be understood for what it is, the desperate attempt of a murderer to try to mitigate his guilt. The members of the court will be under no illusions of the fact you are a liar, so in any event, no one will give your words any weight."

Wickham knew he had shot his last bolt and it had been very far wide of the target. Unless there was a miracle, his life would not be of a long duration.

~~~~~~~/~~~~~~~

Saturday morning the three cousins were joined at the militia encampment by Lord Matlock, Bennet, Bingley, and Hurst. Just before dawn, Wickham was led to two wooden posts, their bottom portions sunk into the earth.

Wickham was stripped above the waist and then manacled to the posts. His left hand and ankle to one, the right hand an ankle to the other. He was already whimpering before the first stroke had been administered.

The whining of the former officer was drowned out by Forster's booming voice as he read the offences which had led to Wickham's flogging. At Richard's suggestion, Forster had agreed to cut the number of strokes in half to twenty. The miscreant would recover sooner and be on his way to London for trial that much quicker.

Forster removed his uniform jacket and then his adjutant handed him the cat. He pulled his arm back and then brought it forward with force. Wickham screamed in pain as the leather ends tore strips of flesh from his back as blood started to drip from the wounds.

Thankfully, he had fainted dead away after the third lash had been delivered. At the end of the twentieth stroke, two soldiers held the limp form of George Wickham up while two others unlocked the irons from his wrists and ankles.

As Wickham's unconscious person was carried to the medical tent, the men who had been witness to the punishment began to disperse. Except for Bingley, who was on his way to Lucas Lodge with his future father-in-law, the rest of the men from Netherfield Park made for Longbourn where they would all break their fasts.

It had given none of them pleasure to witness Wickham's suffering, but it needed to be done. The next time any of the three cousins or the Earl would see him would be at his trial. If he was found guilty, as they expected he would be, some of them would be there as witnesses when Wickham was sent to meet his maker.

~~~~~~~/~~~~~~~

"Now the unpleasantness is over," Mary stated as she sat next to Richard in the drawing room after everyone at Longbourn had broken their fasts, "we can concentrate on the positive. You will be my husband in less than two days!"

"As you will be my wife, my beloved Mary," Richard responded with pleasure. "Are you looking forward to spending time at my parents' home in Ramsgate for our wedding trip?"

"Very much so," Mary replied excitedly. "Some sea bathing will set me up for life."

"It is still warm enough at this time of the year, so sea bathing there will be," Richard stated.

"It pleases me we are spending the first night of our marriage at Rosings Park," Mary informed her fiancé. "We have not seen Anne since she gifted you the estate and everything else…"

"You mean *us*," Richard insisted.

"As soon as we are married it will be us," Mary corrected. "I am counting the minutes until I marry you," Mary revealed after a slight pause.

"As am I, as am I," Richard agreed.

CHAPTER 34

Regardless of the fact Andrew and Richard would have liked to spend Sunday in the company of their fiancées, it was not to be. At the family dinner held at Netherfield Park on Saturday, Fanny Bennet had sweetly, yet firmly told the Fitzwilliam brothers the next time they saw their respective lady would be when she was walking up the church's aisle towards him.

On this final Sunday before the double wedding, the Netherfield Park Party had worshiped at St. Edward's in Meryton rather than the Longbourn village church where they would be meeting their brides in holy matrimony the next day.

After the ceremony, everyone would be travelling to Netherfield Park for the wedding breakfast. Between the mothers of the brides and grooms the wedding breakfast's arrangements were well in hand. The countess was on hand in case there were any last minute details which needed her attention before the celebratory meal on the morrow.

There was a fair amount of jealousy when, after the meal which had been enjoyed subsequent to returning from church, Darcy and Anna boarded a coach for the three-mile ride to Longbourn.

Darcy had felt somewhat smug that the embargo of not coming to the Bennets' estate did not apply to him. Even more pleasing was Elizabeth inviting Anna and him before she departed Netherfield Park yester-evening.

The love he felt for the magnificently beautiful—inside and out—fascinating, sometimes infuriating, intelligent, impertinent woman burned brighter than Darcy could have ever imagined possible. When he was apart from her, a piece of himself was missing, but when in Elizabeth's company he was complete.

If his getting out and pushing the coach from behind would have caused the three miles to Longbourn to pass faster, Darcy was certain he would have done so. Opinions of others who would see him thusly be damned.

He looked across to the forward facing bench where his sister sat looking happier than he had ever seen her. Being in the company of the Bennet sisters had done wonders for Anna in helping her to leave her extreme shyness behind her.

Since coming to Hertfordshire, Anna no longer demurred or even hesitated to exhibit on the pianoforte when she was asked—even if it was before more than one or two and some of them were not family.

He had been the overly proud nodcock who had not wanted Anna to associate with the Bennets. How much did he not owe Richard for giving him the kicks in his rear-end he had needed to begin to re-evaluate his ways?

When he thought of the disaster which could have been because of his own dunderheaded obstinacy in employing Mrs. Younge and refusing to verify her characters, Darcy stopped himself as he heard the voice of the lady he loved beyond reason in his head telling him her philosophy about the past.

'I hear you Elizabeth my love,' Darcy thought. His pondering the almost disaster with the companion evoked the fresh memories of yester-afternoon when the three of them who had visited the criminal in his gaol cell arrived back at Netherfield Park.

It was time to dismiss Mrs. Younge. Even though she, like many before her, including Darcy's beloved father, had been manipulated by Wickham, her agreeing with his plan had shown a monumental lack of judgement which would never allow her to work as a companion again, and certainly not retain her position in the Darcy household.

Anna's co-guardians had made their way up to the bedchamber where Mrs. Younge had been moved after the scheme had been detected. One of the trusted footmen was on duty in the hall outside of the door.

They did not think she would be so reckless as to try and escape, but Richard had suggested the footmen as a precaution and Darcy had agreed.

"It is good that your trunk is packed, Mrs. Younge, you will be transported back to London today," Darcy had told the former companion. "You will receive your wages up to today, as well as an additional five hundred pounds, which will be handed to you when you arrive at the address you will provide to the coachman."

"I thank you for the reward after I assisted you to capture George…Mr. Wickham, even though you were under no obligation to do so," Mrs. Younge stated gratefully.

"Mrs. Younge, if it were my choice, I would not have paid anything," Richard had responded. He still felt anger at what the woman had agreed to do. "Please remember we could have had you arrested for defrauding my cousin." Richard had paused for a few beats as he brought his anger under control. "You understand we will have men watching and if you ever try to pass yourself off as a companion again, you will feel our wrath. If you are ever tempted to do something you should not, do not forget as a peer, my father is able to sign transportation orders."

Mrs. Younge then solemnly swore she would abide by the terms under which she had not been arrested and tried. It was after all the best thing for her own self-interest.

As soon as the cousins had her sign a document acknowledging the terms under which she was free to go, a footman had escorted her to a waiting carriage to convey her to London.

Darcy was brought out of his rumination when he felt the coach begin to slow. He looked up, blinking a few times and saw they were arriving at Longbourn. His thoughts of Mrs. Younge were forgotten as his senses heightened in anticipation of seeing Elizabeth momentarily.

Hill showed the Darcys into the drawing room, and much to the older Darcy's disappointment, only Aunt Fanny —Darcy also called her by that name—and the two youngest Bennets were present. They were informed the Gardiners were calling on the Philipses in Meryton.

Greetings and curtsies and a bow were exchanged while Darcy tried to mask his disappointment Elizabeth was not present in the drawing room.

Fanny smiled widely. "If I were you, I would go to my husband's study. I believe he is playing chess against Lizzy," she informed Darcy who lit up with pleasure at the information.

"Thank you, Aunt Fanny; I believe I will take your suggestion." Darcy looked over and saw Anna was as happy as could be as she and the two youngest Bennets were chattering between them. He made for Bennet's study.

As gratifying as it was to see Elizabeth, her reaction when Darcy was bade enter the study was everything for which he could have wished. Her whole being lit up with a welcoming smile for him.

"You will win soon, Papa," Elizabeth asserted as she tipped the white king. Both men reading the board knew the opposite was true—Bennet, because he understood how keen Lizzy had been to see her suitor, and Darcy who was greatly pleased she was willing to concede defeat to be in his company in less time than it would have taken her to beat her father at chess. Neither called it to her attention.

She had indicated when she reached the point that she loved him she would give him a sign. Darcy was able to read the signals Elizabeth was sending his way clearly.

"Bennet, may I address Elizabeth in private?" Darcy requested; his eyes never left the beautiful emerald-green orbs looking right back at him.

His daughter gave him a nod. "You have ten minutes, you know the restrictions," Bennet granted as he stood and exited his study. He set the door about three quarters closed.

With Elizabeth standing with her back to her father's desk, Darcy sunk down onto one knee in front of her. He reached and took one of her hands in each of his own. "My dearest, loveliest Elizabeth, when I requested to court you, I told you that you entranced me from the first moment I saw you, and my heart was in danger of becoming irrevocably yours.

"Elizabeth, these few weeks spent courting have proven my suspicions correct. You have completely captured my heart, to my unending joy. You are the best woman I have ever known. Your character is above reproach, you are good, kind, and worthy of the highest accolades.

"You grow more beautiful each time I see you. Your lavender fragrance intoxicates me, and your very presence overpowers me with a longing to be ever by your side. You see before you a man who is without hope unless you consent to become my wife. Only you can complete me, and I am yours— mind, body, and soul.

"My dearest, beloved Elizabeth, I love you with every part of me. With every beat of my heart, with every breath that I take, I become more and more yours. Death would be preferable to a lifetime spent without you. You are my love and my life. Will you marry me my darling, magnificent Elizabeth?" Darcy looked up at his beloved's face from his place on one knee. All of his hopes and dreams where poured into that loving look.

"Hmmmm, I think I need time to think about this," Elizabeth teased and then loosed a tinkling laugh.

"Teasing minx," Darcy responded with a huge dimple revealing smile on his face.

"William, my dearest William, it has been since shortly

after you requested the courtship that I knew you and I were formed for one another. I could not, even in my worst nightmares imagine my life with any other by my side," Elizabeth began.

"Similarly to what you declared on that day, I have fallen deeply, irrevocably, hopelessly in love with you. You are the very best of men and as there is none other I would ever agree to marry, yes William. Absolutely yes, I will marry you."

It was the work of an instant and Darcy was standing up again, Elizabeth's hands still gently clasped in his own.

Seeing permission in her eyes, Darcy leaned forward towards his fiancée. Closing her eyes Elizabeth felt the gentle pressure of his lips on hers; she grasped the lapels of his coat and felt his hands move down to her shoulders and then around her back pressing her body closer to his. He broke the kiss gradually, pulling his head back so he was able to look into her eyes to make sure she wanted more. What he saw was an affirmative and the ignited fire of passion.

He leaned forward once again and captured her lips with his own. This time he proceeded to show her what a kiss between those newly engaged and in love felt like. It was slow and deep, soft, and stirringly thorough.

Elizabeth felt warm sensations radiating all over her body, all the way to the pit of her stomach and even lower, to her most private of spots. His kisses spurred her to respond with a natural sensuality and a depth of passion which made Darcy not desire to stop. He had known all along she was a passionate woman, but her reactions to him were beyond anything he had ever dreamed.

After a little while Darcy pulled back again. Elizabeth felt almost lightheaded, dizzy, while at the same time bereft of his lips on her own. His kisses had sent her mind reeling, her heart racing, and her breath was ragged. She smiled as she blushed; he was staring intently at her. The looks did not last long as before either knew it, their lips were once again drawn inexorably one to the other, hungrily seeking the physical contact they both craved.

There was a knock on the door followed by the sounds of Bennet clearing his throat. By the time Elizabeth's father entered the study, the newly engaged couple had created some distance between them.

Bennet said nothing but there was no missing the red and swollen lips his daughter was sporting. "Is there something you would like to ask me Darcy?" Bennet enquired nonchalantly.

"There is, but I need to canvass something with Elizabeth quickly, if I may," Darcy averred.

"Go ahead," Bennet allowed, "or do you need privacy? I did allow you ten minutes, so I am surprised you were not able to discuss everything you needed."

It was amusing to see Darcy's colour heighten and match the blush Elizabeth was showing. He had made many changes, but Bennet still enjoyed discomforting others from time to time.

"No, there is no need for you to leave, as your input will be valuable," Darcy stated. He looked into his beloved's shining eyes. "If your father grants my petition, what say you we wait until after the wedding and celebration on the morrow to make the announcement, so we do not distract from their time?"

"I was about to suggest the same, what think you, Papa?" Elizabeth questioned.

"My opinion would be premature unless there is a certain question Darcy would like to ask me," Bennet grinned.

"We were placing the cart before the horse, were we not," Darcy opined. "Bennet, I asked for Elizabeth's hand in marriage, and she has done me the supreme honour of accepting me. We request your permission and blessing."

"If I were a blind man I would be able to see the emotions which seem to pour off each of you for the other in waves, so yes, you have both," Bennet granted. "As to your question, Lizzy, speak to your sisters and William you speak to your brothers-to-be. I will wager they will urge you to have your engagement announced at the wedding breakfast."

"We cannot keep this from Mama and our sisters in the drawing room. I suggest we have Hill summon Jane and Mary from their packing in their chambers so you can inform the family, Papa. I will speak to Jane and Mary about the timing of the announcement a little later when we are alone," Elizabeth proposed.

Bennet agreed with his second daughter and rang for Hill after which the butler went on his way to pass the request onto the two sisters upstairs.

~~~~~~~/~~~~~~~

"We are all to be sisters," Georgiana enthused after the announcement was made. "William thank you for proposing to Lizzy, she is such a wonderful person."

Lydia and Kate nodded their agreement vigorously. "And now we will have three brothers when not long ago, we had none," Kate pointed out.

"I used to want to be the first one married, now I am perfectly happy to be the last," Lydia stated. "Lizzy and William, I am so very happy for you two."

"Lizzy, you will be a very happy woman," Fanny told her second daughter as she hugged her to herself. "Three daughters engaged to men of honour; God has been very good to us."

"If only you and William had become engaged some weeks ago, we could have had a triple wedding on the morrow," Jane stated wistfully.

"It is impossible now. Everyone would see it as a terribly patched up affair," Elizabeth responded. "Besides, we need a little time as it is so very new. Also, unlike you two, I have not shopped for my trousseau yet." Elizabeth paused and looked at her sisters who would marry on the morrow. Rather than wait, she decided to ask their opinions now while William was still present. "We feel we should wait until the day after your wedding before we announce our engagement in public. We do not want to take away from your celebration on the morrow by drawing attention from you."

Jane and Mary looked at one another and both nodded. "That, Lizzy dearest, is stuff and nonsense," Jane announced as Mary nodded her agreement. "Announcing your engagement at the wedding breakfast will add to, not subtract from, the celebration."

"If you are both sure," William verified.

"William will talk to Andrew and Richard when he returns to Netherfield Park to make sure they do not object to an announcement being made at the breakfast," Elizabeth indicated.

"There will be no objections from them," Mary stated with surety.

A carriage was heard followed soon by the voices of Lilly and Eddy Gardiner who entered the drawing room ahead of their parents. Elizabeth and Darcy's excellent news was shared, and the newly engaged couple received fresh rounds of congratulations from the returning Gardiners.

~~~~~~~/~~~~~~~

On his return to Netherfield Park, Darcy was wished happy by his family and friends there, and just as Mary predicted, neither Andrew nor Richard had any objections to an announcement being made on the morrow.

Aunt Elaine called Darcy aside. "Your parents would have been very happy for you, and they would have loved Lizzy," she told her nephew as she hugged him.

"Of that I am sure." As he spoke Darcy inclined his head

to Richard in thanks.

A little later, in the sitting room between Richard and Darcy's bedchambers, the three cousins drank a toast to them finally becoming brothers.

~~~~~~~/~~~~~~~

At Longbourn, Jane and Mary were *treated* to the prewedding talk. It was given jointly by their mother and Aunt Maddie and the two brides discovered they received pertinent and helpful information, especially as their aunt was able to fill in gaps in their mother's knowledge.

At the end of the discussion, they found themselves anticipating their wedding night with their respective men with no lingering feelings of trepidation at all.

CHAPTER 35

Mrs. Bennet was overjoyed as she sat and watched two of her deserving daughters marry the men they loved in the Longbourn village church. First, the rector conducted the service for Jane and Andrew.

Jane Bennet looked resplendent in her shimmering light blue gown. Andrew stood opposite her in front of the altar his eyes locked onto hers. He was wearing white trousers, a white ruffled shirt with a pale blue cravat which matched the colour of his bride's gown. His vest and jacket were navy blue with silver threads running through the fabric. Andrew's attendant was Lord Sed Rhys-Davies, the Marquess of Birchington.

As would be expected, Elizabeth was Jane's maid of honour, who was fighting to keep her attention on the ceremony occurring at that moment. Her distraction was her fiancé who was standing up for Richard.

Try as he did to attend Richard, Darcy's eyes were very much fixed on the person of Elizabeth as she stood behind Jane in an extremely fetching hunter green silk gown. Her hair, which he could not wait to see free from all restraint so he would be able to run his hands through her tresses, was piled on top of her head with some of her enticing curls hanging down next to her cheeks.

Kate was very proud and honoured Mary had chosen her as her maid of honour. So many positive things had occurred in her life ever since she had realised blindly following Lydia, or anyone else for that matter, in all she did was not the way to live her life.

Here she was a month from her come out into society armed with a promise from Aunt Elaine she would sponsor Kate for both her presentation to the Queen as well as a season in London.

Lydia Bennet sat next to her mother watching her four sisters. She felt no envy that she was the only sister who was neither a bride nor a maid of honour. She had felt envy, but after many conversations with Mrs. McPhee, Lydia understood, and then accepted, the fact another's positives did not subtract from her own.

She had a goal to work towards. If she kept behaving as she did now, kept being educated, and worked on her ladylike accomplishments, then after Lydia turned eighteen, in less than three years, Aunt Elaine would do the same for her as she would for Kate in the upcoming little and full seasons.

Bennet sat next to his wife, right next to the aisle and could not have been more proud of all of his daughters. The four he was watching near the altar as well as the one seated between her mother and Anna.

At times he would remonstrate with himself about how much better his family's life would have been had he not hidden himself away in his study. As now, whenever he allowed his mind to go to that darker place, he remembered Lizzy's words about the past and accepted although he could not change the past, he could do what he was doing now. Ensuring his wife and still unmarried daughters would have secure futures. Longbourn was his to bequeath to whomever he chose. There would never be hedgerows in his wife's future.

He was brought back to the present when Mr. Pierce announced Lord and Lady Hilldale to be married in the sight of God, the church, and the assembled witnesses.

Jane and her husband, along with their attendants, moved off to the left of the altar and their places were taken by Mary and Richard. Kate and William took their positions behind the bride and groom respectively.

Mary's gown was silk in a light shade of pink with a shimmering transparent gossamer overlay. Like his brother, Richard's cravat matched the colour of his beloved's wedding dress. His trousers and shirt were pure white while he wore a dark green waist coat and jacket.

"Dearly beloved..." Mr. Pierce intoned for the second time that morning. As would be expected, there were no objections and soon enough vows were recited and rings exchanged.

As they did during the previous ceremony, both Elizabeth and Darcy silently recited the vows one to the other as the couple being married did so.

After the final benediction the rector pronounced the Honourable Mr. and Mrs. Richard Fitzwilliam to be man and wife. All that remained was for the two couples and their attendants to make their way into the registry office where the register was open to the relevant page, resting on a stand on a table in the centre of the room.

While first Jane and then Andrew signed their names. Darcy leant close to his fiancée's ear. "It will be our turn soon," he said so only Elizabeth could hear.

Elizabeth felt a frisson of excitement as his warm breath caressed her ear. "We have to set a date first," she whispered. Before Darcy could respond, it was Elizabeth's turn to sign the register.

"It is a great pity the other two Bennet sisters are so young," the Marquess stated to his friend as they waited for Mary and Richard to sign their names.

"Kate is almost eighteen," Andrew pointed out, "not even two years younger than my new sister, Mary. However be warned, titles and wealth do not impress the Bennet sisters."

By the time those who had been in the registry rejoined those in the nave of the church, only the extended family, the

Hursts, and Bingley along with his fiancée remained within.

Wishes for happiness were bestowed on the two newly married couples liberally. Once the hugs, kisses, and backslapping had been exhausted, the family group with their close friends made the short walk to the manor house where their coaches were waiting for them in Longbourn's drive.

Everyone except for the newlyweds departed. This left two open landaus in the drive, one pulled by a pair of matched greys and the other by a pair of bays.

"What say you Brother and Sister," Andrew drawled, it is more than five minutes since the last carriage departed, should we board our conveyances and depart for Netherfield Park?"

"Yes, I think they have enough of a head start," Richard agreed, "also, we may request our coachmen make it a slow drive."

So decided, Andrew handed his Jane into the lead landau and Richard did the same for his Mary into the following one. Before they joined their wives, the brothers each had a word with his coachman.

With that accomplished they climbed aboard their respective coaches and with a little lurch by each one as the horses strained against their traces, they began to move up Longbourn's drive towards the gates and the turn to Meryton.

~~~~~~~/~~~~~~~

Mr. Nichols nodded to the two footmen standing outside the ballroom doors. Each man pushed his door open and took up station in front of the half he had opened leaving the doorway clear for the butler.

Nichols entered some feet into the ballroom and then struck the floor three times with the base of his staff. The result was a quiet settled over the guests inside.

"My Lords, Ladies, and gentlemen it is my honour to announce Lord and Lady Hilldale and the Honourable Mr. and Mrs. Richard Fitzwilliam," Nichols intoned in a strong, clear voice. The butler stood off to the side next to one of the footmen.

A cheer rose from the assembled revellers as soon as the two married couples entered the ballroom. Once they had passed the doors, the butler walked out of the room in a stately fashion as his footmen pulled the doors closed behind them.

Per their prior agreement one couple went left and the other right and began to greet the guests, thanking them sincerely for being with them to celebrate the momentous day. A little less than an hour after arriving at the celebratory meal, the two sets of newlyweds sat down with their family.

At that point Bennet stood and cleared his throat which cause the guests to pause their conversations and look at him expectantly. "It is my great pleasure to announce the engagement of our second daughter, Elizabeth, to Mr. Fitzwilliam Darcy."

The news was met with much approbation and a flood of congratulations for the newly engaged couple.

"Mama your insistence we eat and drink this morning was absolutely correct," Jane stated and then kissed her mother on the cheek after the fervour over the announcement of Lizzy's engagement had died down.

"Mother and Father, we thank you for instructing us to break our fasts before the ceremony as well," Richard stated.

"And now you all need to have at least a little to eat and drink here," Madeline pointed out.

Plates with some of each of the various foods on offer at the buffet tables along the one wall appeared on the table within moments of Madeline Gardiner's statement. Carafes of lemonade and water were provided along with glasses.

The four who had married that morning each took a little to eat. Eating reminded their bodies how hungry they were so before they were done, most of the food and drink brought for them had been consumed.

"Jane, I envy you going to the Lake District with Andrew," Elizabeth sighed. "William tells me Pemberley is not far distant from the lakes so I am sure we will visit there soon enough.

"Andrew shared with me the house, Lake Vista, is aptly named. You can see at least three of the lakes from within it," Jane related excitedly. "Even though it is the opposite direction, we will be at Hilldale House tonight. Andrew does not want our wedding night to be at an inn." Jane blushed deeply as she shared the last.

Elizabeth made no comment which would have increased Jane's embarrassment. She just held her older sister's hand until Jane felt ready to speak again.

Meanwhile, Richard felt a contentment he found hard to put into words. He was married to the woman he loved more than he could ever have imagined loving anyone. His Mary adored him as much as he did her.

If that was not enough their futures were secure—many times over. He looked at his wife and found her looking back at him with a look of absolute adoration. How he deserved the love of this woman he would never understand, but it was everything he had ever wanted and so very much more.

"We should depart soon as it is almost fifty miles to our estate," Richard told his beloved wife.

"It is fitting we will be at Rosings Park for our wedding night," Mary replied. "We will have time to be with Anne in the morning before we depart for Ramsgate, will we not?"

"Most certainly. It is not many hours from the estate to my parents' house," Richard informed his wife.

"In that case, I will go and change," Mary stated as she put one of her hands over one of Richard's.

She stood and went to speak softly to Kate who was sitting with Anna, Maria, and Lydia. The three sisters made their apologies to Maria and followed Mary upstairs so they could assist her in changing into her travel attire in the suite at her disposal.

While Mary was changing, Jane made her way to the chambers she would use accompanied by Elizabeth and their Aunt Maddie.

"My Jane is a viscountess," Elizabeth sighed as she assisted her sister out of her wedding gown. "I will miss seeing you every day Janey, my dearest sister."

"And I you, Lizzy," Jane averred with a hug. "Do not forget, once you and William marry, when we are in the country we will be a little more than five hours by carriage from one another, and when we are in London we will be less than a mile distant."

"My rational mind knows all of that. However as happy as I am for you and Mary too—in fact I am overjoyed for both of you—Longbourn will seem very empty without you."

"Will you and William not set a date soon? You are so in love with William that once it is set and you marry you will forget all about us," Jane teased.

"I am ardently in love with him, am I not," Elizabeth stated with a dreamy look on her face. "Although that is true, I will always miss you two."

"As I will also miss you and everyone at Longbourn. I am sure Mary will as well." Jane responded. "Enough maudlin thoughts! Andrew is waiting for me; it is time."

"You will both discover, if Jane and Mary have not already, how quickly—especially when you love him—you cleave unto your husband," Madeline told her nieces. "You will never stop missing the family of your youth, but with him you will construct a new family, one which will be your first priority, especially once you are blessed with children."

The three hugged and made their way back to the ballroom, arriving shortly after Mary and the three youngest sisters. Once farewells were made in the ballroom, the two couples departing on their wedding trips headed to the front of the house, followed by the extended family, where their coaches stood ready in the drive.

~~~~~~~/~~~~~~~

When Elizabeth and Darcy re-entered the ballroom they saw Charlotte and Bingley sitting and talking with the Hursts. "Elizabeth, would you object if we were to share a wedding ceremony with Miss Lucas and Bingley?" Darcy suggested. "He has, from the time I met him, been almost like a younger brother to me."

"Charlotte is my best friend outside of my sisters, so you will hear no objection from me," Elizabeth averred. "If they agree, so do I."

Darcy walked over and requested Bingley and his fiancée join him and Elizabeth. They conveyed the suggestion to the two.

"I have no opposition in principal; however you know my parents are not in a position to host a lavish celebration," Charlotte responded.

"Charlotte, have I not told you more than once I will bear the cost above what your parents are comfortable spending?" Bingley reminded his love.

"This celebration was not very costly at all," Elizabeth pointed out.

Knowing her friend did not like frivolous things and although not as frugal as she was, Charlotte was assured. "In that case, as long as our parents agree, I would like to share the ceremony with you two," Charlotte agreed.

"In order to find a date, let us make for my study and look at a calendar," Bingley suggested.

As there were two couples, they did not feel the need for an additional chaperone. On entering his study, which was characteristically somewhat untidy, Bingley found the calendar under some papers on the desk.

To make sure the two sets of newly married Fitzwilliams would be returned from their wedding trips, the first day of October, a Monday was selected. It was a matter of minutes for them to return to the ballroom where the celebration was ongoing.

~~~~~~~/~~~~~~~

In the afternoon the Darcy coach arrived at Longbourn for brother and sister to visit their Bennet family. Neither Fanny nor Bennet had any objections to the idea of the double wedding or the date the couples had chosen.

At the same time, Bingley arrived at Lucas Lodge and very soon agreement was given by Lady Lucas and her husband to the choices which had been made for the wedding.

CHAPTER 36

The former de Bourgh coach arrived at Rosings Park in the late afternoon of the day of the wedding. Mary and Richard had been too occupied one with the other to notice Mrs. Deacon, as she sat in the garden watching some of her brood playing, and said children waving to them.

Since they had cleared all possible prying eyes in Meryton, wife and husband had fallen into one another's arms and had expressed their love and longing for one another. Not having seen each other for a full day before the nuptials had been difficult for both which led to their absolute need to be as they were while the carriage carried them farther and farther from Longbourn.

By the time they had reached the first rest stop, they had satisfied their need—for the moment—to be connected with their lips. There had been two more stops along the way and eventually they had reached their estate.

As their lips were much engaged at the time, neither had noticed where they were or the turn into the drive which led to the manor house. They were snapped out of their passionate embrace when they felt the coach begin to slow.

They had sent an express to notify their senior staff of the approximate arrival time so it was not a surprise as they, along with three neat rows of servants, were standing under the extended portico to welcome the master and new mistress of the estate.

What surprised Richard greatly when he alighted was to

see a beaming Anne standing there also and holding onto her companion's arm. Richard turned back into the cabin of the conveyance and handed out his wife.

They went directly to their cousin. "Anne, we are more than pleased to see you, but you did not need to stand outside to wait for us," Richard stated warmly.

"Since I have known I no longer have the responsibility of the estate and the dependants on my shoulders, I have felt much easier," Anne insisted. She inclined her head to her smiling companion. "Believe me, Jenki would not have permitted me to be outside unless I was feeling rather well."

"We are very happy to see you Anne, and it is very gratifying you feel so much better," Mary said in greeting as she took her new cousin's hand in hers.

"We thank you all for being here to greet us," Mary addressed the servants and staff, "as you may or may not know, we leave for our wedding trip on the morrow. When we return it will be my pleasure to meet, and get to know, each of you."

Richard nodded to the butler and housekeeper who dismissed the servants to return to their posts.

~~~~~~~/~~~~~~~

Richard led his bride up to the completely refurbished master suite. "Richard, this looks so welcoming now," Mary exclaimed when she entered the sitting room between the mistress's and master's chambers.

"Mary," Richard approached her with a passionate look on his countenance, "we have not discussed this, but do you want to sleep in separate chambers, or would you be happy that we share a bed every night?"

She blushed a deep scarlet, but held her husband's eyes. "Aunt Maddie did tell us it is common for those who make love matches to share a bed. It is my choice to do so," Mary replied softly, watching from under her eyelashes. The look of pleasure which suffused Richard's face told Mary how pleased he was at her response.

"The housekeeper informed me there will be a maid to assist you in your chambers, and a bath with nice hot water waiting for you," Richard related. "How long should I give you before I come to you?"

"I think an hour will be more than enough time," Mary responded.

~~~~~~~/~~~~~~~

An hour later, as Mary stood in her sheer nightgown covered by a silk robe, there was a knock on the door. Richard entered. He was dressed in breeches and a banyan revealing part of his chest and his legs, ankles, and feet below his breeches.

Mary's breath hitched as she found her husband very attractive and the event she had been anticipating since *the talk* the night before was now close at hand.

For Richard's part, he could hardly fathom the beauty he saw before him. Her hair was down, cascading down her back, and the robe over her nightgown clung to her body revealing the very shapely figure below it.

He extended his hand, which Mary took and he led her back through the sitting room into his—their—bedchamber. Once Mary was safely past the door, Richard kicked backward with his good leg and pushed the door closed.

Without any words, Richard removed his banyan revealing his chest to his wife. Mary stepped forward and ran her hands over the scars from his days in the army. She loved the feel of the light brown downy hair on his chest.

She took a step back and not feeling at all self-conscious, Mary allowed her robe to fall off her shoulders and pool on the floor behind her.

Richard was frozen in place at the wonder of the sight of his wife. All of the shapes he had seen under the robe were now revealed to him as her nightgown left little—nothing actually —to the imagination.

Still without a word, simultaneously, Richard opened and lowered his breeches while Mary allowed her nightgown to fall to the floor around her feet. Seeing the big scar on Richard's left leg, Mary stepped forward and softly caressed the surface of his wound.

Without warning, Richard, who was already completely aroused, scooped up his wife and gently placed her on the bed. He began to worship her body while guiding her in her desire to do the same for him.

As he began to minister attention to her breast, Mary arched her back and let out a moan of pleasure. It was not her last moan that night.

As she had been told was possible, there was some pain the first time she and Richard joined, but not as much as she had been informed it could be. Afterwards, both had rumbling bellies as they had skipped dinner. Richard put on his robe, rang for Brown, and requested trays to be delivered to their sitting room. After the meal, they enjoyed one another for dessert.

Having repeated their coupling multiple times, they did not get much sleep until the early hours of the morning. Subsequent to that first time there was no pain, only pleasure.

~~~~~~~/~~~~~~~

The next morning, after breaking their fasts with Anne, and spending another hour or so talking with her, Mary and Richard were back in their coach on the way to Bayview House in Ramsgate.

~~~~~~~/~~~~~~~

The month in Ramsgate for Mary and Richard and at the Lakes for Jane and Andrew passed far too quickly for either couple. As much as they were regretful to depart their respective locations where they had enjoyed their honeymoons, the time had arrived to journey home and then into Hertfordshire. The next wedding was barely ten days distant by the time they departed Ramsgate and the Lakes.

Both brides had received letters from Lizzy during the third week of their respective wedding trips. She had not wanted to write to her sisters until at least two weeks of their honeymoons had passed.

Neither couple had been surprised by the date of the wedding as Lizzy had told them she and William would pick a date which they were certain would allow the two couples to arrive with time to spare.

However, that there was to be another double wedding, this time with Lizzy and Charlotte getting married in the same ceremony was unexpected, but the news was welcomed by all concerned.

In her letter, Lizzy told how she and Charlotte had been shopping for their trousseaus in London and how their respective fathers had been left to worry about only the cost of the wedding breakfast as each fiancé had insisted on covering the cost of the vast wardrobe his bride to be would need. The two men had agreed each fiancée's father would pay for his respective daughter's wedding gown.

On the way back from Ramsgate, Mary and Richard stopped at their estate for a few days. Mary used the time to meet all of the servants as she had promised the night of her wedding and she began to learn as many names as she could. Her excellent memory came into great use in that particular endeavour.

At the same time, Jane and Andrew made a stop at Hilldale in Staffordshire. Jane had not seen her husband's estate before so it was very important for her to do so and to meet the staff and servants.

It did not take long for those employed at the manor house to fall in love with their mistress and recognise what a nice lady she was. Lady Hilldale was very down to earth and never put on any airs and graces.

Given the limited space at Longbourn, both couples were to be hosted at Netherfield Park. That estate was no longer leased by Charles Bingley as he had purchased it during the newlyweds' absences.

Mary and Richard would arrive the Thursday before the wedding and Jane and Andrew were to arrive the next day. The two brides-to-be had eschewed a prewedding ball. That decision had allowed the eldest and middle Bennet sisters more time to spend at her respective estate.

~~~~~~~/~~~~~~~

The Fitzwilliams were vastly pleased to see Elizabeth, Kate, Anna, Lydia, and William waiting to greet them alongside Bingley. No sooner had Richard handed out his wife than she was surrounded by the gaggle of her sisters with much kissing and hugging and not a few tears being shed.

"Bingley, William, it is good to see you two again," Richard extended his hand to each.

"Being married is apparently good for you, Richard," Darcy pronounced. "You are hardly limping at all."

"My leg feels the best it has since I was wounded," Richard agreed. He turned to Bingley. "It is very good of you to welcome us to your home. Have any of your family arrived from the north yet?"

"They will arrive on the morrow, and before you ask, Caroline, who is being courted by a local man in Scarborough is with them," Bingley averred. "She is not the Caroline you all remember from when she was here last. Under my aunt's guidance, and not forgetting what you told her, she has made some considerable changes. The man who is courting her is not even a gentleman, never mind of the *Ton*. He is a very successful merchant who is reasonably wealthy. From what I have heard, they seem to love one another."

"Will we meet this paragon with whom your sister is in love?" Richard enquired.

"No, Humphries cannot get away from his business at this time, but Charlotte and I will see him when we sojourn in Scarborough as part of our wedding trip," Bingley explained. "Fitzwilliam, I must thank you for not only putting me on a much better path, but for making Caroline realise she needed to change. We have our sweet and kind sister back thanks to you."

Bingley led the group into the manner house. As they walked, Richard placed his hand on Darcy's shoulder. "Are you ready for Monday?" he asked.

"It has been quite some time since I have been prepared to marry my Elizabeth, so yes, I cannot wait for that day to arrive," Darcy stated as he watched his fiancée chatting happily with Richard's wife as they walked arm-in-arm into the house with the three younger girls following them.

"I thought I was besotted, but William, you are completely mooncalf for Lizzy," Richard grinned. "On another subject, I believe my parents are to arrive with Jane and Andy on the morrow, is that not correct?"

"You have the right of it, they planned to meet at Hilldale and travel together to Hertfordshire," Darcy confirmed.

~~~~~~~/~~~~~~~

The Saturday before the wedding, the Fitzwilliams and Darcys were present at Longbourn where they joined the Bennets, Gardiners, and Philipses for a family dinner. Bingley and his family were doing the same at Lucas Lodge with the Lucases.

Fanny Bennet had to wipe a tear of joy from her eye as she looked around the table and saw all five of her daughters present, her two sons, future son, and the rest of her extended family.

Ever since she realised just how correct Richard had been when he had been so brutally honest, she had a very large soft spot in her heart for him. When she thought about how much better their lives were, not to mention the ending of the infernal entail on Longbourn, she felt nothing but gratitude.

At the conclusion of the meal, Fanny led the ladies out of the dining parlour leaving the men to their drinks. "Rich and Andy, you heard Wickham was tried while you were on your wedding trips, did you not," Darcy verified.

"I had not been informed, but I assumed it had occurred," Andrew stated as he blew a cloud of blue-grey cigar smoke out.

"Forster told me the approximate date of the trial when I saw him at our wedding breakfast," Richard revealed. "I assume he was found guilty?"

"Yes, no matter how much he tried to deny that he had confessed to his father's murder, there were too many credible witnesses who heard him make his declaration, not to mention when he admitted to trying to harm my late father," Darcy reported. "Anna's name was never mentioned and he was found guilty after a short deliberation by the jury. He was hung at dawn the next morning."

"That miscreant will never harm another innocent or leave ruined merchants behind him again," the Earl stated before he took another deep pull on his cigar.

"Darcy," drawled Philips, "did I not hear you made the officers from whom that brigand had borrowed money whole?" Darcy nodded. He neither needed nor wanted public accolades for what he had done. He had refused to allow Andrew and Richard to assist him in paying what was owed. Like it or not, Wickham had been connected to the Darcys and he had felt responsible to repair the wastrel's damage.

The men finished their smoking and drinks soon after. The two recently married men were more than keen to get back to their wives while one soon-to-be married man wanted to be in his fiancée's company more than anything he could think of. None of the other men were less interested in rejoining their wives either.

~~~~~~~/~~~~~~~

On Monday, the first day of October, as Bennet walked his Lizzy and Sir William escorted Charlotte to the Longbourn Village church, autumn was evident all around as the trees were already half bare and the remaining leaves were reds, browns, and golds as they prepared to fall to earth as well.

Jane followed Elizabeth, holding the delicate bouquet of flowers her sister would carry up the aisle with her. Maria Lucas was behind Charlotte performing the same office for her. The remaining Bennets and Lucases had entered the church just ahead of the two brides.

The instant Darcy and Bingley saw their fiancées' mothers enter the church, they both stood up straighter knowing their wait to see their respective lady was almost at an end. Just like it had been with the previous wedding, Darcy had not seen his Elizabeth the day before.

Jane was the first one up the aisle, her eyes fixed on her husband as she walked. Bennet with Elizabeth on his arm followed. As soon as she passed the inner vestibule door, Elizabeth's eyes sought and found her groom standing to the right of the rector.

Darcy had to remind himself to breathe when he saw his Elizabeth in her ivory gown. She wore a matching wedding bonnet and of course some of her curls were visible in the front and on the sides.

Once Darcy collected his bride and walked to stand back in his place next to Richard, Maria Lucas began her walk up the aisle. She was followed by Sir William with his eldest daughter on his arm. Bingley guided her to stand to the left of the rector with Hurst standing to his side.

Much like he had the previous double wedding, Mr. Pierce conducted the service for Elizabeth and Darcy and then for Charlotte and Bingley. Like all couples before them, the newly married couples signed the register as did their witnesses.

Congratulations flowed when the newlyweds emerged from the registry and not too much time thereafter the newly married Darcys and Bingleys were on their way to Netherfield Park to join those celebrating their union with them.

~~~~~~~/~~~~~~~

"So, you are off to the Lakes, not Seaview Cottage?" Richard verified with his new brother while the latter was waiting for Elizabeth to change.

"We are. I will take Elizabeth to Seaview in the summer so we can enjoy sea bathing in the cove," Darcy confirmed as his eyes were fixed on the stairs waiting for his wife—how well that sounded—to return after changing into her travel attire.

The Darcys were taking the example of Jane and Andrew insofar as they would be at Darcy House for their first night as husband and wife and depart from London the next morning.

"Rich, I must thank you again," Darcy clasped his brother's hand. "Had you not taken charge and whipped me into shape, I am not confident I would be married to my Elizabeth today, or at all."

"William, even though we are now brothers indeed, I have always thought of you as such and you must know I would always have done anything to protect you, even from yourself," Richard stated.

"Excuse me for overhearing, but I want to second what my newest son said. If not for you forcing me to take a long hard look at myself...I hate to think what would have befallen my family," Bennet insisted. "I will never forget you were instrumental in getting Collins to break the entail."

Richard inclined his head. Before they could speak any

more, Elizabeth was seen approaching surrounded by her sisters and other family members. The newly married Darcys were accompanied to their coach by the ever-expanding family.

There were many waves and a few tears shed as the conveyance made a turn and was out of sight.

"God has been very good to us, very good indeed," Fanny told her husband as they followed the rest of the family back into the house. "By the by, I have missed two months courses."

With a smug look on her face Fanny left a speechless husband in her wake.

EPILOGUE

Rosings Park, Easter 1825

Richard sat on a bench in the park with his beloved wife leaning comfortably against him. Never in his wildest dreams when he had been close to death after the injury at Talavera in '09 did he envisage the contentment and love he felt with Mary.

In August of this year, they would be married for fifteen glorious years. Each and every day during his marriage to his Mary, Richard had found new and more reasons to love his wife, something he was sure would occur until he drew his last breath in the mortal world.

At not yet five and thirty his Mary looked as beautiful, possibly more so, than she had the day they had joined their lives together. Understandably, after birthing five children the lines of her figure had softened a little. That fact in no way changed the innate beauty of his darling wife.

A little more than a year after the wedding, Mary had been brought to bed with her first lying in. Somewhat longer than twelve hours later the heir to Rosings Park, Lewis Richard Fitzwilliam had been born.

Thinking of his first son brought a smile to Richard's face. Lewis was thirteen and would begin his studies at Eton in September upcoming, a few weeks after he turned fourteen.

Lewis had been followed a little over two years later by Anthony Thomas—named for Anne, and three years later Reginald Paul joined the growing band of brothers. Just when Mary and Richard had begun to despair they would only be blessed with sons, two years after Reg, as he was called, Mary bore Anne Mary and five years after her, just when they thought there would be no further little Fitzwilliams, Franny —Frances Elaine was born.

During the family meeting at their estate this year, Franny's second birthday would be celebrated which, given the date of Easter, fell two days after that holiday on the fifth day of April.

His thoughts drifted to his brother-in-law and cousin, William. Due to the fact their love for one another had grown while walking in the groves and visiting the glade the first time Lizzy had visited Rosings Park in 1810, it was no surprise they were walking in what was by far their favourite place in Kent to ride or walk.

Lewis as the oldest male cousin was leading a ride around the estate—under the watchful eyes of Biggs and Johns —for those of his siblings and cousins who were old enough to ride. That group consisted of three Miss Darcys.

Elizabeth and William had the opposite when it came to their first three of now six children. They had all been girls. The Bennet matriarch's worry about entails had reared its head briefly until she had been assured there was no entail to heirs male on Pemberley or any of the other estates.

The first Miss Darcy to be born in September 1811, was Priscilla Beth, called Cilla, the next, born in June 1813, was Wilhelmina Jane, called Willa, and then in February 1816, Annabeth Madeline joined the growing ranks of Darcy daughters.

Everyone in the family, her husband and parents most of all, were amused no end that all three Miss Darcys, if not in looks, but certainly in character, were very much like their mother. Cilla was blond like Aunt Anna, but had her mother's emerald-green eyes and petite stature. Willa looked just like a smaller version of her mother in hair, eyes, stature, and complexion. Annabeth had the same coloured hair as Elizabeth, but she had the Fitzwilliam blue eyes and was taller than her two older sisters. In character, she most closely resembled her mother. Darcy loved all of his children, but especially his daughters who were so much like their mother in so many ways.

In mid-1818, Elizabeth had felt the quickening of her fourth child, which led to the birth of Bennet Robert—Ben— in November of that year. The next two born, Robert Thomas in 1820, and the youngest of the Darcy brood, Phillip Edward, was born in January 1823.

As he caressed his wife's shoulders, Richard noticed Jane and Andrew walking on one of the paths through the park at a leisurely pace. He remembered his sister's anguish thanks to the fact after five years of marriage she had not been in the family way except for once some months after the wedding which had ended in a miscarriage before the quickening.

Richard was well aware that regardless of how much Jane berated herself for not bearing him an heir, or any child for that matter, Andrew had soothed his wife with the fact that by then, Mary and Richard had three sons so the future of the Matlock Earldom was secure, even if they never had a child of their own.

Just when Jane had despaired she would never be with child, she was blessed with that state in the sixth year of her marriage to Andrew. On Christmas day 1816, a son and heir, Ian Andrew was born. The celebration of the Lord's birth took on a very special meaning from that day forward.

Since then, the new Viscount Hilldale's birthdays had been celebrated on the day after Christmas so Ian would have a day which was his own to commemorate his birthday. Thinking of his nephew, who was eight, produced a measure of melancholy as it reminded Richard his father was no longer on the mortal coil.

Less than two years ago, having not quite reached his seventh decade, Lord Reginald Fitzwilliam had gone to sleep one night as he always did, and never woke the next morning.

His death had elevated Andrew to the earldom and made Jane the new countess. As sad as she was, their mother had much to do visiting grandchildren, great nieces and nephews, and the extended family, which had grown rather massive over the years.

His thoughts returned to his brother and sister-in-law's family. Barely a year after Ian's birth, Elizabeth Mary—Bethy —had been born. She was followed three years later by Elaine Catherine—Ellie. Since then, there had been no more children granted to Jane and Andrew, but rather than think about how many they did not have, they rejoiced in those with which they were blessed.

"What has you grinning?" Mary asked her beloved husband.

"I was just thinking that although Lewis is the eldest male cousin, he has an uncle who is slightly older than he is— something Tom never allows him to forget. The story of Fanny Bennet shocking her husband at the celebration for the double wedding of Lizzy and William and Charlotte and Bingley was famous within the family.

Six months later, on the ninth day of March 1811, Thomas James Bennet arrived in the world. His birth meant even had the former heir presumptive not joined in breaking the entail and no simple recovery pursued, he would have still been displaced and without any of the remuneration he had received.

When she finally bore her son, Fanny Bennet was not yet forty, although she would be in a matter of two months. With his daughters making such advantageous matches, Bennet had not settled on which one would be heir, but Tom's birth had made that decision moot.

It still amused Richard, his brother, and brothers-in-law that they had a brother almost thirty years, or in Andrew's case, more than that number, younger than themselves. One of the things which irked Lewis and some of the other cousins, even though they knew Tom only jested, were the times when the latter would remind them of his status as their uncle.

"I was one who thought Mama had decided to repay Papa for all the times she was the object of his jokes by making sport of him, only to be proved wrong when Tom was born," Mary admitted.

"If that was a surprise, what was it when Kate became a Marchioness?" Richard reminded his wife.

Lord Sed Rhys-Davies, heir and only son of the Duke of Bedford had met Kate in Town after her coming out. At the end of the season of 1811, he began to court her. With the blessing of his parents and his younger sister Marie, who had become a close friend with Kate, he proposed, and was accepted by her in August of that year.

They had married a few days after Twelfth Night in 1812, a few months before Kate turned twenty. So far, much to the Duke and Duchess's delight, Kate had borne four children. Until then, very few Rhys-Davies bore more than one or two children.

In keeping with tradition, the firstborn son, birthed in 1814, was named Sedgewick, called Little Sed. Next were two daughters, Rose and Hattie, spaced about two years apart and finally another son, Albert, who had been born just over a year ago.

"It was, but they are so very happy together, where are they by the way?" Mary enquired.

"I believe they are sitting in the drawing room with your parents, Mother, and the Gardiners," Richard replied.

Gardiner no longer ran the day-to-day operations of his business; it was in the very capable hands of his son Eddy, who had married the daughter of a very wealthy fellow tradesman two years previously. His wife was with child.

As soon as it was clear Eddy could run the operation without him, Gardiner had fulfilled a promise to his beloved Maddie and purchased an estate, Willowmere, three miles the other side of Lambton from Pemberley and in his wife's much loved Derbyshire.

Lilly had married the second son of an earl in 1818. The older brother had died in a reckless curricle race and not a year later, the Earl had followed his heir and left the mortal coil. The daughter of a tradesman was now the Countess of Granville.

So far, she had presented her husband with two sons and a daughter. Her parents could not have loved their grandchildren more if they had tried.

Gardiner had continued to produce much better than expected returns on the investments made with him, and there were none in the extended family who did not invest, including Bennet who had begun to send Gardiner money shortly after he changed his ways.

"It is a pity Aunt Hattie is in mourning for Uncle Frank or she would have been here as well," Mary mused.

Frank Philips had passed away from heart failure some four months previously. His law practice had been taken over by his former clerk, Michael Ross-James. He was another brother-in-law as he and the former Lydia Bennet had married in June 1815, just before Lydia reached her majority.

Thanks to Mrs. McPhee, who had remained as Lydia's companion until the latter reached the age of eighteen, her charge had only gone from strength to strength in all facets of her life. The young lady then bore no resemblance to the brash, flirtatious girl who had been on the road to ruin at fifteen.

As much as Lydia had begged her companion, who she lovingly and in jest called *Nanny* McPhee, not to leave her, the companion had explained she had taught Lydia everything she could and it was time to move on as she already had employment waiting for her with a family with younger children of both sexes who were in need of her services as a governess.

Even after the teary goodbye, Lydia never divulged what Mrs. McPhee had said to her that first meeting which had helped put her on a path to a good and proper life.

The clerk had joined Philips in his law practice in late 1811, and for the first few years Lydia would hardly even look at him, or any other eligible man for that matter. After she had her promised season in London subsequent to her companion's departure, Lydia returned to Longbourn.

From that point, a friendship between the two developed until in February 1815, Mr. Ross-James requested and was granted a courtship. Two months later they were engaged which led to the wedding in June of that year. They had a son and daughter, born in 1817 and 1822, respectively and Lydia was heavy with child again.

Hence the Ross-James family had remained in Meryton so Aunt Hattie was not left alone while the rest of the family was in Kent.

Richard looked up and saw Anna walking with her two youngest children—twins—a son and daughter who were almost three. Anna shared a season with Lydia and not long after her coming out ball, she met Viscount Westmore, Wesley De Melville, son and heir to the Earl of Jersey.

At the time she was nineteen and he four and twenty. They courted and were married in less than a year. As happy as she was in her marriage, the only small regret she had was that Westmore was in Essex, not close to any of the other family estates. However, they saw each other in London for the seasons and their frequent visits between family estates, like now at Rosings Park.

With her co-guardians' hearty and unreserved blessing,

Anna was married in late 1814. On the second day of the year 1816, a son and future Lord Westmore was born and named Robert Cyril after his two grandfathers. A daughter, Annabeth, arrived in late 1819, and then the twins in July 1822. One was named Sarah for her paternal grandmother while her brother was William after his mother's brother.

The Bingleys and Lucases sometimes were present for the Easter gatherings, but not this year. Richard had been sad to hear of Sir William's passing some three months previously. The precise reason for his passing was not evident, but he had been well into his sixth decade when he was called home to heaven.

For that reason Charlotte and Charles Bingley and their son and three daughters were absent. As far as Mary and Richard were aware, the Hursts and Humphries were spending time at Netherfield Park in an obviously muted celebration.

Hurst's father had gone to his eternal reward seven years previously when he and Louisa Hurst moved to Winsdale in Surrey as he took over as master. After many years of trying, a son arrived two years before the senior Hurst passed away. Not long after, Mrs. Hurst delivered a daughter, but there had been no more children.

From everything they had heard, the former Miss Caroline Bingley, Mrs. Humphries since May 1811, never reverted to her former self and was as contented as could be with her role as wife and mother.

Her husband's business more than provided for her and their three sons and daughter. Like her mother, Miss Humphries had a dowry of twenty thousand pounds. It was, however, her mother who eschewed London. Since her move to the north she had not been back to Town. That meant her daughter would be brought out in Scarborough society when she reached eighteen. Ideas of being members of the *Ton* or first circles never crossed Mrs. Humphries's lips.

She had been in contact with the Bennet sisters from time to time over the years when they were in Hertfordshire at the same time she and her family were visiting Netherfield Park. No envy was felt or displayed for the four who had made such advantageous unions and were part of the *Ton*.

Richard's eyes flicked towards the de Bourgh family crypt which was between the park and the rest of the graveyard at Hunsford. Anne, dearest Anne who had gifted them the estate and all that came with it, had passed away just over a year ago.

Without the pressure of the estate and her late mother trying to constantly undermine her, Anne had lived years longer than any of the doctors had predicted. Although she never travelled away from the estate, Anne had a fulfilled and happy life as spinster aunt to the Fitzwilliam and Deacon children as well as all of the rest of the offspring of the extended family.

A special treat was when Aunt Anne would take two or three of the children riding with her in her pony pulled phaeton, something she had continued to do until a month or two before she passed away.

Her former companion had not expected the bequest of half of Anne's dowry. She had gone to live out her days with her daughter and grandchildren, thus enabling them to buy a much larger dwelling and live in a style they had never imagined they would.

The afore mentioned Lady Catherine had passed less than two years after being ordered to the cottage because of her despicable attempt to have Richard murdered. It was guessed that her constant raging against her situation had brought on a massive apoplexy.

She was buried with the rest of the commoners in the Hunsford cemetery, nowhere near the family crypt.

As it was getting late in the day, Richard stood and

pulled his Mary up to him. They kissed deeply and then hand in hand made for the manor house.

~~~~~~~/~~~~~~~

That evening after dinner and musical entertainment, the children were sent up to the nursery and their chambers. Not long after the older generation said their goodnights and made for their chambers.

Within an hour, some of those remaining in the drawing room were yawning and on their way to their suites. Eventually only Jane and Andrew, Mary and Richard, and Elizabeth and Darcy remained.

Darcy lifted the snifter of brandy he had been nursing for some time towards Richard. "To you, Rich, my brother. As I have each year since I married this wonderful woman," Darcy inclined his head to his lightly blushing wife, "I drink a toast to you for steering me, and others, onto the path we should have been on. You can take charge any time you like."

There was a chorused "Hear hear!" from the other four in the room. It was Richard's turn to colour slightly.

"All I did was what needed to be done." Like always, Richard tried to minimise what he had done. "At times, I know I gave offence, but I suppose things did work out for the best in the end, did they not?"

There was some laughter and giggles from those around him. Jane raised her wine glass. "To our brother who we love, the master of understatement," she toasted.

A repeat, and more hearty "Hear hear!" rung out in the room.

"Thank you, I love you all too," Richard responded.

~~~The End~~~

BOOKS BY THIS AUTHOR

The First Mrs. Darcy

A Change of Fortunes (Republished & Re-edited)

Much Pride, Prejudice, and Sensibility
- Without Enough Sense

Lady Catherine's Forbidden Love & Love
Unrestricted Combined Edition

A Curate's Daughter

Mary Bennet Takes Charge

Admiral Thomas Bennet

Separated at Birth

Jane Bennet Takes Charge - 6th book
in the 'Take Charge' series

Lives Begun in Obscurity

Mrs. Caroline Darcy

Lady Beth Fitzwilliam – Omnibus Edition

Anne de Bourgh Takes Charge – 5th book
of the Take Charge Series

Mr. Bingley Takes Charge – 4th book of the Take Charge Series

The Repercussions of Extreme Pride & Prejudice

Miss Darcy Takes Charge- 3rd book of the Take Charge Series

Banished

Lady Catherine Takes Charge – 2nd book
of the Take Charge Series

A Bennet of Royal Blood

Charlotte Lucas Takes Charge – 1st book
of the Take Charge Series

Cinder-Liza

Unknown Family Connections

Surviving Thomas Bennet

The Discarded Daughter - Combined Edition

The Duke's Daughter: Combined Edition

The Hypocrite

COMING SOON

A Change of Heart – the 2nd book in the 'Change Of' series – November/December 2023

Printed in Great Britain
by Amazon

29587149R00207